Nov 2020

To Sirca

Karen & Evan,

Looking forward to
being closer to you again.
Thanks for your support.

Gideon x

16/40

PORTICO

GIDEON BURROWS

NGO.MEDIA

1

Alice Harding momentarily stuttered as the man entered the lecture theatre. She gathered herself, took a deep breath, carried on. The man sat at row 20, crossed his arms and glared directly at her. He sat on the last row. Where it was dim. Hard to see from the brightly lit platform below.

He was not part of her usual crowd. Way too old, and too smartly dressed. She could see that even from his outline in the dark. On a Friday morning, she'd usually pull 20 or 30 undergraduates into this much too large space. Many of them she'd got to know, some she could name personally. She liked most. Tolerated the rest. But none of them wore a suit and tie to lectures. Not even fellow lecturers or professors. This man wanted her to know he was there. He was making a point of it, she thought. But he didn't want her to be able to see him clearly. Not yet.

Harding shifted in her flat shoes and straightened her back. She concentrated on the words before her: a few concluding paragraphs summarising the competing arguments about the causes of recent riots on the outskirts of

Paris. She delivered them to the front few rows, deliberately keeping her eyes below those on a higher level.

She felt a slight nausea at the overwhelming presence of the mysterious man on the twentieth row. She rushed her final lines, almost stumbling again, but recovering to deliver a tone which indicated the lecture had finished. She did not expect applause. That wasn't what happened at an undergraduate lecture at Oxford University. Certainly not for a fresh PhD student who was barely out of the junior common room herself. Undergrads began to gather their things together, shuffling A4 pads into rucksacks. A few of the showier students closing laptops, their Nokia and Samsung flip phones switched back on and glowing with messages.

Harding took the opportunity the shuffling offered to glance up to the top row. He was still there. Far older than she first thought. Perhaps forty even. Dark black, neatly set hair. He sat still and upright without notebook or bag. Unmoving. Just staring. Whoever he was, he wanted to make her feel uncomfortable.

She began putting her papers together and unplugged her laptop from the HDMI set up. She removed her gown and stuffed it with her computer into a bag. Academics were obliged to wear gowns when lecturing. It was one of many conventions she hated about Oxford. But today taking it off was a convenient way to show her students she didn't intend to hang around.

A few familiar students came to the front anyway, hoping to chat and to offer a few questions. This keenness she usually welcomed. In fact, she loved it when her undergraduates came to explore her subject a little more.

Most times, Harding would walk with them up the wooden boarded steps of the lecture theatre, then along the marble tiled corridors which echoed with their chatter about freedom of speech, revolutionary movements or extremist politics. The conversation would continue as the small group accompanied their lecturer down the ancient marble staircase, only dissipating when the building known as Exam Schools released them onto High Street. There the noise and bustle of cars, bicycles and tour buses made it impossible to talk. She was less than five years older than some of the undergrads, and felt more akin to them than her more senior colleagues.

Today though, she wasn't up for chatting.

"I have to get back to Mansfield today."

Harding really did need to get back. Her recent appointment as Junior Dean was demanding her time and attention. Mansfield was one of the smallest colleges of the university, but with less than a month in the position, it was a role Harding had yet to successfully make her own. And the man at the top of the lecture theatre was beginning to unnerve her.

The *proper* way for a lecturer to leave the lecture he or she had just delivered - at least according to the turgid Oxford University Handbook - was by the side door. Harding had never entered nor exited through the lecturers' entrance. It was a snobbish idea.

Her students stood quietly, waiting for her to gather her things and join them. If she went with them, she would pass the man, clearly waiting for her. Would there be be strength in numbers? Could she theoretically, find herself too engaged in chat to notice him as she passed.

"Ms Harding, you spoke of the cultural significance of murals in the poorest areas of Paris as catalysts for community solidarity among the poor there."

It was one of Vicky's questions. She always had at least

one. Harding tried to show a piqued interest. This might be a good topic to lose herself in as they left the theatre.

"But don't you think that if a mural has aggressive or violent symbolism, that it encourages rather than discourages communities to be violent? Take Northern Ireland..."

Vicky continued her question. More like a statement, thought Harding, only half listening. She glanced towards the top of the theatre again. She felt ready to lead Vicky and the other undergrads out.

In the pit of her stomach, the slight churning felt familiar. For a few months now, Alice Harding had had an eerie feeling she was being watched. Not stalked so much. Just very rarely did she feel quite *alone*. The visit of this man to her lecture stirred the same deep worry.

Much of what she had to say was not too pleasing to certain special interest groups. She knew that from the mail she received at the Porters' Lodge at Mansfield, where it was kept piled up for her rather than delivered directly to her rooms. Extremists from the left and right would write. Some sent unpleasant packages - though so far at least, nothing with any wires or batteries inside. They were from those intent on nurturing long past wrongs, and playing them out into current aggression. Wounds that the injured felt couldn't be healed, certainly not by a young university lecturer who asked: 'isn't it time we all just got along?'

It meant Harding was almost always on edge. An unknown person in her familiar space? Well, that was bound to ring alarm bells.

The man sat there, his arms crossed still. Staring.

The way he was dressed made it clear he didn't belong in Schools attending lectures. He was too neat. Too perfectly turned out to be a fellow lecturer or academic.

She knew the old-school lecturers who sniffed, coughed

and limped around the university and her subject matter. Nationhood, imperialism, tribalism, extremism. Most had become rusty and stuck in repetition of the same old tropes. African nations are *bound* to continue their aggressive little wars. Violence is *built* into the Islamic psyche. Communism will *always* lead to dictatorship, because the theory is built on the endemic weakness of its subjects.

Good old 'Christian Western Values', imposed upon the world, had mostly brought peace, prosperity and development. And when it had been rejected, well, that's when tensions emerged. Any associated prejudice and racial violence and discrimination? That was no more than tribal rejection of the gift the West had to offer.

Thus extremism, terrorism, tribalism was the fault only of those who perpetrate it. There was nothing to learn from it. Dusty pages of history to be rewritten again and again, but not - Harding imagined - to be learned from.

Her own position was different. Extremism, she believed, needed to be called out before it became history. Discover and observe its causes before and while it occurs, not after the fact. Violence and upheaval should be challenged and changed. It was everyone's personal responsibility to confront hatred and extremism. Only by uniting could reasonableness and peace become the norm.

No. The man on the twentieth row was no academic. The more she considered him, the more sure she was that she'd seen him before. The smart suit. The staring eyes. Perhaps on the other side of a road. In the blink of sunlight reflected on the window of Blackwells bookshop. Sitting straight and upright, on a bench as she'd pedalled her sit-up-and-beg around Radcliff Square. Or outside college. Standing against a wall at The Tuck Shop, on the edge of Mansfield Road. All familiar places to her. All places she'd pass daily. She realised now how easily she could be stalked.

She swallowed back her fear, disguised it from her students as a cough. If it wasn't the first time he'd hung around, it wouldn't be the last.

"I really must get back to Mansfield," she told her students again. "I don't have my bike."

Harding stepped back from her students, snatched up her bag and strode away. She had said it louder and more pleading than she might have. Harding shook her head and left by the side door, her students still embroiled in the half discussion Vicky had prompted.

A change of route and routine would clear her head.

The Junior Deanship had brought pressure. On paper she was supposed to take care of the general welfare of the undergraduate students at Mansfield, a rabble of some 200 late teens high on booze, ProPlus and privilege. But she'd welcomed the responsibility. It came with new rooms at the college and a small stipend to add to the hourly rate she was paid to lecture on her PhD themes. And, so far, she'd had to do little more than chastise a few students who'd decided to stage a late night drunken race around the quad during a fire alarm.

The pressures from the Senior Common Room were different. The professors, lecturers, the Master, the Dean. All the other academic staff at Mansfield were friendly in their own way, but many brought with them eccentricities and stubbornness that she'd somehow found herself having to manage too.

Men - and it was mostly men - who appeared barely to have seen the other side of the fence of their boarding schools and rugby pitches, let alone seriously considered the world beyond. Within the sandstone college walls, these senior members remained as stuffy and turgid as the dusty overwritten academic texts that were protected like sacred relics on the top floor of the college library.

As Junior Dean, Alice Harding wasn't *supposed* to be responsible for these ageing academics. But she found herself compelled - informally at least - to bridge the gap between the old and the new. The student touched up by his geography professor. The undergrad accused of plagiarism of another's work, by a tutor who was obviously motivated by her own prejudices. The dichotomy between the staid conservative values of the many older academics at college, versus the rebellious, progressive and naïve opinions of the kids fresh from sixth form.

Harding pulled the exit door to the lecture room behind her and heaved her bag onto a shoulder. Her shoes scuffed along the marble tiles, echoing around the narrow corridor. A mix of logic and intuition allowed her to navigate behind the lecture theatres on the second floor, and down a spiral staircase leading to another corridor. At the end of it, a small room full of ancient oak lockers stacked against a wall. Before her, a solid door would take her onto the street.

Harding pushed the handle down and gave the door more of a shove than it needed. She tumbled out onto High Street, with its bustle of buses heading to the city centre. Students and tourists walked unawares this way and that, along the pavements in animated conversation.

She took a breath.

On her bike, she would normally cross the road here, straight across from Schools and onto Queen's Lane by the coffee shop. It would eventually bring her onto Castle Street and close to the crossroads that would lead back to college.

Fighting uncertainty and perhaps too much caffeine that morning, Harding took a direct left and continued up High

Street to cross the road closer to the busier shopping area. From there she could cross through the always busy Covered Market.

Outside the Shepherd and Woodwood clothes shop stood the man, just as straight, solid eyed and determined as he had appeared sitting in the twentieth row of her lecture. He wore a neat dark blue suit, a dark crimson tie and polished shoes. Outside the shop, he might have looked inconspicuous. To Harding, he looked terrifying.

Whether on a grand or personal scale, those most threatening to peace, stability and even personal safety should be confronted. Called out. The majority should take control. The individual should stand up for themselves, calling on others to support them. The victim should be supported to speak out before they become the victim. Show up, embarrass, estrange those who oppress, discriminate, divide, threaten, spread pernicious and dangerous beliefs. Beliefs that could lead to extremism. To indoctrination. To violence.

Understand it. Call it out. Confront it. The rest will follow.

It was time to approach this stranger and ask him, 'what the hell!?' She took stronger strides towards him, grasping her bag tightly, ready to swing it and the heavy laptop inside. Her heart beat faster.

She watched him as her looked her, directly up and down, as she approached from 15 metres away. He abruptly stood away from the wall and began to approach her.

Her stomach turned again. Harding swore as she bailed out. Rejecting her own academic theory in favour of her gut instinct for safety. Sticky fumes from a nearby cafe had not helped her nausea. She checked the High Street quickly and gambled correctly that she would be quicker than the pink number five to Cowley heading her way, as well as the cyclist in a flowing skirt who was attempting to cut up the inside of the bus.

To the right there was no traffic and she was quickly across, retracing her steps on the opposite side. Ahead again was the Queen's Lane Coffee Shop and its back alleys. But Harding knew of a more open route back to college.

St Mary's Passage was wide, decorated each side with rails plastered with posters for upcoming concerts and plays. Before she ducked into it, Harding took a side glance back towards the gown shop. He was crossing the road, only with less luck than she had enjoyed.

Harding moved with long, quick strides past St Mary's church. She thought of the self defence classes she'd been offered as a student. Protect yourself. Carry your solid keys in your hands. Don't go down dingy passageways, particularly if you're being followed by a strange man, who you're sure is following you and you've a feeling you've probably seen before doing exactly the same thing. Why hadn't she attended? Such classes would, she imagined, be especially valuable for those who had a particular interest in controversial issues like race, women's rights or, say, for example, researched and lectured and spoke publicly about extremist groups, and what individuals, as well as authorities, could do to confront their threat.

Harding glanced back again but there was no one behind. Her pace lifted as the tall sandstone walls of Brasenose on one side and St Mary's on the other finally opened up onto Radcliff Square.

Out in the sunshine, Harding slowed up. She felt safer here. She neatened her hair and brushed away sweat that had gathered on her eyebrows. Once back at college, Harding could lock the door of her recently upgraded rooms, drop her heavy bag and think more clearly. She would report it - whatever it was - to whomever you were supposed to report this kind of thing at college. The Junior Dean. Only that position, it appeared, had been occupied by someone totally incapable. She'd definitely go on a self defence course. Confront. Call out. Shame.

Run away, more like.

The strength of Alice Harding's thesis on personal responsibility to challenge violence and extremism was weakening around her, and in real time. The disappointment of the thought brought her to a stop on the cobbled surrounds of the Radcliff Camera. She gazed up to the top of the library, and its greening eighteenth century dome. The picture postcard of Oxford. A precious building full of precious works.

Works so cherished and important they were protected by a uniformed guard who sat behind its doors and who electronically checked the university pass of everyone who went in and out. There were no unplanned visitors permitted in the Radcliff Camera. Just members of the University and their books, and papers, and maps, and desks with green lamps and little slips of pink paper to tell knowledge seekers where to go for a book not currently on the shelf. No books were allowed to leave the building. And no strangers were allowed in.

Harding took another gaze at the dome and smiled.

Almost at a sprint, she headed through the gate, moving quickly towards the dozen concrete steps leading to its narrow oak door. She fumbled for her pass, swiped it, and with a familiar nod the security officer allowed her to pass into safety.

Harding descended from the security desk, down a spiral staircase towards the bottom floor of the Radcliff

Camera. How many hours had she spent here? English. Humanities. Theology. The books she'd read or dipped into across her academic interest in social anthropology.

At the bottom of the spiral, she turned right instinctively, heading for her usual place. Seat 398, positioned with another desk under a dusty narrow glass arched window looming above. It was to this place she'd come for most of her studies in the library over the years. Her place of peace and solitude and thinking.

Sitting opposite, in seat number 399, cast in shadow by the green lamp under which she'd done so much work, was a man. He had dark, neatly cut hair, and was wearing a neat blue suit and a dark crimson tie.

"Alice Harding," he almost whispered, rising to his feet and extending a hand. "Why don't you take your seat?"

2

The man has needs.

Every man has needs. But this man's needs are very particular. Very specific. Very illegal.

But a man has needs. And a man with needs as strong as these, well, sometimes there is no choice.

A dull grey cursor blinking on an otherwise black screen. *What are your needs?* The rhythmic flash asking.

He knows he should not be here. But his needs. Too much to bear. He types. A list of needs appears. A long list. They are as desperate as the cursor to find him what he wants.

*Lolita needs. *AskingForIt needs. *Choke needs. *CreamPie needs. *DeadPan. *DirtyPlay. Disgusting needs. Not the needs he has.

A blinking cursor at the bottom again.

Asking the question.

The man feels more desperate. He presses the arrow key. A new list.

*GoHome. *KKKRevolt. *HangingwithGays.

No. Not those needs.

*OKComputer. *HackedOff. *CodeBusters.

His hands are shaking.

Desperate. He should not be here. He should escape. Swipe *escape.*

*CuttingRemarks. *SpectatorsOf. *RopeWorks.

He reads. Hesitates. Maybe. But not now. Now he has other needs.

*LegallyHigh. *LegallyLow. *WatchingU.

The man with needs takes a breath. Perhaps. The cursor begs the question.

LegallyHigh he types. He swipes.

A new list. *DeathBeComesHer *GotTheSnuff.

He cannot read on. He feels sick. Not his needs.

BACK he types. The list clears.

The cursor questions.

LegallyLow. He hits return.

*CanOfCoke. *Pharmacy.

No. Not those needs. Not now at least.

*GoneMissing. *CallTheCops. *SwagBag.

He hesitates. The cursor blinks on.

GoneMissing he types.

A new list. Names, dates of birth, places. He picks one, and types it against the unending blink.

The screen clears. A single paragraph remains. The man with the needs reads closely.

Ron McClay, estimated age 59, last sighting in South Derry, 1984. UVF, murdered my dad. Released early, re-identity in exchange for peace agreement. Should have rotted in hell. Never Surrender. Reward for positive ID. More if ends in accident. Contact direct.

A cursor blinks beneath the paragraph.

BACK he types. He should not be here.

*GoneMissing.

The cursor blinks like a question again.

NEWPOST he types.

The screen clears. The cursor blinks. The man with needs begins to write.

3

The door to the TriCab slid open and Curtis Soren squeezed his bulky six foot frame into the cramped cockpit. He slid his slate into the dashboard holder, and gave it the usual hard knock to make the connection points mate. His screensaver flipped over to reveal the TriCab logo, beneath which was written the question the speakers around him also asked in a smooth male tone.

"Good morning, Mr Soren. Where would you like to go today?"

"Social Ministry."

"I'm sorry, I do not know that location. Would you like to try again?"

"Ministry for Society and Communications." Soren said, chopping the words into unnatural chunks.

"I'm sorry, I do not know that location. Would you like to try again?"

Soren shook his head, swore under his breath and swiped away the logo. Newer versions of his slate were supposed to be better at voice recognition, but he'd not bothered to upgrade.

He selected his email screen, chose the top email and searched it for the address listed in the press invite before swiping the highlighted link.

"Thank you. Please fasten your safety belt, Mr Soren."

Soren did so, then swiped the mute indicator. The cab would cost more without his having to watch or listen to advertising. But, he wasn't paying. His email flipped over to the TriCab logo again, with a question written below it: "How would you like to pay today?"

Soren swiped the logo of SkyCloud Media. It was a limp pastel coloured depiction of a child's fishing net attempting to catch clouds. He made sure he didn't swipe anywhere close to his personal account. Not that there was much to spend on taxis in there. Or on anything else.

His screen flipped, revealing his personal desktop. The door autoclosed and the taxi buzzed into electric life before it pulled smoothly into the traffic.

The slate predicted a 20 minute journey across London, plenty of time for another look.

Soren swiped open his feeds, personal messages and social, and looked again for any hint of what he would be wasting his time listening to this morning.

The hashtag #endit was beginning to drop in the ratings, replaced again by tags on fashion tips, celebrity gossip and the latest tech. Nothing was dominating like #endit had over the last few weeks, but it wasn't holding the top spots as consistently as it had.

Fellow newsgatherers had not mentioned they had been invited to the MinSoc press briefing. He'd not bothered to post about it himself either. He posted as infrequently as he could.

Twenty years ago, when Soren first got into the game of what was barely still called journalism, he could rely on some personal contacts within the government to help him write stories. Or, as it was now known, generate unique content.

But these days, insider leaks mostly turned out to be kite flying by one of the ministries, using newsgatherers as a test bed for potential new policies. Nothing of any substance came from those sources anymore. Civil servants didn't need newsgatherers to test their kites. There were many thousands of users on the social, willing to offer simple 'yes/no' questions on their slates in exchange for money off their electric cab rides, weekly drone deliveries or music subscriptions.

He still attempted to write critical stories about social media, questioning their tactics, the collection of data, the monopoly social media organisations had developed over everything from shopping to entertainment, communications to the damn TriCab he was riding in.

Curtis Soren pulled his vape from his jacket pocket and took a long toke, drawing the minty flavoured nicotine into his lungs. The chemicals budged his mood from boredom to mere resignation. In a way, it was surprising SkyCloud had been invited to the MinSoc press conference at all. It was one of the only organisations that did - and then only occasionally - criticise the too close relationship between some of the social media companies and Government departments.

The screen on his slate flipped again, and he felt the TriCab lurch to the side of the traffic and come to a slow stop.

"Vaping is not permitted on TriCab journeys. That's for your safety, and for your health in future. I am obliged to remain stationary until your vaping equipment is safely stored."

No mute button could prevent this remonstration. The strongly toned words came to him on his slate as well as over the cockpit speakers. It was exactly what Soren had expected. Two vapes and you're out. TriCab would still charge the full fare. He pushed his vape back into his jacket pocket and breathed out slowly through his nose, covering the message on his slate in swirls that quickly evaporated.

His prepayment would spare him the antivaping personal and community health video that those taking a free or discounted ride had to see. The social was choosy. The relatively well off got an occasional ticking off if they broke the rules. The poor were subjected to an onslaught of lessons on how to live their lives, in exchange for a cheaper bus or cab ride. The TriCab slipped back into the traffic and his slate flipped back to the previous screen.

Soren swiped his slate to blank and stared out of the window. He'd needed the nicotine to quell the frustration still stinging his brain after his argument with Will Grey this morning.

Grey was the editor, publisher, advertising manager and all round pain in the arse who ran SkyCloud Media. He was a friend, but his approach to journalism was about as limp and pastel as his logo.

Granted, Grey had kept the business running with what was left of his family money after the second and third waves of Covid 19 and the big financial crash of 2021. And he'd been generous enough to take Soren on again last year, after he returned from self imposed exile for five years, away from London, away from civilisation. Though he was not a little shy of reminding Soren of the debt. Soren was one of a small number of other specialist newsgatherers, a weather analyst, a few editorial coders, and a half dozen advertising coders and salespeople at SkyCloud.

SkyCloud was able to get good traction on the social - so Will Grey was able to pay its staff an industry level wage - but it was hardly the hotbed of decent journalism Soren and Grey had been engaged in when they worked on the *London Herald* together. *The Herald* had been one of the last surviving newspapers. It had finally gone to the wall in the early 20s when its benefactor had given up on print and moved into web video.

Like the other newsgathering organisations to rise from the ashes of print, SkyCloud was mostly a churner of pre-arranged, pre-written information from Ministries, corporates and the PRs of celebrities that Soren and his colleagues had to reshape. His copy needed to contain the most popular keywords the coders supplied for that subject, and the social coders would try to get traction on as many feeds as possible. The advertising coders made sure the most profitable ads surrounded the copy, and the result was food on the table for everyone. But not much else.

As long as readers stayed glued to their screens, the money would come in. Every aspect of that idea sickened Soren.

"Our readers love exciting social news," Grey had argued when Soren had harrumphed at being sent to cover today's press conference at the Ministry for Society and Communications.

"New social tools, same old story from MinSoc," Soren had argued. He predicted that within minutes of the release of information, whatever this exciting social news was about, it would be all over the social feeds. And old news by tea time.

"Yes, and we need our readers to get the information from SkyCloud," Grey had replied.

Soren had heard it many times. If SkyCloud didn't keep

its stories at the top of the feeds, and in front of as many eyes as possible, its advertisers would drift away from the platform.

In other words, Soren should swallow that outdated idea of breaking real news, and bring back some reader friendly copy. Otherwise make room for someone who'd rather move slightly up in the world from package picking for drone deliveries to take his place.

Soren had argued with his editor anyway. He and Grey went back a long way and he had reason for his scepticism. When he'd reluctantly returned to work with Grey it was on the understanding he could write what he wanted, follow leads that he might uncover. Grey had granted his wish, but the need to constantly turn over copy had left the idea of Soren's independent, new and exciting journalism on the sidelines. It wasn't what readers - SkyCloud's readers - wanted.

That morning Soren had waved his hand towards the younger staff who had arrived before him, with their gigantic headphones, staring and swiping, typing and successfully speaking into their slates. He could speak as openly as he liked to Grey. They wouldn't be able to hear him through their noise cancelling headsets.

"Can't you send one of these guys to the Ministry for their latest dose of social bling? What about Harrison? She's keen and up with the tech."

"These guys are busy, Soren. Tracking the feeds. Keeping up their networks. Gathering social traction. You're gathering dust."

"They write about celebrities," said Curtis. "Clothes. New technology on the corner of every high street. The latest bloody slates for sale, all of which they have and I don't."

"You choose not to update yours."

"That's not the point," said Curtis. "I used to write about politics, about war for goodness sake, homelessness."

"I'm sorry the world became so very uncomfortably nice for you, Soren, but this is what we do here. These gatherers generate stuff others want to read and share, and that's what gets the job done. You want to write about politics, fine. The Ministry is awaiting your so very highly esteemed visit in about thirty minutes' time. You are supposed to be our current affairs correspondent, after all."

"Politics? There's nothing of any interest coming out of that building today. When was the last time there was?"

The closest Soren had come to current affairs at SkyCloud since he'd come back to journalism was the #endit campaign, a sudden and brief uptake in interest in human rights in an otherwise apathetic world of social users.

For years, well before the newspaper industry had failed, social media publishers had been pushing out sensational stories about scrounging foreigners smuggling themselves to the UK to get on benefits and live the life of luxury. Apart from celebrity hairstyles and the latest tech, nothing gained more traction on the social than a bit of good old fashioned bigotry.

The newsgathering organisations knew it, the advertisers knew it, and users of the social loved to argue about it. The death of Rasalina Mazeika had been an unfortunate illustration of the fact.

Mazeika was twenty one-year-old trainee junior school teacher from Vilkaviškis, a small town on the southwest border of Lithuania. According to police reports, she had been sent over to England by a drugs cartel who'd organised the transfer over the dark web, where they sourced a fake passport and documents for her. Probably considered too smart for her own good - too likely to snitch - the young woman's body had been found washed up on a beach in Suffolk, her abdomen cut open to reveal where bags of cocaine had probably been removed from her stomach. Next to the bloated seventeen-week-old body of her never-to-be-born first child.

XLSMedia, a direct competitor to SkyCloud, had hedged its bets and put out two equally sensational headlines. First, about another woman selfishly risking her and her baby's life to scrounge for overly generous benefits. But then another about the dark web, and how criminal gangs were using it to traffic drugs and people. Some of whom, with their unborn children, ended up dead.

The two stories had performed equally well on the social. There were readers on either side who lapped it up, and reposted their own sensationalised opinion that fitted their prejudices and audiences.

Then someone - no one knows who - had placed the hashtag #endit to the end of the dark web story. The tag had rushed up the ratings and XLSMedia quickly deleted the other story as if it never existed.

The public had chosen.

Cynical? Perhaps. But Soren questioned whether it was really any different to SkyCloud testing two different headlines about a skin softener, to see which attracted most visitors to its website.

#endit became a UK wide phenomenon for two weeks, and spread across the globe for just over a day. At first a heartfelt plea for change and the banning of the dark web. Then quickly leapt on by newsgatherers and anyone else with something to gain to improve their ratings.

Such was the social, and Curtis was disgusted that he had come back to work in it.

Will Grey had opened his door and invited Soren to step out of his office.

"This press conference is as close to current affairs as you're going to get just now, Curtis," he said. "Your cab is just a slate swipe away."

Grey mimicked doffing his cap to the older man.

"Or if you'd prefer, there's a new Vegan Vodcast you could try socialising with as part of our series on kitchen trends."

"Asshole." Soren didn't wait for a response. After the press gig, he'd seek out one of the east London backstreet cafes still selling meat - preferably via some greasy, stinky, questionably sourced kebab.

Soren checked the small mirror provided on the dash of the TriCab. Without having to worry about driving, electric car riders had more time and ability to worry about how they might look on arrival. Soren's only concern was that he would look as bad as he felt, after another night at Ned's.

He appeared older than his 44 years. Felt even older. Wispy greying hair, sunken dark eyes, a rough unshaven face. He was slightly overweight - he could ask the TriCab by how much if it bothered him - and his ragged suit smelled musty, with a hint of sweat. Had he even showered this morning?

Soren took out his vape again and breathed in a long grateful drag. His slate screen flipped and the TriCab remonstrated with him, before pulling over and automatically opening its door, an electronic bell sound pinging impatiently. He snatched the slate from the dash, bashing it out of the slot with his fist, while pictures of rotten lungs and crying children emerged on its screen. SkyCloud would be charged for the whole journey and he'd have to explain it to Grey. But hey, got some real news for you there buddy: SkyCloud still allows ads from vaping brands on its site, so who's really paying the bill?

Most people only had one slate, and as far as the social and public services was concerned that was perfect. People could pick up their benefits in slate coin, be rewarded in SC for using public leisure facilities or clocking up a healthy number of steps, or participating in healthy food initiatives delivered in restaurants. Taxes, wages and credits for taxi rides, as well as communications with schools and public services, ID, passports, health certificates, appointment reminders all came through that single slate too.

If citizens had two slates they couldn't swap SC between them, they could only access their government account with one of them, and social companies allowed only one single log in, and that had to come via a single slate, not multiple ones. The single slate policy had, he admitted, helped manage the fourth Covid 19 crisis in 2026, by allowing very accurate track and trace. After that, it hadn't occurred to the world to go back to multiple devices. Why would they?

Soren had tried to write stories about the creep of the one slate world, the threat to British sovereignty by restricting citizens to all communications through one method, but they'd dropped off the feeds within hours of posting.

The Ministry was still another mile or so away. Soren asked his slate for the time. It ignored him, but the slate of the young woman waiting to get into the TriCab he'd just vacated seemed happy to oblige. The woman smiled and tilted her head awkwardly, as if to apologise that her slate was so much more modern than his. She got into the

TriCab, leaving Soren to calculate that he just about had the time to go by foot. To vape a little more. And to think.

Theft of slates had long been a thing of the past. Once the technology had moved from passwords to fingerprints, there was no point stealing them. Unless you were going to take someone's finger too.

Soon, the slate companies had that covered. Once set up, in one of the ubiquitous communications stores of course, slates became so attuned to their owners that they could only be used by them. Something about microgyroscopes in the devices, magnets sensing the way owners used them, held them, swung them as they walked.

Soren had stopped upgrading not long after that. After years of tweaking recharging plugs and ports to force users to buy new devices every two years, the slate manufacturers had finally agreed to a standard magnetic charging platform built into universally compatible mounting stations. The companies had promised this would never change, however developed the hardware and software would become in the future.

Soren's last upgrade was one of the first to fit on the now ubiquitous charging stations found on desks, coffee shop tables and in stores across the country. But now, his version was pretty old technology. It just about recognised his voice and his walking gait. The rest was pot luck. They *wanted* him to upgrade. He'd held on to his old, far out of date slate, as a small rebellion. Defying the creeping control that updating was bound to bring. But it wouldn't be long before his became so obsolete he'd have to concede to a new one.

Curtis Soren held up his screen to the laser panel mounted on the strengthened glass double doors at the

Ministry of Society and Communications and they slid across to let him in. Somewhere a camera would have checked his physical build and facial features, matching them against the information his slate had just delivered.

A map emerged on his device, guiding him up an escalator and around two corners of corridors before he emerged in a triangular open plan space designed to funnel the twenty or so bodies standing around through another security gate, this time staffed.

The security guard wore a smart blazer, with the MinSoc logo sewn onto her breast pocket. It represented the top curve of a radar, with a dot emitting three curved bars. It was the symbol that used to flash then appear solid on electronic devices when they were connected to the internet. Like most government insignia, it had a modern comfortable feel about it. Underneath the radar appeared the words: *Always Community. Always Connected.*

"Mr Soren, if you would please step through the security arc." Another electronically generated voice.

He did so and was cleared with a green light, as he expected. Only the usual warning flashed up on a welcome screen that vaping was not allowed inside any building. It was the same technology as the front door of the building, only with added metal detecting. Standard practice at airports and train stations. And when someone was about to be in the same room as someone high up in government.

At least that might be something interesting.

Following the flock, Soren entered a small conference suite, which was comfortably furnished with warm wood panelling, a soft maroon carpet. There were ten rows of comfortably upholstered chairs in the same royal blue and light purple trim as the Ministry's upbeat logo, neatly laid out with an aisle down the centre. Each chair had a docking station for its user's slate.

He took a seat at the back and surveyed the crowd of fellow newsgatherers. Fifty-fifty in gender, he estimated. Racially diverse. Very modern. Very London. Not one of them older than him, most barely out of their twenties. The dress code was decidedly informal, jeans, t-shirts, a dyed haircut or two. Soren straightened up the lapel of his own jacket, and ran his fingers roughly through his greasy hair. He wished he'd worn a tie.

Some chatted with each other quietly, but most stared, prodded and swiped at their slates. Some screens didn't require a touch at all. Soren shook his head as he watched a young freckled women in a patchwork dress moving her hands this way and that in front of her slate. Windows were opening, moving, slipping and scrolling quicker than he could track.

He slotted his slate into the armrest and banged it slightly with his right clenched fist to make the connection. A twenty-something looked over at the noise, but Soren dead eyed him until he looked away.

Soren was about to begin his own swiping, for any smallest clue about what the hell he was doing here, when his slate faded and the logo of the Ministry expanded smoothly from a dot in the centre of the display to eventually take up the whole screen. Looking around, Soren noticed each slate in the room had lit up in the same way, casting a white glow against the faces of their owners. The lights in the room had dimmed slightly, exaggerating the luminescence - or was it dominance? - of the tech.

A door opened at the side of the room and three people entered. Two sat down on the chairs at the back of the slightly raised stage. The third, a tall man barely scratching his forties, moved to the lectern at the front. He made a swiping movement, and a large screen lit up on stage with the Ministry logo. Underneath were the hashtags #MinSoc #endit.

Soren read the words and sat up a little straighter. Maybe Grey had been right. Or maybe this press conference would be another example of a young woman's death being used to gain traction in a world with a very short attention span.

The man at the lectern stood silently as if waiting for applause to settle. Soren took the wait as an opportunity to assess the speakers. The man at the lectern wore a suit and a bright striped tie, loosely knotted, top button undone. He was blond with wisps of hair rising to a slicked over quiff at the front. Lanky, holding his hands against the lectern limply as he stood waiting for the crowd to come to a hush.

To his left sat a slightly younger man, stiff black hair, with a five o'clock shadow. He had dark trousers, finished with bright white sneakers crossed under the bottom of his chair like a school boy. He wore a white polo shirt, with short sleeves and no tie. Clearly he'd left his cap back stage, but was definitely delighted to be here.

And to his left sat a woman. Older. Probably older than Soren. She wore a formal suit dress in light blue, pressed neatly and buttoned up to a collar at the front. She held her hands in a neutral pose on her lap, clasped together. Streaks of grey ran through her otherwise brown hair. Dyed, Soren imagined. The impression she offered was formal, authoritative.

And her face?

Soren shuffled in his seat, uncrossed his legs and felt his stiff back force him into a yet more formal upright pose to match hers.

He felt the slightest shiver run down his spine.

"Ladies and gentlemen, and those identifying as other," the lanky blonde man began. "You are all very welcome here at the Ministry of Society and Communications, and I would like to express my thanks to you for coming this morning. We have a lot to share with you and we hope you will stay.

"In fact, I make no apology in bribing you to do so," he added, with a wave towards the back of the room. "We have fresh coffee, pastries and fruit, as well as a chat with us all, in exchange for the fifteen minutes or so of your time you've so kindly allowed us to take."

The speaker tittered to himself, closely followed by mumbling approval of his audience. They had turned to look at the treats that had been brought into the back of the room. Soren turned too, his gaze falling to the fresh coffee beans stacked in a bean-to-cup machine, ready to grind out his third caffeine hit of the day. He looked for cinnamon scones and found them. Satisfied, he turned back to the woman on the stage, squinting to try to see her face more clearly and wishing he'd sat closer to the front.

The speaker waited for the excited murmur to calm, his intention to lighten the atmosphere in the room clearly achieved.

"Many of you will know me already," he continued as a few nodded their heads. "Those who don't I hope I will get to know. My name is Harry Godspeed and I am assistant national director here at MinSoc. Don't get too excited by that title. I'm merely the chair here today. My job here is to introduce two speakers who sit far above my own seniority and pay grade, let alone my knowledge. Or security clearance."

He paused to allow another small laugh from the crowd. The man had charisma. Was this how all Ministry press conferences went? A show and a joke, with pastries and chirpy chat for afters?

"Today we are going to be talking about the social. Why else would you be here, right? But I'm delighted to offer you the latest news straight from one of the biggest social companies in the world. Adisa Zane is here, Driver of Coding at YoYo."

Soren sighed and shook his head. The rest of the room gasped at the announcement. YoYo was magic dust. One of the main social communication platforms worldwide. The man sitting on the stage wearing schoolboy trainers knew it. He nodded slightly as the atmosphere grew warmer. Sweet pastries had just taken a step down as the main attraction once the speeches were done.

Godspeed smiled at Zane, then towards his audience who gradually came to focus on him again. "Mr Zane will be answering questions about the initiatives we have to share with you today, but before he does I'd like to introduce my boss, and our national director here at MinSoc, Amanda Ward."

Soren heard the name and squinted again towards the middle aged woman. He couldn't place his discomfort.

"My colleague Amanda Ward is going to make the official announcements today, on behalf of the government. At the end, all three of us will answer your questions, and I hope - if you guys leave us any - join you for pastries and coffee."

Soren watched as Ward approached the lectern, and Godspeed took his seat. Immediately, Godspeed started swiping above the screen of his slate.

"Friends, we really are very pleased to welcome you here

to the Ministry," Ward said. Her voice was strong but welcoming, sincere. As she began, each of the audience's slates flipped to reveal a picture and a mini biography of the speaker. "I do know many of the Ministries here can be stuffy and formal, but I hope you'll appreciate we try - we're trying - to do things differently. We're committed to participation and openness, and on that count we have some very good - and I know interesting - news for you to collect, and share with your audiences and users today."

She smiled back to her colleagues on the stage, and they nodded to the audience with approval. In turn the news-gatherers shared glances, smiles and nods with each other.

Ward looked towards her feet, and took a moment for the whole room to become silent. She looked up, her face serious.

"Unfortunately, each of us in this room cannot have escaped the recent devastating story of Rasalina Mazeika, a young woman who had her whole life ahead of her. I do not wish to go over the terrible details here, except to once again express our sincere regrets and thoughts to her family and friends in Lithuania. It is a shame to us all and a national embarrassment in the UK that that we were unable to prevent Ms Mazeika's life being cut short in such a brutal manner."

The room fell into total silence, as if a moment of reflective respect had been called for. Soren shook his head and crossed his arms. Ward broke the silence after about twenty seconds.

"Though this poor woman's loss of life is not the reason for what you are about to hear, the case has highlighted and solidified the necessary measures I aim to outline.

"The hashtag #endit is not our own, but as you will see, it is one we at MinSoc fully support."

Soren glanced down at the biog of this serious woman. Her CV photo showed her slightly younger, with the grey strands missing from her brown hair. The skin tones had been touched up to smooth out her age to an indistinct middle age. It wasn't 'done' to include age on biographies.

Comparing the picture and the woman standing at the front of the stage, Soren judged her age as maybe five years older than he. She was ten times more confident, and God knows how many times more comfortable in this atmosphere of collect and share, manipulating audiences and users.

"Today, I aim to outline the Ministry's new strategy for online safety. I think you'll find it a landmark in the way we all use social across everything we do. Most importantly, I know you'll feel that we're making the social - and therefore the very communities we live in - safer places to play and to socialise, to share and to work.

"I won't pretend this hasn't been a challenge." The woman smiled, and looked over towards the YoYo Driver of Coding, who offered a mock apologetic smile in response. "But we've come to some monumental agreements that simply present the best of all possible solutions."

Soren tried to garner what the woman was actually saying. He concluded she had said very little so far.

"The internet and the social has been a great place for us to share, unite, socialise and discover. But around every corner, behind every swipe, has been the danger of stumbling - our children stumbling - upon something they should not be seeing. The very existence of social had provided space for the best in society, but also the very worst. Either in full sight of those who do not want to see it and share it, or behind dark walls and secret codes where users are able to carry out hateful, distasteful, prejudiced, illegal activity with impunity. The sad death of Rasalina Mazeika is the latest and most visible example."

Amen, answered the crowd. Or they might as well have done, such was the shaking of sad heads and squeezing together of buttocks in unity.

"You will know," continued Ward, her voice rising ready to deliver her next carefully practised lift, "that in the past, our social friends have resisted any kind of intervention from civil servants, let alone elected government officials, to clean up and restrict this negative side of what we all benefit from. They have said it is too complicated. They have said it is a matter of freedom of speech. They have said we must allow space for these negative communications to exist on their platforms.

"It has been nearly twenty years since the government of the time had to begin passing legislation to impose an official duty of care on these social platforms, backed up with heavy fines. The companies fought back, claiming what they called the higher ground and the right to a free market. They spent their users' money to attempt to keep the status quo. The occasional fines government did impose meant nothing to these multi billion outfits. They barely covered the state's legal fees.

"Ladies and gentlemen, friends, the last few decades of this approach have not worked. Fanatics have become more fanatical. Insulting, racist and bigoted communications have been targeted at those in and out of the public eye. Children have been exploited. People have died at their own and others' hands, directly as a result of the hatred that has been shared through the social. Our children... and our future children," Ward quickly corrected herself, looking up at her young audience, "need protection."

She took a sip of water, and appeared to take a few breaths to calm herself.

"I'm getting carried away here." Soren wasn't sure whether those words were scripted or not. He assumed they were. "I'll try to stick with today's announcement, which I know you will find as appealing as we have found it challenging to agree with our colleagues."

The slates glowed and flipped onto a blank page, with the Ministry's logo in the bottom right corner.

"Working with our colleagues from social companies we have finally agreed to a set of norms for the social space." She took a breath. "To more effectively seek out and restrict negative commenting, bullying and harassment across social media platforms."

A corresponding bullet point appeared on Soren's slate.

"There will be a complete banning of extremist groups from these platforms, and social media companies will create rapid response teams who will seek out and delete any accounts that promote such content."

Another bullet mark flew across screens.

"And finally, and this to me is the most important announcement of the day, we have agreed with our colleagues in the social industry that the dark web - that pernicious, criminal, hidden, protected, secret and disgusting part of social that shames our society - will be shut down. Totally and completely. Its protagonists, its creators, maintainers and users will be tracked down and banned from our digital world."

She paused. "Together, we *will* end it."

Soren sat up at this. It was quite a promise.

"Every tool, and all of the knowledge our friends in the social companies have used over the last generation to make our lives easier and more productive, will be turned upon those who would seek to hurt for their own personal pleasure and gain."

Ward took another sip of water, her cheeks glowing.

"These policies are what we have to share with you today. So sensitive, and certainly delicate in terms of negotiations with the social companies, that we didn't feel able to pre-share them through the usual channels. As the country's leading information gatherers, we felt you - our friends - should be the first to know. To thank you for your continued support of MinSoc, we would like to give you the opportunity to be first to share this news among your networks."

Ward looked up from her slate and surveyed the room. It was silent, many of the newsgatherers reading the policies outlined on their slates. A few looking over towards Adisa Zane from YoYo, waiting for his time at the lectern. Soren knew for many of them, this would be the story of their careers. An entirely safe web and social community, announced under their watch. For the brainwashed social newsgatherers, this would be a story to be swiped into the digital archives of history. It would be instant messaged from generation to generation. And they were wetting themselves to have been there.

For Soren, the challenge of how Ward and the social companies would destroy the dark web was the big question. It would take more than a hashtag.

"And though there will be opportunities for questions later, please don't ask me how we managed to finally bring the social companies around the table on this. Success sometimes requires private negotiations. Nevertheless," another glance towards Zane, "we have achieved our aims. Simply put, the internet and the social will be entirely better places to be as a result of this work."

Ward gave the impression of speaking off script as she concluded her remarks.

"Friends, naturally there is plenty more information to share with you. It will be available as a swipe when you leave the room. After you've joined us for the treats the Ministry has laid on for us. I'm no techie, I don't know *how* these things are being achieved as we sit here in this building, but I know they are. And I know it's a great thing. I believe in our humanity and our will to be better."

She paused, then it was if she was trying to make eye contact with every person looking in her direction.

"I can only welcome the exciting social times to come. As a fellow social user, as the national director of this Ministry, and... as a mother."

The crowd of newsgatherers broke into soft applause as she left the platform. Soren uncrossed his legs, stretched his back, then sat lower in his chair before crossing them again and gazing at the woman who had just spoken.

Ward retook her seat, freeing up Harry Godspeed to take the lectern. Slates across the room flipped to the Ministry logo.

"Well, I'm rather excited about all of this. But it gets better. And that's because I'm now pleased to introduce Adisa Zane. He's been at the heart of this project on behalf of YoYo, and he's here to answer any of the more technical questions you might have."

Slates flipped to a short biography of Zane as he took to the microphone, amidst far stronger applause than had been offered to Ward's emotional speech. His photo was of the wackier variety: a selfie taken after some mud splattered running escapade, or perhaps a caving trip. The kind of photo heading up pretty much every under-thirty's social feed. Chuckles spread across the room as it appeared on the audience's slates.

Soren had time to take in the key ideas from the man's biography. MIT, of course, stints at Google and Twitter. Lots of Partnerships, Memberships, Trusteeships and Champions, most at social start ups Soren had heard of, but wasn't exactly clear what they did. Or had done. Some, he knew, had failed because the companies didn't know either.

"Hi folks, I'm Adisa - or Adi for short." The young man spoke with the confidence of a thirty-something millionaire. Soren was surprised he hadn't made the hashtag sign with his fingers as he announced himself.

"I'm delighted to have been invited to chat to you all this morning, and to share this exciting news. Thanks for having me."

He paused as the audience nodded their approval. One person clapped, then retreated embarrassed.

"Well, I work for YoYo. I'm Driver of Coding at the Village," the man's voice lifted at the end of each line, as if each statement was a question. "It's hard to describe what I do, but it's all around exploring what YoYo could do next with the platform. We test a few things. I'm nobody's boss, though. But, don't tell that to the people who work for me."

Another titter from the crowd, and he grinned at the response.

"Anyway, you can get a full priority update on our main feed just as soon as we're all done here."

More giggles. Soren saw a few trying to swipe their screens already, though the MinSoc logo stayed put.

Zane adopted a more serious tone.

"No, I'm here on behalf of pretty much all the other socials too. Together we have agreed with the Ministry to put in place these policies. For the greater good."

There was silence in the room.

"Our consortium, we call it Portico, covers all messaging platforms, internet providers, social feeds. Podcast and music stations, forums, news feeds, advertising providers. Anything on your slates right now."

It occurred to Soren that this man had little idea about the politics behind what he was sharing. He was a techie and had been sent as a crowd pleaser. Toeing the line, little chance of speaking out of turn. He was the coder that Ward wasn't. And not the politician she was.

"Anyway, my bosses have been talking to the bosses here at the Ministry, and especially to Amanda Ward and Harry Goodspeed. We at YoYo and all across Portico have been convinced that it's time we gave back as an industry.

"More formally, I guess," - Zane looked down at his slate for the first time since he had begun speaking - "we recognise our responsibility in society, our privileged place among our users, and our debt to those who have loyally used our platforms as we've developed and improved over decades."

He spoke it as a child does, when they're learning to read the alphabet by rote.

"We've been convinced strong action is required, and understand our privileged access to knowledge and experience puts us in the ideal position to use it to achieve the aims of this programme. We've gained a lot, now we're going to give a lot."

"Oh," said Zane, looking up at the audience and faking the gesture of speaking behind his hand, "also I guess we've got gazillions of dollars to make these things happen."

The crowd erupted in laughter, and then applause. Even Soren smiled, though he quickly pulled it into check.

Godspeed took the microphone again and waited for his audience to settle.

"Well, we have limited time for questions now, and some time for the three of us to share coffee with you before the national director must leave us for other business. And Adisa, I'm sure, is keen to get back to the YoYo Village."

"You know how this works," he continued. "If you'd like to pose a question, just type it into your slate, and by the power of the social we'll be able to choose who's best to answer it. I'll give you a minute or two to get going."

Soren observed his fellow newsgatherers, as their slates flipped and a box appeared with an onscreen keypad. Some prodded away, breaking only to lean over empty seats like sneaky school pupils trying to spy on each other's work.

Soren tapped the question box on his own slate, prodding the letters with a clumsy forefinger.

"Who decides what to ban?" he typed, then swiped to send.

"Thank you, your query will be considered by the panel," the slate responded. He looked up to see the three on stage. Their slates glowed as the questions came in. Godspeed conferred and then swiped, this way and that, above his slate.

Soren's slate pinged.

"Thank you. Your question is dealt with in the accompanying material you will be given after this session. Do you have another question?"

Soren tapped his screen again, punching the letters out a little harder this time.

"Who's in charge? The Ministry or the social companies?"

"Thank you," his slate responded again, before pinging

the same response. The after material would answer his question.

Soren uncrossed his legs, straightened up and looked towards the stage. Godspeed and Ward were leaning together into Godspeed's slate. Ward gazed over in Soren's direction, squinting as he had towards her earlier.

He reached for his vape then remembered the sign at security. He stabbed at the question box one more time.

"When do we get our coffee?"

A second later Godspeed smiled and Ward laughed.

Soren's slate pinged.

"Thank you for your question, which will be considered by our panel."

When chatter in the group became louder than the occasional pings from the newsgatherers' slates, Godspeed swiped his own screen and everyone's slate returned to the Ministry's logo.

"Well thank you very much friends," he said, taking to the lectern. "There's been some very interesting questions posed, and obviously there'll not be time to go through them all, but we'll do what we can.

"First, to Amanda Ward, executive director, if you'd like to take this one: 'Why has the Ministry decided to take these actions now?' Thanks for that question, and I think it's a good one. Let me quickly start and say my colleague here will be modest in her own answer, but suffice to say I have been lucky enough to work with Amanda for a number of years, and I know social safety has been a major concern of hers - a passion even - since we started working together. She's been determined, might I even say stubborn, with the social companies on this. No surprise, then, that her appointment has coincided with this programme being instigated. But anyway, sorry Amanda, the floor is yours."

Ward stood and spoke clearly, the mic in her own slate clearly taking up the sound and broadcasting it throughout the room. "Really, Harry, you do speak too highly of my powers, but thank you. It's been a pleasure to work with you."

She turned to the audience.

"To be honest, it's really a case of the socials seeing sense after two generations of controversy. Perhaps the #endit campaign has reinvigorated what we were working on, but I'm so glad the public and the Ministry appear to have been on the same wavelength for some time.

"We've all seen the good social can do, but we've seen the damage too. Granted, we've had to push the companies, and yes, initially they pushed back. We've threatened, they've threatened, there have been a lot of difficult conversations in dark rooms. But I think we've come to a good place. It's not my doing, it's a partnership that has been a long time coming. Yes, it's been a passion of mine for a long time. Way before #endit. Many parents like me have been horrified by the dark web in particular. So I see these policies as something I'm lucky to be able to present to you today."

Zane nodded along with every word.

Godspeed took control again. "Okay, a question for Mr Zane here. Which companies are backing this new scheme?"

He sat up and smiled.

"All of them," he responded quickly, not even rising from his seat.

Now he did rise. "Like Mrs Ward says, this has been a partnership effort. Lots of social bosses talking to social bosses - I hear some of them actually met, like, in person."

He looked up for the laugh.

"I don't remember when Gum first came on the scene, but I know the early social company's founders said the core value of the platform was: 'Don't be evil'. Well, maybe we in the social community lost our way somehow. But the world changes. And we changed too. I don't need to tell you #endit was the most shared hashtag in the history of the internet in the UK? That told us something that was staring us in the face. Time for change."

Godspeed spoke again: "Well, we're all grateful for that, I'm sure. But Adisa, while you're standing, we might as well move onto another question for you from the audience. How did you get into working at YoYo? What's the secret?"

The crowd of newsgatherers laughed and shuffled in their seats, shifting their bodies towards the stage, as if to hear better. Soren reached for his vape again.

"Harry, please," he said, laughing. "This always comes up. I guess it's a lot about being in the right place at the right time. And showing real interest in social, I mean, *real* interest. Sharing, commenting, using. Opening up your life. Networking. Knowing the right people. And working hard."

The lifting tone at the end of each line grated and Soren stopped listening. He tried to swipe away the logo, but it stayed put. No outgoing media, he reckoned. Not until the press gathering was done. No headstart for anyone, until they left the building and then they were free to frantically tap away at their slates, competing to be first to post. All he wanted was a puff on the vape in his pocket.

A few more questions were posed to the panel. One regarding funding for the initiative - government seed funding, backed up by the social companies who would implement it for free. One about online porn, which everyone lapped up but Amanda Ward took seriously and answered directly, "as a feminist and mother".

The policy would erase or prevent any porn, video or otherwise, that had not been certified as consensual and legitimately made by a registered adult entertainment production company. This so called 'Safe Porn' certification was already in place, and had governed the porn industry for the last five years. Any porn of any sort that was not certified or appeared on the dark web would be removed. Again, the dark web would be deleted entirely, beginning bit by bit as the social companies worked together to bring it down.

"It's important to say," Godspeed added, "that we quite understand that as we bring in certain and very fair limitations to what people can share over public forums, the underground sharing of information is likely to increase. That's why we've included our work on eradicating the dark web as a priority too. We have a whole team working in the department alone, in partnership with our social associates."

Zane took a question about how hate speech, discrimination and bigoted content would be tracked down among the billions of pages and messages posted every day. He waved it off with the simple answer: "Our whole company is built by hackers and geeks. We know how to track that stuff down and delete it, just give us a slate and we'll write the code."

He took two more questions with delight, about his own work and how incredibly useful YoYo had been to users whose job depended on sharing great news. How best could newsgatherers use the tools the social provided?

Soren continued to ignore the fawning, only lifting his head when he heard Godspeed say there was time for just one more question, a very pertinent one, which he believed would be from the back row. He looked behind him, before

43

realising the question Godspeed was indicating was to come from him.

Catching up, Soren stood. He was faintly surprised that his question had been the only one identified as from a particular person.

"Curtis Soren, SkyCloud Media. My question is about," he fumbled for his slate, which was blank except for the Ministry logo, "er, decision making. Who gets to make the call about what's permitted and what's not?" He looked up to see Ward and Godspeed slightly raise their eyebrows in unison. Zane just looked bemused. "Who's going to ultimately be in charge?"

"Oh, sorry." This time it was Godspeed's turn to fumble with his slate, swiping above his screen. "I think you'll find technical questions, and far more of all the complicated details like those, are contained in the information you'll all get when you leave the room this morning."

He stood.

"I think we expected your question to be about," he indicated the back of the room, and forced a huge grin onto his face, "coffee and cake?"

The crowd took his joke as an invitation, detaching their slates and rising quickly. They seemed torn between heading for the coffee and pastries, or joining a growing queue to speak to boy wonder in the sneakers from YoYo.

Soren dropped to his seat and smacked his slate on the left hand side to release it. Finally, the logo disappeared but it remained seared into his retina. He blinked to clear the image, staring into the distance. When his eyes cleared, they found Amanda Ward's own eyes which were staring directly at him. Then she quickly turned away to Godspeed. The man's grin faded as he leant over her. They swiped his slate together, then Godspeed nodded. Ward walked out of the side door.

Godspeed used the mic built into his slate. Few were listening anyway. "I'm afraid Mrs Ward has been called away on other business, but of course myself and Mr Zane here will take coffee with you and hope to offer you any further information you require."

Soren didn't bother staying. He had nothing to say to these social obsessed clowns. His vape was calling.

Inside the TriCab, Soren swiped his slate to video call his editor.

"So, tell me all about it," said Will Grey. "What's the scoop?"

"No big news. Just a bunch of kids claiming to make the world a better place by restricting basic freedoms and pushing out more advertising."

"I like it, especially the advertising part." Grey was joking, but only just, thought Soren.

"They're going to hunt down and wipe out extremist groups and those with very strong views from the socials. We've seen all those promises before. Only this time, the socials appear to be on board. Maybe half heartedly. It's yesterday's news, and I'll believe it when I see it."

"And?" said Grey.

"So you've seen the posts the other newsgatherers have already posted?"

"Yes, and I'm impatiently awaiting your own contribution, so?"

"Right - as you *already know* then - they're talking about destroying the dark web. Easy as that. Hunt it down. Pull the plug on the servers. Lock out its users. Goodnight everything awful in the world, hello sunshine."

"And you doubt they can do it?"

"I didn't say that," replied Soren, reaching for his vape, then thinking better of it. "Not overnight, though, and the dark web will grow for sure once the other measures have been brought in. So it won't be simple. And I question whether it can or should be done, at least in this way."

"Hold on," said Grey. "You've seen the traction #endit got. You still question whether it's a good thing to get rid of the dark web. Child porn? Human trafficking. Extremist groups?"

"You know it's more complex that that."

"No. It *used* to be more complex than that. Take a look at the feeds, Curtis. The socials are going wild with the idea. #endit is already back up the feeds."

"I haven't looked at that yet."

"Then you're way behind everyone else that was at that bloody press launch. And behind the times. I'm looking at the feeds now and there's no sign of SkyCloud on any front page. That's your job, my friend."

"I'll put together some copy and post it now," said Soren,

"Swipe it to me first. I'll get it onto our front page. Just the basics. You can do something more indepth when you get back."

"You don't trust me to post it myself."

"In your state of mind just now, Curtis, I'm not sure I trust you with anything. Over recent months you've sneaked out some criticism of the socials that haven't pleased our advertisers one bit."

Grey signed off. Soren wiped through the feeds. The hashtag #darkwebdoomsday was trending alongside #endit.

No doubt it had been created by the newsgatherers from InfoCom.

InfoCom, twice as big as SkyCloud, were always first out of the starting blocks with the hashtags. Other newsgatherers, then their readers, picked up the tags to share. In the last fifteen minutes, #darkwebdoomsday had become the dominant tag. Attempts from other newsgatherers - #socialsafety #endsocialhate #MinSocPledge - had quickly shuffled down the feeds, victims of the social's Darwinian survival of the fittest algorithms.

Soren pulled up InfoCom's original post. It had so far been re-shared over 4,000 times.

MinSoc and socials end all child porn. No more hate on feeds and web. Safer social. Safer society. #Darkwebdoomsday #endit, followed by a link to MinSoc's web release on the story.

No newsgatherer would have had time to write their own story on the release yet, so the link to MinSoc was as good as they could muster. InfoCom had a knack for keywords that would get readers into a fluster. And for creating posts a reader couldn't possibly disagree with.

Soren scrolled to the Ministry of Society and Communication's own social feed. *Our three point plan to keep you safer in the social world. Thanks to our friends on the social for all their hard work, #endit.* Then a link back to the MinSoc webpage release.

A moment later, MinSoc posted again with the same words. Only with *#darkwebdoomsday* added to the end. Within seconds, the post began getting shares and re-posts by the dozen.

Soren swiped through more relevant posts. Some just factual: three point plan, partnership between MinSoc and the social corporates, radical shakeup of social posts. Others were more fawning: great news, protecting our kids, MinSoc success on online equality. Some merely boastful or grubbing for favour: thanks to MinSoc for the coffee and cake, great to meet you #AdisaZane, #YoYo, and row after row of those emoji animations Soren despised.

#brownnose, Soren might have added.

He reached for his vape, and took the telling off from his TriCab as it pulled to the curb. It would give him a sliver more time to put together his own post. The trick was to post something new. Otherwise, he might as well re-share InfoCom and keep them high up in the rankings.

MinSoc new Exec forces socials to keep broken promises.

The newsgatherer put his vape back into his jacket, and swiped the delete key.

MinSoc Exec #AlisonWard impressive as she forces socials to delete dark web. Passion for a safer social welcomed. Questions remain about responsibility, #endit

He looked over his copy. He sighed and added *#darkwebdoomsday* to the end of his line, quickly swiping it to Grey with gritted teeth.

Only a couple of times had Soren coined a hashtag that had gone viral. Once only because he'd been first to stumble upon the near homonyms *#princeprints* when covering a story about some stolen artwork by a member of the then recently defunct royal family. The second more thought out: *#nomonkeybusiness* after MinEnv announced the final closure in its long term programme to shut all zoos.

His slate pinged with a message from Grey.

Love the celeb angle. Harrison getting a pic of National Director. Wasn't so hard, eh?

Soren blew out the remains of steam from his vape, directing it at Grey's message. He felt sick with the concession he'd made.

He swiped the feeds again. More praise for the policies,

each beginning to be separated from the main announcement. Each newsgatherer was searching for their own angle.

Socials promise anti-bullying action was at the heart of one emerging strand.

No to spreading #selfharm say socials ran another.

Dark web, no place to hide, and many other variations on that theme, which Soren read closely.

#Safeporn left intact, ran one rather pleased with itself idea. It climbed the rankings quickly, with sharers adding a wink or blush emoji to the end of the text. Soren knew where that strand had started.

Then there were various strands on the worthiness of #YoYo, #socialsafety, #socialcorps and #MinSoc in general, most accompanied by #endit. All were struggling to make middle ranking in the rush of posts.

Soren knew these would soon plummet, and the dilution of too many hashtags would smooth out the socials' excitement on the subject. It was a matter of hours before users would move on.

That's when Grey would lean on Soren to either find new angles on this morning's announcement, or to earn his keep by seeking out an original story to keep SkyCloud in the rankings. Was there something about MinSoc's new openness to newsgatherers he could latch onto? A 'view from inside MinSoc' about the furnishings, staff and top tech security? Or, God help him, patch together some of Adisa Zane's answers to create a five point superguide to getting a job in the social. He knew that would fly easily with SkyCloud readers, but he'd rather chew off his own fingers.

Soren's slate pinged as his post appeared in his feeds, then watched it slowly drop through the rankings.

MinSoc Exec #AmandaWard impressive as she unites with

socials to tackle dark web and hate online. Passion for a safer
social welcomed. #endit #darkwebdoomsday

"Fucking editors," he said aloud. Grey had deleted his
note about unanswered questions. He was barely getting
away with anything critical these days. Grey had to keep
those advertisers absolutely delighted.

The post was accompanied by a picture of Ward. Ten
years younger at least, far more informal than the one on
her biog. A holiday shot, perhaps. A smiling freckled and
bronzed face, with soft lips highlighted by the sunny coastal
view behind her. A warm picture. She was beautiful.

He looked at the picture more closely.

Soren took to his slate, and swiped open the info pack
he'd picked up at the news release. The photo and the biog
in the pack were the same as when she'd spoken on stage.
MinSoc's public face. Harrison had found the picture somewhere else.

He swiped open the image browser on his screen and
began to type in her name.

Then he noticed his feed.

His post had begun lifting in the ranks, as others had
added or commented on his line. Grey's edit had stayed
intact, but the hashtag #AmandaWard had been given a
halo by some of his readers. It was something rarely
awarded to anyone who wasn't a celebrity posting from a
children's hospice, or a dog who'd rescued an old man from
a flood.

It was uplift Grey would be excited about. But Soren had
his own reason to be interested. He peered into the eyes of
the woman in the picture.

Who are you?

. . .

"Looks like you've scored there," Grey said as Soren walked into his editor's office. It was on the second floor of a building close to Old Street roundabout in central east London. Some of the young staff looked up from their screens as he entered. One or two even removed their headsets.

"She was just there to make the announcement. A pretty picture doesn't make a story."

"It does in this game," said Grey.

"It wasn't even my post," argued Soren. "You edited out my rightfully expressed doubts, and Mia," Soren swung round to Harrison's work station, which was empty, "added the fairy dust. You think we'd have got that kind of uplift if Ward had been some male, ugly old duffer?"

"You shouldn't be so hard on yourself."

"Piss off, Will. Anyway, we've got the traction haven't we? Will you kindly let me get on with earning you some more money?"

"Fine, a post concentrating on Ward then," said Grey. "Her background, her motivation, how she brought this thing about."

"A puff piece."

"If you like, you know I'll edit for shareabilty anyway. Mia can seek out some more pics of this famous-for-fifteen-seconds MinSoc national director. Think you can get an interview?"

"Nope. She didn't hang around for questions at the end. In fact…"

"Will you try?"

"In fact, she was due to stay for coffee, but suddenly changed her mind when I started asking awkward questions."

"Mmm, that could be something. Now we're talking real newsgathering," said Grey.

The editor swiped up on his slate. "Nothing yet, but I reckon you've got about forty-five minutes to get something worthy of that halo out there. That means sharing with me in thirty."

"Jesus. Where's Mia with her magic wand?" Soren asked.

"I'll call her back from lunch."

Soren threw his overcoat onto the back of his chair, and slumped into it. He'd missed coffee at the Ministry and it wasn't like any of these chumps was going to get one for him. He slotted his slate into the battered mounting on his desk.

The newsgatherer pack featured Ward's picture, along with the dumb grin of Adisa Zane and the smarmy, smartly dressed Harry Godspeed. Same biographies as they'd been given at MinSoc.

Ward had recently been appointed national director at MinSoc, a position only government ministers had power to control. After graduating from Cambridge, and mastering at University College London in politics and economics, she'd been brought up through the traditional establishment path: work experience periods across Ministries with the civil service early in her career, then an overseas placement to East Burundi with a charity for two years. French was just one of four languages she spoke. Then she'd come back to London and Edinburgh, where she'd specialised in communications, tech and social media.

She had been a junior at the Ministry of Society and Communications for a year, before being promptly promoted to assistant national director. Then just two months ago, she was made national director. As high as one could go in this Ministry. Obviously, hot property.

Other Ministries worked differently, but Soren had tried to pay as little attention to civil service mechanisms as possible. They made his head hurt and if written up, would hardly make ad saleable copy.

Soren copied and pasted Ward's biog onto a blank page.

A more detailed release about the new policies had been provided as part of the press pack, the same one Soren had glanced at on MinSoc's website during the initial social frenzy.

Each of the policies was outlined in a little more detail, in bullet points designed to be copied and pasted directly into social shares. Soren had already seen some word for word shares drop through his feed.

The release was short on fact and detail, long on pledge and fuzziness. There was lots of 'delight about partnership' and 'hard work to agree terms', then more on the 'benefits to social users' and society in general. That MinSoc would be 'cleaning up the social' was the most often repeated phrase. Nothing more than he'd been offered at the press conference earlier in the day.

Soren copied a short formal quote from Ward and pasted it beneath her biog. Hardly halo material. He looked at the clock on his slate. Ten minutes had passed.

He looked over to Mia Harrison's station. Still empty. She had only been at SkyCloud for a month and was already taking liberties. He liked that. As well as her cynicism and general disrespect for everyone. He looked around him at the informally dressed delinquents that made up the majority of the rest of the SkyCloud staff. She wasn't one of them. But he could do with a little help right now.

Soren opened the Frequently Asked Questions document supplied by MinSoc and scrolled through quickly. A long list of the project's social partners had been provided.

Their participation was being led by the four biggest social companies in the world. Together, the big four had become known as Portico - representing the four huge pillars that held up grand triangular entrances to buildings in ancient Greece and had been ever present on churches, parliaments and important buildings since.

There was a quick primer on the history of Portico. Over the last decade there had been a myriad of social media companies, each competing to do the same thing. Eventually they began buying each other up and merging, in order to serve customers better (according to the primer). Facebook bought WhatsApp. Amazon bought up the biggest webspace providers. Then they merged with Google, in an attempt to compete with Facebook, who by that time had also partnered with YouTube. Instagram held its own, but picked up TikTok and Snapchat on the way. Spotify bought up anything sound related, like Amazon's former platform Audible, only then to be taken over by Apple and its own iTunes platform. What had finally emerged was a new set of four major internet giants, working together to serve their clients better. The American companies Wonderfish, Talk, Gum, and the British YoYo.

Soren knew the rest. The untold story. The companies had faced huge anti trust suits launched by governments, users and smaller social media firms because they were taking over the whole market. But like a shapeshifting octopus the socials had restructured, and reworked themselves - including their names - to avoid the strongest cases against them. By establishing Portico, the companies had agreed to work together to keep prices low by sharing resources and data, and not overlapping in services. Instead they pledged billions in projects and innovation for the poorest and disenfranchised, and promised to create effective internal markets. Companies serving the public - shops, slate providers, webspace sellers - would still compete against each other to serve their customers by advertising and taking advantage of the Portico partners' functions. It didn't seem to matter if the competing companies were - at the end of a long labyrinth of ownership and offshore trusts - owned by the Portico companies anyway. No one cared who was at the end of the chain, as long as goods were affordable, accessible and deliverable the same day.

Soren looked again at the material about cleaning up the social. Yes, the project had direct government approval. Yes, the Ministry of Security was in on the project. Soren typed in to his screen, on his writing pad app: *'who supplies intelligence?'* The socials had agreed to implement all of the measures required through their own budgets. 'Good news for taxpayers, and a fair compromise by our social partners.' Would they provide all the data too, or was MinSoc going to share what it had with the socials?

Then Soren came to the question he'd been looking for.

'How will decisions be made about permitted content and permitted groups?'

This initiative, the FAQ revealed, had been five years in the making. It had been widely consulted upon among social user groups, victims' charities, the police and others, and had been scrutinised by government committees and executives at various ministries.

Soren copied the term *'widely consulted'*, to his writing pad, adding a question mark.

Policies would be continually reviewed with special interest groups and stakeholders, and updated accordingly. The exact mechanisms of these decisions will, by necessity, remain undisclosed in the interest of social, community and national security.

"Basically, whatever you like," Soren said aloud.

"Whatever I like?"

It was Mia Harrison, holding the coffee that had delayed the return to her station. Soren looked at the cup first, feeling a dryness in his throat, then up at Harrison who took an exaggerated sip.

"What I'd like," said Soren, leaning back in his chair, "is for you to find out more about Amanda Ward. To fill out this bullshit PR provided by MinSoc."

"Cambridge. East Burundi. Language specialist. Career civil servant. Enough for you?"

"No, I need more than the biog posted on the website. Let's start with where you got that picture?"

"Which one?" said Harrison, obviously trying to wind Soren up.

"The social pic."

"The sexy 'by the beach' shot?"

"Time is ticking, Mia," said Soren. "We're currently trending with that photo, but losing traction with every minute. If you don't want Grey chewing both our arses, you'll work with me on this, rather than gloating over the halo."

Soren's slate pinged.

"?"

It was from Grey. Rude bastard.

Soren stood and looked towards his editor's glass cubicle. He saluted, sat and looked back up at Harrison.

"Well?"

"Okay, so I figured I'd delve into her biog a little more," she began. "There's nothing more on the MinSoc website except what you have there, but there were a few loose ends to grab at. First, she went to Cambridge. I couldn't turf anything up on her there, but it wasn't like I had that much time."

Harrison took another sip of coffee.

"Then I looked around the various Ministries where she'd done work experience. All very tight on their information, as they tend to be about civil servants. At least until they rise to the top of the ranks. Don't want to highlight the ghosts in the machine I guess."

"Which leaves?"

"Which leaves the charity in East Burundi, where Amanda Ward took a two year voluntary placement. I did a search of some of our national funded projects out there, but turned up nothing on any of those. Then I looked at the French charities working close to the lakes there in East Burundi, because of the water in the shot? Naturally, Mademoiselle Ward brought up no search results, but a little guesswork, and a little squaring of the years she was supposed to be abroad in French Africa, and..."

They said it together: "Voila?"

"I found the pic in a charity PDF of an annual report published by *Ligne pour les Pauvres* in 2009. Her name is not there, and I don't speak French, but you don't overlook a pretty face like that. It was Lake Rweru."

Harrison leaned her backside against Soren's desk, crossed her arms and raised her eyebrows.

"Okay, have an apple," said Soren, holding up an empty palm which Harrison mimed taking from. "Well done you. We have a little background. She's a good person at heart and her East Burundi work - if I can push that French annual report through Cambio - should give me enough in English to polish that halo. Could you take another look at Cambridge? Got to work quick though - those 250 words aren't going to write themselves."

"Sure," said Harrison with a smile.

Soren had already turned back to his slate. Harrison continued to lean against his desk.

"Thank you," he said, extending the *you* and dismissing her with a wave.

"I'll find some more sexy pics for a longer piece we can put out tonight," she said. "Our 600-word follow up isn't going to look very good without them."

A minute later, Harrison had pinged across the *Ligne pour les Pauvres* report to Soren's slate. He fed it through Cambio to translate it. The result was mucky English but enough for him to pick out the salient points.

Amanda Ward had worked with the French organisation, which according to its annual report 'worked in partnership with its dedicated volunteers and generous corporate sponsors to improve social communications channels among the most deprived communities in the world.' Quite a mission thought Soren, but there was more. 'Social media was a lifeline to poorer towns and villages, allowing them vital connection with larger settlements, towns and regional government.'

Soren shook his head. No need for bread and water, when you can message your chums. He skipped through the charity report until he reached a double page spread with a picture of little brown kids running around with kites, their mums comparing tiny mobile phones. One speaking into hers. A big quote, running along the side in bright bold letters:

'Focus on mobile and emerging social communications quickly develops the economies of the poorest people in the world. And helps engender democratic government.'

Ah, those days when the social was going to save the world, thought the newsgatherer. Got a problem, new technology to the rescue. Let's not mention the cyber bullying, dark web and state control that came as part of the package.

He opened up his draft document:

MinSoc National Director brought social to the poorest in the world. Now she's protecting the most vulnerable from its darkest corners. #AmandaWard, 😊

Ward - at least as far as Curtis Soren's story was concerned - would make out that she had used her growing expertise and passion for electronic communications, super-charged at Cambridge and working at various government departments, to uncover majority world solutions with the help of first world technologies.

Soren created additions to the story from other broken English text he'd been able to unscramble from the charity report. He topped and tailed it with the highlights of this morning's announcement.

A back-of-a-postcard profile, but not too bad for thirty minutes' work. He tidied up his literals, checked spellings of place names against the original report, and set the document up for swiping to Grey who was again peering in his direction.

"Want a bit more sparkle for your copy?"

It was Mia Harrison again. She had crept up beside him and was scanning what he had just written. She gently placed her slate in front of his, and pressed the small red arrow in the middle of the screen.

It was a video cast from MinSoc. The page's viewing figures were already jumping up in triple figures. It had been posted ten minutes ago.

"The Ministry of Society and Communications is delighted to share with you a personal message from our own National Director," the text read alongside the bottom of the screen. The video description read: 'A personal message from Amanda Ward, as a civil servant and a mother'. At the end of the description was the hashtag #AmandaWard.

Alongside were posted two halo emojis.

Soren and Harrison watched the full ninety second video together, before Soren added the broadcast directly into his copy and swiped it across to Grey.

The East Burundi story and the video would work well together. Concentrating on the national director's voluntary work would create great uplift for his profile of Ward.

"She really is something," said Harrison, almost purring.

"Behave," said Soren. "There are still lots of unanswered questions about this whole 'clean up the social' thing. I'm only getting started on this woman."

Harrison took a final gaze at the woman who Soren had paused on his slate. "Well, you know where to come if you want some help."

The short queue in front of him was made up of office workers who barely looked up from their screens as they handed their cups to the baristas. Without speaking, they in turn swiped the cups against a glass pad, then filled them with whatever concoction appeared on their screen. The drinks machine had already begun to prepare the brew. Pop tunes echoed slightly too loud over speakers built into the ceiling.

The staff stood there, slumped and grumpy, resigned to a job that amounted to little more than moving a pre-ordered over sweet hot drink or sandwich from one space to another, before ungrateful, distracted customers. A sickly stink of synthetic sweetener, coffee liqueurs, rancid milk and body odour hung in the air.

Soren had left his slate in the office, a personal rule which he rarely broke when it was time for coffee. Not that information was easy to escape. Even in Carlos' place, a constant newsfeed ran across digital panels behind the counter and around the top of the room.

Soren looked up at a large LCD screen, which was muted in the corner of the cafe. On it, in the top left hand corner, sat the InfoCom logo.

At the newscaster's desk sat a very young woman relating the day's headlines. As she spoke, keywords appeared on the screen to her right, including, he noticed, #endit and #AmandaWard.

On the left of the screen ran the name of an online shop selling the formal pink jacket she wore, the designer of her dress and its price. Thus went also her lipstick, blusher and eyeshadow. And the name of the jewellery shop from which shoppers could purchase the delicate silver broach on her lapel and the necklace that hung ostentatiously across her chest.

Soren allowed a few customers to go past him in the queue as he read the list of trending hashtags moving along a wall feed.

His take on the story was still running, Soren noted with a smile. *#darkwebdoomsday* too, which he was less pleased about, and other emerging tags. Other subjects of the day, which he had missed that morning while he was at MinSoc: *#Strictly10,000*, *#fiverforafortune*, *#TriCabSlowDown*.

The hashtags meant nothing to him, and everything to the two dozen kids around him manically staring into their slates and swiping above them. Only a few chatted over their drinks and snacks. The tags would be celebrity stories, he assumed, or else some not very clever advertising dressed up as news.

On his way in this morning, Soren had searched the feeds for his own stories and shares and was pleased with the results. But he'd also searched for any negative responses to his stories. Actually, he'd searched for anything negative at all about the new MinSoc policy. Words like 'freedom of speech', 'civil liberties', 'criticism'. He couldn't find anything. Just like Will Grey had lifted 'questions remain' from his own story about the developments, anything doubting the policy was conspicuous by its absence.

That was strange. Even the most popular films and books got some negative posts and shares, trolls and philistines usually. *#AmandaWard* and *#darkwebdoomsday* seemed to be running without negative criticism or questioning at all. True enough, he didn't quite understand how the social worked. But it was something he thought he should talk to his editor and Mia Harrison about.

He tried to put it out of his mind, because now was coffee time.

"Ah, Mr Soren!" said a man from behind the counter, his round belly bulging between the grumpy teenagers shuffling cups under the coffee machines.

"Carlos," said Curtis, with as much warmth as he could muster. He handed his cup to the coffee shop's owner.

"Good to see you as always, sir." His booming Italian voice cut through the low chatter and the constant pinging of slates. Carlos swiped Soren's cup. "Ah, the purist as always," he beamed, brushing his hands on a coffee stained cotton apron. "Black americano, extra shot, no sugar." He pushed a girl with pink hair away from her machine, and filled the cup himself, running boiling water through the nozzle before beginning to make the drink. He shook his head at Soren, and raised his eyebrows in the direction of the various flavourings, sweeteners, milks, cremes and additives listed on the video board behind him.

"So what is the latest news in the land of newsgathering? Tonight's final? Tax rises? The latest coffee flavours?"

Though tired and too often repeated, Soren liked Carlos' quips. He never failed to joke about himself and the coffee business which, like Soren, Carlos believed had become as stagnant and copycat as newsgathering.

In fact, Soren liked Carlos' place a lot, despite the sullen staff and the tinny music. At least it had staff. All of the big chains were now self service. Your own microchipped cup did all the hard work of ordering your drink, while the coffee came out of the machine with the remnants of the last person's drink still in the nozzle. Soren had often found the pure black Americano he craved bubbling with a greasy film of oat milk, or a sickly hint of buttermint. If you wanted a plastic tasting sandwich, or a pre-wrapped gluten free, low sugar brownie, you merely swiped your slate against the vending machine. The coffee and food was cheap from those machines. You got what you paid for.

At Carlos', though not deemed strictly safe according to MinHealth guidelines for cafes, his buns and teacakes were laid out in neat rows behind a glass screen, instead of ready packaged in air tight containers. Treats slick with grease, chocolate and icing sugar. And if you asked nicely, one of the teenagers would look up from their slate for long enough to hand you one on a bamboo plate.

"Something to eat, my friend?"

Soren remembered the pastries he'd left behind at the Ministry in favour of a vape.

"Okay, Carlos, why don't I take one of your cinnamon loops?"

"Perfect with your coffee, I think," said the owner.

Carlos handed over the freshly brewed coffee, and slipped the pastry onto a plate, along with a blunt bamboo knife. He waited, and silence hung in the air between the men.

"Shit, sorry." Soren pulled back his sleeve and pressed his fingerprint onto a metal plate. Old tech, but the only other way to pay if you'd left your slate in the office.

"Ah, that's no problem Mr Soren, Curtis, you're always welcome here. It would have been on me, but well..."

Yeah, like crap it would be.

"Always good to see you, always good."

Carlos was looking along the queue for another familiar face.

Soren took his coffee and cinnamon loop to his usual table, far away from the window facing the street. He pushed the slate mount to the side, and brushed someone else's crumbs onto the floor with his sleeve.

He hadn't done a bad job this morning, and maybe even had felt a tingle of excitement when Harrison and he had pinned down the East Burundi angle. The kids around him would have been sharing that story for the last hour, and quietly he'd been at the centre of that. He hated the social, but at least he'd been able to write something close to meaningful.

The policies MinSoc had laid out this morning had been popular. And what was there to argue about? Discriminatory language and bullying to be banned. Hate speech called out and eradicated. Extremist groups, their voice taken away to protect their victims and the public. And the dark web: the space on the internet that was the last standing ground for all that was evil in the world - the child porn, the terrorists, the drug smugglers, the people traffickers, the murderers of Rasalina Mazeika and her unborn child - to be taken down, piece by piece.

There was no doubt the dark web had played a long and ugly role in some of the worst the nation could even know. The bombs and acid attacks in first decades of the 2000's. Millions of pictures of children, even toddlers, being abused. Container after container of dead migrants washing up on southern beaches. Police hauls of cocaine and amphetamines, destined for deprived city schools. Hard right gangs of extremists attacking Muslims and Jews with machetes as they left mosques and temples. Far left groups organising violent protests.

If you took the story at face value, which was pretty much how communication on the social tended to present things, the policy seemed a good one. The rough edges of any complex story just got smoothed away by restrictions on word counts, or the desire to share as quickly as possible. Hard to swallow ideas quickly morphed into more digestible nuggets.

The policy even had a feel good factor about it. The socials had, for so long, said they wouldn't - couldn't - do anything about the most shadowy corners of the landscape they maintained. Then with a wisp of her wand, using the #endit campaign as if she'd started it, Amanda Ward had bewitched them: they'd given in and would use every coder they had to shine a bright light into the darkness and smash to pieces everything they found there.

And yet.

Soren looked up again at the hashtag rankings. The halo was still trending. No one was really looking behind the policy. Surely there were others who felt they wanted to understand more, before giving the trend a lazy thumbs up or a smiley face. Those who *relied* on the dark web, for example? Would they take this lying down?

The social wasn't to be trusted. The companies behind it even less. Soren looked down, took a slug of coffee and a mouthful of his pastry.

"See this, Mr Soren?"

He almost choked on the cinnamon dough as he looked up to see Carlos' belly waving beside him beneath the stained apron, all a little too close to Soren's face. He looked up to meet the coffee shop owner's gaze. He was gesturing towards the newsfeed running behind the counter.

"She's doing a good job, this woman."

Soren chewed quickly, and gulped.

"My daughter, ah my daughter Mr Soren. She spend too long, way too long," he gestured towards his customers, "on these bloody screens. All sorts she looks at. Fifteen years, and who knows what she see. I can't see what she see - I try, Mr Soren, you would too if you have a daughter - but I don't have the swipe or fingerprint, see."

He flailed his fat fingers, helplessly. Soren suppressed an instinctive revulsion, deep in his gut.

"Pah, fingerprint. I am her father. Her mother worries. Her brothers, older see, they worries. We all worries."

Soren took an opportunity. "So, you don't worries," he gulped a few lumps of dough back down his throat, "- worry about who controls what we see? Who gets to decide?"

"Mr Soren, Mr Soren sir, I don't know how they do it, I don't care. But I like that they do it. Naked kids? Gangs? Drugs? Nasty comments because you black, or yellow, or Italian, whatever..."

The man faked a spit to the floor. A few heads momentarily lifted from their slates.

"You're doing a good job, man," Carlos patted Soren's

shoulder. "A good job to write good stuff. Too much bad has gone before. We need more happiness."

Carlos switched to his salesman face again.

"You're doing a good job too, my friend," said Soren, raising his cup, then awkwardly also the half eaten cinnamon loop that was still in his hand. He waved them both at the coffee shop manager.

Carlos waddled away, pulling a grubby hanky from a back pocket and blowing his nose with it.

"I have *got* to get to Ned's," said Soren aloud.

Soren took a TriCab from the office, this time swiping for payment from his own account. He had sneaked back to his desk to pick up his slate, and asked Harrison to tell their editor he was going to work from home.

He would be putting together a bigger profile of the MinSoc national director. Maybe a 10-point feature, full of juicy keywords and links to other feeds. The kind of article Grey liked, and the advertisers' algorithms liked even better. He needed space to gather it all together, ran the line. Soren knew his colleague didn't believe his excuse for leaving the office.

The electric vehicle dropped him on Greek Street, deep in an area of London that was famous for secret political machinations. And before them, its establishments of debauchery and prostitution.

All that had gone of course. Politics now took place on white boards, via online polls and video conferencing. News conferences like the one Soren had endured that morning were few.

And sex? Sex work was barely recognisable. Strictly regulated by the Empowerment of Street Workers Act 2024, with very high minimum tariffs for clients. It was well governed and delivered in clean and safe pleasure shops. Trade unions for women and men who sold sex had been established, and they had easy access to civil servant champions right at the top of the Ministry of Employment.

The grubby porn shops of Soho were long gone, with a few remaining sex stores as present and unremarkable as pharmacies. Buying a dildo or sexy négligé was no more clandestine or embarrassing than shopping for shoes or upgrading your slate in store. The latter probably brought most shoppers to a higher state of arousal.

Ned's was a pub, plain and simple. One of many in this square mile, but few punters visited it. Or even knew of it. The landlord appeared to have done his damnedest to keep it that way.

The place sat between two tall terraces that had been converted into offices for advertising companies. It didn't feature a sign announcing its name, nor the ever changing screen of drinks and food offers that would power up when potential drinkers passed by other pubs.

Soren wasn't even sure it was called Ned's. He wasn't sure the place had a name at all. He pushed open the door, removing his long coat. He opened a wooden locker in the tiled corridor and placed his coat and his slate into it. Then he closed the locker, secured it and removed a thumb sized bronze key.

He ran his finger along the ridges of the metal, enjoying the feel of it, and then dropped it into his pocket. There, the weight of it felt good too. A physical object, in a world of passwords and swipes.

The bar was small and quiet, just five or six other customers. An aged gentleman sat on a stool on the other side of the bar. He looked up as Soren entered. He climbed down from his perch and reached for a heavy bottomed cut glass from one of the shelves.

Soren approached the bar.

"Whisky?" The old man rasped out the word. He pushed the glass under the optic, and let a shot of McCraken flow into it. He looked across at Soren, who nodded. He pushed the glass up for a second measure.

Soren took the drink and sipped. Then he took a longer draw. Now alcohol content had been restricted, it was harder to get the hit. He let the cut glass swing between finger and thumb, then knocked it a couple of times on the bar.

He pulled out his vape, raising his eyebrows to the pub landlord, who gave a grizzled smile.

"You know the MinHealth rules on vaping inside."

"And when to break them," Soren replied.

He took a deep toke, then left the bar to find a seat on a long bench on the opposite side of the room. It stank of warm leather and had patches of slightly newer material sewn in where generations had worn away the cushioning.

Two middle aged men sat in a corner with glasses filled with the same deep golden whisky he had. An older man and woman sat together further along the bench, in silence, each with half pints of brown ale, barely touched. He blew scented steam into the air and watched it fall, before taking another slug of the spirit.

He'd been coming to this bar for more than twenty years. He looked again at the familiar walls, dark and yellow stained with cigarette smoke from decades ago. There were framed pictures of well known journalists of their time: George Orwell, Alistair Cooke, Christopher Hitchens, Marie Colvin. Some were pictured with celebrities, others with politicians.

Between them were hung framed cartoons, satirical masterpieces taken from newspapers when they were at their critical best - Martin Rowson, Chris Riddell, Steve Bell, Ronald Searle. Their subjects stretched, squashed and morphed to satirise their personalities, politics and misdemeanours. Winston Churchill as a bowler hatted bulldog, Margaret Thatcher a terrifying hook nosed bird, David Cameron with his condom shaped head, Boris Johnson as King Kong, swinging off the Big Ben tower. Minor members of the royal family as refugees, as they exited stage following the death of the Queen and the public movement to grab back the royal estate. Emma Lewis, the third female prime minister, with her distinctive hard set eyebrows and ever scowling face. Their half page cartoons were as detailed, scathing and questioning as any thousand word editorial.

A 280-character post via the social? Forget about it.

Along one wall were pasted newspaper front pages announcing historic stories, national turning points. The Death of Churchill on the front of the *Daily Telegraph* in 1965. The *Daily Mirror* picture of Margaret Thatcher in tears, in the back of a car taking her from Number 10 for the final time in 1990. 'It Was The Sun What Won It' two years later. The mesmerising full page photo of an American firefighter climbing the stairs at the World Trade Center before it crumbled - September 11th, 2001. A woman with her face covered in bandages after a multiple terrorist attack on London in 2005. 'Diana Dead': the only words on the front page of the *News of the World* one morning in August 1997.

Front pages that were poignant. Terrifying. Earth shattering. Funny. Pages that meant something, then promised you the full story on pages 2,3,4,5,6 and 7.

Soren thought of the couple of hundred words he'd produced today, half regurgitated from press releases supplied by MinSoc and swiped into the social with barely a moment's consideration. Void of even an ounce of criticism.

The landlord brought Soren a new drink and cleared his empty glass without a word.

Rumour was that Ned - if that was his name - would rather be taken out of his bar in a coffin than allow those newspaper covers to be papered over. How old was he? By Soren's judgment, nearing 80. He would have been a young kid when Churchill resigned in 1955, so maybe the real Ned was the landlord's father. Or maybe it was his father's father who first pasted newspaper front pages on the walls. In a dark corner, preserved by a perspex frame, was the front page of the *Daily Herald*, available for a halfpenny. It was from Wednesday 4th August, 1914.

'England and Germany at War'.

Soren felt at home.

He didn't know whether that front page was real, or just a copy. He certainly wouldn't get an answer from Ned. The man rarely spoke, and certainly not about politics or scandal or celebrity. Or himself. His gruff voice was limited only to asking if you wanted another drink, or whether you'd finished the one you had. Discretion.

For decades, Ned had been a listener. When Soren had started coming here, there had been a lot to listen to.

Soren looked around at the few other drinkers this evening. Twenty years ago, by this time in the afternoon, the bar would be packed with newspaper journalists who had finished their shifts, or were dropping by for a snifter before going back to write the overnights. Politicians and celebrities, even a minor royal or two, might be found hidden in the dimly lit bar, huddled in conspiratorial corners allowing not so subtle slips of the tongue. They'd gather in a small courtyard in the back, to smoke cigarettes, cigars, the occasional pipes.

MPs visiting the bar, in between division bells, rubbed shoulders with hacks from the nationals to share their real opinions. Often in direct opposition to the policy they'd just been whipped into voting for. Politicians from opposing sides would drink together, their combative day job left in the wooden lockers with their coats and parliamentary passes.

West End stage actors headed to Ned's to avoid groupies and stalkers post-show, or to drink a stiff one beforehand. To pin down journalists for a good review, in exchange for the inside track on their next production or film.

The politician at the heart of a scandal, the reporter who broke the story and the actors who played them in the stage show a generation later: all drinking in the same bar, from the same glasses, sitting on the same worn leather benches.

For a brief time, Soren had been part of that mêlée. He'd seen the last days of the Boris Johnson government, and the beginning of the re-emergence of moderate Labour. Within these walls, he'd been briefed by MPs in favour of and in opposition to Britain leaving the European Union. He knew what each of his confidants really thought, whatever they said on the Today programme at 8.10am the next morning.

Brexit had, of course, failed. Marred by corruption scandals and accusations of dictatorial machinations under the Johnson government. But by that time, politicians had begun to communicate directly with their audiences, online, though profile pages and video casts. The need for newscasters, the need for Ned's, was beginning to ebb away. Then multiple waves of Covid 19 had changed the way pubs and bars served their customers anyway, creating a takeaway society. Moving even human social interaction online, which over time people got used to.

Then began to prefer.

Had Ned noticed the change? Soren had gone away for five years. When he had come back, everything seemed to be different. Ned's was empty, the bar propped up only by a few nostalgists like him. He imagined they too drank there for privacy, to nurse memories and heal wounds.

For Ned, perhaps the change had been so gradual he hadn't noticed the difference. Instead of rebuilding Parliament, the public - scandalised by the cost - had demanded that MPs found a new, more modern way of debating and making decisions. The official Online Parliament had been born after the third national wave of Covid in 2024, with rooms in elected politicians' own homes or constituency offices converted into sound proof communications booths. From there they could participate in debate, and vote as motions came up for discussion.

MPs could stay close to their constituents, and it saved an enormous amount of taxpayers' money that had previously been spent on second homes, constant travel and dodgy expense claims. Their London replacements were far poorer paid civil servants like Amanda Ward, who did the leg work and research, wrote and implemented the policies.

Everyone won, except the journalists. And Ned.

Celebrities too had turned to online videos and social feeds, employing professional gurus to protect their reputations. More than a decent living could be made hosting a celebrity channel, sharing beauty or health tips with online followers. Somehow that was more appealing than flirting with semi powerful hacks in grubby Soho bars.

Soren watched Ned as he polished the bar, and moved glasses around, as if he was expecting a mass of customers any time. With his ban on electronics in the bar, that was unlikely. Who would want to be without their slate?

Had Ned introduced the ban in a hope to retain the custom of politicians and celebrities who had something to gain from the privacy and atmosphere within the walls of the bar? Or was it as a final gesture of defiance when the social had taken over?

Either way, he'd created a single island of peace, in a too connected world. One which, when Soren had returned from his five years away, he had desperately needed.

He smiled. Maybe he would offer to take over the bar, when Ned was done. Anything would be better than churning out re-hashed press releases.

This morning had been rare. He didn't believe the crap Godspeed had said about this being something extra special, awarded to a select number of journalists in exchange for their support. There was something else going on. A rare old feeling emerged in Soren. The sniff of a story.

He stared into his empty glass, and tried to think. He knocked the glass on the table. Ned delivered another double.

An hour later, Soren stumbled back into the corridor and fumbled with the key to collect his coat and slate. He tried to balance, and swiped the slate against the glowing Exit sign a couple of times. On the third sweep, it was read by the sensor and the door opened.

It was the only concession to new technology the landlord allowed, Soren guessed. How else would Ned get paid for the four double shots he'd just drunk?

4

Soren slid into the familiar deep well in the cushion of his sofa and placed his black coffee on a side table.

He used his feet to budge aside the morning's breakfast bowl and a few empty cups, clearing just enough room on the coffee table to put his legs up. The table was heavy oak, once pristine, an object he had once loved and shared. Now it was stained with cup rings, spilled drinks and scuffing from the heels of his shoes.

He took a long drag on his vape, so deep he coughed up the steam. He soothed his throat with a swig of coffee, then pulled over the slate which he'd thrown onto the sofa when he'd entered his tiny apartment.

He swiped on a dim reading light behind the sofa and began to read. It was the same material he'd been given this morning, but he looked again at the FAQ document, and the more detailed policy outline. He swiped to the notes he'd scribbled.

'*Intelligence?*' and '*Widely consulted?*'

Three more questions had occurred to him as the

whisky flowed at Ned's. He added them to the list on his writing pad.

'Transparency?'

'Tested/trialled?'

'Criticism?'

Soren's stomach rumbled. Apart from the cinnamon loop, he had not eaten since he'd emptied a bowl of protein flakes this morning. The one he'd kicked to the side to put his feet up.

He took another slug of coffee.

Soren swiped to bring up MinSoc's website and visited the page covering this morning's announcement. He scrolled down, then stabbed at the orange button that invited him to open an online chat. A line appeared, with a small flashing robot at the front.

"Good evening Mr Soren. How can the Ministry for Society and Communications help you this evening?"

He typed: "I'm seeking more information on rules governing social guidelines, outlined today."

"Please wait, Mr Soren, while I investigate your question."

Almost immediately, another message appeared.

"Thank you. I have just messaged you the latest information on the Ministry's announcements regarding new actions and policies regarding the internet and social media. I hope you find them useful. Do you have any further questions?"

Soren's slate pinged and he opened the same documents he'd seen a dozen times already.

"Who will make final decisions regarding acceptable and unacceptable content under the Ministry for Society policies released today?"

A moment's pause. His slate pinged again.

"Thank you. I have just messaged you the latest information on the Ministry's announcements regarding new actions and policies regarding the internet and social media. I hope you find them useful. Do you have any further questions?"

"Why don't you fuck off, and find me a human being to answer?" He swiped it.

"Mr Soren, I am not permitted to respond to abusive language. The Ministry for Society and Communications is committed to helping page users where we can. Do you have any other questions?

"I am a journalist -," Soren scrubbed that. "I am a newsgatherer with SkyCloud. I would like to request an interview with the National Director of MinSoc on today's policies regarding social media for my readers."

"Please wait, Mr Soren, while I investigate your question."

"The National Director Mrs Amanda Ward is not currently available for interviews by newsgatherers. Information has been provided to approved outlets. We are pleased to share a Video Cast, which we would be delighted if you would share on your feeds. Do you have any other questions?"

The video started up automatically. It was the same one that had been published earlier, with its double halo emojis.

Soren looked closely at Ward's face as she spoke. The way her cheek bones raised as her mouth moved. The thin line of her lips. Harrison was right, she was beautiful. And the way she spoke, rounding out her words as they rolled out, was charismatic, almost charming. He liked watching her, and restarted the clip when it finished. He pulled up the pic released by MinSoc and the waterside picture Harrison had tracked down from East Burundi.

There was something. He maximised the East Burundi photo on his slate, then cupped his hands around her face, attempting to exclude her hair.

He swore and swiped the light behind him to a brighter level. He restarted the video and cupped the woman's face in his hands again. He watched her talk, listening intently to the way she pronounced her words.

He held the screen inches in front of his face, then at a distance, squinting. Then he paused the video, and swiped open the MinSoc chatbot box.

"Good evening Mr Soren. How can the Ministry for Society and Communications help you this evening?"

Curtis Soren took a very deep breath.

"I am a newsgatherer with SkyCloud. I'm seeking an interview with Alice Harding."

"Please wait, Mr Soren, while I investigate your question."

Soren rubbed his eyes and breathed out with a yawn.

His slate pinged.

"I'm sorry, Mr Soren, I do not know anyone of that name within the Ministry of Society and Communications. Do you have any other questions?"

He flung the slate and it bounced off the far arm of the sofa. He wiggled further into the cushions and fell asleep.

5
————

The man with the needs has new needs. He knows where to look.

He types. He looks at lists. The cursor questions.

CuttingRemarks he types.

He looks.

SpectatorsOfSuicide he types.

He looks.

RopeWorks he types.

He looks.

He looks because he needs to know.

6

Soren was woken by the bright sunlight cast through the window of his living room. He hadn't bothered to close the curtains the night before. It was the kind of light that tells you it's already half way through the morning. He sat up, his neck painful. He wiped his hands across his face and felt a crease in his cheek where he had slept against the armrest.

He stretched, reached out for his cup of cold coffee, stared at the gloop in the bottom of the cup and the greasy layer that had formed on the top. He put it down again. He reached for the slate which he'd knocked onto the floor during the night.

10.14 a.m.

There was a missed message from Harrison early doors, one from Grey at 9.05 a.m. and another at 9.30 a.m., another missed message from Harrison, and then a missed video call from Grey about twenty minutes ago.

Soren wiped the sleep out of his eyes and returned to the messages.

"Our lady is top of the charts again this morning. 😎😎."

Didn't she ever sleep?

Grey's message read: "News breaking and you're not here. Hope to see you very soon."

Then twenty five minutes later: "Soren, your day should have started half an hour ago."

Then Harrison: "Grey's on the prowl for you. Where are you?"

He swiped a vomiting emoji, with a question mark back to her, then opened up his social feeds.

"SkyCloud: #AmandaWard names top 10 hate groups and posters taken off the social. Right and left extremists, jihadis and paramilitaries in the firing line. #banned10"

Soren swiped a second post to Harrison. "Thanks for posting for me. Nice pun." He'd never used puns in his own copy.

His slate pinged.

"That's why you're chief newsgatherer! Get your arse in here, before Grey does something drastic. Like promotes me."

Soren took a few swipes at his news feeds. Other newsgatherers were already breaking down the announcement, picking up and running with the various groups Amanda Ward and her halos had banned in the first few days of her strategy. By the end of the week, groups which theoretically only existed in the social world would simply cease to be. And those people suspected of being behind the groups, dealt with by the police if crimes had been committed.

Soren wondered at the words being pushed out by MinSoc. Selling drugs and weapons, trafficking people, sharing images of abuse: sure, those were crimes. But posting, sharing, reading - were they to be crimes too now?

Each newsgathering organisation had taken a group or two in a particular area, and provided examples of the posts that had been carried on their now banned pages and websites.

The pages themselves, Soren discovered with a quick search, had already been replaced with a MinSoc logo and the words: *This page has been removed to protect you. For more information, please visit the Ministry for Society and Communications*, with a link.

It was 10.45 a.m. He took a quick shower and was in a TriCab by eleven.

"So, what do we have?" Grey's tone across the video call was cross, but resigned. The newsgatherer was going to get his balls broken when he arrived, but for his editor the priority was a new angle on the story. SkyCloud needed something to create uplift in the rankings. "Something new and exciting I hope," Grey said.

As ever. Sensation sells.

Soren tapped his fingers on the dash of the TriCab, a rhythm that helped him to think and apparently annoyed the hell out of Grey. He tapped a little louder.

"Okay, I'll go to some of the interest groups. The charities and campaigners. See if we can't find a real life story or two of those previously harmed by the bad guys."

"Anything stickier?"

The newsgatherer tapped louder. "I shall not stop until I find a new and fully fledged celebrity angle. A 100 million view Vlogger who's been attacked by Jihadi crack dealers. Will that do you? Maybe a video of an aged Tory busted up by some militant lefties?"

"That's what I'm talking about," said Grey.

"Will do."

"Meantime, I'll get one of the coders to put together a list of keywords."

"Of course you will." Soren shook his head.

Grey swiped off without saying goodbye, and Soren opened the new MinSoc release. He copied and pasted some statements and the list of 10 groups into his writing pad. For each banned group, he searched for and listed a charity or campaign group likely to welcome the news.

To temper the ball busting, he swiped the list to Grey to pass onto the coders. God, was he beginning to think like them?

"Let's start with those the far right like to target," he said aloud. He pulled up the pages for the British Association of Jews, Pride UK and The Immigrants Collective. None had created official responses yet, so he swiped a message to each of them asking for a quote or two.

"And if you have a celebrity -" - he deleted that - "high profile figure available for an interview, I'd appreciate a rapid response."

He flipped up a video chat to Harrison.

"And what do you want?" she said. Since day one, she'd always looked bright and ready for the day. "You look like shit."

"I was working late." She didn't look convinced. "Can you meet me at Carlos' in ten minutes?"

"Carlos'?" asked Harrison. "Will is already on my back about following up on the post I set up three hours ago - no problem, by the way, you're welcome - and you want to meet for coffee and buns?"

"I thought we could compare notes."

Harrison said, in a mocking accent: "Okay, Mr Soren. Always a pleasure, Mr Curtis sir. But you buy the drinks, yes?"

. . .

The coffee shop owner was absent, so Soren was able to collect his coffee and cinnamon loop with merely a grunt from a surly barista. Harrison was already sitting at his usual table with her own coffee.

"So, what's the scoop?" she said as he sat opposite her.

"Alice Harding. Mean anything to you?"

"Nope, never heard of her. You trying to set me up?"

"She's Amanda," said Soren.

"What?"

"Amanda Ward. Alice Harding. I think they're the same person."

Harrison sat back in her chair, and crossed her arms.

"At least, I mean, they look the same."

"Aha? You want me to go on a date with Amanda Ward? I might well consider that, if I wasn't married of course."

"Alice Harding. No date. I think I used to attend her lectures at university."

"I have no idea what you're talking about," said Harrison. "You went to Oxford. Ward went to Cambridge and she has no record of any postgrad stuff anywhere near where you've been."

"No, not according to her CV. But her biog was enough for you to track down a near 20-year-old photo of her in a tiny African country, in an outdated charity annual report, written in French."

Harrison looked pleased with herself. "Okay, who's this Alice Harding?"

"That's the point," said Soren. "Harding was a lecturer - young, a PhD I think - at Oxford. In social anthropology, or something close to that. I did PPE, but I used to hang out at lectures that interested me."

"Ever poking your nose where it doesn't belong. So, what convinces you that Amanda and Alice are the same person?"

"They look the same," Soren said, a little hesitantly.

Harrison laughed.

"That's all you've got? There's a lot of women in the world, Curtis. Some of them resemble each other."

"Maybe she was on secondment or something. But listen Mia. She disappeared." He took a sip of his coffee.

"Disappeared?"

"Well, not in a kidnapped way. Just, the next time I turned up to the lecture, she'd been replaced by someone else. It wasn't my faculty, and the new lecturer wasn't half as interesting. I stopped going. I barely noticed she'd gone. Until she appeared in the feeds yesterday."

"And at the press conference you went to," said Harrison. "Why didn't you talk to her then? Your long lost lecturer?"

"I was sitting at the back. I couldn't be sure. And her hair was different, her voice. God, she's nearly thirty years older. So am I, and she would have had five or more years on me." Soren reached for his pocket, then remembered he couldn't vape in the coffee shop.

"And memory can be fuzzy, especially after an afternoon at Ned's," said Harrison.

"It was her. It *is* her. She left the press conference when she saw me."

"And you've checked with MinSoc?"

"Yeah, but try getting anything out of them. The ChatBot had never heard of an Alice Harding. And Ward is not giving interviews."

The two sat in silence for a beat, taking swigs of coffee.

"So?"

"So," said Soren. "Will is on my back about getting a longer piece out about today's banned list. I've made some progress with the campaign groups. He'll definitely go for them, if there's something from any celebs I can get to speak publicly. Perfect click fodder. I also want to look into why everyone has fallen head over heals with this policy, and I can't seem to find anyone online who is criticising it."

"Which leaves me digging around in the undergrowth after your old crush."

"I'm just saying it's worth a look, and you're much better at the detail than me. Leave me with the words. *In the firing line,* so to speak."

"Bastard," she responded, then waited for a moment. "Okay, I'll do it. But I think you're missing something."

Soren turned towards her, with raised eyebrows.

"Grey is not going to publish this. Every woman has the right to change her name, if that *is* what Alice-Amanda has done in your special world. No news. If you got it through at all, it's the kind of random factoid that drops through the social like the crumbs tumbling down your chin right now."

"Thank you, Mia," he mumbled through stuffed cheeks.

The woman swiped the video call closed and Soren stretched his fingers. He'd been prodding the screen of his slate for nearly half an hour during his interview with Vanessa Vintage.

Soren had only needed a few headline quotes for his longer piece on how charity organisations were responding. But the presenter of Vanessa's Queer Queen Resistance Vlog had taken the opportunity to give him the full history of the trans resistance movement. And her own long track record of achievements.

Soren was pretty sure his editor wouldn't give a hoot about Queer history, as long as Vanessa's Vlog had more than 200,000 followers and would be re-sharing the piece Soren was about to write.

His slate pinged with a message from the coders, who had provided a list of artificial inteligence generated keywords to include in his copy. Within an hour he'd swiped 500 words to Grey and twenty minutes later it was climbing the ratings.

#AmandaWard was taking a lot of halos, to the delight of Vanessa's Queer Queen Resistance Vlog's re-share, which was itself taking hundreds of likes, hearts, pride flags and re-shares. His piece was gaining similar traction via the other organisations he had mentioned or quoted, all warmly welcoming the banning of their long standing social antagonists.

#CurtisSoren, imagined Soren. With a halo emoji to boot. The taste of cinnamon rose into his mouth as his stomach turned at the thought of what he'd spent the morning doing: churning out journalistic junk food for the masses to chomp on with relish. Not a critical or questioning word in his copy. Or anywhere else as far as he could see.

He messaged Grey to ask if he was free.

"At least we're back up in the rankings," Soren said by way of hello as he entered the office. His editor scowled at him from behind his slate.

"You went AWOL yesterday afternoon, and then were very late this morning."

"I was working from home."

"Yes, so Mia claims. What's on your mind?" asked Grey.

"Amanda Ward," Soren stated simply, for the second time that morning.

"Well, she's certainly become popular since you ordained her yesterday. Have you come in for my gratitude?"

Soren considered which way to take this. He didn't want to put Harrison's little project in jeopardy.

"No, it's just that she makes me uncomfortable. No one seems to be bothered by what she's doing on the socials."

"That's because she's doing a good job. No Ministry national director has ever got this kind of traction. Halo after halo. They're loving it."

"But I can't find any real criticism of what she's doing," said Soren.

"Perhaps because most people don't really object to, you know, banning neonazis or closing chat forums for paedophiles? My guess is, people think those are, generally, *good things*."

"Yes, but I've found nothing negative on the socials at all. The social companies themselves used to battle against this kind of restriction - freedom of speech, they'd say. Then suddenly they just roll over because Amanda Ward clicks her fingers?"

Grey sighed and invited Soren to sit with a wave of his hand: "Curtis, look at the praise they are getting for doing it. Some kid over at the YoYo Village must have done the sums and realised they either go with this, or they face restrictions from MinSoc. Higher taxes. Warnings and disclaimers all over their sites. Potentially, boycotts from advertisers if campaigns like #endit continue to get really good traction. And it looks like they made a good call, because it's all halo emojis for the social companies all over the rankings."

"And any criticism?"

"Either not being posted -"

"Unlikely."

"Or more likely dropping down the rankings. Negatives are far out-trended by positive posts. Social users are liking what they see."

"But I've searched for negative comments," said Soren.

"Curtis listen, I've spent my life in this industry. I'm not sure you've followed it as closely I have. We post stories that people like to read, like and share. They get boosted up the rankings, so those posts get read more, shared more and so on. The nature of the social these days is that people like to share good stuff, make recommendations to their friends. All the haters, the trolls, they've moved to the dark web. And MinSoc is onto that nasty side of the web too. No advertiser wants their keywords dropping, so they expect us to write copy that goes down well with audiences. Everyone wins."

"I get that. But what about personal posts? Individuals making comments, sharing ideas, questioning the access socials have to our information?"

"Wake up, Curtis. People don't care anymore. We swapped it all for cheaper shopping and free music ten years ago. The socials know what we like, they give us more of it, and we lap it up.

"You can't close Pandora's box. And who wants to, when you get free same day delivery on your shopping orders and money off your next VeganMac?"

"Doesn't the truth matter?" asked Soren, pulling out his vape and toying with it in his fingers.

"Not so much as that VeganMac, my friend. And anyway, the *truth* is that everyone loves MinSoc just now. They're doing a good thing and Amanda Ward is getting justly praised. Publish anything else, and we lose our readers and your shares."

"Where's the scrutiny? The questioning?", asked Soren. He knew he was on a losing streak. Will Grey had allowed him to post negative and questioning copy about the social on SkyCloud before, and his stories never gained much traction. There was an underlying question about whether

Soren was really earning his keep. The truth mattered back on *The Herald*, and what happened to that paper? It had crashed and burned. Soren knew he was five years out of date, probably more.

"Questioning isn't our job. It's sharing, content generating, nuancing."

Soren baulked at the idea that *nuancing* a Ministry's press release was his vocation. "So you think critical posts are just dropping through the adoration of MinSoc and the socials? So far down they're invisible."

"Look, I know where you're going with this," said Grey. "You think MinSoc is deleting unfavourable posts about them? Or the socials are?"

"Not just unfavourable, but anything negative. Anything critical. Anything even questioning the policies. My most inane question about where the buck stops was shut down at the press event yesterday."

Grey laughed. "That's paranoia, Curtis?" Then he went on more sympathetically. "Listen, you've earned your place here. If you want to go around laying into the most popular policy for years from the most popular Ministry in the government, released by a national director with multiple halos, then please go ahead and do it."

Grey paused.

"But not on SkyCloud."

The newsgatherer knew his editor had him pinned. Soren couldn't work anywhere else - no other newsgathering organisation would have him given his grumpy reputation (and let's be honest, his age in a young industry), let alone publish him. Many didn't publish government, police, current affairs or Ministry news at all, let alone anything with a hint of criticism. Celebrities, fashion, cooking, shopping and the like were all far more swipe and like friendly.

Soren considered - as he had before - setting up alone. His own personal blog, where he could express his own views, seek out and tell his own investigative stories. But buying webspace for that kind of enterprise had become prohibitively expensive for individuals. While buying up most of the website hosting companies, the big four platforms had made publishing, messaging and sharing on their platforms easy, and completely free. Operating outside of the Portico platform was as pointless as it was expensive, even if Soren had the knowledge of how to do so.

Companies big and small just used the Portico platform to most effectively reach their markets. Without Portico, Soren wouldn't be able to get even close to the viewers he needed to sell an advert or a paid-for link, let alone make a living.

And his critical or questioning articles if they were posted on Portico? Grey was right on that. They would sink without a trace. No one reads the second page for search results, and Portico algorithms favoured commercial biased stories that could have adverts wrapped around them.

Hence the SkyCloud business model. There was no money in what Soren wanted to write. Thanks to Ned's, he was already late on this month's rent.

"I guess I better get back to work then," he said.

7

The greasy cup from two nights ago and the cereal bowl from the morning before that, a small pool of milk at the bottom now curdled and stinking, were the first to go into the hot soapy water.

Soren swiped up a late 90s playlist on his slate, and hummed along to *Daysleeper* by REM as he did the dishes and wiped down the surfaces.

Soren had put in a good afternoon's work, following up leads for Grey. Playing the good boy. He'd found some other hero personalities keen to jump on the hate group banning bandwagon, and converted them into keyword friendly copy, with a #banned10 hashtag to round it off.

Many of his fellow newsgatherers went for a smoothie after work on a Friday, but he never could picture himself sucking on a pink straw, surrounded by garish wallpaper and happy chat. He wasn't sure Ned's would be a good idea either, his head still dull from the night before.

The next best thing was a little housework. It helped him to think. Besides, the waft of sweat and rotting food had turned his stomach when he'd entered his flat twenty minutes ago. Funny how that smell was never there when he had a Scotch or three in his belly.

After REM and a few inevitable adverts, his slate began to reverberate with the spiralling guitar riffs that began *Special K*, the Placebo track. Soren tapped his foot to the track celebrating ketamine and love, as he washed up and by the end had even run a sponge around the inside of the SpeedyCook.

He cut a corner off a PackOSoup, placed the pack inside the SpeedyCook and set it to low.

His slate pinged just as the next set of adverts were getting underway. He swiped Harrison, and the adverts moved to a corner box leaving most of the rest of the screen free for the video call.

"You're not still at work?" he asked.

"And *you're* not cleaning your kitchen."

He smiled.

"So, did you manage to find anything out about Amanda Ward?" asked Soren.

"Or Alice Harding?" she replied. "On the latter, not a lot. First part of the morning, I was convinced you'd lost your marbles. Then remembered those had rolled away years ago, so carried on looking.

"If there was an Alice Harding at Oxford during the time you were there - or five years either way - as an undergrad, PhD, lecturer or even floor cleaner, I would have found her. There's not a single record for her online. Not in the Bodleian library register. Not in any of the college records and not in the social anthropology faculty."

"Maybe I have her name wrong," said Soren. "I'm sure it was her."

"I tried a few variations on her name, but still no joy. So, I looked for Amanda Ward at Oxford too. Same result. All the same bases, none of the data shows an Amanda Ward across the whole university - or on the electoral roll."

"You've been busy," said Soren.

"I went through Ward's biog as supplied by MinSoc, and tried to widen out the different roles she'd supposedly filled. As you know, the Ministries are as tight as a duck's arse on information about civil servants - unless they start getting halos it seems - so had no joy there. So, I went back to the charities, and particularly *Ligne pour les Pauvres.* No results, at least not in my French, so the picture remains the only thing we have to go on."

"So we're back to where we were."

"No, we're back to university. No trace of her at Oxford."

"Yes, you told me that."

"But Ward went to Cambridge, duh. That's what her biog said, remember? And there she is, true to the words on her CV. She did PPE at Jesus College from 1998 to 2002, a first class student. I have her library card, a pass for the Fitzwilliam Museum and her college digs rent record. She played violin in her college orchestra, and in the Cambridge string ensemble and orchestra. Ms Perfect was even captain of the university hockey team for Michaelmas term in '99. I've checked all the online data, such as it is, and peeked behind a few firewalls too. It all checks out."

"So MinSoc are telling the truth. I just imagined her in Oxford?"

"In black and white in Cambridge, yes. But not in colour."

Soren scratched his head. He was developing a headache. "Go on."

"Let me swipe you a file," she said.

Soren's slate pinged and he opened the file which contained three high resolution images.

One was a picture of a group of around fifty late teenagers, dressed up in tuxedos and ball gowns, sitting or standing on a stage, each holding a musical instrument. The picture was formally posed for the camera.

The second was similar. Soren estimated two hundred students, dressed smartly with gowns over their shoulders and mortar boards on their heads. They were standing in raised rows before an impressive stone building in the midday sunlight. The perfect group shot.

The third picture was less formal. A bunch of around twenty rowdy girls, in matching sports skirts and tops, surrounding a central player in leg pads, holding a helmet. Each of the young women held a hockey stick aloft in apparent celebration.

"Yep, got them," Soren scanned the images quickly.

"And what do these pictures all have in common?"

Soren glanced again. The mortar boards, the colours of the hockey kit, the instruments, particularly the string section. He took a deep toke on his vape.

"That's right," said Harrison.

"She's not in any of them," said Soren.

Ping, went the SpeedyCook.

The sachet of PackOSoup was steaming hot. Soren had to use the tips of his fingers, swapping every couple of seconds, and swearing with the burn at each swap until he managed to get the liquid into the bowl he'd just washed up.

A few dashes of lumpy tomato and lentil spilled onto the counter he'd just cleaned. He opened the fridge looking for bread, but only found an imitation of a loaf spotted with green mould. He closed the fridge door again.

He swiped up the volume on his slate and took the bowl

to the table with a spoon and a coffee. He stared out of the window as he ate.

Amanda Ward had had an illustrious career at Cambridge. Top of the populars, according to the paperwork. But scratch the surface a little deeper and she was as good as invisible.

Harrison had found no references to her in more recent social posts of those who might have been her friends at the time: old hockey mates, possible tutorial partners. She hadn't appeared in any reunion group messages she could find, nor any photos of college or orchestral gatherings. Apart from her official one at MinSoc, she had no personal profile page on the social, and as far as Harrison could see, never had.

Nor even on the fledgling social media sites like MySpace or FriendsReunited which had sprung up not long after Ward would have been at university. Those platforms had quickly been overwhelmed by the forerunners of the social, but they still had archives stored on one of the Portico platforms if you knew where to look.

This was a woman who was at the top of her game at university, and now the top of her game at her Ministry, yet was pretty much absent otherwise. There was some standard documentation, but nothing social or physical placed her at Cambridge at all.

Harrison had signed off with the question: "If you're convinced Amanda is Alice, and something doesn't smell right, what are you going to do next?"

"I really don't know," he'd replied.

"That'd be a first," she said.

He had swiped her away and laughed, and not because she was wrong.

Soren closed the curtains, picked up his bowl, spoon

and coffee cup and placed them in the sink. The toppled sachet leaked the remains of the soup onto the counter top. *And that's why cleaning is a waste of time,* he thought to himself. He returned to the sofa and picked up his slate.

He peeled back the protective casing from the side of the screen, and felt around for a small depression in the hard shell. This he held for three seconds, until the glow of the slate went to deep black, then to nothing.

He took it to his bedroom. His bed was made, but only just. A week of used clothes were spread across the floor and flung over the back of a chair. He closed the bedroom curtains, then placed his slate in the top drawer of the cheap unit that had come bundled as part of the sorry sparse furnishings of the apartment.

He closed it, then opened the bottom drawer. From underneath a couple of sweaters, he pulled out another slate and returned to the sofa.

This slate was smaller, and so out of date he had to swipe hard at the screen to get it to respond. It requested a username and password, which Soren punched in after a few moment's hesitation.

The social account of Jess Andrew opened on the screen, along with a photo Soren had taken from an online catalogue. Her face was plain, unremarkable.

Soren swiped up the social, and slowly and deliberately typed out a direct message, using his fake profile:

JessAndrew: *#Amanda Ward, who are you really? Never got to meet you at Cambridge. I wonder why?*

He read the comment three times, took a deep breath, and swiped the post from his outbox.

8

The man has needs.

Others have answers.

I have truth. Send money directly and will return with detail. *nineyards

Specialist person hunter. However you want it. Specialist in your case. *youtong

Former officer at London Met. Full details of incident and re-location. *mikey342

The man with the needs looks closely at the third response. The cursor blinks in askance.

mikey342 he types.

The cursor waits. The man with the needs waits.

Plate: WV4R 985. 1,000 sc total, three batches. More on delivery of first payment. 333 sc to 40-40-55, 18945634.

The man with the needs gulps hard. He sees the words and his stomach churns. The man with the needs makes a direct transfer.

Transfer made, types the desperate man with desperate needs.

He waits. The cursor waits.

Florent Road + Farmer's Hill. Correct? 333 sc to same.

The man with the needs' guts crawl. His breath lifts. His heart thumps, desperate. A small 'fuck' escapes dry lips. His needs will be met.

The desperate man with the needs makes another online transfer.

Transfer made, he types.

He waits. The cursor waits.

9

Though he'd not worked overnight, Soren had prescheduled some social posts to go out to keep the SkyCloud audience warm. A few more minor celebs celebrating victory over prejudice had agreed to provide exclusive quotes, which Soren set up to release every four hours.

The morning's ritual with Carlos had been endured, and Soren was halfway through his Americano before he spotted the plain black BMW sitting outside the coffee shop.

There was no question of who the two passengers in the BMW were, one sitting in the driver's seat, the other directly behind him. Nor what they were doing, waiting outside the cafe. The newsgatherer decided to take extra time to finish his coffee, watching the unmoving figures in the car outside.

Finally, he collected his overcoat from the back of his chair and moved to the door, waving to Carlos on his way out. The driver of the BMW opened his door and climbed out.

"Mr Curtis Soren?"

"Yes, officer. How can I help you?" Soren took a toke on his vape.

"I'm Chief Inspector Miran Burman from the Metropolitan Police. Would you like to swipe my ID?"

Soren pulled his slate out of his satchel and held it up against the officer's device. His screen lit up with a one page breakdown of the Inspector's credentials, including his photo and the Met Police crest.

The officer's screen lit up with a similar biog of the newsgatherer, who blew out the steam from his vape.

"My colleague and I wondered if you might spare a few moments to talk to us?"

Soren studied the officer. He was around ten years younger. Plain clothed, apart from the Met insignia sewn into the left chest of his polo shirt. He had a full head of dark hair, kept smartly, was cleanly shaven and had eyes that were alert and inquisitive.

"Of course," said Soren. Neutral.

Burman opened the passenger seat of the BMW, into which Soren lowered himself. Burman walked around the front of the vehicle and dropped into the driver's side. The inspector inserted his slate into the dashboard, and it lit up before dropping to a dull glow.

"Mr Soren, this is my colleague, Sergeant Leanne Lee."

Soren swung round awkwardly to nod at the woman in the back. She had shoulder length black hair over a pale and stern face and wore the same Met issued polo shirt as her senior. She held up her slate, but Soren shook his head.

"What's this about inspector? I have to get back to work very soon."

"We'd like to talk to you about posts on the social. Specifically about, or directed towards, the Ministry for Society and Communications and its staff," said Burman.

"You think I've committed a crime?"

"Mr Soren, I think you know how this works. Under the

Crime Prevention Rapidity Act of 2026, I can access permission to convert this car into a custody suite and we can do an official interview, with you under caution. Everything will be recorded, and you will be sent a transcript as per your rights."

Soren remembered when that legislation had been brought in. Reduce paperwork for on-the-streets cops. Reduce time wasted bringing suspects and witnesses to physical buildings. Swipe, record, carry out the interview, then decide whether to press charges. It had gained lots of traction for the Ministry of Justice, who had pledged to cut the cost of policing while raising police pay.

"I'm happy to talk off the record if you are, inspector?" He looked to the back seat. "Sergeant?"

"Good then," said Burman.

"This is a delicate time for MinSoc and the Ministry of Justice, as you know," he continued. "We in the police have been given the task of tracking down every nasty shit who's set up hate speech groups from anywhere within twenty miles of Trafalgar Square. That makes us busy, and it makes the Ministries pretty jittery about protecting their civil servants - the ones shaping the policies."

"And what does that have to do with me?"

"Nothing. But there's been a feeling in MinSoc of, shall we say, pressure they don't need? We all know where that kind of pressure leads. The referendums in the mid 2020s. The attacks on MPs. The blurred line between chats and abuse over social platforms, forceful inappropriate questioning from journalists, out and out threats against..."

"Against women politicians," said Lee from the back.

"Yes, it all got pretty itchy if I remember," said Soren. "And if I'm not mistaken you guys were running round in circles, trying to decide if this or that comment was a credible threat, and missing those that did turn out to be."

"My predecessors, perhaps. And people got hurt," said the inspector.

"Two women were killed because they supported Brexit, if I remember, Mr Soren," added Lee. "A female Labour politician was murdered because she didn't."

"You're not the only newsgatherer we're talking to. We just want to... keep the current tone. Some of the groups banned from the social yesterday are pretty upset, according to our insiders. Obviously, we're on top of that.

"But among newsgatherers, we think you can help us temper any wider hysterics while this policy is properly rolled out. Ultimately help us to protect the good people who work for our Ministries, and for society."

"You sound like a Ministry robot," said Soren.

"As you know, the Metropolitan Police operates entirely independently of the government and its Ministries. But we're obliged to act on any intelligence we're passed from them, including carrying out arrests of those perpetrating hate speech or harassment."

"So, the new MinSoc policy should make your life easier then," added Soren.

"It'll make our job a little more difficult tracking down the extremists, but we'll still get info about those trying to post or set up groups - direct from the socials, even though it won't appear in public."

"And you get the halos for tracking them down."

Lee said from the back, "I've seen your work, Mr Soren. The social loves it."

"So, more of the same, I think," said the Inspector, before adding: "And maybe less of the pressure... on individuals trying to get good work done."

"I have no idea what you're talking about," said Soren. "And I do need to get back to work, if I may?"

"You are entirely at liberty, sir."

Soren grunted.

"Please, let me swipe my personal contacts to you," added Burman. "I meant what I said about independence. We're on the same side, no?"

Soren nodded and the two men pressed their slates together a second time. He left the BMW, which pulled out silently behind a TriCab and into the traffic.

Soren walked through the door of SkyCloud's open plan office, and headed towards Harrison, intending to update her on his strange conversation with the police. Before he reached her station, she'd pointed towards Grey's office.

Soren raised his eyebrows. She shrugged her shoulders.

He about turned and headed towards Grey's glass cubicle. *Here we go.*

He entered, coughed and closed the door behind him.

Grey was deep into his slate, but stood when Soren entered. He put his slate aside, before inviting Soren to sit. His face was one of delight.

"Good morning, Curtis. Having a good one?"

"Yes, I think so?"

"Your ratings are sky high for your story on MinSoc and all those charity responses on the banned ten."

The poor man was even speaking in hashtags.

"SkyCloud is getting all the traffic and traction," Grey continued.

"Well that's good news. Obviously your chat did me some good yesterday."

"Blummin Valerie whatshername swiped me this

morning to say sales of her beauty products are going through the roof."

"*Their*, not her," said Soren.

"Mmm? Well, the ad coders are onto her popularity and re-sharing, so getting loads of good traction in the feedback loop. The snowball effect, working well."

"Does this mean I'm up for a pay rise?"

"Ah, better than that, Golden Boy"

"I'm not sure there is anything better than that. I had PackOSoup for dinner last night."

"How about an interview - face to face - with the national director of MinSoc?"

"Amanda Ward?"

"I had a message from her office this morning, and I followed up with a video call with her diary secretary to pin a time down."

"Today?" asked Soren.

"Three, this afternoon. You're to go to her office."

"In person, face-to-face? Not just a video call?"

"Face-to-face," Grey confirmed. "So you better get yourself fully abreast of all the tags in the feeds just now, and any re-shares and comments on your overnights. And put on a tie. You're on your way to a full personal profile, and InfoCom will be spitting with jealousy."

Grey looked down at his slate and began swiping around. He looked up again. "Why are you still here?"

"You're the boss. I'll put out a few more positive one liners, after I've taken a look at the lie of the land, just to keep her warm for my arrival."

"This is big news for us, Curtis. Don't mess it up."

Soren left his office and headed towards Harrison, who was watching him every step of the way.

"What the hell just happened?" he said.

. . .

It didn't occur to Soren to vape during his TriCab ride to MinSoc. The follow up posts with the charities' reactions to the #banned10 were getting great traction. It was mesmerising seeing his words rising and falling, then rising again on the feeds.

He took the opportunity to look over the few notes he did have on Amanda Ward, and her supposed time in Cambridge. This he'd collected together on a single document, which he'd fingerprint protected. He needed to think carefully about how to use this information during his interview with the national director.

He buzzed through security as quickly as he had two days before, then approached the reception desk to declare his name and his appointment with Amanda Ward. A temporary permit was swiped onto his slate by the uniformed receptionist, before he took a seat at the end of a plush sofa to wait.

The man who came to collect him was the same who'd introduced his boss on the stage during the press gathering last week. He was dressed just as smartly, wearing the same bright stripy tie.

"Mr Soren, I'm so sorry to have kept you waiting," he said, extending a hand. "Please, please, come this way.

Soren glanced at his watch. The man was two minutes early.

"I'm Harry Godspeed, assistant national director here at MinSoc. Mr Soren, it has been a busy morning, as you can imagine, but we're delighted to have been able to make time for you. I'm sure you have lots of questions and the Ministry here has lots to share."

"Curtis."

"I'm sorry, sir?"

"Call me Curtis."

"Oh we do like it informal here, Curtis. Thank you. Would you like a coffee?"

"Yes, please, black, no sweeteners or flavoured goo." Godspeed swiped his screen, then led them through some double doors. "Curtis, is there any reason why you are unable to use the stairs? Perhaps, a disability." He said it in an over emphasised soft and sympathetic voice.

"I don't believe so, no."

"Ah, good," he sprang back to his normal tone, which had a public school polish. "Only two flights anyway. Ministry policy is to use the stairs unless there's good reason not to."

By the end of the second set of steps, Soren was slightly out of puff. Next time, if there was one, he might ask to use the lift. He'd grunted single word answers to Godspeed as the man scampered above him, wittering about the weather and whether Soren had had a decent TriCab ride.

"We'll be happy to cover the cost of that, by the way. We're all delighted with the copy you and the folk at SkyCloud have been putting out about our initiative to clean up the social."

Maybe his web editor had been right: give more, get more.

Godspeed swiped them out of the stairwell and into a corridor. Then he guided Soren through another door which opened into an informal meeting room. It was banked on one side with floor-to-ceiling glass windows overlooking the Thames at London Bridge. Before the windows sat two wide sofa chairs, with a coffee table placed between them. On the table was a pot of coffee, steam rising from its spout, and a plate of two cinnamon loops. They could have come straight from Carlos', only they were larger, glossier, stickier.

"It's an amazing view, isn't it?" said Godspeed.

"It sure is," said Soren, eyeing the pastries. He looked up to see Godspeed smiling.

"We're very lucky to have this building to work from. It helps us all to be more creative in our daily grind."

The man is a walking talking training module, thought Soren as he took a seat.

"Curtis, I shall be right with you. Please enjoy your coffee for a moment."

Godspeed left the room. Soren took a look around him. There was a video camera on the wall, in the top corner. Not unusual, for a Ministry building. On the table, close to the cinnamon loops, was an empty slate mount. On the wall before him there was a wide screen of the sort Soren had seen downstairs at the press event.

He poured the steaming coffee, noting no milk had been provided. He used his fingers to take a cinnamon loop, before noticing a delicate set of tongs had been provided for that particular operation.

He sniffed it, then took a bite, savouring the cinnamon kick, then washed it down with the wonderfully dark and bitter coffee. He took another mouthful, but swallowed quickly as the door opened and Godspeed entered with his own cup.

"Sorry Curtis. Oh, those cinnamon loops are to die for, aren't they? I'd join you but..." he patted his stomach in an unashamedly camp way. "You know how it is."

As Godspeed sat, Soren put the loop onto a plate and pushed it away. He took a slug of coffee.

The pair waited in silence, a question hanging between them.

"I was expecting to see Amanda Ward?" said Soren finally.

"Ah, yes, I'm so sorry, Mr Soren." He paused. "The national director was called away to the Ministry of Health this morning. Very sudden, but duty calls. I think they're looking at social messaging about healthy eating." The man stopped abruptly; his eyes had blinked towards the half eaten cinnamon loop. "Or it might have been school based health checks."

"Oh, can we rearrange? I appreciate your time Mr Godspeed, but I really was counting on meeting Amanda Ward."

"Amanda has asked me to stand in her place. Speak on her behalf. I am delighted to do so. And I have the clearance to answer any questions you have, Curtis.

He leaned forward: "You'll understand I hope, we don't find time for every newsgatherer to come for a direct interview in MinSoc."

"I was hoping to do a profile on Mrs Ward."

"I see." The man paused for a moment. "I can see how that could work... yes, that would be good. Perhaps you could do one about me? I've worked very closely with Amanda on every aspect of the policy. Right from the beginning in fact."

"Not quite the same, I think. Not meaning to be rude."

Godspeed dramatically waved hands towards his face, as if fanning himself, but grinned. "And no offence taken, I'm sure." He took a sip from his drink.

He spoke again, this time in a more serious voice: "I think it might be very difficult to make the national director available at another time. You're already here. So am I. So?"

The newsgatherer hesitated.

"I can see a few angles," Soren conceded. A new official

face to add to the story wouldn't hurt. The trendy kid from YoYo had got some traction after the early announcement, but disappeared once the fawning had stopped. Amanda Ward was still hot, but another personality from MinSoc would be a good addition.

"Can I say, Mr Soren... Curtis. We've been so delighted on the uptake of your posts about our initiative. The traction has been something we've not really seen since this Ministry was set up. You seem to have an eye for the real human lives we're trying to touch. Not just the dry facts and lists. You're telling the real story behind our policies. The children. The victims.

He continued: "It's those we had in mind when negotiating with the social to get this work done. At the end of the day, Amanda and I, our colleagues, we're just civil servants - we're not allowed to talk about individual cases. But behind every banned group, every brutal comment taken off the internet, there's a real family. Someone hurting who won't hurt any longer."

Godspeed started to fan himself again. The newsgatherer watched him as he looked down at Soren's slate, apparently checking if his little speech had been recorded.

"Sorry, Curtis. We all really feel it here at MinSoc. It's what we were established to do. Change lives."

"Mr Godspeed, let's not get carried away. I used to be a newspaper hack, I've seen good and bad in equal measure." He took a huge bite out of his pastry.

Godspeed straightened his tie. "Of course. So, if you're happy to proceed, I'll have my biog messaged to you once we're done here."

"A biog. Or something more detailed?"

"You're welcome to send any supplementary questions

about my background and credentials. I'll even send you some holiday snaps." Soren thought he saw the man wink.

"And the national director?"

"I think if we leave here today with a relationship of trust, we might be able to release more than the biog you already have. The rules are quite strict about civil servants as you know. We may not release anything that might indicate any political preferences, or information that might compromise a team member's privacy or safety.

"But if you're happy to continue in the same positive vein as we've seen from SkyCloud over recent days, then I think there's a lot we can do together."

"I won't need, nor request, any permission from you to publish what I want to write," said Soren.

"Of course not, Curtis. If there is something I can't answer today, then I won't. If there's something I'm not sure of, we can follow up and get back to you. The rest is all up for grabs. And, if you don't mind my repeating, it's all yours. Exclusively."

Soren peered down at the glistening Thames beneath. It was so clean he could see the glint of individual fishes swimming in the shallower waters towards the bank. When he'd worked on *The Herald* ten years ago, the river had been brown foaming sludge full of litter and oil from tourist boats. He took a sip of coffee.

How an earth had he allowed this stitch up? He'd come here to challenge Amanda Ward on the basic questions on freedom of speech, and potential back scratching between MinSoc and the socials. Now he'd leave with nothing more than a puff piece about a Ministry nobody, with a few anodyne factoids to pepper the guff.

And meantime, MinSoc was treating him like their messenger. Leave the building and get nothing; stay, eat the damn pastries and take home more crumbs to push out more halos for MinSoc on the social.

The idea that Godspeed would send detailed on-the-record responses to his more challenging questions was laughable.

Soren thought of Grey, waiting at his desk for the big scoop.

"Okay, Mr Godspeed. Please explain to me how this works. MinSoc is pledging to rid the social of hate speech, not just from organised groups, but from individual posts. Who gets to decide what does and doesn't amount to hate speech?"

"A very good starter, Curtis. And it's not just hate speech. We're targeting comments that personally criticise people based on their appearance, sexuality, gender, race, beliefs. It's a long list."

He continued: "We've been working on this for a long time. Five years ago we engaged a group of consultant organisations - and no I'm not at liberty to name them - to do a wide analysis of the worst sides of the social. Not just ugly words, but looking at the effects of negative posts. The consultants not only looked at the phrases and posts, but specifically where they linked in with actual events - criminal or otherwise - that happened offline. May I give you an example?"

Soren was making brief notes on his slate. He nodded.

"Where the police or the Ministry of Justice had identified particular posts, or trends of posts, that had led to a rise in, say, self harm among teenagers - even specific cases - we could harvest that data, take the phrases and words used, and create some idea of those posts or trends most likely to be harmful to social users."

Soren felt a shudder, but raised his head as if waiting for more.

"This was, of course, all top secret. We had to monitor from behind the scenes to create a real picture we could work with after launching the policy. Like I say, it's been five years at least in the making.

"The consultants also engaged with randomly selected groups of social users - both online and offline - and we whiteboarded the feedback. The result was a list of phrases, words and patterns of behaviour on the social that we could now use to monitor and remove posts. And where necessary pass information to the police. Of course, that's how it began. It will be an ongoing process, as the project rolls out."

"Meaning?"

Soren heard Godspeed gulp.

"Well, say hashtag #fag gets red lighted in the system," said Godspeed. "It won't take long for the homophobes to find some other word, or emoji, or whatever to say the same thing. Once that new tag or trend begins to spread, we'll be able to identify it, and take the necessary action."

"Until every word in the language has been red lighted?"

"That's a cynical view, Mr Soren. Our modelling suggests words or phrases will become recycled, and then so dispersed that they'll no longer work as insults or hate speech. A kind of self filtering. From here, it all gets very technical. That's where the socials themselves are involved. They do all the technology that does the job."

"So I can't just choose a particular word or a phrase, and ask for it to be banned?" asked Soren.

"Absolutely not. And nor can I. And nor can Amanda. And nor can YoYo. You can report it, and if enough reports come in, then the system flags it and the cogs begin to turn. It's all very clever, but a bit above my head."

"So, it's the social doing what it does best, I guess," said Soren. "I know the world of social advertising well enough to understand how they exploit this kind of trend to sell adverts."

"Exactly, they'll be exploiting negative *trends*, as you put it, to clean things up. And the really exciting thing is this: as the social companies continue to get better at creating algorithms for better targeted ads, they'll use that improved technology to improve the clean-up coding too."

Soren shuddered inwardly. Arms firms used the same justification: creating and selling drones and smart bombs to dodgy regimes enabled them to transfer better technology to civil industry, supporting innovation and saving money. He didn't buy it.

Soren finished the cinnamon loop before speaking again.

"You mentioned the socials and their role in this. For a long time, the heads of those companies were fanatically resistant to any policing of their feeds and functions. And as they merged they had all the power to resist any government intervention at all on what they published."

"And resist they did," said Godspeed.

"So why the change of heart?"

"Exactly that. Heart. Protecting what a bunch of geeks called 'freedom of speech', according to their own definition, became untenable when their own platforms were resulting in children being exploited, teenagers harming themselves, politicians being physically harmed.

"The early 20's were a wakeup call, I think. Teens carrying machetes into schools, because someone had disrespected their gang on the feeds. The *MeToo* movement. *Black*

Lives Matter. The near riots over Brexit, after groups organised gatherings online. The second and third waves of Covid. The confusion between real information and fake news? I guess they were on the brink of users turning on the social, blaming them. The politicians tried their best to pass the buck. Even tried to legislate"

"Yes, and the socials resisted for so long," said Soren. "Even won court cases in the US, protecting the right to freedom of speech. Users were hardly about to abandon their platforms. What changed?"

"Lots of things," said Godspeed. "But I guess, my theory at least, is that one of those things was the opportunity to change the world while making bigger profits as a result."

"Always the profits."

"Such is the world. Along came the climate change movement, right. All over the globe, as a result of kids communicating on social, then coming out on strike outside their schools, governments started to listen.

"The socials picked up the trend, and multiplied it. Every company, charity and government department realised there was traction in changing their practices, then - if I may speak frankly - marketing the hell out of what they'd done over the social. In a virtuous circle, support for actions against climate change gained bigger and bigger support."

"All more money for the socials, and halos all round for bringing it about," agreed Soren.

"Look out of the window, Curtis. The river is clean. The air is clean. There's not a fossil fuel vehicle allowed within fifteen miles of London Bridge. Trends steamrolled, change happened, and the socials were able to take the credit. You saw the audience at the press conference. The reaction to Adisa Zane?"

"And now MinSoc and the socials have agreed to apply the same model to other *issues of concern,*" said Soren.

"Exactly. Starting with those issues we've identified over the last five years. Issues that have a real negative effect on our communities, that we've identified as of concern to citizens. Or dangerous for them. The end it campaign for example."

"And the socials are all willingly on board?" said Soren.

"I have to say that Lucas - Lucas Simmons, the chief executive of YoYo? - has been pushing the changes particularly strongly in the UK over recent months. He, out of all the Portico heads, has been the prime mover. Without him, we wouldn't have launched right now. But he's brought the whole of Portico on board earlier that we were planning to."

"All very neat and tidy, I have to admit." There was doubt in Soren's tone.

Godspeed gave an obviously frustrated sigh. "It's a work in progress, Curtis. There will be blips. But if we can reduce gang violence, make children safer, protect them from abuse, stop hate crimes, that's got to be a good thing to aim for. And it's in our interest to make this known, in the right way. Hence our invitation to you today."

There was a comfortable logic to it all. And there was certainly a lot to work with for an extended profile, though the technical aspects wouldn't be of much interest to Grey or his keyword coders.

Which itself proved Godspeed's claim. Good news sells.

"None of this is really news to me," said Soren. "You could deduce most of it. What I don't understand is why there hasn't been any questioning of what you're trying to do? I can't be the only one asking these questions? And when I did, at the press conference last week, I was ignored."

"I'm sorry about that, there was only time for a few questions."

"Which you chose from the stage, ignoring two very legitimate ones of my own."

"Which is why you're here, Curtis. There's only so much one can say in a press launch, particularly when it's the biggest thing we've done at MinSoc since the Ministry was founded. We had basic information in the press pack. We didn't want to complicate things at that early stage."

"You ignored me. You avoided any hint of criticism."

"My job was to make our new policy look as good as it really is, I make no apologies for that. But you're here now, and I hope have the answers you've been seeking."

"We've barely scratched the surface. Amanda Ward took to her heels as soon as I asked about accountability. That's not democracy, nor in the interests of the community." Soren realised the volume of his voice was rising.

"I apologise on the national director's behalf. Her leaving was not in response to your question. She had an urgent family matter to attend to. As you know, we're not permitted to speak about personal issues, even if we wanted to."

"But why should I believe you won't shut down critical comments or legitimate questions like mine on the social itself? Because I'm seeing nothing but halos."

"I'd like to think we deserve those halos," said Godspeed. "And I can assure you we have no intention of closing down discussion or debate on our policies. The intention is to screen out posts that might be harmful for users and the community at large."

"So if I criticise your policy of, say, banning nazi sympathising groups on the social, it'll stay in place."

"Well, I suspect it won't be very popular."

"Not the same thing."

"The algorithms have been set to highlight any posts, comments or groups that might lead to the kind of damage we've been talking about this afternoon. I don't believe it would pick up a post that merely criticises the removal of a group or post. Like I say, I'm not a techie, I'm not sure how it works.

"But I do know at MinSoc, Amanda insisted on a human stage in any intervention - at least in the early stages of this partnership. Your critical comment, if picked up at all, would be passed to one of our wider team, to make a final decision about whether it should be published."

"Theoretically, a hell of a lot of work if you get a lot of criticism," said Soren.

"That, I don't know about," said Godspeed, then added: "If I may speak frankly again, Mr Soren, you appear to be very cynical about the whole project today. But I don't believe you've posted any criticism, have you? So why would anyone else?"

He was becoming tetchy, Soren detected. "I'm just trying to get clarity," he said.

"Well, maybe I can be a little clearer. It is very early for this whole programme. Ten organisations are very upset that we have removed them completely from the social. Many, many more, I can assure you, are very upset that we're in the process of dismantling the dark web. Tensions are running high and we've all seen how that can spill out. We're being particularly vigilant about any messages sent directly to the national director, or any heads of the social."

Soren wondered whether Godspeed knew about his little encounter this morning.

"Perhaps, and this is strictly off the record," he waited for Soren to nod, "we're being tighter on the reins to begin with, to keep things as calm as we can. But at MinSoc we're certainly not afraid of criticism, nor do we have any intention of banning questions."

"A benign dictatorship."

Godspeed didn't pretend to hide his annoyance now. "Hardly. The point is worth repeating: we - the public - expressed our disgust at these groups, these attitudes online. We - the public - called for them to be banned, or screened out in our own comments and posts. We - the public - out-trended the negative posts and comments, with positive ones. Our priority is the sovereignty of the UK and the freedom and safety of our citizens.

"Five years of monitoring and understanding people's posts across the social had told us a lot of what we need to know, and will tell us more into the future. That is, you might say, a type of democracy."

"A *type*, I suppose," said Soren. "Only, we didn't know we were part of it."

10

___

From the TriCab, Soren swiped Grey and updated him on what had taken place at MinSoc.

"I spoke with her secretary directly," Grey protested. "The interview was supposed to be with her."

"I guess they changed their mind. Didn't ring true to me. I was ambushed by Godspeed into interviewing him instead."

Soren waited for Grey.

"Okay, actually I think this could be good. A new personality for the story, something exclusive for SkyCloud. We can make the most of it."

"I was thinking the same thing. There's certainly lots to say. The readers won't go for the techie stuff, but they'll love the socials unite, five year project, community involvement angles."

"Let's do some mini posts on each of those which we can drip feed over night. Put a halo around this Godspeed's head, but get Ward in there too. Then finish off with a full profile of Godspeed to go live in the morning."

"Will, it's already after five," said Soren.

"You better get on it then."

He swiped off, and Soren swiped Harrison who, as expected, was at her station in the office.

He related the afternoon's events to her, then asked: "Don't you think there's something not quite right here? Ward not showing up for an interview she arranged?"

"She was called away urgently, wasn't she?" asked Harrison.

"To the Ministry of Education, apparently. Any truth to that?"

"I'll check. Any juice on Alice Harding?"

His slate pinged. It was Godspeed's biog, sent personally from a MinSoc no reply email address. It was twice as long as Ward's had been.

"Sorry, can we catch up when I get back?"

"At your service, sir," said Harrison. Her face disappeared as suddenly as Grey's had a minute before.

Harry Godspeed was assistant national director at the Ministry for Society and Communications. He'd been personally appointed by the elected Minister, who did all the hiring and firing at the top end of the civil service.

Not that civil servants got fired, as such. They were just shuffled around depending on how good they were, and how popular among their colleagues and ministers. There were plenty of vacancies at the Ministry of Waste, Sewerage and Refuse that loomed for those not on top of their game.

Godspeed, like Ward it appeared, had a glowing track record. He was a graduate of Edinburgh University, previously schooled privately in Suffolk. A master's degree in social studies at Imperial College London, then selected for the civil servants fast track at the first time of application. He'd landed at the Ministry of Environment as a junior, before moving to MinSoc where he'd apparently climbed the ranks to assistant director. It wasn't hard to see where he was heading.

The biog outlined his out-of-work interests. He too had done placements abroad, as part of his MinEnv work. Eastern Europe - first in Romania and Bulgaria, then in Slovenia, which had been rapidly climbing the GDP ratings to become one of the strongest economies in the region.

He'd been a competitive swimmer through school and university, though didn't seem to have won any awards for the biog to brag about. His personal interests were listed as baking, badminton and walking his two adorable pekingese dogs, Lulu and Sadie.

Soren was spared a photo of the handbag dogs, but the mugshot of Godspeed was formal, in his familiar suit and tie, with the MinSoc insignia sewn into his jacket lapel. He had blond hair, flicked over at the front, and an impeccable pine coloured complexion surrounding bright white teeth.

It was more than enough for Soren to package into a keyword heavy profile. Throw in some photos of the dogs, maybe a cake or a loaf of sourdough, and the likes would soon be pinging in. To be honest, Soren had enjoyed his hour and a half with the charismatic young man, including their mild sparring.

He'd spoken a little more about the dark web, and how difficult that was to track down and erase. This he wanted to do off the record, which Soren had agreed to. It would be more like a war of attrition, he'd said, than a straightforward delete of webspace. There wasn't a single dark web but a network of singular cells, each with its own codes and continually renewing passwords.

Godspeed had admitted he wasn't quite sure how it worked, but users could disguise themselves and the slates they were using by bouncing their heavily encrypted coded messages, videos and pictures across an array of data servers the world over, making them next to untraceable.

The only way to destroy them was to endure the process of becoming part of the dark web, learn the processes, gain the codes and then to trick users to reveal something about themselves, or link their dark web personas with their public social profile in some way. Then the Ministry would have the data to close them down. Offline, they could then be arrested and compelled to reveal their codes and tactics. Any UK based channels could be closed down, and channels coming into or out of the UK cut off. Information would also be passed around internationally, so individual nations could implement their own actions regarding the dark web.

"Can I offer you a metaphor?" asked Godspeed. Soren nodded.

"All this is very techie, but imagine that all internet communications - posts, socials, messages anywhere on the internet - run in and out of our slates into big wide pipes. Those pipes carry chunks of information to big processing stations, before they are sent abroad through more pipes. Once out of the UK, the chunks of information are put back together at other stations and become the full message again, before reaching the slates of other users. That's massively simplifying what happens, but in essence we believe heading off that dark web data, once we've discovered who's producing it, at the processing stations is the way to go.

"And that same basic principle is what individual countries can use to manage internet communications within their own nations. Most internet traffic in the UK, for example, runs through YoYo servers - YoYo is the processing station in the the UK pipeline if you like - so YoYo can manage what's posted or not on the Portico platforms in the UK. It's why our working with the Portico partners is so important. Banning those ten organisations this morning was a case of switching off their access to the distribution servers, then erasing their pages."

Soren thought he understood.

Godspeed put himself back on the record: "To start with, taking down the dark web is going to be a full job of work. The international aspect of it is enough to make your head spin, but we've experts on the case. And what we're doing is already bringing results. With more finesse, we hope that we'll be able to automate more and more of the process, bringing the whole network to collapse. Moore's Law - the quicker we get onto the technology part, the quicker the whole process will become."

For all his reticence over free speech, even Soren could see the logic.

"Is the dark web as big as made out, though?" he asked. "Sometimes if feels like politicians blame it for anything they haven't been able to prevent. A terrorist attack - it's the dark web. A child pornography ring - that's the dark web too. Rasalina Mazeika - dark web again. Feels like a good way to pass the buck, because if anyone has any doubts: well, they're hardly going to go looking for proof."

Soren had leaned forward and said pointedly to Godspeed: "I wouldn't dare to type 'child porn' or even 'dark web' into a search engine. The Met would be knocking down my door."

"I can assure you, Mr Soren," Godspeed was talking in his sympathetic voice again, waving his outstretched fingers. "*I've* seen some of the stuff on the dark web. It does exist, it's massive and that's the problem. It would horrify anyone who saw it - any normal person, that is. Whether the politicians use it as an excuse, that's not for me to say. I'm strictly apolitical, as you know."

"But what about the right to a private conversation?" asked Soren.

"That's when we get back into the discussions we started with," said Godspeed, and he was right. Soren had already got the feeling their interview had turned full circle and was becoming repetitive. There was no more to say.

He'd decided right from that first gaze onto the Thames that he would steer well clear of his questions about the connection between Alice Harding and Amanda Ward.

The two had parted on good terms, with Godspeed assuring him that any supplementary questions really were welcome. He'd swiped his personal details onto Soren's screen before guiding him back down the two flights of steps, and seeing him to the wide doors of the Ministry of Society and Communications.

"Contact me any time," he'd said with a warm smile.

Back at the office, Soren headed straight for Harrison's station.

"It checks out," was her immediate response. "Ward *was* at MinEd today, she wasn't avoiding your interview."

Soren raised an eyebrow. Harrison continued: "According to the release material, it was a long planned launch of a Ministry of Education series of guidelines on childhood obesity. She wasn't initially billed to speak as far as I can see, but she was on the paperwork from today, biog, photo and all. And it's natural MinSoc would be involved. The Ministry of Health was there too."

She showed him the press release. MinEd was to increase periods of physical education at schools, but with special provisions for those kids who might already be too unfit, too shy or self conscious to participate with the rest of the class. For those families identified as needing it, the offer of free softly-does-it education on healthy eating. Even experienced chefs coming into their home to show them some basic quick meals. For those most in need, low cost boxes of fruit and veg each week. An emphasis on positive messages, which is where the social would come in.

"Could we go through MinEd to get an interview with Ward, do you think?"

"Already tried. They just referred me back to the paper-work, there's a quote or two to use. In her speech, she barely mentioned the new social policy. She said the social was the ideal platform for pushing out health and exercise messages. And that she hoped the new guidelines on the social comments would reduce bullying of chubby kids."

"Chubby kids?" asked Soren.

Harrison giggled. "A banned word in the new MinSoc world, I suspect. *She* said 'based on body shape or type'. Or something like that."

"Okay, so we're no further on finding out why she's avoiding difficult questions."

"I'm not so sure about that," said Harrison. "Have you seen the socials? She's all over them again, halo emojis all the way. Way out trending Ryan Irons."

"Ryan Irons?"

"National director at MinEd? You'd think he'd be getting all the credit, but Ward is sprinkled with gold dust. They're crediting her for the obesity stuff, as well as the social stuff from the last few days."

Soren swiped through his feeds, spotting mention after mention of Amanda Ward, with halo after halo.

Loving your work #AmandaWard. Time we used every proven tactic to save our children.

Sensible ideas from #AmandaWard 👮 today at MinEd on exercise for kids at school.

My kids might not thank you now #AmandaWard, but I do and they will in the future.

Ready for my food box #AmandaWard. Literally a life saver.

#AmandaWard 👮 my daughter is very conscious of her weight. I think one-on-one weekly walks with a health buddy is spot on. Thank you.

Good work getting the social under control #AmandaWard. Healthy, safe, community focused - exactly as it should be.

He noted MinEd were getting a fair amount of traction, with InfoCom's *#MinEd♥OurKids* riding the top of the ranks. But his posts with his own halos for Ward were still well up there too.

Soren asked: "Could you write a few positive stories using those posts, and the MinEd release?"

"Like I don't have enough to do."

"I've a hunch if we keep pushing the Ward angle, we'll squeeze out another video cast from her. Meantime, I'll blow some smoke up Godspeed's backside and the two can play off each other."

"It'll keep Will happy," said Harrison. "But why the about turn? I thought you were against this fawning click-bait stuff. Sounds to me like you've gone native."

"That's the impression I'd like to give. Somewhere soon they're going to slip up and maybe I can bait Ward out of hiding. We might then get to the truth about Alice Harding."

"So that's what this is all about."

"This question of freedom of speech and who makes the choices hasn't been pinned down. Even from Godspeed today. I came away with more questions than answers. But yes, Alice Harding is one of my questions too."

"You still think that's worth pursuing?"

"You saw the photos," said Soren. "I'm sure it's same woman. Which means something doesn't add up. I have to clear this up, find the truth."

"You better be damn sure it's the same woman if you publish anything," said Harrison.

"This kind of stuff is why I became a journalist thirty years ago. I'm beginning to realise, it's what still keeps me here."

Harrison looked up. "That's why I came here too, Curtis. Exciting, isn't it?"

"Yeah," he replied. "Just don't let on to the boss. Don't want him to suspect I'm enjoying the damn job."

That afternoon, time passed quickly as the two newsgatherers churned out positive copy. Harrison concentrated on the MinEd initiative, giving extra weight to Amanda Ward's role. Soren wrote some short posts to develop the MinSoc socials story, following up with a fawning profile of Godspeed.

Soren's short pieces focused on the way MinSoc had consulted over five years, before beginning to restrict hate speech on the socials. The policy, he argued, would be all the more effective because it was based on evidence of where negative posting on the social had led to real life negative incidents. He almost found it convincing.

In another story he gushed about the work Godspeed and Ward had both done to persuade the socials to come on board, painting the companies as reluctant bad guys who'd finally seen the light. He had paused, and made a quick side note about Lucas Simmons from YoYo. Godspeed had said he was a keen driver of the changes. What finally made him give way? Maybe he could be set up for a follow up piece.

In another story, Soren had tried as best he could to explain how machine learning plus human intervention would govern how hate speech was tracked, assessed and dealt with. He threw in the words 'online democracy' and 'community government' as if he knew what they were, and asked: is this the future for how all decisions will be made? Grey and MinSoc would love that.

A final short story concentrated on freedom of speech, and Godspeed's reassurance that the community had been at the heart of decisions about what should and shouldn't be allowed. And that widespread consultation, as well as strong analysis of posts over social media, had helped MinSoc pick the first ten organisations to be banned from the social in the UK. He followed up with some more quotes from grateful victims' groups, who had assured readers that their audiences would be safer as a result.

Deleting the dark web, he added as an afterthought, was a work in progress, according to Godspeed. But since only a minority used it, most would not notice. Except, he added for emphasis, the poor children, abused women and men, trafficked individuals like Rasalina Mazeika and her family, who would soon no longer be subjected to the horrors the dark web had created. The mention of Mazeika, he was all too aware, would give the story more traction. He added an #endit hashtag.

Soren had then worked on a long profile piece on Godspeed and his background. He praised the man for his community work in Slovenia, noting the coincidence between his time there and the upturn in the country's economy. He emphasised how Godspeed had been working with Ward from the outset, helping to shape the whole programme. He finished the piece relating for readers the smart suit, striped tie and shoes Godspeed had worn, something he knew to wish the ad coders at SkyCloud would be able to track down and attach pay-per-click advertising. The MinSoc photo of Godspeed was an attractive one, which itself would do no harm either when posted along with a picture of his oh so cute handbag dogs and soda bread loafs.

When he looked up from his slate, Soren noticed Harrison had left the office. Only Grey and a single overnight newsgatherer were still there. It was after 9 p.m.

Soren swiped the last of his pieces to his editor, so gushing it made him sick. After two minutes, Grey pinged back the question: "Drink?"

Soren approached his glass office and waited a moment for his editor to swipe the articles he'd just written into the social.

"A good day, Curtis. I don't think I've ever seen you work so hard." Grey closed the glass door, then poured a splash of Scotch into one glass, then a double into another. He handed Soren the larger measure.

"So you felt you got your answers about freedom of speech?" asked Grey, with the air of someone who was not quite gloating, but wasn't far off.

"I don't think it all adds up, but what Godspeed said about how decisions were consulted upon rings true. Maybe the social moves so fast, I hadn't realised how quickly all of this had happened."

"I sometimes feel that too," replied Grey. "Though I can see it from the financial perspective. You remember when every web page we opened, every App we opened, asked us if we agreed to their terms and conditions? Did you ever read them? I never did. We were so desperate for content, we swiped away our right to privacy, plus who knows what else.

"But turns out that might have been a good thing, if the data we shared, the websites we visited, the posts we wrote, ended up informing a massive transformation in the safety of the socials. Like Godspeed implied, we were doing good without knowing about it. We didn't know what was good for us, but our surfing swiping selves did?"

"We can't go backwards, I suppose," said Soren.

"Well, we could all individually opt back out again. How to go about it, I have no idea. Let alone anyone wanting to. And why should they?"

Soren agreed. The data the social now had was so comprehensive and constantly evolving, even if he opted out or closed his accounts completely, there's enough there to know what *people just like him* were thinking, doing, wanting, believing.

"I'm no exception," Soren said. "I grumble about the social, but I have no idea what they have on me, nor how to remove myself. And I need the social for my job."

"We all do, and to live our lives," said Grey.

He poured Soren another large drink.

By the time the newsgatherer had pressed himself into a TriCab home, the two had near finished the whisky. Grey had pressed the remains of the bottle into Soren's hand as he left. Drinking alcohol was strictly banned in TriCabs, but he felt it would be worth the wait when he got home.

Soren swipe ordered a pizza, and was pleased to see the delivery pod at his door twenty minutes later when his TriCab pulled up. A swipe of his slate opened the heated compartment and he took the 12" to his apartment along with the bottle.

He kicked off his shoes, lay on the bed and feasted while

he swiped through his feeds. Each of his posts on MinEd and Godspeed was getting great traction, with Godspeed earning a few single and double halos. Harrison's posts on Ward were getting good ratings too.

It was as if Godspeed and Ward's ratings were competing against each other, rising and falling in popularity as each post, comment and like came in. A mini horse race, played out in real time with a potential audience of millions. The pair's ratings were scoring better for SkyCloud than Soren had ever seen.

He drained the bottle, and pressed the shutdown button of his slate. He leant over from the bed, and pulled out his other, older slate from the bottom drawer.

He had to try his password a few times this time, his mind fugged by the booze, but eventually got it right. He swiped up a personal message, and through blurred vision began typing.

JessAndrew: #*Amanda Ward* 👓👓, *congrats on your health initiative today. Couldn't find you in the pic of your own hockey team at Cambridge? Maybe I should be looking for Alice Harding?*

He swiped the message into the world.

Soren leant over from the bed to poke his legacy slate back into the bottom draw. Within five minutes he was asleep. Two minutes later, beneath the layer of sweaters where it was kept, his legacy slate pinged:

ClariceKing: #*JessAndrew. This is all far bigger than you think. Best left alone.*

11

It was only by chance that Soren saw the message from ClariceKing. Through a headache and scrunched up eyes he'd fallen out of bed and into the soak of a hot shower. He picked up his sweater from the floor, and the stink of whisky, pizza and sweat was overwhelming. Probably time for a change.

He opened the bottom drawer to get out a new jumper and spotted his legacy slate. Unusually, the screen was still mildly glowing. Only then did he remember last night's probably too hasty message, and wondered if he might be able to undo it.

He puzzled at the message posted directly to him, from ClariceKing - a tag he'd never encountered. Officially, citizens should only have one social account - the Portico partners liked it that way because it was easier to maintain data on its users - but Soren himself had got round it with the help of a trusted coder. It was surely not beyond Amanda Ward to do the same. Certainly with the social power she commanded.

Sat half clothed on his bed, Soren began prodding at the

screen. But his still wet fingers made a mess of the letters he was trying to type. He took this as a sign. He was neither a believer in fate nor in any of the gods. What he was a believer in was that there was a very strong chance he was still drunk from the night before. The pulsing in his head, and his memory of his little telling off by Inspector Burman yesterday, led him to close down the slate before he did something stupid.

In his TriCab, Soren swiped through his feeds. His profile on Godspeed was gaining great traction, with re-shares clearly liking the personal aspects to his piece. Apparently, they liked seeing the people who worked in the Ministries close up, and hearing the voices behind the machine.

Godspeed and Ward's socials initiative was the best thing to come out of MinSoc, and now social users understood it was actually *their* own work (albeit without their knowledge). A few sharers had tried out tags #newdemocracy, #voteviasocial and similar, but none had really taken hold. Like so many others, they would be gone by lunchtime.

Brandon & Faulks, the tailors of the suit Godspeed had been wearing during the interview, was trending too - and their own marketing company was making hay, putting out further images of the assistant director wearing B&F clothing, as well as other personalities and celebs.

A few other companies were jumping on board, claiming that Godspeed wore their fragrance, or their shoes. And in one case, used their toothpaste. The man did have exceptional teeth, but there was no evidence either way that #BrighterWhite was the secret behind the sparkle.

The government of Slovenia had also picked up the Godspeed article, and was re-sharing it, topped with phrases enticing tourists to enjoy one of the most beautiful, peaceful and strongest economies in Europe.

Grey would be pleased, and Soren wasn't surprised to receive a message congratulating him as the TriCab pulled up outside his office. He took it as an invitation to be late, and headed across the road to Carlos'.

The coffee shop manager was as delighted to see him as usual, and pulled Soren to the front of the short queue to give him personal attention.

"You are the master of good news, Mr Soren," he said, taking the newsgatherer's cup and, Soren noticed, not swiping it. He filled it with steaming coffee, and placed a cinnamon loop on a bamboo plate. "Please, be my guest this morning. This cafe is a happy place today for your work. I like this Amanda Ward woman. She is a mother. She feels it. She understands."

Soren sat at his usual table, thanking Carlos for his gesture. The sickness from last night rose again, and he looked down at his pastry with only mild disgust. A hit of hot coffee soon settled that.

"My daughter say, the social has become kind place. Balloons, rainbows. Not evil messages and bullying. Her friends," he said, "feel they can chat again. They are free."

"Well Carlos, that's great news," said Soren, trying to smile. He thought he could just about manage the question: "How old is your daughter again?"

"I tell you, Mr Soren, she fifteen. But before, on her screen, bad things. Always nude men and ladies. Cruel messages. Now, she says, kindness. Sweetness. Like cinnamon, yes?"

Soren raised his eyebrows. As far as he knew, the policy was only beginning its roll out.

"Yes, Mr Soren. She asks for more time on her screen

from now on. Yes, I'm happy. Spend more time, because it is a good place now. Like this coffee shop, you agree, Mr Soren?"

Soren took a moment to decide, looking down at the coffee and pastry he'd just been given by the owner.

"It's great news, Carlos. I'm happy that this new policy is working for families."

His social smart daughter had obviously twisted the yet-to-be implemented policy to her benefit. It was a very long time since Soren had been fifteen. He had no idea whether he would have even considered questions of freedom of speech, rights and data protection. These days, he assumed, there was no distinction between a personal and public life lived on the social.

Soren usually obeyed his personal policy to ignore his slate when in Carlos' enjoying his morning coffee. But the message from the mysterious ClariceKing this morning had made him jittery. Maybe he too was morbidly addicted to his own slate and the social. When the ping for a new message arrived, he couldn't help but haul it out of his bag for a peek.

It was a message from Mia.

"Heads up Curtis 😇. Mystery man has been snooping around Will Grey, and is heading your way."

"Thanks," Soren swiped back. "And thanks for all the good work yesterday. More to share, W.T.S."

"W.T.S?"

"Watch This Space! Get with the chat, Harrison."

"T.W.A.T." she swiped back.

He smiled and placed his slate back into his bag. He took up his pastry, savouring the cinnamon warmth at the back of his throat as he stared out onto the street.

A moment later, he was coughing up a piece of dough. A

casually dressed man in jeans, polo shirt, bright white sneakers and a cap had walked slowly past the window, peering in. Then he opened the door and walked in Soren's direction.

"Mr Soren, your editor Will Grey said I might find you here," said Adisa Zane.

The YoYo electric car was so conspicuous in its branding that it turned the heads of pedestrians as it carried Soren and Zane towards the Village. The two men sat side by side, with Zane's super modern slate in the driving position. Soren wondered whether YoYo's Driver of Coding had even been old enough to have a licence when human driven cars were still the norm.

YoYo's predecessors had gradually taken over the whole of the former 2012 Olympic site in east London, filling every vacant warehouse and space, before buying up the pool, velodrome and football stadium too. These days the sports facilities were made available primarily to YoYo employees, but the company had also bought up and bank rolled what used to be West Ham United FC, now known as the YoYo Hammers.

Perhaps a disinclined nod to the local community's needs in the social company's massive land grab in the east of London, Soren thought.

During the first half of the journey, Zane had explained to Soren that YoYo was very pleased that SkyCloud had taken such great advantage of their platform, and that the work he had been doing in particular was causing lots of traffic that was advantageous to the company and its aims. Soren wasn't delighted at the praise, but kept his mouth shut.

In the spirit of being more open than in the past, YoYo would like to show him around their 'labs', and had set up a short face-to-face with a senior figure in the company. Grey, he said, had been delighted to release him for the day.

Zane turned to his slate and began swiping through messages and feeds, which Soren took as indication he should do the same. Or look out of the window, which is what he did. Watching the other electric cabs, cars and trams, as well as the pedestrians, all moving in a slow and seemingly mechanic symphony helped him to think.

It had been a weird few days. One in which he'd transformed from cynical newsgatherer grumping about the social, in Ned's obsessed with the demise of journalism and freedom of speech. Now he was in danger of becoming the social's loudest cheerleader. The louder he cheered, the more luck came his way. Now he was sitting in a YoYo electric car, on his way to an interview that fellow newsgatherers would bite off their swiping arm to be offered.

But there was something else. Soren knew there was nothing special about his copy. He had a talent for spotting a story, but so had any number of other newsgatherers in his industry, especially his so called rivals at InfoCom.

Everything he'd benefited from in the last few days had been handed to him on a plate. If anything, he'd pushed the wrong way. But it had bounced back smelling of roses.

Say what you see, he had learned as a junior hack. And the way he saw it right now, Mr Curtis Soren was the darling of the social and he'd done nothing to deserve it. Except make a crappy attempt at doing his job along the lines Grey wanted, rather than being led by instinct.

The puzzle of Amanda Ward, Alice Harding and now ClariceKing was one which he couldn't make sense of at all.

Adisa Zane interrupted his thoughts.

"We try to do a lot of good here in London, and everywhere we work," he said, indicating new roads, shop fronts and clean, neatly laid out green spaces with children's play areas, as the car crossed the River Lee and entered the YoYo complex.

Some of the new housing built after the Olympics the company had set aside, generously subsidised, for its own employees; the rest it provided as social housing. Zane explained that the company now offered more subsidised housing than all of the surrounding boroughs put together.

"Diversity and community are our core values," Zane said, sounding like he sincerely believed it.

Soren considered the landscape around him. Could it be that YoYo, MinSoc, the whole new social policy, was just as it seemed? A good thing. Done for good intentions. The company wins. The social wins. The Ministry wins. Carlos' fifteen-year-old daughter wins.

Hell, he thought, gazing at the ultramodern dashboard in the electric car he was riding in, even he was winning right now. And if Zane's attitude towards him over the last twenty minutes was indicative of the rest of the morning, he was about to get the full love bomb treatment.

Soren steeled himself against the thought. All the cinnamon loops in the world wouldn't turn him away from an honest assessment of what YoYo was about to show him. And what the as yet unnamed figure would say. He had his own reasons to mistrust the social. Reasons that would never go away.

The car pulled silently around a grand fountain.

"Fresh from the Lee river, of course," said Zane indicating the water. "With the roof of every YoYo building covered with solar panels, and the hydro spinners in the river, this whole village is sustainably powered. And we have a sanitation plant on site, to clean our waste before it re-enters the Lee as clean as we took it out."

The building itself was enormous. It was four storeys high, but stretched in either direction further than Soren could see. Over the wide electric doors shone the words Welcome to YoYo HQ in full branded lettering.

Soren noted Zane did not need to swipe his slate to enter the building, and inside a wide bright grey reception area there was no sign of security equipment, or even a security guard. To the right, in a space far larger than the SkyCloud offices, were half a dozen clusters of on-brand sofas and easy chairs, each surrounding low coffee tables with inbuilt slates. Soren watched people swiping the air above them, not even touching the screens. New displays, spreadsheets and diagrams appeared on an accompanying larger screen next to each cluster.

"This is workspace for our visitors, or really anyone who just drops by," explained Zane. "Would you like to take a seat? Just swipe for a coffee if you'd like one."

Soren took a seat, expecting Zane to join him.

"It's been a pleasure to meet you Mr Soren. Big fan, sir. Big fan." He extended a hand.

Soren stood again awkwardly to shake the man's hand, before Zane disappeared through the double doors they'd entered by. Not a moment's rest for the Driver of Coding, it seemed. What's the next big idea he's working on. Tele-porting between YoYo Villages in different countries?

He leant over his coffee table, and swiped up what appeared to be an internal search engine and typed in a query.

"Please find below a list of YoYo offices across the world. We operate in every country, but have 12 registered YoYo complexes in capital cities, and another 25 smaller offices in key countries."

There was no mention of teleporting. A matter of time.

Soren noticed an increased tension in the room. Conversations at other clusters became quieter, and others wandering the reception area stopped talking completely. Some just stood and stared.

A middle aged man, with a bald head and a neatly trimmed, barely visible beard, had entered the space. He wore thick, black, rectangular glasses which emphasised light blue eyes. He wore jeans and a casual sweatshirt with the YoYo logo embroidered on his left breast.

He chatted in a friendly way with the two receptionists before moving on to a group of visitors, who stood in silent attention as he welcomed them to the building. Then he did the rounds at some of the sofa clusters, shaking hands and laughing with some of the other guests. Finally, the man approached where Soren sat. Fifty pairs of eyes followed him.

The newsgatherer felt compelled to stand and to shake the man's hand. It was a face he recognised from numerous video casts and posts.

"Mr Soren, I am personally delighted to welcome you to YoYo. My name is Lucas Simmons. I'm chief executive of this outfit. I'd love to show you around."

"I hope you had a pleasant journey to the village," said Simmons, leading Soren around the vast reception. He smiled and nodded to other visitors as he passed. The man's accent was hard to place, certainly eastern European, but softened into a middle class London tone picked up from living in and around the capital for at least a decade. Soren made a mental note to check.

"It was very good of you to bring me here. Your electric cars are really something. I've never seen such technology."

"Ah, we try to be ahead of the curve, of course," replied the other man. "But I guess you and I both know there's a place for tradition too. I still have a hybrid Maseratti Gran-Tourismo 2021 in a lockup in the Village. Can't drive it around London, of course. But wouldn't give it up for the world."

His language was clear, not stuttered like Carlos', but the English idioms jarred with Soren's hangover and didn't sound quite right. Like they'd been learned, rather than picked up naturally.

"You're a vaping man I see?," asked Simmons. "Ah, to dream of an LD Blue cigarette! You know the brand? Russian. Illegal now, of course. No filter, if you can imagine such a thing."

"I always smoked Camel. Now it's mint and cinnamon vapes. And no intention to give up either," said Soren.

"And I'd bet a cigar every now and again, if you can get hold of one?"

"A long time ago, when I could," said Soren. "No chance now, not in London anyway. The best I get is to treat myself to a flavoured vape, they call it Pure Cuban Cigar. And just one mind, on Christmas morning."

The two laughed and Soren's lungs pulsated at the delicious thought. The guy oozed charisma.

Simmons slapped Soren on the back, and led him down a corridor which opened up into an enormous open plan office. A few dozen workers looked up in unison, smiled towards the two men, then went back to work. Captain on deck.

The office was hardly distinguishable from a very large coffee shop, with circular, square and double desks placed seemingly at random around the room. About half the stations were occupied by single workers wearing headsets. Others sported a couple chatting, or sometimes a larger group, with slates and smiles, in deep discussion.

A single glass wall opened up at the back of the room onto a tennis court - currently hosting a game of doubles - surrounded by ten or so outdoor training machines. On these, three fit looking women were squatting, twisting, lifting and peddling.

To the right of where the men had entered were a series of laminate planks covered in soft cushioning and brand colours. They were arranged in groups of four, slightly leaning out from each other around a raised table. In the corporate font on the wall above was written, *Think On Your Feet.*

Simmons smiled at Soren's puzzled look, "I guess the designers thought the guys here would get more blue sky thinking done standing up? Never seen the point myself."

Yet one of the clusters was being used: three people, chatting excitedly and wildly gesturing, occasionally swiping a slate.

Along the left wall stood a bank of kitchen units, a small staffed hot drinks stand, and seemingly unlimited shelves of snacks, fruit and soft drinks.

"Only one thing missing," said Soren. It was Simmons' turn to look puzzled. "Where are the bean bags?"

He slapped the newsgatherer on the shoulder again. "In time, Mr Soren. This is a work area. Life and Leisure is on the second floor."

"Work?" Soren scoffed.

"Yes, this work area is mainly administrative. But there's

a lot of new ideas coming out of here about how we can streamline our work. Get bills paid more quickly. Keep better track of partner expenses. Improve how we communicate with each other around the complex. Even down to ordering stationery - not that we need much of that these days."

Another laugh.

"You'll find, Mr Soren, we're firm believers here in the accumulation of minor gains. Shave a little time here, save a little money there, reward staff to increase production somewhere else, and what do you have? In one room, close to nothing. But rolled out across YoYo UK... or even worldwide? That's quite a transformation. Small ideas, huge results. Now add all those huge results together."

"More and more lovely money," Soren almost spat. It was the first time he'd felt uncomfortable around the man.

"I think money ceased to be our priority a long time ago, Mr Soren. I'm sorry if I gave that impression." He sounded genuinely conciliatory. "It gives us the opportunities to put what we've learned to work for the good of everyone."

Soren attempted to hold back the anger welling deep in his chest.

The YoYo boss continued: "Better communication for other companies, for individuals, new ways to reach the poorest, more effective ways to keep climate change in check. If nothing else, simply employing more people of all skills and backgrounds, disabilities, abilities."

"Have you brought me here just to show off, Mr Simmons?" His friendliness towards the man had begun to drain.

"Far from it, and I do apologise. I get carried away and I know you have your own questions about what we're trying to do here. Please, just two more areas I'd like to show you."

The chief executive led Soren back to the reception, where a YoYo electric car was waiting for them at the main doors. The trip was short, during which the men made small talk about the onsite creche and the company's family-friendly policies on childcare.

"Do you have family, Mr Soren?" Simmons said.

"Tell me more about the coding systems," replied Soren after a moment.

"Of course. That's where we're heading now. The eggheads," he smiled.

The car pulled up at a massive, square copper coloured box. It had been the venue for handball, fencing and badminton during the 2012 London Olympics, and was the central arena for the Paralympic Games the same year. Inside, its three floors had been separated into smaller offices, each laid out more formally than the admin offices he'd just been shown. Through soundproof glass, the two were able to watch men and women in casual clothing using touch reactive LCD walls to demonstrate ideas, construct flowcharts and draw mind maps, while others swiped at slates. They took side glances at Simmons, then carried on perhaps slightly more intensely than they had been.

In other rooms, coders worked in partially segregated booths, facing each other. There must have been a hundred at least, Soren estimated.

"A strange layout," Soren commented. "It's like they're playing battleships or something."

"Hah, I remember that old game," Simmons replied. "I guess it's not so different. See that woman there in the yellow scarf? And her partner opposite?"

The woman was very young, perhaps early twenties, wearing a bright blue over-the-ear headset and nodding her head gently in time with whatever music she was listening to. Before her sat a slightly older man, his 'Rather Be Listening to Rock' t-shirt revealing a lizard tattoo on his right arm. The rhythm of his head indicated a far quicker, rougher beat. His headphones had a skull and crossbones sticker on them.

"Ander here is writing code for one of our projects - let's say for slightly improving how your slate detects a swipe above the screen."

Soren felt for his slate, for a moment embarrassed that it was a touch only model.

"And Rocky here, he's checking Ander's code as she's writing it. If she slips up, he'll suggest a change, or maybe a better way of doing it. Then after ten minutes, or a natural break in the code, they'll swap over."

"Accumulation of minor gains."

"Precisely, though this is something coders have done for a long time, if not in real time like this. Remember open source software? Same idea. It may cost more to employ two people to write the same code, but if the outcome is better and more efficient, and has fewer bugs, well that's a job better done in a shorter time."

Soren made a mental note. It was rich material for his article. Literally a gaze inside the machine.

"On site, we have more than 4,000 employees, a whole bunch of freelancers, and we also obviously bring in remote workers if we're getting close to the launch of a project or need some external testing."

At the end of the bank of offices was an open plan space, with the same kitchen units, coffee and snacks area as the administration department. Soren swallowed hard, noting the dryness in his throat.

"You're almost ready for a drink I imagine, Mr Soren. You'll allow me just one more indulgence I hope?"

The two men rejoined their car, which took them half a mile away from the main complex, into a more remote area of warehouses with a security guard at its entrance. The guard swiped open the barrier after a single glance at the car's passengers.

The pair left the car and went through a small entrance; a set of electric doors was opened by an unseen security system. They were greeted by a woman wearing jeans and a YoYo branded polo, her curled black hair tied back smartly.

She greeted Simmons and welcomed Soren after her boss had introduced him as a newsgatherer from SkyCloud.

She looked Soren up and down, then handed over two thin sealed compostable green bags. Soren's was marked 'Large'.

"If you don't mind, gentlemen," she said, swiping open a door through which they entered into an airlock room with pegs and benches.

"Sorry for the dramatics, Soren," said Simmons with a thin smile. He tore open his bag and pulled out a white full body overall made of the same flimsy compostable material. This he began to pull on over his clothes. Soren did the same, then pulled the provided compostable bags over his shoes. The two men pulled up their hoods, the elastic securing uncomfortably around Soren's chin. Soren hung his bag on one of the pegs.

Simmons waved at a camera on the ceiling. An electric door on the other side of the room opened, and the two men left the chamber, their bodies fully covered.

Inside, the warehouse was cold and tasted artificially dry. A low buzzing hung in the air. A handful of fellow overall suited bodies moved around long alleyways of shelving containing great metal cabinets. Their overalls were far thicker, blue in colour, and had their names written

- in the company font of course - across shoulders and chests.

Charlie. Claire. Mulab.

Each of the tall aisles of buzzing cabinets was labelled with a number, and as the two men proceeded down aisle 18 opposite where they'd entered, it became clear the crossing corridors were labelled with letters. The two reached 18-J before Simmons led them to the right, past 19-J, 20- and 21-.

Soren estimated there must be at least another ten aisles, while the depth of the warehouse might just accommodate the rest of the alphabet.

Spinning above them, huge fans pushed cold air onto the buzzing cabinets, through Soren's overalls, his clothes and onto his skin. He shivered.

"As you might have guessed, these are our main servers for the greater part of the UK. The physical location of this part of the social I suppose," said Simmons, also with a slight shiver in his voice. "Though obviously we have backup sites in secret locations. Each constantly updates each other, via satellite. It's basically impossible to lose data."

"It's enormous," said Soren.

"It's the engine room of what we do. There's not a message or swipe in the UK that doesn't come through this warehouse one way or another. Or one of the three we have on site."

"And how far does that data go back?" asked Soren.

"As far back as the pre-existing companies we took over held their own data."

"Nothing is deleted?"

"That's the idea. Everything is backed up," said Simmons.

"A data graveyard?"

"We like to think of it as a living, almost breathing, up-to-date information bank, built above an immense historical library of data going back twenty years. At least."

"That's what worries me," said Soren, barely audible over the buzzing of miles of aisles of information. "What if I want my data to be deleted, forever? Gone. What about those pictures of kids being abused? Will *they* still be lurking in this immense historical library? As you put it."

Soren's fists were clenched and red. He wasn't sure if it was because of the cold.

"I think it may be time for that coffee," said Simmons.

The office of the chief executive of YoYo was split into three areas, each separated by a floor-to-ceiling glass panel. Together they made up the size of a small sports hall.

One half featured the same random array of tables and sofas Soren had seen in the administration section Simmons had first shown him. A dozen staff milled around, or worked at their stations or at a window bench over-looking the complex.

Another L-shaped space through double glass doors was where Simmons welcomed his visitors. There were comfort-able sofas, as well as a more formal oval table surrounded by branded chairs.

The two men passed through the first area, greeted with smiles and nods from his staff. In the middle space, on one of the tables, stood a steaming pot of coffee along with an array of pastries and sandwiches. A bowl of glistening fruit had been laid to the side.

From here, Soren could see Simmons' private office through another floor-to-ceiling glass panel. He had no desk, but various standing and sitting work stations, a coffee table surrounded by three armchairs, a large LCD screen on the wall behind them. There were a few frames stuck to one wall, close to a full length window overlooking the River Lee. From what Soren could see, they were family photos, a small map in a frame, perhaps some certificates or awards.

The room was pristine, and it occurred to Soren that it was barely used. Simmons appeared to be a man who did his business on the move, chatting to employees around the complex, meeting everyone - whether managers, or coders, or canteen workers - in their own workspaces, or along corridors, or in one of the many leisure or coffee facilities. This was not a man who summoned employees to his private suite.

Simmons swiped the doors closed and invited Soren to sit.

"I suppose that massive data bank told you how I take my coffee?" he said.

"And that you're keen on cinnamon loops, and don't eat meat?"

"Christ!" replied Soren.

"I'm joking. It's only what's published on your personal profile, anyone can access that. For the record, my own vice is the pecan foldover, but you know, no nuts on site, etcetera. Even for the chief executive."

"PC gone mad."

The two men laughed at the ancient phrase. It had been a long time since nuts of any kind were allowed in public places or offices. MinHealth rules.

Simmons poured the coffee, and Soren took a few triangles of granary sandwich - cucumber and cheese - onto a plate. The other man took some grapes, then a single sandwich. They ate and drank in silence for a while.

"Oh, for a cigarette now," said Simmons. In spite of himself, Soren was in danger of liking this man.

"You're wondering if I'm really charming, or it's all just a show so you write good things about me?"

Soren shook his head with a smile, and put down his empty plate. Damn the man.

"Okay, so let's start with my key question," asked Soren. "What am I doing here? I suspect you don't roll out the red carpet for every newsgatherer with a pulse and a slate."

"Curtis... can I call you Curtis?"

Soren didn't feel like he could refuse. He nodded.

"Curtis, I'd be delighted, we all would, if you took away from your tour today, and my personal time with you, a positive view of our company. We can talk about the detail, but I hope you're getting the idea that we're trying to do good things here."

"I'm getting that message from you, yes. But I do have questions."

"And I'm very much keen to hear them and answer as honestly as I can. But before that, I'd like you to understand something." Simmons put down his coffee.

"All of this is an ongoing project. It's been many years in the making. Not just YoYo itself, but also the latest social oversight project with the Ministry of Society and Communications. We've been working with MinSoc for at least five years. Longer actually, which is another part of the story.

"To make this happen, we've needed to recruit the very best in their fields and bring them into the fold," he continued. "The brain boxes, those at the top of their game. We have a whole postroom dealing with CVs and letters from people who want to work for YoYo. But we're not just about those who want it the most. We want those with the most talent, the best fit, those who 'get it'."

"So, you want my article to focus on your amazing recruitment strategy? I think you might need to talk to our advertising department," said Soren.

"I'm not sure you're understanding me, Curtis." The man had let the smoothness of his London accent go a little, revealing something a little more stuttered and guttural beneath.

Soren sat back in his chair. The man was right, "I'm not sure I am."

Simmons smiled, "Mr Soren, I'd like you to come to work for us."

Soren choked on hot coffee, and had to take a deep breath to avoid coughing up over the pastries.

He released a full belly laugh. "You're joking, right?"

Simmons picked up a bun, perhaps protecting it from anything else about to spurt out of Soren's mouth. He placed it on the plate in front of him and leant forward. "On the contrary, I think it's the soundest, most sensible idea some of us here have had for a long time."

Us? He was being mocked, surely.

"Bullshit. I am probably your most vociferous critic, Mr Simmons. I have personal reasons for being so. But also it is my job. Or at least it was my job, to question everything you and the rest of the social does. You can and have harmed lives, however many you now claim to be attempting to improve. We may joke about the old days together, but everything you've shown me today has left a bad taste in my mouth."

"Please, explain that to me," said Simmons calmly.

Soren clenched his fists, as he had in the server room: "Tech wash, if you like. The pile of CVs in your post room, the gleeful awe of those you schmoozed in reception. We've all been so overwhelmed by your company's novelty, the sparkling new, the *amazing work* you claim to have achieved. We don't look past the gloss. Hell, most of us don't look up from our screens to meet people eye-to-eye any more."

His tone was fierce now: "And then people get hurt."

Simmons paused, before replying: "You can't argue that we're not making the world a better place. Friends have been able to communicate better than ever before; companies are more productive; we've been able to look at the world on a local, national and global data scale, and have been able to use that information to improve communities, to slow down climate change, to halt down the progression of disease. It was our tech that put a stop to the fourth global wave of Covid, remember."

Soren had the feeling Simmons was purposely pushing him to the edge.

"Yes, all branded in your bloody YoYo colours, with a happy smile on your face. But what about democracy? What about personal relationships? What about the big questions? What about getting a coffee without having a chip installed in a bloody YoYo branded smart cup. We've all become automatons, caught up in your big net, and have allowed ourselves to be... part of your machine. All for a discount on some streaming service you're trying to sell us, or for a cheaper cab ride to one of your events.

"And the worst thing is, Mr Simmons, is that we're all doing it willingly. Blindly. I don't know when we put up our hands and said, '*yes, take us away to your magic paradise*'. But it happened, and now it can't be reversed. There *is* no reverse gear. Just like in your YoYo taxis."

Soren paused, allowed his anger to dissipate.

"And at one time people believed the earth was flat,"

Simmons replied, sounding amused. "Then they discovered we were a spherical rock, a tiny dot in an infinite universe. There was no reverse there either."

"But there was adaptation," argued Soren, calmer now. "We took the new information, we used it to reshape our lives, our myths, but we still had autonomy. The freedom to disagree, to debate. The world you have created is a bubble that your users, your employees, most of the world, have been seduced into. We've forgotten how to look outwards."

"You're right. We're too internally facing," said Simmons. "We've got ourselves into an immense virtuous circle. We can't see the real world."

"You're *creating* your own world, that's the point," said Soren. "Then it circles around itself. Get on board, or get left behind."

"So, what do we need Mr Soren?" It felt like the conversation was coming to a climax.

"That bubble bursting, someone not caught up in the whirlwind. An...", Soren caught himself, and shook his head before finishing his sentence. God, he needed a vape. "An outsiders' view."

Simmons leaned back in his chair, and smiled again.

"Mr Soren, let me say it again. I'd like you to come to work for us."

12

Curtis Soren asked for some time out. He really did want that vape.

"Why don't you take an hour, or so? Have a wander around the campus. Think things through," Simmons had said. "Just ask for me at reception when you're ready to talk some more."

"If," Soren corrected him.

Simmons had called an assistant, who had packed up some of the leftover sandwiches and a pastry into a paper bag and given it to Soren. The assistant had then led him back to the ground floor and out of the main building. A YoYo cab was waiting for him.

On the built in dashboard screen, Soren had selected what looked like a leisure spot next to the Lee. Swiping deeper into the map had brought up pictures of benches surrounding a children's playground. He swiped above the screen, and the car pulled around the fountain and off towards the river.

Soren sat on a bench and watched some swans paddling

up and down the river. Once, this part of Hackney Marshes had been a no go area. The only moving things in the Lee back then were empty beer cans and filthy nappies. A small group of ducks waddled up to where he sat, and he threw a few crumbs in their direction.

Soren knew Harrison should have been his first call, but he somehow didn't want to break the peacefulness of the little lunch spot he'd found.

Soren had immediately, but politely, refused Simmons' offer. After angrily boxing himself in by the time Simmons had asked a second time, he'd taken a deeper breath and thought about what he was proposing.

He wasn't sure if the offer was to buy him off, or honestly to use his critical eye. He considered both in turn.

Surely Simmons hadn't made the mistake of thinking Soren would be bowled over by the chance to work at YoYo. Simmons was smart. He could never have grown the company to what it was by offering money and status in exchange for obedience and silence. If he had thought Soren would go for that, then he was a fool. Simmons might be charming and gregarious, overzealous at times, but he was certainly not an idiot.

In which case, perhaps the offer had been made in good faith. Perhaps Soren could bring the eggheads at YoYo down a peg. Open their eyes to a reality beyond the swipe. If employees, and perhaps wider users of the social, could start to see truth and discussion as more valuable than sharing fashion tips or buying the latest tech, then surely that would be a good thing.

The social would need to be far more critical of itself - not only its founders and its champions, but the government, the everyday users. The social had become an inane vacuum, consuming people into self obsession. Their looks, their so called friendships, the size of their houses and bank accounts. Ironic to call it the social when it was anything but.

Then there was the issue of privacy. The seeming impossibility of opting out. Once the social companies knew you, your profile, your likes and dislikes, they not only could use the data about you to make more money for themselves, they could also tempt you to buy things you didn't really need. To get you to spend more time and more money on their platforms. Buying. Gambling. Spending. More self obsession.

And there were always negative consequences: Soren knew that alright. And Amanda Ward knew that too. The price we pay for the social could result in actual harm. A terrorist or racist attack, online bullying, self harm among kids. A fatal road traffic collision because one of the drivers was more interested in messaging her friends than paying attention to the road.

It was too high a price to pay.

He shook his head.

"What exactly would you expect me to do?" Soren had asked Simmons in his office.

"Just be yourself. Tell us from the inside what we're doing wrong. Guide us in the things that make people feel they're not safe, that their information is not safe, that their rights have been taken away."

He paused. "Can I speak frankly, and off the record?"

"Shit, this whole thing is off the record," said Soren. "My editor would knock my block off if he got a sniff that I'd come here to be offered a job."

"Thank you. Getting into bed with MinSoc has felt

extreme for us here at YoYo. We've always been proud of our independence, and have previously banned only the very worst material on the social. The rest," he had held up his hands to emphasise his point, "was freedom of speech.

"But lately we've felt we had no choice but to lean in MinSoc's direction. Our users, the Ministry's research, they've all pointed in that direction. But it's all a muddle. The lines are blurred, and like you say, we can't find the reverse gear."

"It's a lot to expect of one man," Soren had said.

"If compensation is your concern, Curtis, I can assure you that won't be a problem."

"That was not what I meant, and you know it. If you collectively, with all those hundreds of warehouses of data, don't know how to handle the future, what do I have to offer?"

"MinSoc have the best of intentions, but they've not modelled where all this ends up. I think you have the critical eye that can help our senior staff to understand where our limits should be."

"MinSoc told me your whole project was based on years of data, consultation, posts and feeds. All the knowledge you need is there," Soren argued.

"That's their naivety, and it also makes a good story. Life is more than data. People think something, but write something else. There's a whole load of fake news in the socials, and most users can't tell the difference. And once they click one conspiracy theory, they get more and more. Users are only presented with stuff our algorithms tell them they already like. MinSoc call it democracy. I'm worried it's the opposite. What happened to truth."

"Well, we agree on something."

"We agree on a lot, I suspect," said Simmons. "How long

until we start voting for our politicians, our leaders, through the social? Based on questionable information?"

Soren added: "How long before the social assesses from our feeds and preferences what we *probably* want from our leaders in future, then votes on our behalf?"

"Exactly."

"You seem to have a pretty clear picture of this yourself," said Soren. "Why do you need me to keep you straight?"

"Because my personal investment in the social is too great - financial, historical, reputational," Simmons replied.

"So why the sudden about turn? Why now?"

"I have my reasons," the chief executive said. "And you've got me on a good day, because I prepared what I needed to say. Most of the time, I get caught up with the flow of what we're doing here. And as you know, I'm only the head of YoYo. We're partnered, under the Portico deal, with the other three biggest social companies in the world. Their CEOs don't think the same as me. There are a few at the top of the social around the world who wouldn't give these questions the slightest consideration. But here, right now, we need an outside perspective."

Simmons had paused, choosing his words very carefully.

"I have been very affected by the #endit campaign over the last month. It changed my mind, if you like. I now know we need someone who has a personal interest in seeing Portico fail. So we can be sure it doesn't."

Soren looked up from his packed lunch. He had potential to do good, by forcing the social to look inwards. To give it some limits as a critical friend. Or would he just be another pawn in the game, brought in and bought out to keep quiet; thinking he was doing good when everything he had to offer would really be a drop in an ocean of self echoing noise.

Soren looked towards the ducks at his feet. A mallard, a female and a single chick just shedding its first layer of down. He threw the remains of his pastry at the birds suddenly, and they scattered. He watched them regather on the other side of the Lee.

He pulled a worn photo of his wife and daughter from the rear pocket of his jeans and stared at them. There was no answer in either of their faces.

He took out a vape and blew steam into the air. The duck family returned and he emptied out the remains of the paper bag at their feet.

"Naturally I have some further questions," Soren said. The company head had ordered new coffee and had the fruit bowl replenished, but he had held back on the sweet treats.

"Do you mean for our press interview, or your job interview?" The man no longer seemed quite as charming as he had before lunch.

"I need to know more about how YoYo came about. Where it stands in the internet and social world?"

"The Portico project?" asked Simmons.

"Yes, Portico. I know the basics, but I need to know how it all fits together."

"This is entirely off the record?" Soren nodded, and Simmons continued: "Then you'll know YoYo is a UK based company, of which I'm chief executive. But we're a global company. The same would be true of the other three biggest 'functions', if you like, on the web. Three more companies just like ours, only doing different things - the other three are based in the States."

"So, YoYo handles the social, then there's Gum, Talk and Wonderfish?" asked Soren.

"Exactly. Gum handles search and find; Talk handles messaging, picture sending and online chat and video; and Wonderfish our shopping, online transactions, the financial stuff. Together we are the four pillars of Portico."

"Working Together To Widen The Web, if I'm right," said Soren.

"That slogan is six years old," said Simmons in an embarrassed tone. "But I guess that's the general gist. Previously we all worked separately, all trying to make the world a better place..."

"More profit," interjected Soren.

"A better place, in our *own way*. But the heads of these companies didn't take long to realise we were competing on key things - messaging, streaming, server space and most importantly data about our users. To start with, we'd dip into each other's functions: using each other's platforms to advertise, or buying up messaging, even buying data and space from each other."

"So, it made sense to merge," said Soren.

"Not merge, exactly, but to come to a sharing agreement. Working together we could deliver a far better service for our users. The chief executives of the big four know each other very well. This MinSoc project is far from the only partnership we've worked on together.

"So now your average users can message and chat and post between them, or in groups, or do some searches through Gum, and the partners in Portico can use that data to predict their behaviour, meet their needs better, and of course deliver the advertising that helps them discover the things they want to buy. But we're also better able to deliver health messages, public policy advice, the things you most need to know for your own situation."

Simmons continued, excited now by the track he was on,

and newly charismatic in his manner. Soren took a new coffee.

"Say I announce to my friends and family over the social, run by YoYo, that my partner and I are going to have a baby? Or I start searching for new baby advice on Gum? Of course, I'm going to start getting advertising, placed around my feeds, for things new parents might want: cotton wool, baby shampoo - I don't know, that was a long time ago for me. But that's useful, yeah?"

"Intrusive, but I suppose convenient," replied Soren.

"Convenient, exactly. But we can do more than that. Say that, from the mix of pooled data, it's been identified that you're poor, or living in a deprived area, or have special needs? Then as a result, MinHealth sends you a parcel of baby goods completely free of charge. Then sellers from Wonderfish take the opportunity to contribute a care box, which its advertisers pay to send out to you. That child begins their life with the things they need, not what their parents can scrape together."

"Previously, there were forms to fill in, applications to make, waiting lists to join if you were in need. Now, those who need get it for free and without a hint of stigma attached. Those who don't need a free care box? Well, they might get advertising for more expensive stuff, luxury stuff - our algorithms have a pretty clear idea of their social class, their purchasing power, even their tastes. They might get some free samples. But they *buy* the expensive stuff, and the profit earned there easily pays for the free boxes for those in need."

"I believe they used to call that socialism," said Soren. "And you're telling me we need high technology to bring it about. But isn't that at all scary to you? That the social, or

Portico - even the government - knows what you want as quickly as you do?"

"Or even before you do," said Simmons. "That's not scary. It's exciting. Adapting to the world we live in. There have been so many things we've invented we didn't know we needed. And now, we can't live without.

"You're old enough to remember, Curtis, just about, when there were shops on every high street? People got itchy when those shops started to shut down. They wanted their butchers. The tiny toy shop. But boy, wasn't it more convenient to drive to a big shopping centre and get everything you needed in one Saturday afternoon trip? Free parking, cheaper prices, more choice.

"Well, what happened next? Those big shopping centres started to close too. Because it became more convenient to get online, to buy anything we wanted at the swipe of a slate and have it brought to our door, within one specified hour, at our convenience, in an electric vehicle. Did we carry on the big weekend shop? We did not.

"And things will change again. Smart fridges that automatically order the food you need and robots that swipe into your home and put it away for you, perhaps. Now Gum knows how old your nephew is, it might ship out some sample toys to you to choose from for his next birthday. If you don't want them, send them back for free. Whatever, I don't know, and that's what we're trying to find out here, so we can deliver the 'What ifs...?'."

"Is this supposed to be reassuring? Because I don't want a robot coming into my apartment," said Soren.

"No, but you sure as hell like those cinnamon loops being ready for you every time you walk into your local coffee shop. Technology has allowed us to work more, if we want to.

Spend more time with the kids, if we don't. Women have been liberated by technology, freed from some of the home responsibilities that previously fell to them. Those dead high streets? Now, they're alive with communities, playgrounds, events.

"There are microbusinesses' products and experiences to enjoy, rather than mundane daily shopping trips to endure. There was a time when most thought the rise of the Portico was threatening society, locking us indoors waiting for the next package. It's the opposite."

Soren knew what was coming next. He'd heard it so many times when he'd criticised the social.

"When was the last time you took a business related flight, Soren? When was the last time you drove a fossil fuelled car? Ten years, I bet. The climate crisis demanded innovation, transformation. And we delivered. No more traffic jams and massive car parks, just electric cars delivering goods to our doorstep. No more flights for meetings, just immersive video technology that's far cheaper, far easier and just as effective as meeting in person. Plus massive improvements in energy efficiency thanks to big data, automation and behavioural nudges over the social.

"Portico has always been about that better place. And I'm not saying what is good right now will always be the best. It'll change again, and we'll need to change with it. That's why we need the very best in their fields to join us on the journey."

Soren cringed at the phrase, but felt in danger of agreeing with the man. He checked himself. His role, whether outside or inside of YoYo, would need to remain ultra critical. Finally he spoke.

"Okay, but say I was to join your scheme. Go with the inevitable, as you may or may not have convinced me is the case. Will I have full freedom to say, write and post whatever I wish, no matter what the consequences?"

Simmons paused, apparently considering: "Internally, you will have absolute freedom. Most of my colleagues here will welcome the criticism. What reaches the outside world, that has to be a different story. But the actions we take as a result of your input? Well, my hope is that they will become apparent over time, in how we change as a company."

Soren attempted to cast a line for his story.

"And I suppose that YoYo's algorithms are already designed to screen out any direct criticism of the organisation anyway?"

"That's a strong accusation, Curtis. I agree, theoretically, that our algorithms can monitor for negative language and attitudes towards our company, but it wouldn't automatically ban or delete them. There's a human element, a PR team if you like, that monitors what people say so we can gain from that knowledge. And protect the company if we need to."

"So, that's freedom of speech banned there, already."

"No, that's preventing libel, fake news. It's our own platform, why shouldn't we closely monitor what our own users are saying about us?"

"Because of the virtuous circle you've already talked about," said Soren. "If the negative stuff is screened out, only the positive survives. And it might not be true, and you lose the perspective you need. Surely that's obvious. And I'm not even on your payroll."

Simmons said: "The more you speak, the more desperate I am to have you working here. But I think you overestimate what our algorithms are capable of. We needed MinSoc's help to implement their own rules, find key organisations and monitor attitudes and traffic over five years."

"Which brings me to MinSoc, actually," said Soren. "What exactly is your relationship? You would need to work with them quite closely to implement their plan. What's in it for you, if you're restricting the very data you've spent the last ten minutes claiming is the gold dust on which Portico operates."

"Our relationship with MinSoc is very good, and since Amanda Ward has taken over there, even better. I've worked with Amanda for a very long time. She's a specialist in communications and I'm convinced what she's trying to do is for the best. Will we lose data? It depends on how you look at it. I think the whole of Portico is moving towards the total eradication of the dark web, and there's no data on there any of us want.

"As for negative posting and groups on the social, I think it's a matter of slow shift. As we take away the opportunities for people to express hate speech, or gather to share odious views, I suppose the aim is to dilute them. Amanda and I have talked extensively about this very nuanced thing, and have worked closely with MinEd and independent psychologists to understand how it might work. Those most likely to post offensive comments, those most drawn to hate speech, those fanatics who set up groups, those most likely to express negativity: they're those most in need. The bullied becomes the bully, right?"

"Maybe," said Soren.

"Well, if you're the poorest of the poor. If you feel your job is unfairly taken by someone else who's not like you. If you feel the system is against you. If you live among those who bark your own views back at you, you remain encircled in your own warped sense of what the world is really like."

"So, you want to change what they think?"

Simmons ignored the question. "By identifying those most likely to post hatred, we can smooth out the corners. Okay, we're not exactly going to send them care packages, but we can use what we know about them to meet their needs, answer their concerns. Racists still have kids, right? They still go shopping. They still have daily needs. They still use the social. These are all opportunities to take the anger away by engaging with them in a positive way."

"You will always have extremists, motivated by extreme, immovable points of view," said Soren.

"Yes, and if our data shows that those few people, and I do believe the numbers are minimal, continue to act, post or attempt to organise disgusting behaviour, then we will already have the data the law needs to prosecute them. But even if they were locked up, there would be programmes to rehabilitate, change views, calm tensions. In simple terms, we're trying to do some rehabilitation work before it gets to crisis level."

"This sounds like an awful lot for a social media company to be taking on," said Soren.

"It is, but we're not doing it alone. We have the Ministries on board, partnerships with charities and justice organisations. We're working with Amanda Ward to pick off the low hanging fruit before it gets even close to going rancid. We're learning as we go. We're not deleting groups in a vacuum. That's the nuance we're not getting across just now, and which might anger those who suddenly find their social accounts have gone down.

"We know the social can only take us so far. We need human beings for the rest of it. Human beings like you."

"And like Mia Harrison, my partner at SkyCloud?"

Simmons considered for a moment.

"Mr Soren, my only interest is to make YoYo, and Portico better, and our interventions more effective. I believe we've earned our spurs so far. So, if your colleague is valuable to you, and will contribute to making what we do better, then sure, there's a place for her here on the fourth floor.

"Right next to yours."

13

It was a twenty minute TriCab ride across London, then just a ten minute wait until Soren could take a train from Paddington to Oxford. When he was at university, the London to Oxford train would take about fifty minutes. Now, the Ministry of Transport's trains - complete with technology supplied from Japan's bullet trains - could make the journey in half that time.

Soren enjoyed watching the tight urban sprawl of London as it spread out into Reading, the train's only stop before Oxford. Patches of green space here and there to distinguish between the two cities. Then he began to relax as the train suddenly passed into purer countryside, through the greenscapes and hamlets of the Pangbournes, the Hagbournes and Moulsefords. In this part of the world, every village boasted an Upper or Lower, often a West and East too. Each with a bridge over the radically smaller Thames, until the vast waterway became thin channels along which Oxford students would still row before dawn, walk and run in the morning, and punt across on lazy summer afternoons.

He'd visited Oxford a few times since matriculation. First, to collect his 2.1 undergraduate degree from Magdalene College. Then, in the first few heady years following college, to revisit friends in hidden pubs and to attend wild balls organised by keen second year students.

Then there was the annual Mayday celebrations, a feast of drinking and stupidity, where rich boys threw themselves off Magdalene Bridge, to the ire of Oxfordshire Police and the despondency of the poor doctors and nurses working accident and emergency that night at the John Radcliff.

London life had taken over. With new friends, and a relationship with another UCL journalism student beginning to blossom, the City of Dreaming Spires had lost its attraction.

Soren decided to walk from the train station to the centre of town. Despite criminal modernisation, the close cobbled streets, tall sandstone buildings and traditional shop fronts still stirred his heart. A cab ride couldn't do them justice. At St George's he crossed into Broad Street, marvelling at the mix of the old and the new. Tiny alleys and passageways remaining, but cornered by AutoCoffee vending machines, social newsfeeds, LCDs and ever changing shop window advertising feeds that clearly knew what you'd last considered buying on your slate.

Before reaching the King's Arms, he turned right up a dozen steps and through four massive pillars. Before him stretched a broad rectangle of gravel, with corridors to other squares leading ahead and to the right. He had not been to this place for over twenty years, yet still knew the path to take to the main entrance of the Bodleian Library.

Soren knew from his time at Oxford that it is a quirk of the University that its library has had the right since 1910 to demand a copy of every book, paper, pamphlet and brochure published in the UK. Its catalogue actually runs back to the 1600s, and has some treasured books from the 15th century. It was a workable, enforceable system, until online publishing took over the book industry and the internet became the primary source of knowledge (and false knowledge). The university's narrow corridors and long shelves could no longer keep up.

In huge chambers below the libraries themselves, all interconnected, and in safe deposit warehouses buried in the Oxfordshire countryside, there still sat millions of pages. Knowledge. Conjecture. History. Fiction. Personal diaries. Essays and doctorate theses. And far more besides.

It was another quirk of Oxford University that any student who has studied there, presuming they weren't thrown out for some wild misdemeanour like jumping off a bridge on Mayday, can remain a life long member of the Bodleian. And had access, free of charge, to the lot.

Soren stood in the centre of the square and sighed. He knew it was pure privilege. But today, for the first time in a long time, it was one he was pleased to have.

The young librarians at the main desk fussed over the older man, until they had tracked down the member of staff Soren had been messaging over recent days. The librarian was in his twenties, with neat brown hair, a smart shirt but no jacket, and a badge which offered the name Adrian.

Soren swiped his slate to confirm his identity, and Adrian checked his name against college records. Magdalen College. One of the biggest, richest colleges in the university. Magdalen, so said the legend, owned pretty much all the land in a straight line between Oxford and Cambridge. The librarian appeared to stand a little bit more upright as he read from his own screen.

"PPE at Magdalen? How did you find reading there?" he asked.

"Very different then, as you can imagine," said Soren. This man would have been a toddler when he was strolling across Magdalen Bridge on his way to Exam Schools for a lecture, or more likely nipping into the cheaper undergraduate bars at Queen's and St Edmund Hall. "But quite beautiful. I've not been back for nearly a decade. I hope nothing has changed."

"Nothing, and everything I suppose," said the librarian, smiling and pointing to Soren's slate. Back then it was against university rules to bring an ink pen into the Bodleian, let alone use a screen or an electronic device. Soren appreciated the man's apparent jealousy. His envy, even.

"As per our messages, I've brought up from the stacks the records you've asked for. I'm surprised about how detailed they are. I do hope they're of use to you."

Soren thanked the man, and took the folder to a private bench. The green lamp above the desk cast a dim light over the crisp papers he was about to go through.

The information was set out in black type, on neat grids on faded A4 paper. Three or four pages for each lecture day at Exam Schools during the three terms of 2003/4. Soren did the sums quickly in his head. Eight weeks of lectures per term, five days in a week. Skip a few days, and there might be four or five hundred pages to get through.

Finding his own lectures didn't offer too many problems. Familiar names popped out at him, and the faded memory of the titles of his PPE modules oozed back into his consciousness. Political analysis. Microeconomics. Comparative government. Economic transformation.

Next to each was written the time, room and lecturer

scheduled to deliver the session, and their college. He read names of his old tutors, trying to picture each one: Dr A Helmsbury; Rev. P. Falkner; R. H. Cooper. They merged into one, though Soren knew at least some of them must have been women.

But PPE lectures were not what he was looking for. First he browsed, then took a more structured approach to searching through the lecture schedules, beginning with the first lecture day of the first term, Michaelmas.

Unable to remember the exact titles of the lecture modules he would attend for personal interest, he tried to recall instead the subjects that had attracted him the most. Society. Anthropology. Heuristics. Population. All close, but not quite right.

It took him an hour to find it. In the first week of Trinity term, on a Friday morning at 11 a.m., Exam Room 12. Community History. The lecturer, an A. Harding, PhD Student, Mansfield College.

He skipped five pages at a time, and viewed the same information for each of the next four weeks, Friday at 11 a.m.

Then in week six, Trinity Term, at 11 a.m., Exam Room 12, the lecture wasn't there. In week seven, it had returned, but lectured by a Dr. R. Burnside, St John's College.

A. Harding, PhD student at Mansfield College, had disappeared from the lecture timetable.

Soren was correct in his recollection that Mansfield was no more than a ten minute stroll from the main Bodleian building, up New College Lane past the King's Arms.

Unlike many Oxford colleges, the entrance to Mansfield wasn't protected by a high wall, or huge and ancient oak gates with small doors cut into the wood to make an entrance. Instead, low metal railings jammed with bicycles and electric scooters locked to them, allowed Soren to look directly into the college and its small circle of grass in the centre.

He crossed the road, then lingered for a moment at the *No Visitors* sign. Two female undergraduates walking across the road began heading purposefully towards the college. Walking a few paces behind them, he fancied he might appear to any onlooker as their tutor, or perhaps a father being taken to see around the college by a slightly embarrassed student walking two paces in front.

The entrance to the college was so wide, it would not have really mattered. He was soon into the college grounds and he followed the students as they circled the quad - *No Walking On The Grass* - and up to the building with the tower.

Despite its ancient grandeur, the building's oak doors had a small black screen with a red light at shoulder height. One of the young women swiped her slate and the door unlocked with an audible clunk. Soren quickened his pace, and slipped through the door. He took a chance.

"Excuse me, the library is on the second floor, is that right?"

The young woman turned, took a single glance at him, no doubt taking in his well worn suit, leathery wrinkled skin and greying hair. Her smile was one of polite respect.

"Yes, it's at the end of this corridor, and up the stairs," she pointed to her left. "Do you want theology, or other subjects?"

Soren remembered Mansfield was originally a theological college. His research had shown the college still produced ordinands for the Church of England today.

"Where might history be?"

All three of them smiled, caught out for a moment by the existential question.

"That's in the main library," said the other young woman. "Follow the stairs to the right past the SCR, and it's there on your left."

The women turned right, and headed up some concrete steps towards a queue of students waiting for lunch.

He followed the corridor to the left, then swung around a grand staircase which spiralled gently to a landing. A sign pointed to the theology library, and to the senior common room. He continued up until he reached the double doors of the main library.

He pushed, but the solid wooden panels only rattled on their hinges. A pull did no good either. A red light blinked to the right.

Soren used a palm to shade his eyes, and gazed through one of the small panel windows in the door. Inside stretched meticulous oak shelves on either side of a wide alley, glossy with polish and lit in an amber haze by the high stained glass window on the facing wall. He could see dust floating in glowing rays bouncing off the shining floor.

But there were no students in sight, nor on the stairs or corridors around him. Feeding time. It had been so easy until now. He waited for five minutes, in the hope that a student would skip lunch, or be late leaving the library so he could slip into the door which, no doubt, they would so politely hold open for him.

He took to the steps again, stopping at the landing to consider whether the theology library would be any less protected. Probably not, and probably not what he was looking for anyway. He stopped instead outside the door marked Senior Common Room, and peered through a single small glass panel. From what he could see, the room was richly decorated, with books across some low shelves. To the right was a fireplace, clean and ready to be lit, with a mantle above it. And above that sat a large acrylic portrait of a woman in formal Oxford robes, trimmed across its edges in the Mansfield red and green. Presumably she was the current principal of the college.

He pushed tentatively at the door, which creaked open, and slipped inside. Two clusters of arm chairs sat at either side of the room, the larger cluster close to where the fire might be lit. This was clearly the place where senior members of the college, its lecturers, professors and clerics, took time to rest, socialise and read. With no lock on the door, no flashing LED, surrounded by portraits and canvases of the college, it felt as if this room had stood still for the last hundred years as the world whizzed by outside.

Next to the principal's portrait ran a tall flat wooden column in a frame, with the names of former principals etched into the wood. From 2026 the position had been held by Baroness Virginia Woods. The same name was written beneath the portrait, confirming his assumption. When Soren had been at Oxford, the Principal of Mansfield had been Diana Walford, a big name in tropical disease prevention.

The temptation to sit in one of the easy chairs by the unlit fire and pull out his vape was strong. Just for a moment. Tradition, memory, authority, determination. A world before the social, clinging on resolutely.

Through the window of the SCR, Soren could see the quad. Students had begun leaving the dining hall, and were making their way back around the circular lawn and onto tutorials or their digs. Some were chatting in twos and threes. Most were staring into slates, swiping across their screens.

He sighed and turned away from the plate glass window, heading towards the door. Before he reached it, he noticed another etched wooden board. At its head, chipped into wood and painted in gold effect leaf, were the words Junior Dean. Beneath ran a list, beginning in 1995 and running to the present day. He traced up from the current Junior Dean. And there it was: covering just one academic year, 2003-04, the name etched into the wood. Alice Harding.

It took Soren just eight minutes at quick pace to get back to the Bodleian, and another few minutes to track down the librarian he'd spoken to earlier. Adrian assured him the library would have what he wanted, but it might take an hour to call it up from the stacks.

Soren left the library and took an expensive but nostalgic lunch and a pint of pale ale in the King's Arms, among tourists and students being taken for a late lunch by their parents. The young woman behind the bar already knew the kind of ale Soren liked, and her slate had a short list of suggestions for his lunch today, all based on his social profile he presumed.

He returned to the Bodleian via a longer route past Jesus College to clear his head from the haze of a second, probably poorly judged pint.

Adrian handed over a single leather bound book and Soren took it to the same empty desk he'd used that morning. Beneath the hard leather outer, he found the actual cover. It was really just a thick pamphlet: the Mansfield College Year Book 2003/4. There she was, filling the whole of page 24: *Junior Dean: Alice Harding, PhD Student.*

At the top of one column was a colour head and shoulders photograph of her in college gown. He looked towards the reception desk, where Adrian was fussing over another reader. His colleague was directing a tourist, telling him it was pronounced 'maudlin' not '*mag*dalene', and no, sorry, tourists are not allowed inside Oxford colleges.

Soren quickly took out his slate and took a picture of the page. He then cropped the image. He brought up the beach picture Harrison had found, and the photo officially released by MinSoc. He lined up the three mugshots against each other. Harrison would be able to run them through some facial recognition software. But that really wasn't necessary.

Alice Harding and Amanda Ward were clearly the same person.

14

Behind the floor-to-ceiling glass wall of the SkyCloud offices, three colleagues were failing to keep their whispered argument from penetrating into the wider office.

Soren had briefed Harrison about his visit to Oxford the day before, and presented her with the three mugshots, as well as the evidence he'd copied from the Exam Schools lecture schedule. The two had rushed to Grey with the story: Amanda Ward, national director of MinSoc, had given - or had been given - a false history. They had the evidence.

Initially, Grey had listened carefully. The mysterious disappearance of a young woman, a whiff of scandal round a high ranking civil servant: a long buried journalistic instinct began to stir. But he became annoyed that Soren had gone to Oxford to dig around without agreeing it with him first. He then became angry when Soren mentioned a secret source of information that might imply the connection between Amanda Ward and Alice Harding was 'bigger than you think'.

He was furious when Soren refused to reveal the source. Harrison grumbled too, but went with her colleague's word.

"I don't see where the news is here," said Grey. "A woman has a right to change her name. Who knows what's behind that? Domestic violence, witness protection. If you're right about it being the same woman anyway."

"Look again at the pictures," Soren said. "Tell me it's not the same woman."

"I think Curtis is right here," said Harrison. "Anyone can see it's the same person."

"But why does it matter?" asked Grey. "We've been writing about Amanda Ward and gaining loads of traction. Our readers love what she and MinSoc are doing. The features you did on Godspeed were very popular. There's no news here, so why burst the bubble?"

"What you mean is there's no advertising keywords. That doesn't stop it being newsworthy and readable. Something is going on, and if we publish what we know, perhaps Ward will come out of hiding and talk to us, exclusively."

"Or go directly to InfoCom," said Harrison. Soren shot her a glance. Thanks a bunch.

"I still think this is a distraction," said Grey. "YoYo love us. You've not written up your visit to the Village yet. That's a cracking story. Haven't you got enough to do? No, instead you go off to Oxford chasing an ancient memory."

"So, you're saying no? You won't publish?"

"That's about the size of it."

"We don't have to work here you know, Will," said Soren, a few decibels too loud.

"Curtis?" Harrison said, grabbing his arm.

"No, in fact, we both have plenty of other options."

Soren hadn't intended this. Not at all.

"Yeah, where are you two going to go to earn a decent living? Have you seen my inbox? It's full to the brim with CVs."

Harrison said, "Speak for yourself, Curtis. I don't think we're quite at resigning stage yet."

"You think people don't know my name, Will?" said Soren, angry now. "Well fuck you. Lucas Simmons offered me a job when I visited the Village. Me and Harrison. You wouldn't believe the benefits."

"Lucas Simmons? *The* Lucas Simmons. That's unreal. You, Soren, working for YoYo." He laughed out loud.

"Hold on," Harrison said, turning to her colleague. "You never told me that. What are you playing at?" Soren gave her a look she knew well. It said, just go with this. I owe you a mountain of cinnamon loops and a bucket of Carlos' best coffee if you just *go with this.*

"I think I'll leave you boys to it," she spat. "Let me know when you've decided what my future is going to look like." The hinges on the door rattled as she left, sending shivers of vibration across the glass wall, almost fierce enough to crack it.

Grey sat at his desk and looked up at Soren.

"So, easy as that is it? I've supported you, given you pretty much a free rein since *The Herald* closed. And when you came back, crawling out of the woodwork. And now you're selling *me* down the river. And for what, a job at the heart of everything you hate? Fuck off Curtis."

Soren sat, and placed his flat palms in the air.

"I'm sorry. You're right. I didn't mean to...," he hesitated. "No dirty tricks here."

"It certainly feels that way."

The two took a moment.

"I turned Simmons down. Of course I did. I haven't even told Harrison, that wasn't fair on her. But I turned him down because I want to write the truth. Look at the photos, Will, please."

"I should sack you anyway," the editor snarled and shook his head. He took Soren's slate and his eyes flicked between the pictures. "So, Amanda Ward is Alice Harding. So what? Convince me that's important."

"Look at the way the social is going. There's a movement towards criticism and questioning being removed. In fact, Simmons said as much to me. We're self censoring. We're not talking about things that matter, not challenging those in power. With a muted voice, we won't know that our fundamental freedoms have disappeared until it's too late."

"'First they came for the communists,'" said Grey.

"Exactly. I can't even get my questions about MinSoc policy through their PR. They invite me to a press launch, co-ordinate puff piece interviews with Godspeed instead of his boss, but every time it gets challenging, they clam up. Simmons was on and off the record like a, well, a yoyo, with regard to his relationship to the Ministry. And Amanda Ward is at the heart of this. But if her background is a lie, if the story they're telling is a fiction, and if we keep retelling it without question, we're nothing but part of the problem."

Grey opened his bottom draw, and pulled out a bottle of Scotch. It was before midday, but he didn't need to ask.

"I feel like this goes deeper for you, Soren," he said, pouring a double which he pushed across his desk. He splashed a finger width for himself.

Silence held between the two as they both took deep sips from their glasses. Soren enjoyed the burn. "You know what the social did to me, what it has done to me." He paused for a moment.

"The social is not your enemy, Curtis. It was different then. You can't punish it."

"Don't say it: don't you dare say it. I've heard it all. Don't say it was bad luck. Don't say...." His eyes began to well. But he felt relieved. The two friends had shared many moments like these. He was just about due one.

Grey's own eyes softened. "You can't punish Amanda Ward. If anything, she's bringing things towards the way you might like them to be." He took a very deep breath. Tentative: "With the dark web, I mean."

Soren sat silent, far away.

"It's not Ward, of course," he said finally. "But she's part of the system. She's helping to pull up the blinds that she's hiding behind herself."

Grey sipped from his glass.

"Okay, old man. Here's the deal. Go and write your story. Work with Harrison to make it the best damn feature you've ever dared to type. I want everything. Every connection. Every implication. Oxford, Cambridge, MinSoc, Godspeed, bits of Simmons where he went on the record. The whole story of Harding and Ward and why it matters. We'll add the pictures, question the hypocrisy, the stonewalling from MinSoc."

"And you'll publish?"

"We're journalists, right?"

"We are," said Soren.

"So we do this properly," said Grey. "Before we go live, I want to put each and every allegation directly to MinSoc. If possible to Amanda Ward herself. We won't send your article, but we'll send her a tight list of questions. Plus your evidence. We'll give them 24 hours to respond."

"Won't they race to cut off our story, put out some puff to InfoCom, if they know what we're going to say?" said Soren.

"You want journalism, well that's journalism," said Grey. "Like the old days. A right to reply directly, or to get something out before we can. If they come back with a good explanation, one that checks out and might make SkyCloud look like fools, we spike the lot. If they come back with an admission or an official statement, we incorporate that."

"And if they don't reply?"

Grey downed the dregs in his glass, leaned back in his chair and smiled.

"We publish, Soren. We publish and be damned."

He queued for a black coffee at Carlos', intending to clear the fug from the whisky. The fug was quickly replaced by nerves when he saw Harrison sitting at their table waiting for him.

"What the actual fuck?"

"I'm sorry, Mia. I never had time to talk to you about what happened at the Village, and then Grey had us up against the wall."

He'd never seen her cross before. She usually responded to any challenge with sarcasm, or wit.

"You had no right. Putting my job on the line? Using me to blackmail Will to agree to your selfish aims. I ought to slap you right here and now. Or shove that pastry right in your face."

Soren opened his arms: take your best shot. I deserve it.

She took a sip of latte instead.

"Sorry Mia," he said again. "You're just about the only friend I have around here. You deserve far better from me."

"Too right mister. You are officially a shithead and a bad friend. This shall not be forgotten."

"Agreed," he replied.

Now she smiled. "So, how many gazillions were we going to be paid at YoYo?"

"Many, many gazillions," he replied. "And all we have to give up is our souls."

She smiled again. The tension washed away as they sat in silence. Soren tentatively began nibbling at his cinnamon loop.

"Actually," said Soren, "Simmons is genuinely charismatic. Do you have any idea where he's from? His heritage? He speaks with an accent and used to smoke Russian cigarettes."

Harrison shook her head. "I'll try to find out."

"Well, his heart is in the right place. At least, that's the impression I got. I haven't pinned down his change of heart about the social, suddenly allowing the haters to be banned when Portico has been so against it. But he seems to have realised the social is taking us to hell, and he's afraid of what he's created, I think."

"He said that to you?"

"As good as. So I'm not so sure who's pulling the strings right now. Portico? Simmons? Government? Or just MinSoc? Nobody is talking."

"And our story will smoke them out?"

"If you'll still work with me on it," said Soren.

"I've already started. While you boys were playing kiss-and-make-up," she said. She stood abruptly and headed for the door.

Soren asked Carlos for a bamboo bag to take his cinnamon loop back to the office.

"It's a good piece of work, guys. Very good."

It ought to be, thought Soren. It had taken him and Harrison nearly two days between them to put the full series of features together, and back it up with quotes taken from various press releases and freedom of speech charities.

Grey read through the main feature article a second

time. Four pages of closely printed text on his slate. With a quick pen he scribbled here and there, threw a few question marks into the margins. The slate converted his handwriting into small boxes filled with his comments, alongside the onscreen type.

"Do you think we've gone in too hard on the headline?" asked Soren.

Questions emerge about MinSoc head's real identity

"Not hard enough," Grey replied, scratching out the title with his quick pen.

Lies surround MinSoc head Amanda Ward, he wrote into the screen. It converted into a headline in solid type.

"We're doing this properly, or not at all."

Harrison and Soren glanced at each other with a barely visible smile. They thought it might go this way. Once Grey was convinced, he'd be full steam ahead.

"Okay," the editor said. "A few changes, questions and typos, and we're good to go. Do you have the questions to put to Amanda Ward?"

"I do," said Soren, swiping them across.

He took a moment to look over the allegations. Soren had taken care to ensure every controversial part of their feature had been covered: that Amanda Ward and Alice Harding were the same person; that the CV distributed by MinSoc for Amanda Ward had contained false information; that Amanda Ward did not attend Cambridge University; and finally that Amanda Ward had avoided contact with Curtis Soren from SkyCloud on two occasions, first at the press release for the new social platform when he started to ask difficult questions, and second for a pre-arranged face-to-face interview.

The page of questions invited Amanda Ward to give a

full and honest interview to SkyCloud about the implications this presented for her work and policy.

"I think we should send the three photographs too," said Grey. "Show them we mean business. And say something about Soren having his own private source of information."

"Great," said Harrison, and Soren nodded.

"Big question for you," said Grey. "If MinSoc only allows us to use chatbots to communicate with them, how are we going to get these questions to Amanda Ward and get her to read them?"

"Aha," said Soren. "MinSoc have already opened that door, especially for us."

He swiped up the private contact details of Harry Godspeed: *Contact me any time.*

15

Soren entered Ned's alone. He'd tried to persuade Harrison to go for a drink somewhere else, perhaps something to eat, but it was already late by the time the pair had left SkyCloud.

Grey had sent the questions to Godspeed, and they'd spent the rest of the day tightening up their copy and - though they wouldn't admit it - expecting something, anything, from MinSoc that would prove their story right.

Anyway, they'd probably spent too much time together and though Soren was a loner, Harrison had a wife to go home to. Jessica had already put up with Harrison working late two nights in a row.

He walked toward the bar, surveying the near empty pub. How did the landlord keep it open? No devices. No music. No kids. No kind welcome when you walked through the door.

It was exactly why Ned was able to keep his place open, he thought. Suits a certain type of temperament. Soren sank onto a bar stool and felt entirely comfortable as he leaned against the bar.

Ned took his time to come over, finishing his conversation with the bottled beer guy, a permanent fixture at the other end of the bar. He took a cut glass on his way to Soren, and drained a double from the McCrackens optic, no ice, before placing it before him.

There was always this moment. Were the two to strike up conversation, or would Ned go back to his chatter with the other drinker. It was always the customer's decision, one of the reasons Soren came here. Drink quietly alone, if you like. Grumble with others if you don't.

"Thanks," Soren said, and turned away. The landlord returned to the other end of the bar.

It had been a strange few days. The first time Soren had actually felt the bite of a story for a long time. He realised he hadn't had time to take his usual opportunities to stare at his feet in misery. Or at the wall, mesmerised by the traffic, or the mothers and their children walking down pavements hand in hand. He'd not given the ever present gnawing feeling in his stomach the chance to take hold and paralyse him.

That gnawing in his guts returned now, and he tried to fight it off with a slug of whisky. Only his stomach wrenched even more with the drink, polished off with the feeling of guilt. Had he - what was it? - *enjoyed* the last few days? Had he forgotten, just for a few moments?

Never. Just distracted. The last two days had not been happy; they'd just been busy. He squeezed both fists tightly, his nails digging into his palms until they began to bite skin and his knuckles ached.

Better. The physical pain takes the guilt away. So does the drink. Now he felt free to think of the past. He knocked his glass gently on the bar, and Ned came with a refill.

Soren was deep in thought when the woman opened the

door and entered the bar. A tall, stout man in a suit followed her but stood where they'd entered. The atmosphere in the bar changed. Soren looked over at the tall man, who continued to tower over the only entrance and exit to the place. He looked into the mirror behind the bar, and saw the woman reflected in it taking a bar stool next to him.

Soren shook his head, and took a slug of whisky.

"I wondered when you would turn up," he said. "Should I call you Amanda, or Alice?"

Ned approached them, and Amanda Ward ordered a whisky and water.

"And for the suit?"

"Oh, nothing," Ward said. "We're not staying long."

Soren interrupted: "He'll have a tonic water, no ice."

He turned to include Ward in the conversation. "And he'll be pleased to sit there by the door with civility, I'm sure."

Ned nodded and Ward waved at her colleague, indicating he should take a seat.

"First time in this pub, Amanda?"

She looked around. The dim lights, the old style bar, the gruff barman pouring their drinks.

"You could say that," though it didn't look like the place phased her one bit.

"Yeah, it's more Turf Tavern than King's Arms," said Soren. "And nothing like some of those newer bars down George Street."

The Turf had been an Oxford pub hidden out of the way, down back alleyways, unreachable except on foot. A traditional place, almost secret, where the fire was always burning, the real ale was on a pull tap, and the chatter of students and tutors drinking side by side meant no music was ever needed to create an atmosphere. Soren hoped it was still the same today.

"Have you been back to Oxford lately?" he asked.

"What's this about, Mr Soren? I don't have much time," Amanda repeated.

"I presume you got our questions? Have you come to give me an interview? If so, this is hardly the place. Or are we off the record?"

"Mr Soren, my even being here is off the record, if you don't mind. Can I ask, what is your interest in me?" Ward's clipped tone indicated she wasn't used to repeating herself.

"I used to attend lectures by you at Exam Schools. Your PhD was really interesting: extremist groups, if I remember. I used to drop by to hear you speak. Then one day, you just disappeared."

"I don't remember tutoring you," she said.

"No, I wasn't one of your students. It was just, your lectures were more interesting than those I usually attended. You had good ideas. I was even considering swapping courses. But then, Alice Harding just disappeared… *poof!* And then… *ping!* … you reappeared as Amanda Ward, national director of MinSoc."

"You haven't answered my question, Mr Soren. Why are you interested?" The third time of asking.

To the newsgatherer Ward came across as impatient, like a school teacher who has heard it all before. He felt like she regarded him as a bit of business. He just had to be dealt with, so she could get on with more important things. She had walked in here like she owned the place.

"I'm not sure. I guess the changing of names, changing of histories, is interesting. But it's more what you have to do with the social. I have my reasons."

"Okay, Mr Soren."

"Please, call me Curtis, since we're getting to know each other properly. Finally, since you keep running away," he added.

He felt he'd taken her down a single peg, no more.

"Curtis, completely off the record, you are correct," she said finally. "I was Alice Harding, I did lecture at Oxford, and now I am Amanda Ward. And Amanda Ward is doing great things for the UK for the social. Tempering the hate speech, increasing opportunities, reducing crime. You've written it yourself, and added the halos. Isn't that enough?"

"And Clarice King?" he took a deep drag from his glass, and stared at her reflection in the mirror behind the bar, making eye contact.

She gave him a puzzled look. "I've never heard that name," she said.

It annoyed him.

"I'm not interested in scandal, Amanda. I'm just interested in how in this age of data, you were able to disappear and change your identity. How could you manipulate the social that way? I thought it was set in stone. Once online, always online. Yet you seem to have deleted yourself. How can that happen?"

"I didn't delete myself. It was done for me. For the best of reasons."

"Always the best of reasons, I've heard that before. And it makes me sick." Soren's heart began to cave in. He took some deep breaths, then tempered his mood with the smoky burn of whisky. He waved the glass at Ned, ordering another.

"What do you mean, makes you sick?" The question felt patronising. Poor little boy, doesn't understand.

"Those in power, those connected to power, they can just *disappear*. The rest of us, we just get tracked, and pigeonholed, and gathered up, and spat out with advertising tailored to our needs. The bog roll we use, the brand of vape I smoke. It's all there in some dataset and I can't just - *disappear*."

Amanda Ward's voice wavered. She glanced towards the man by the door. She apparently chose her next words carefully.

"You're very angry with the social, I can tell that. But this whole thing is bigger than you think."

Soren slammed his glass down on the bar, hard enough for Ned to look over, and for the suited man at the door to slightly rise from his seat.

"Where have I heard that before?" he snarled. "Why are you even here tonight?"

"To exchange."

Soren turned from the mirror and looked at Amanda Ward directly. His voice softened. "So, what do you have to offer and what do you want from me?"

"I have the truth about Alice Harding to offer, but it's bigger... it's complicated. And from you..." She paused a long time, before draining the remainder of her whisky. "I want to ask you to temper the story about me."

"Ahaha," the journalist shook his head. "Of course you do."

"Listen, I'm not asking you to stop the story completely. Just, I don't know, hold off. Until everything is clearer. The bigger picture. If you can hold off, I think we can give you an exclusive."

"Exclusive access to the big picture you and MinSoc will feed to us, like we're dolphins nodding our heads for sardines?"

"It's not like that," said Ward. "There's more to say. Surely that's good for you."

"My editor is crawling all over me to get this story out. Do you know how hard I had to push to get him to run it at all? Are you going to respond to our questions?"

"Officially, that's not our plan. You agreed this little chat would be off the record, too."

"Then we'll run the story. I don't know if I could get SkyCloud to pull it even if I wanted to. Which I don't."

Ward looked around the pub. Her tone had changed. Was it real, or just part of her act?

"Please, Curtis, you must try. It'll set everything off kilter if you publish."

"Set what off kilter?"

"That's what I have to share with you. But I need trust, and I sure as hell don't want to talk about it here."

"So, I'm supposed to go back to my editor and say what? I've changed my mind? Let's spike the last three days of work and publish a special about Celebrity Dance Off instead?"

Through the mirror, Soren could see Ward's face blush red, not with embarrassment, but with fear. She stared into her glass, now empty.

"Another drink?"

"No, I have to go. Thank you anyway, Mr Soren."

"I got into journalism for the greater good, Amanda," he said. "Am I to believe what you're asking for is to further that cause? Or is it smoke and mirrors, buying time so you can get another fake story out before we tell the truth?"

"Nobody knows I'm here Curtis. If they did, I would be in very deep trouble. With MinSoc, with Portico, with everyone. My family might not be safe."

The fear rose in her face again.

"Then I'll try to hold the story," he said finally. He waited for a moment and called Ned over with a request for a pen. Something that would be strange in most other pubs in London, where a swipe would do the same job. Ned complied without question.

"When can you meet me?"

They agreed a time after the weekend, and Soren wrote down an address. She looked at it, gave Soren a quizzical look as if questioning the location, but he had turned back to the mirror.

"Thank you," she said. "For the drink. And..."

"I'll try," he said. He shook his head, ashamed at the concession he'd made. Amanda Ward stood and thanked Ned. Then with her assistant, she left the bar.

Soren ordered another double, promising himself it would be his last.

16

"You have to be joking, right?"

It was 10.30 a.m. and Soren was travelling in a TriCab to the SkyCloud offices. Grey was on his slate, so furious his picture rattled with every thump on his office desk. He had received no response from MinSoc, no notification of any response from Godspeed from Harrison or Soren, and was just about to begin the process of getting the stories online to catch the lunchtime news feeds. And the primary author of the biggest story they'd worked on for years was very late and obviously hungover.

Soren stifled a belch of vomit as the TriCab swung around in the traffic.

"I'm just asking for a little more time. I have reason to think we should hold on to the story for a few more days."

"Have you heard from MinSoc or Godspeed?" Grey asked, his voice gnarled with anger.

"No, not as such."

"Then why the hell shouldn't we push the button? Yesterday you two were desperate. I'm putting my reputation on the line for this."

"Sources," said Soren limply. "I can't talk about it like this. I'm on my way in now."

"We'll miss the lunchtime feeds," said Grey. "MinSoc as good as have the story, they'll close it down if we wait a moment longer."

"I don't think so. Please, trust me. I think we can wait another day."

"I can't believe this."

"Or two," Soren added.

"Two? That'll be Sunday. Jesus, Soren, this had better be good. Because if you and Mia aren't in this office by noon convincing me with cast iron evidence why we shouldn't publish, I'm pressing that button for the six o'clocks. Understand?"

"Yes, I understand. That's very fair," said Soren. Grey disappeared from his slate, and Soren knocked his head against the window of the TriCab. What was he doing? He couldn't think straight with this headache, let alone make sensible decisions. And if Grey was angry, God forbid the next call he had to make.

Soren swiped, and quickly Harrison appeared on the screen, the rest of the SkyCloud office behind her. "Oh dear, old man, what have you done?"

"Meaning?"

"Meaning, I'm looking at a very angry man in a glass box, pacing up and down, and a very crumpled and hungover, grey haired old man on my screen. And putting two and two together."

"Always so smug, Miss Perfect."

"Mrs," Harrison reminded him.

"Mia, I want us to hold back on the story. It's not ready to go yet."

"What? Grey told me MinSoc hadn't responded. We're

all ready to go here for the lunchtime feeds."

"Things have changed."

"Has Godspeed been in touch?" There was excitement in her voice.

"No. And I've received no response to our questions."

"So, what the hell? Publish and be damned. All stand together." Now it was her voice rising to a peak, bouncing around the TriCab and landing squarely at the centre of Soren's headache.

"I have a new source. We just need to hold on to see where it leads?"

"What source?"

"Now, Mia, I know how you feel about journalists protecting sources." It was a low blow, and he knew it.

"Oh, you fucker. This better be good." She disappeared from his slate. This was definitely becoming a habit.

A moment later, his slate lit up with a message.

"Carlos'. Now!"

Soren swiped for the coffees. Harrison was once again already at their usual table. He bought her a shortbread square, which she didn't even look at when he sat down. He'd picked a decidedly greasy cinnamon loop for himself.

"I'm not speaking to you, so you better just talk," she said. He hung his head and went for the pastry.

She flung out her hand and pushed the loop away. "No eating. Just talking."

He took a sip of his Americano instead. Waited a moment and began.

"I had discussions last night with a source, very high..."

"Discussions? Online or in person?"

"I thought you weren't talking?"

Harrison made a zip motion across her lips.

"Thank you. I had a conversation last night with a very senior source about Amanda Ward. I think if we publish our story as it is, somehow we're not getting to the whole truth. And my source says, it might put people in danger somehow."

He waited.

"I'm going to discuss with the source again, and we've agreed SkyCloud will get exclusive information. It'll improve our story and set out the truth."

"The truth as your source wants it to be," said Harrison.

"No. We decide where that source's information fits into our story. We need to judge its credibility against what we already know, and whether what we thought we knew matches up too. The way I see it, by holding on, we can double check our own information about Ward, and have a stronger story."

"And you're sure this source is sound?" asked Harrison.

"I'm absolutely certain. How reliable the story is, we'll have to find out."

"Secret squirrels. I love it. Is it someone from MinSoc?"

"Now, Mia. It's best we don't speculate. You know the game. I need your trust on this."

The two sat in silence for a few minutes. Harrison allowed Soren to eat his cinnamon loop, and she pecked at the shortbread he'd bought her.

"You know, I envy you Soren," she said eventually.

"Why on earth would you envy me?"

"Ah, you know. Late nights by yourself, drinking. No rules. Get in when you like, eat what you like, get an easy ride from Grey when you turn up late. Me, I'm a typical working mum. Concessions to Jessica here. Having to apologise for working late there. Kids to drop at school."

"You don't know my life, Mia," was all Soren could say.

"I'd like to. But you don't share. You seem so angry all the time. I think you need a friend."

"You are my friend, Mia. At least I hope so."

"I mean, outside of work."

"Let's get out of here. I need a vape." This time it was Soren's turn to stand abruptly and head for the door.

Harrison joined him outside, against the wall of the SkyCloud offices where Soren had stopped to vape.

"I didn't mean to pry, Curtis. I'm still new here, don't really know my way - *around* - I guess. Just know, I like you. I think we work well together."

"We'll see about that," said Soren.

"What do you mean?" Harrison sounded hurt. "I think we've got on well together so far."

He smiled, and placed his vape into an inner jacket pocket. "I mean, we now have to go together and convince Grey not to swipe our story into the world."

Soren looked at the online map on his slate, a platform called Streetwise which, thanks to Simmons, the journalist now understood was run by Gum: the search and find column of Portico.

He'd used it hundreds of times in his work, but never really thought about what, or who, made it possible to find any street or location in the world, and either create travel directions to it or to zoom down on a particular place from above. Or how you could switch to a 3D view of that place, view it from 360 degrees, and then zoom to a street level view and look at the houses, buildings and fields around.

Once you could zoom in at street level, you could visit shops virtually, follow their social pages, and even buy goods they offered you based on your interests. If there was a car, or an electric scooter or even the double glazing in a house you zoomed in on, Gum could show you the brand and options for purchasing the same, or similar. The tech wasn't real time enough to show you where your friends were right now, but Gum could show you pictures in 2D or 3D of where they *were*, according to the last signal from their slate.

Right now, the red droplet hung above his sofa in the small apartment he rented close to Islington and twenty minutes' TriCab from work. He knew the picture he was looking at of his apartment was probably not taken today or yesterday by a Streetwise bot, but it would certainly be in the last year. A function he'd once found useful he now found a little scary. He looked out of the window, and waved the bottle of whisky in his hand. Should a little Streetwise drone be taking new pictures just now, there he would be, out of focus, behind a second floor window, getting drunk for all to see.

He wasn't sure he was ready for what he was about to do, but the whisky helped.

There was a time when he'd planned to make a home in South London, right on the outskirts near Esher where the urban sprawl gave way to little patches of green space. He'd not even been around that place for five years.

Tonight, drink and slate in hand, would be the closest he'd been. He poured himself a deep measure before beginning, fingers shaking, to type the address. The red droplet quickly zoomed across London in a south westerly direction, coming to rest above a suburban street.

He rubbed his eyes, purposely hurting the sockets, preparing himself for what he was about to see. There, on his slate, was the double roof of a simple semi detached home, the last-but-one building at the end of a cul-de-sac. He checked the garden, a messy affair by the overhead photograph. There was a small shed towards the back, and what looked like a slightly raised patio leading to double doors at the rear of the building. Though the picture showed a caged trampoline, and there were kids' toys sprinkled and rotting across the garden, he was sure this was the correct one. The picture could have been taken any time in the last few weeks.

He squeezed his hands into fists, so hard that his nails dug into the skin. It hurt as much as it usually did. Not enough. He zoomed in on the property. The view flipped to the street. With some manoeuvring, Soren was able to bring the house into view.

Number 61.

The frontage was more or less the same. He was unexpectedly angry that the door colour had been changed from blue to black. A Christmas wreath hung across the door. He felt the welling of sickness in his stomach. A small family car, perhaps an electric Corsa, sat on the driveway.

Soren pushed away the slate, and rubbed his eyes again. He took a deeper than expected drag on his vape, and washed it down with a harsh slug of Scotch. He couldn't bear to type in the other address, so decided to trace it with his fingers instead. He picked up his slate and reverted to the overhead view of the cul-de-sac, and quickly traced a line with his finger from number 61 to the end of the road. He was surprised how easy it was to follow.

He turned left, up a few streets, and then joined the main road with his finger. In his mind's eye, he drove south along the A road for about a mile until his finger hit the end of the slate screen. He swiped gently down, revealing more of the map.

His breath quickened as he took a right off the main road, onto a side road heading into the country, and proceeded on it for another half mile. There he stopped. Where Florent Road and Farmer's Hill crossed. He pushed the screen, and the red droplet moved to where he had pressed.

Could he do it? After all this time?

Soren zoomed into the map, so far that it flipped to street view. He took a deep breath and scrolled around the 360 degree panorama. Fields, hedges, a farmer's gate. And country roads leading in four directions. Puddles captured and stretched into weird shapes by the Streetwise camera. Four roadways opening up like bubbles, viewed through a fisheye lens.

Nothing more. Just one of hundreds of thousands of innocent, barely memorable junctions in a nation full of country roads. Soren might have passed through that crossroads any number of times without thinking about it.

But to him, this crossroads was important. It was one he'd dared not visit for over half a decade. It was the last thing he wanted, but he'd already committed.

Tomorrow he would have to force himself. He finished the bottle of whisky.

17

The TriCab dropped him off on the main road he'd traced the night before, just before his finger had taken a right onto Florent Road. He remembered from the map it would be a ten minute walk. He'd have preferred it to have been far longer, and idled along the side of the road to take as much time as possible. A few electric cars passed almost silently. Soren sometimes missed the roar and clunk of a petrol engine, the whiff of petrol fumes on busy roads. The hedges were high and unkempt, so he took care to cross whenever there was a tight curve and the few vehicles might not see him ahead.

It had begun to drizzle almost as soon as he'd stepped out of the TriCab, and the grey clouds hanging above promised worse to come. He pulled out his vape, then pulled his jacket tight to keep out the chill. Taking deep drags, he felt a sense of dread as he trod out the half mile. These hedges. These trees. This tarmac. This gate.

They would have been... He could barely think it.

A black stretched Nissan was parked about fifty metres ahead of the crossroads, tucked into the hedgerows where a long gate opened up onto a muddy field. Next to the car stood the same man as had accompanied Amanda Ward to the bar. He stood with his hands in his pockets. He wore a grey suit, covered by a thin blue waterproof layer. He barely acknowledged Soren as he passed, and Soren kept his eyes to the ground.

Ward was standing at the near right corner of the cross-roads, alone and looking stern with her arms crossed. She stamped her flat shoes on the tarmac, trying to generate some heat from the movement.

"Should have worn some better footwear, perhaps?" said Soren, "It's chilly when you get out of the comfort of the city."

"I don't know why you have brought me out here, Mr Soren, but whatever it is you've got to say, can we do it quickly?"

"You really don't know?"

"I thought it might be because you can't get a signal out here, but mine and Tom's," she indicated her companion with emphasis, "are both fully connected."

"Boy, do *I* know you can get a signal here," said Soren. His voice was sad, not angry.

"So, let's get on with it," said Ward.

"Trade," said Soren.

"What?"

"The other night you said you would give me more information about you. Explain why I shouldn't publish the story. I've managed a temporary reprieve, though my editor is spitting like a cat. So, trade. You tell me the truth, and I'll tell you why we're here."

"This is all very childish, Soren. Can't we do this in the car, at least?"

Soren stood in silence. The rain continued.

"Okay, I'll explain," she said. "Care to talk and walk?"

They turned right at the crossroads, and continued down the slight decline of Farmer's Hill. The man followed at a distance.

"I don't know which way to go about this, so I guess I'll start from the beginning," said Ward. "There was a time when I was called Alice Harding. That's my birth name, and the name I took to Oxford with me. I was at Mansfield College as an undergraduate, and stayed on to do my PhD in social sciences.

"I lectured, in aspects of human sociology: particularly on my specific PhD interest of extremism. What leads people into extremist groups? How do they organise? How can we prevent them, or bring people out of their brainwashing? This you already know."

"Yes, because I attended your lectures." The rain had eased only slightly. They passed a farmhouse.

"In my final months at Oxford I became Junior Dean of the college. I was giving a lecture one day, when someone came to meet me. I was scared, as they looked pretty menacing. At that time, if you remember, there was a spate of attacks against students by townies. They followed me, and I ended up hiding in the Radcliff Camera. It was there they approached me. Waiting for me when I got to the seat I'd used since my first year. God knows how he got through security."

"He?"

"I thought for a moment he was from MI5 or the security services." She laughed. It was the first time he'd seen her smile. "You know all those stories of Oxford students being approached in dark corridors asked to become spies, and all that. The man who pinned me in the Rad Cam was so smartly dressed, and so posh, what else could this have been? And given my subject matter? For a moment, I thought I might be the perfect candidate."

"Special Agent Alice Harding?"

"Yeah, that lasted for about five minutes until the guy stopped with the cloak and daggers. But what he had to offer was just about as interesting. He talked about my having a chance to make a difference, to follow up my studies and knowledge on extremist groups, but in a more practical way."

She stopped. Turned around, and began to walk back to the crossroads.

"This gets complicated," she said. "Back then things were moving very fast for technology. The founders of the companies that preceded Gum and YoYo, they were becoming household names, big personalities with lots of power. Facebook. Skype. Twitter. Google. YouTube."

"Brands bigger than countries and having more impact than most," said Soren.

Ward agreed: "The world was in a state - at least this is what the man in black explained to me. Climate change, as we called it then. The twin towers and war in Afghanistan. The invasion of Iraq. Terrorist attacks across Europe. Massacres in Darfur; Iran and North Korea developing nukes. Here in the UK, anti capitalism riots in London, racist attacks, dissident IRA bombings.

"Apart from a few successful campaigns, and too many extremist groups, apathy ruled. Governments were locked in politics rather than action. Election turnout was lamentable."

"So the big tech names thought they could do better?" said Soren.

"They knew they could," corrected Ward. "And they had the money to make it happen. My understanding is that the group of new technology leaders were asked, informally, by the United Nations if they could help straighten things out. Not a penny would be spent by governments, not a single acknowledgement of any connection would be admitted. The tech giants were simply asked if they could help, and given a free rein to get it done."

"That's a huge ask," said Soren.

"All the bigger because no one quite knew what 'get it done' meant. I guess it was to take the will of the people, and to help make the world a better place. One way or another. A few years later, the social leaders started coming together more formally, in a group."

"Portico?"

"What eventually became Portico, yes. All I knew was that, if I agreed, I would be part of a group of expert minds in our particular subjects, tasked with assisting them in that work.

"They had already been monitoring me for months. They knew all my information, stats, every word I'd ever written in essays, and my posts on chat boards - even private ones. For God's sake, they knew exactly where I sat in my favourite library. But because the project was so secret, I would need a new back history."

"So they erased Alice Harding, created Amanda Ward, and placed you at the heart of government."

"No, it happened far more subtly than that, and over years. I grew into the position I'm now at. I earned it, I'd like to say. Changemakers were recruited from all over the world, in lots of different disciplines, and placed in sandboxes, to see whether we could make change happen."

"Changemakers and sandboxes? You've lost me," said

Soren. They'd reached the crossroads again and despite the rain, the pair were so engaged they had crossed and began tramping up the incline of Farmer's Hill.

"Changemakers. I can't remember if that was an official name of the programme, or whether it was something we invented for ourselves. But stick a bunch of experts and charismatic personalities into a single location, give them the very best training and resources, and we would have to have begun calling ourselves something. We spent five years honing our skills, discussing strategies for tackling some of the most challenging scenarios, then were sent out to a test site to see if the project would work. Our sandbox.

"Some left, didn't want what had been offered them or didn't make the grade. They got good payoffs from Portico and a gagging clause in exchange. Others were distributed around the world to test out the Changemakers programme.

"A dozen of us were sent to a small African country, where the government was totally corrupt, democracy had collapsed, and the result was poverty on the one hand, and extreme exploitation of natural resources on the other. A perfect small scale test bed.

"My responsibility was to concentrate on extremist groups, guerrilla fighters, rebel groups, that kind of thing. Not fighting them, but how to create the conditions that would remove the fuel that fired them. Social change. Equality. Dealing with deep seated anger."

The pair had crested the hill, and turned to go back down. Soren spoke: "You're talking about East Burundi. Where that photo was taken of you. The charity was just a cover story."

Amanda was silent for a moment.

"We had the very best minds in the world, and all the data we could gulp. This was five years after I'd first been recruited, and the tech had improved year on year. The social platforms had started emerging, opening up masses of data. It gave us the computer modelling we needed to test different outcomes.

"Our modelling showed that if we used a series of covers, such as charities carrying out social interventions, we had best chance of transforming attitudes on the ground. Meantime, other Changemakers were influencing the East Burundi government, the economy and of course the media. It was all modelled, but it had to be tested out."

"On real people," Soren interjected sharply.

"On a nation of people who were desperate for change. Their lives depended on it. And our five years in East Burundi made a difference. It became one of the most peaceful and economically stable countries on the continent."

"White man saves the day, it sounds like," said Soren.

"Far from it. East Burundi was in that state specifically because of the West's intervention over years, going right back to slavery and pilfering the land for oil and diamonds. That was the point of Changemakers. We worked out very early on that there was no trust for the West. So Portico recruited the best of the best across Africa, and specifically in East Burundi too. The results speak for themselves."

The pair had reached the crossroads again. Tom went to stand by his car.

"So, Portico is still running this Changemakers programme, and you're still part of it?"

"Yes, and no. Once we had achieved a relatively positive outcome in East Burundi, we had lots of lessons to learn. We took that knowledge, and were asked to go back to our home countries, to find ways to put into practice some of the techniques and strategies we'd learned. Each country had different needs. In the UK, it was fossil fuels, extremism, the growing potential dangers of social media, and ineffectual combative governments. There are about a dozen Changemakers working across the UK, in government like me, or in academic or media positions. Trying to change the system from within, if you like."

"But Portico still supports your work?"

"Yes. Financially, there is money available to support initiatives. I don't get paid by Portico, I'm paid to do my job which I rightfully earned as national director of MinSoc. But I won't say my work in Changemakers didn't help me to get where I am. In my work, as you've seen recently, the best resource I've been able to draw on is data - Portico's access to data and the influence that the social is able to have on its users."

"So, just as I suspected. We're being fed what you and those at Portico or Changemakers want us to think, and those who dissent get their comments deleted, or downgraded or whatever. It's what I've heard from my... sources inside Portico itself."

Ward stoped, surprised for a moment. She shook her head, and continued.

"It's not supposed to work that way. It's my job to influence the social, and of course to use the social to the best of my abilities to achieve the Changemaker outcomes," said Ward.

"No, but you're able to create rules on which groups can be banned, and what messages are classed as hate speech, and you're trying to delete the dark web altogether. Portico has given you that power, and it's not earned power. It's not elected power. Just as those East Burundi villagers never gave you power over their lives."

"For the better outcome in the end," Ward snapped back.

"That's not democracy, though. We have a right."

"Look around you, Soren. You can't argue the social hasn't made the world a better place. A little restriction here, some extra influence there, that's all the interventions we've made. And look where it's getting us. People love the anti extremist messaging coming out of MinSoc; people need and want the social in their lives."

"Not all of us."

"No, not everyone. But most."

"I never gave my consent." Soren's voice was raised, and Ward's bodyguard stood just a little bit taller, taking his hands out of his pockets.

"We all did, by shopping, and searching, and using Portico's functions," said Ward.

"No," Soren shouted. "We were sucked in, blinded. You say you're making the world a better place, but no one asked you to."

"Theoretically, our leaders asked us to, at the UN."

"That's semantics, Amanda, and you know it." Soren began pacing around the square of the crossroads.

"Why do you hate me so much? I've told you the truth here. Why do you hate the social? Surely it's great for a newsgatherer like you?"

"It's *not* great for me, don't you see?"

"No, I don't. Please, Curtis, explain it to me. Trade? I think I've kept my side of the bargain."

Soren stood for a very long time. The rain was becoming heavier, but the pair ignored it. The tension was keeping their bodies warm.

"Okay, trade," said Soren, still angry. He walked towards the bodyguard, who stood upright expecting the older man to challenge him. Soren turned quickly, and called out to Amanda who stood near the middle of the crossroads.

"My wife Lucy," he said. "She was coming this way. Well below the speed limit. Ping. Ping. Ping." He was furious all of a sudden. "Ping. Ping. A shared messageboard of secondary school mums, their worthless messages pinging. Again and again up on her mobile phone. *Mum's coffee on Thursday after drop off? How's Rafe getting on with the flute? Does anyone have yesterday's Spanish homework?* Ping. Ping. It was distracting her. Ping. Ping. Fucking ping. She was trying to turn down the volume on her phone."

"Oh, God," said Amanda as he reached her. He swerved directly to her left.

"And down here, down this fucking hill, comes this woman, riding her Chelsea tractor. A big fucking Subaru, four foot something off the ground, speeding. The woman behind the wheel was on some fucking social media site, messaging her friends as she drove, giving thumbs up and likes. She drove fifty miles an hour down this hill, looking at her phone, not at the road beneath her enormous truck. Fifty miles an hour down a fucking hill on a country road, Amanda. With her face stuck into a social app."

Soren approached Amanda, his face now very red, and very close to hers. The bodyguard had begun to approach.

"Ping. Ping. Ping. It was the last thing my wife ever heard."

"Oh, gosh, I'm so sorry, Curtis. I don't know what to say." She waved the tall man away. She put her hand on his shoulder, but he brushed it off.

"That's not all though. That's not nearly all. That woman, driving the Chelsea tractor. She walked away. Not a scratch. She killed my wife with her big truck, and just walked away. "

"But if she was on her phone, she should have been prosecuted."

"And that's the thing, isn't it Amanda? She *was* prosecuted. The police had her pinned to the wall. Her phone showed her speeding, and that she was browsing her feeds at the exact moment of impact.

"But that woman was a social media star. She had hundreds of followers because of her fashion brand or something. The centre of her circle. All her social friends were very vocal on her behalf during the trial. She didn't send loads of messages afterwards, but *they* did. There was this whole disgusting online battle.

"There was so much chat on the social about the incident. So many accusations, speculations, excuses, her supporters threatening boycotts and protests. Saying they were both on their phones. There was a public free for all over the feeds. The judge decided the woman couldn't get a fair trial because so much had been said. They wouldn't be able to find an unbiased jury. She dismissed the case.

"That woman walked away from that Subaru and she walked away from prison."

"I'm so, so sorry," said Ward. "This is truly horrible. I understand, I really do."

"You do not understand," Soren snapped. "Do you know what happened when the social enabled her to simply walk away from killing my wife? She was able to relocate. She disappeared, just like *you* did. Her profile, her chat feeds. Her whole identity was changed to God knows what. All to protect *her* safety. And the details of my wife's death? That disappeared too, all to protect this woman."

"The social. *Your* social, Amanda. *Your* social stopped that woman from going to jail. Then it allowed her to disappear. To continue with her life. While my wife lay right here, under our feet. Dying. Ping, ping, ping as she bled out onto the tarmac."

There was more to say, but Soren felt he might be sick on the road if he tried. He turned to Ward, and looked her dead in the eyes through tears.

"How do you feel about that, Amanda? *As a mother?*"

18

The two had stood in silence in the rain for five minutes. Maybe more. Soren's face had flushed red and was now calming, and Ward's own tears had begun to well up. Though she tried not to show it. There was a choke in her voice when she finally spoke. It was with a tender tone.

"I'm genuinely sorry about what happened to Lucy. It explains a lot, and I'm sorry it had to come to this for me to understand. I don't know what to say. I'm supposed to be a Changemaker, but this I cannot change. I can only hope time will heal."

Soren pulled up his jacket lapels. He sniffed loudly, clearing his head and indicating that his dramatics were over. He'd made his point and now he saw it was wrong to have brought her here, as if she had to pay dues for the pain he'd suffered.

"I'm sorry," he said. "I think we're done."

"I think so too. For God's sake, please let Tom drive us both back into the city."

"Of course, thank you."

In the car, the two sat in the rear while Tom, her body-guard and driver, drove silently. For most of the journey, no one spoke. Soren and Ward looked out of their windows, as the rain drizzled on the increasingly squashed buildings, packed pavements and squeezed in shop fronts. Soren noted how few private cars were driven in the centre of London these days. Instead there were double decker electric buses, with concertina middles, hundreds of TriCabs and other taxis. People passed at crossings unhurriedly on foot or by electric scooter and bike, taking priority over the electric vehicles.

He knew the social had helped to create this smooth hum of transport along London's once most congested and polluted roads. The move to electric, self driven cars had hugely reduced the number of accidents. The number of fatalities in road traffic incidences had dropped year on year for the last five years. Still, too late for Lucy.

What was once called new tech really had made London, and elsewhere in the world, safer places to be. Where once it felt like the world was going backwards - the era of President Trump threatening nuclear war with Iran; the UK isolating itself from its partners in Europe; crippling inaction in the face of the climate crisis - it was clear that things had improved dramatically.

How far had Changemakers been part of this move-ment? Soren thought of Simmons, YoYo and Portico. Simmons had said he and his colleagues had been working on things for a long time, and that he knew Amanda Ward. It began to add up. The predecessors of Simmons and his social media start ups had set up Changemakers before Portico even existed. And even now, Changemakers were placing their agents into the heart of Governments to budge things along faster than perhaps even country leaders wanted.

He was about to ask Ward how well she knew Simmons when the slate in his bag pinged for a swipe call. He turned to her with an apologetic look.

"Go ahead, I have a mountain of messages to deal with." She reached into a pocket in the rear of the driver's seat and pulled out some wireless ear plugs. She slotted her slate into a mount which she released from the door.

Will Grey, SkyCloud flashed on and off on Soren's far older slate, which he held up at a difficult angle to get the best picture in the dark recesses of the saloon car. He swiped open the call.

"Curtis, I've been trying to get hold of you." His voice was not cross, but a little panicked. Soren noted two missed calls, obviously overlooked during his rant at Ward.

"I was busy. Sorry."

Grey peered closer to his screen. "Where are you? You're not in a TriCab. Doesn't matter. Listen, it's Harrison."

"Mia? Where is she."

"She's been mugged, Curtis. Last night, outside of her flat. Jessica called a couple of hours ago. She's in St George's. Was in an induced coma and pretty beat up by the sounds of it."

"Oh, Jesus," Soren almost shouted at the screen. Ward looked up and took out her ear plugs. "What happened?" he said.

"I don't know, she'd only just come round when Jessica called. The doctors had sedated her so they could do some surgery. Jessica has been at her bedside the whole night."

"Okay. Thanks for letting me know, Will. Listen…"

"You should go there, Curtis," he said. "Of course you should."

"Thanks. I'll swipe you when I know more."

Soren turned to Ward, but she was already leaning forward to speak to her driver.

"St George's, did he say?" she asked.

"Yes. Thank you."

"I know she's a good friend of yours." She paused. "Would you like to see something neat?"

"Okay?" said Soren.

"Tom," she said. It was an instruction.

He swiped his screen, and a siren began to sound. From the reflection in shop windows and other cars, Soren could see blue flashing lights blinking back at them from the front and rear of the Nissan. The cars in front gently parted in an exact, gentle, smooth and automatic movement, giving their own vehicle just enough room to move between them.

The path continued to automatically open up, like a widening tunnel. Soren took a glance through the rear window. The electric cars and buses pulled back together into neat little rows. The Nissan was moving quickly through the traffic like a bubble through a straw.

"I'm impressed," said Soren, barely hearing the siren through sound proofed windows.

"It's all automatic, guided by GPS. Is your friend alright? I didn't catch the conversation."

The question brought Soren immediately back to earth. He'd lost so much already. Now his only real friend might be in danger.

"I don't know. She's had emergency surgery. My boss said she's just come round from an induced coma."

Ward put her hand on Soren's shoulder and he felt a gentle squeeze.

"I *need* her to be okay," he said. He fought back tears for a second time that morning.

A nurse showed Soren to the private room in intensive care, where Harrison was being kept under close watch. He knocked and pushed open the door. Jessica was sitting by the bedside, with Harrison's hand in hers. His friend was lying in the bed, her right eye purple with bruising. A drip fed into her arm at the wrist, and her left side was propped up by a stiff pillow.

"Jessica, I'm Curtis. I work with Mia." She stood, and the two instinctively hugged. "I'm so sorry this has happened. How is she?"

"She's taken a huge hit," Jessica began to say.

"Hey, I can speak for myself, thank you." The voice was muffled, led astray by a thick lip and the grog of anaesthetic. Jessica and Soren turned to Harrison and they all smiled.

"Getting back to her old self," said Jessica, with mock crossness. "A nurse has just been in with a horse tranquilliser, so she'll not stay awake for long I suspect. I'll go for now, find myself a better coffee than this piss. Want anything?"

"Latte, extra shot," mumbled Harrison.

"Not you, sweetheart. You're still nil by mouth." The three laughed again until Harrison groaned with pain.

"My sides are literally split open, you bastards," she said.

"No, thank you Jessica," said Soren. "You've put in an amazing shift. Go take your time."

Soren took the seat Harrison's wife had just vacated. For a moment he considered taking Harrison's hand. Instead he patted her gently on the wrist and sat back in the chair.

"Where does it hurt?"

"Ah, pretty much everywhere. I must look like shit. I'm sorry, Curtis." She tried to shift her body towards him, but it was going nowhere.

"You don't look so bad. You've seen me with worse hangovers. What the hell happened?"

"I got mugged, kind of. I never saw who did it, but I heard them pretty well as they kicked my face in. And my ribs."

"They?"

"At least one woman and one man, I think two men. I was on my way back from working late, just coming up to my apartment. It came out of nowhere. They whacked me on the back of the head and I went flying."

"Christ."

"Then they came at me screaming. Lezzo bitch. Freak. Dyke. Queer. That kind of thing. Punching and kicking."

"Wow, that doesn't sound like a mugging. Besides, what did you have to steal?"

"I don't know. There's plenty of very out gays in that area, and I suspect none of them got the beating I got last night."

"You mean you were targeted?"

"They seemed to know me. Where Jess and I, and the girls, live. Soren, you've got to get them protected."

"Have you talked to the police?"

"Not yet. They've been waiting for me to wake up. The staff have been great. Apart from Jess, you're the only one I've seen not dressed in scrubs."

"Well, I'll give the police a call and fill them in, tell them you'll be ready to speak soon. In a way, I hope it was a random attack. Because the alternative could be pretty scary. I'd better tell the police that too."

Harrison groaned a little with tiredness. Soren said he ought to leave.

"No, it's nice to have you here."

"I didn't bring any grapes."

She smiled.

"Talk to me, Curtis," she said. It was the tenderest request. He'd never seen Harrison so vulnerable. For once, she just wanted to listen and be comforted. He was surprised how close the two of them had become.

"Well, nothing much is going on. Spent the morning with Amanda Ward, that kind of thing."

"What?" Harrison coughed, then breathed heavily with the pain the surprise had brought.

"Oh, didn't I mention that? I met her this morning and she gave me some deep info on her background. It all got a bit tense, but I think her heart is in the right place. She dropped me off."

"So she knows I'm in hospital."

"Yeah, she sends her regards. She knows my take on the social. Or at least, what I thought my take was. She's very convincing."

"Gosh, was there any more for our story? Does Will know?"

"His only concern, right now, is you. He sent me over here, though I would have come anyway. But I guess I'll need to outline with Ward what we can say about what she told me this morning. I'm starting to understand where she's coming from."

"Sounds complicated." Harrison was beginning to sound tired. "Tell me about you, Curtis. You're so closed off. You've got me off guard here, time for you to 'fess up."

"Have you not looked me up on Gum?"

"I'm a journalist, not a stalker," she said. "I take friends as I find them, not what their feed says. Tell me your story."

"More like a nightmare," he said, but he smiled at his friend.

"I'll settle for anything, if it takes away the pain in my bloody ribs."

"About time you knew, I suppose," he said. This time he did take her hand, and she closed her eyes and let out a comfortable sigh.

"I was married, before. Believe it or not. Will came to our wedding. Lucy, she was a journalist too."

Harrison smiled.

"We met at UCL, on the journalism course. She went to a rival paper, back when we both worked in the real press. Then she left work, when our daughter was born. Grace."

Harrison opened her eyes gently. She seemed delighted. "You have a daughter?"

Soren hesitated. "Listen, you don't need to hear this now. You need some rest." He wasn't sure he was ready for this either.

"I just want to listen," she said.

Soren waited until he felt he could speak. With his friend lying there exposed, he could do nothing but share. He needed to.

"My wife died in a car crash, six years ago. The twelfth of February 2024. Not far from our home in west London."

"Oh, no. Curtis, I'm so sorry." Harrison's eyes were closed, and her voice was groggy. "So, so sorry."

"My daughter, Grace," Soren gulped, "she took it as you might expect. It was so sudden Mia. She didn't cope." Soren breathed heavily and shook his head. "We didn't cope together. She was 12. We grew apart, she spent more time in her bedroom. Or out with her friends. I didn't know who those friends were. I was too drunk to know."

He wasn't sure if Harrison was awake or asleep. His eyes welled.

"She disappeared. They found her after two days. In an old farmhouse barn. She'd..." He still couldn't say it out loud. He never had.

"They found evidence on her phone. Self harm chat boards. Suicide. Really dark stuff. Looking back, she didn't stand a chance."

He was weeping now.

"I went away. I *had* to go away. For a long time. I still don't understand what I'm doing with my life. I'm trying, but it falls out of focus."

Soren took a tissue from the top of the bedside cabinet, and wiped his eyes. He looked down at his sleeping friend. Peace showed in her face despite the wires running under her skin and the beeping of a heart monitor.

"I guess I better go," he said. "Thanks for listening."

Harrison's face and body didn't move at all. But he felt a very slight squeeze of his hand. He laid her hand down and walked out of the room.

It wasn't difficult for Soren to find the swipe contact for chief inspector Miran Burman from the Metropolitan Police, who had pulled him into his BMW outside Carlos' last week.

"We're on the same side, I think," he'd said. Time to put that to the test.

The officer had been sympathetic. He hadn't heard about the attack, but he said he'd take a personal interest and head over to St George's now. If appropriate, he would take charge of the case. If it had been a homophobic incident, it would definitely be treated as such. Hate crime was taken very seriously, particularly in the Met.

"How are *you,* Mr Soren?"

"I'm convinced there might be more to this attack than a random mugging. I think Mia's family needs protecting. It might be to do with the story we're working on. It's sensitive stuff. Maybe things certain people would prefer us to keep quiet about."

"Do you feel able to share more with me about that?"

"No, it's just a feeling."

"Resources are tight, Mr Soren, for a *feeling.* But I agree we should definitely look at getting Mrs Harrison's family protected, or even moved temporarily. She has young kids, is that right?"

"Yes, I think so."

"Then they would jump the queue. And we'll look into any possible threats to you and your organisation. I've not heard of anything, but things have been quiet since our last conversation."

Soren had felt a small well of, what was it, pride in working with the police? Being agreeable, rather than combative. It felt good to trust. Almost as good as whisky.

When he reached SkyCloud, Grey was waiting for him. He looked haggard and obviously hadn't been able to do any work since Jessica had called that morning.

Soren entered the glass office, and pulled the door softly behind him.

"She's okay. Hardly walking wounded, but she'll definitely pull through."

"Oh, thank God. It's terrible," said Grey.

"I spoke to her, though she was pretty out of it. The doctors say she's had some ribs broken, and her face is pretty mashed up. But she's going to be fine. I've talked to the police…"

"The police?" Grey said, surprised.

"Yes, there's a feeling it was a hate crime. A homophobic attack, but Mia seemed to feel it was more than that. Something connected to our work, even. I agree. I have a contact in the Met and he's agreed to look at any possible threat."

Grey loosened his tie and sat down behind his desk. He dropped his voice to a whisper.

"Are we in danger, too?" He indicated the SkyCloud workers. They were oblivious to what was going on, except that one of their team members had been mugged. Grey had promised to update them.

"The police will tell us that, and I hope act accordingly. Meantime, I guess we'll just wait," said Soren. "I think we should do a story."

"On the attack?"

"Yes, just a small one. Noting that it happened, and that we're fully supportive of our colleague as she works her way to recovery. Something like that. The attackers left her for dead. I want to send them a message that we fight on."

"I think it's good to write a small story," said Grey. "But let's not mention any motive. That's her business. And let's not intentionally try to wind up the shitheads who did this. If they are a threat to us all, we better wait for the Met's advice before going full on."

"Agreed," said Soren. "Don't worry about Mia. She's tough as nails. It was me who fell apart at her bedside. A lot has happened today. I told her about Lucy. And Grace."

Grey sat back in his chair, astonished. And then calm and sympathetic.

"That is *you* being tough, you know Soren. It must have been hard."

"Actually, it felt like a release."

"That's good. Perhaps you should talk about it more. To a professional, I mean. Meanwhile, go write a story."

"There's someone else we need to talk about," Soren said. "Someone I met this morning."

"I wondered where you were. Who was it?"

"Amanda Ward."

19

The two spent the next hour talking through what had happened that morning at the crossroads between Farmer's Hill and Florence Road, what Ward had told him about Changemakers, the test bed in East Burundi and Portico.

"This is a far deeper story than we thought," said Soren. "And something we have exclusively, though I do think we need to clarify with Ward what is on the record and what isn't. She seemed to imply that publishing anything - even that her history had been massaged - would put her in danger somehow, and scupper the whole Changemaker project."

"Surely that's not our problem," argued Grey. "As you've told me so many times, our job is to tell the truth."

"You're dead right. But I have a duty to protect my source. And publishing without cross checking the facts puts Ward directly in the firing line for having leaked. And her intention was the opposite: to ask us to lay it down, at least for now. It was almost an exchange. Wait to publish, and she'd supply more information. An exclusive."

"You're sure no other newsgathering organisation is being courted in this way?" said Grey.

"I'd be surprised. We've done all the leading on Ward, and I have the personal 'in' via the Alice Harding false history. No one else knows about that."

"So what are the next steps?"

"I have another contact, who I think might be able to support Ward's new back story."

"Another source?"

"You could say that," Soren replied. "Once we have that confirmation, and have cleared it with Ward, I think we should publish. It needn't be a cutthroat job. I'm beginning to be convinced by Ward that Changemakers at least began as a good thing. It just needs to be dealt with carefully."

"Well, I need to be really convinced your story is as strong as you claim it is. You seem to have a good grasp on what's going on, but I also know you have an axe to grind about the social. Your job is to convince me, before we do anything else. Work with Harrison as a sounding board, as soon as she's up to it. But I'll hold the story for now. But you've got days, not weeks."

"Thanks Will."

"Go work on that other source," he replied. "And then go home."

Soren retreated from his office and swiped his slate. He brought up Lucas Simmons' personal details. The YoYo chief executive had told Soren he'd worked with Ward for a long time, before Portico. And Ward had mentioned him too. If he was sore about Soren not joining the YoYo team, he might not talk to him. Though he had promised there would be no hard feelings.

There was only one way to find out.

Soren swiped the video call, and it began to ring. After

three cycles, the screen flashed up with a 'Not currently available', followed by an invitation to leave a message. Soren decided to hedge his bets.

"Mr Simmons, it's Curtis Soren from SkyCloud. I wanted to talk about, well, follow up on the conversation we had last week. If you might get back in touch, please."

He swiped the screen blank. He then swiped up Inspector Burman.

"Any news on Kate Harrison?"

"She's stable and talking about the attack," the officer said. "There are lots of leads, but I think you're right that there's a personal element to it. We're inspecting CCTV around the streets outside her home. My colleague Sergeant Lee has been stationed with her wife Jessica. And she'll take her home. The kids are being taken by Jessica's relatives. Can't really say more for now, but we're investigating."

Soren swiped off, and began a short story about Harrison's attack and how SkyCloud wished her a rapid recovery. As he punched the letters into his slate, he realised how much he wanted to write about her that he couldn't: that she was tough and stubborn, but absolutely reliable. Funny, sarcastic and she totally had the measure of men who acted idiotically around her. Like during the fight he and Grey had had yesterday.

His stomach twisted as he remembered her lying on the hospital gurney, wires running in and out of her skin. Genuine pain on her face. He remembered the hand squeeze. He took a deep breath and blew it out again.

He wrote a few straightforward paragraphs on the attack, and concluded with one which stated that the police were following a number of leads. He swiped it to his editor.

Then he took some time to look up East Burundi, to see whether what Ward had told him added up.

The country was one of the smallest on the continent, a little mass of dry land and bush buried in tough scrub, competing for natural resources with Burundi, Rwanda and Uganda, and for fishing rights on Lake Rweru. Angry communities lumped together on inhospitable land when European colonisation had upped and left in the 1960s.

The results had been like so many others across the continent. Poverty and discontent. Men who had been robbed of knowledge by being cajoled into work for the white man, left now with few skills and little self determination. Women and girls with no right to education, and no awareness of what it might do for them. Health was poor. Education poorer. It was a country with a history of tribal spats, and a dysfunctional government continually passed between family members, opposing clans, sectarian sides. A typical basket case created by exploitative colonisers, according to most commentators.

An opportunity, Ward had said.

What East Burundi had had, at least as far as Changemakers was concerned, was the benefit of being small. Just a few million people, living in separate, sometimes disparate clans over 10,000 square kilometres. A great test bed.

East Burundi's second gift to Changemakers was the technology revolution that was blossoming at the time the organisation began its work there. The nation had never had physical telephone lines, except those run through a tiny exchange in the capital Farawana. Outside the city, contact between populations had been by mobile phone and messaging, internet connections via widespread communication towers.

Like the African nations surrounding it, mobile technology became the most widespread means of communication. But only in East Burundi had Changemakers tested the widespread monitoring, tracking and analysis of communication and data. It was then able to create projects that answered the needs of rural and city dwellers, that their data modelling suggested was required. A lot of that including pushing out health and education messages to citizens' mobile phones.

That monitoring, modelling and responding to trends that Changemakers had been able to carry out in East Burundi had allowed the country to develop quicker than it might otherwise have. At least according to Amanda Ward.

The growth in communications ability had been widely credited - Soren read articles online in the *Economist*, on the United Nations website, on the *Bloomberg* financial pages - with the radical transformation of East Burundi. No mention was made of a secret organisation commissioned by the UN. But if Changemakers had supported communication channels, created messages which influenced and educated civilians, and made the country a safer and more progressive place to be born, then perhaps the programme could take some of the credit.

And as the articles outlined and Ward herself had claimed, it was local village leaders and community champions, women in particular, who had been at the heart of the change. Better technology and communcations had perhaps just enabled them to do it quicker.

Soren now wondered whether the people of East Burundi had willingly embraced the monitoring and use of their communications, or whether it had been imposed by Changemakers without their knowledge or consent.

It would be difficult to include the entire story of East Burundi in his piece about Amanda Ward, let alone get most potential readers to give it more than a passing glance.

But it provided good background. He could do a more extended article later.

But what Changemakers might have achieved in East Burundi was different to what Amanda Ward and Lucas Simmons had told him about their plans for the UK. Delivering health messages and education was a long way from screening out opposing views, hate speech or the banning of particular ideas. Soren wanted his readers to make up their own minds. He made some detailed notes, swiped an outline to Harrison and Grey, then left the office.

Opening up to Amanda Ward and then to Harrison about Lucy and Grace had felt like the biggest step Soren had taken to deal with what had happened. He tried to remember what he'd been doing since the crash.

For the first month, trying to hold it together for Grace. To be the understanding dad, to give her the space she needed to deal with the death of her mother. But she, like he, had completely closed down. They had both retreated to their own rooms and pulled the curtains closed.

While Soren had taken in bottles of whisky each night, Grace had taken in her mobile phone and razor blade. She had begun to cut herself, to harm her own arms, legs, the back of her neck where her long black hair would cover the scars.

He had been oblivious. He hadn't *wanted* to see.

It was only when Grace's body had been found at the farmhouse that he realised his grief had been focused solely on himself, not on his daughter when she needed him the most.

What Soren had found elsewhere had helped him to understand, a little, what Grace had gone through. He understood the influence others had had on her. She had blamed herself for her mother's death: if only she'd somehow prevented her mum from going to the shops that day; if only she'd damaged a wheel on her car; if only she'd pretended to be sick; if only...

Mums don't just die. *Her* mum couldn't just die. Soren had felt the same.

Grace wanted to be punished. And she needed to *feel* something. Something, other than terrible, unutterable loss. The pain of a razor blade was a release. Something tangible, rather than the cruelly vacant hole in her life. And now her father too, lost in drink and self pity.

But pain is never enough. The need to overcome the grief grows and grows, just as the guilt grows and grows. Until, one day, only one option seems real. It seems fair and just. But most of all, it's the only way to escape the pain.

Soren had read all about it since Grace had sought that pathway. Always trying to understand the influence the social had had on her. He wished he'd had the foresight to look earlier. If only he could pinpoint the exact moment when her grief turned to more. He could have saved her. They could be living together now. Supporting each other.

Father and daughter. Solid, loving. Filling the chasm Lucy had left behind.

Soren himself had had no one else to turn to. Will Grey had been around when Lucy died, and had tried to support him in the immediate weeks after her death. And two months later, when Grace had died, he had tried to support him again. But Soren was a collapsed man. A heap.

Grey offered his condolences, but didn't speak the truth: that Grace took her own life because Soren had failed as a father to protect her. He had been too consumed by his own agony that he hadn't reached out to cut the rope she'd strung herself up with.

The court case which released his wife's killer kicked his already crumpled body into the gutter, washed it down the drain.

The Herald was closing down, with a small redundancy payment for those like Ward and Grey who had worked on the paper for many years. Grey had taken the money, added it to family money, and established SkyCloud. Soren had taken his, and the measly sum he got from a week long auction sale of his and Lucy's home, and disappeared.

To where, he couldn't quite remember.

Abroad. Dingy hotels and shitty bars, the most he deserved. Seeking sun, seeking cold, seeking anything that made him feel something. Anything.

He stole from shops, just to get caught and beaten up by corrupt police in wayward states. He gambled money away on impossible odds, knowing that he'd lose, addicted to the short lived adrenaline of imagining he'd beat the bookies.

Alcohol everywhere. Opium in Cairo. LSD on Zanzibar. And cannabis. Always the cannabis. So strong that he'd experienced hallucinations, but ones that were never pleasant. Ones that always featured his wife and daughter, the grotesque, distorted image of their yellow and bruised, blood covered faces.

At times he'd tried to follow Grace. But never carried it through. He didn't deserve even that release.

And all that time, and ever since, the need to understand why remained. How had he failed his daughter and wife so badly? How could a young girl cut pain into her own skin, and flail off her fingernails. And how had he managed not to see it? Why didn't he stop her?

Soren hadn't said all of this to Grey and Harrison today.

But now he had said something, the buildup of questioning in his gut had been irresistible. This evening his closest friend would be a bottle of whisky, and his illegal slate.

As so often before, he needed to know.

With two double shots already downed, Soren found it easy to enter that place again.

Soren had needs. A clue that would prove his guilt, and bring his suffering to an end.

He entered his password. Now comfortable, too comfortable. He cruised to his usual channels.

*LegallyHigh

*GoneMissing

He looked for and selected his previous post, from years ago.

He looked at the list. No information. Same as earlier in the week. Same as last week. The week before. The month before.

The man with the needs had been scammed back then. A clever trick to play on someone new and naive.

666. Sign of the devil, the gullible and the desperate.

Provide just enough information to draw in a man with desperate needs, bait him with a possible answer. Then withdraw.

Others had posted similar promises. But now he could smell the scams.

The 666 slate coin he'd paid? It was obvious now.

The number plate. The crossroads where the crash took place. Where his wife had died, her last breath taken on tarmac long before an ambulance had arrived.

All public information, if you knew where to really look. Bait for the desperate. He saw the money he'd paid as his subscription fee, a price worth paying. But he wouldn't be scammed again. His post had run cold, but he couldn't help looking. Just in case.

Habit took him back to the cursor.

*CuttingRemarks. *SpectatorsOf. *RopeWorks.

He read, visiting each one. Trying as always to understand his daughter's final decision. To find the blame he deserved.

Back, he typed. And then he noticed.

*TowardsDeath

A new channel, perhaps another way to understand. He typed the words, tight up against the blinking, questioning cursor.

Curtis Soren gasped as he read the dull white type as it appeared on his dark screen.

The community who had gathered around *TowardsDeath were not what Soren had been looking for. But in a way, they had been looking for him.

Posts had begun four days ago, the same night Soren had met Amanda Ward in Ned's, her bodyguard sitting at the door sipping tonic water. She'd been watched, entering and leaving the building. A poster on the forum said they had followed Ward's car back to MinSoc, where the trace of her had been lost.

That liberal bitch heads back to MinSoc to ban our basic rights.

Fuck her and the liberal elite. Stop immigration. Stop hand-outs. White is right. Blue Team, who's with me?

Among the diatribe and slogans were snippets of information about Ward's movements, and others around her.

Ward spoke at MinHealth today. Scouted her out there.

Saw Gayboy Godspeed flouncing into MinSoc today. Disgusting, flaunting.

Possible sighting of target in jew land, Harrow. More info if poss. I'll look out for the princess. Blue Team!

Target?, thought Soren. Then a few lines down on the same feed:

Who is this guy with the bitch in a pub on Greek Street? Grey hair, long mac. Boyfriend? Another communist wanker? Likes pizza whoever he is?

Soren suddenly felt sick to his stomach. The address of his apartment building was published as part of the post. He clicked a link, which opened a thumbnail picture of Soren stumbling up his front steps with the 12" under his arm.

Lying sucker from SkyCloud, I think. Probably fucking Ward in exchange for fake news.

Soren stared at the next lines on his screen, with his mouth open. The glass of whisky dropped from his hand and the spirit spilled across the carpet. He grabbed the bottle instead, and swallowed a mouthful.

Took down a SkyCloud bitch today: now SkyCloud and Ward know we mean business.

A final reply:

Good work. Time to get this thing underway. Time is running out for comms in this space. Take down the bitch and her boyfriend. Blue Team salute!

Underneath, at least five different contributors. Each had posted the same words:

Blue Team salute!

Blue Team salute!

Blue Team salute...

"Oh God," was the most Soren could muster. He drained the bottle, then threw it across the room where it smashed into tiny pieces.

20

"Mr Soren, have you been drinking?"

It was a fair enough question for Detective Inspector Burman to ask. The officer was at the hospital when Soren swiped him and asked him if he could meet in private. When Soren stumbled out of the TriCab, Burman had been waiting for him in the hospital reception.

"Why, is it illegal?" he replied. "How's Mia Harrison? Is she protected?"

"Yes, I have a female officer at her door," said the officer. "Why don't you sit and I'll bring you a coffee?"

"Can I see her?"

"The officer?"

"Not the fucking officer. Mia, I need to tell her." He was slurring his words.

"She's sleeping as far as I understand. I've been able to take a statement, but she needs to rest. I'm going to speak to her again in the morning." Then more sternly: "Mr Soren, you need to take a seat. Black coffee coming up. Have you eaten?"

"Can't talk here," he slurred.

"Okay, we'll go somewhere else. But coffee first." The officer went to find a vending machine. Soren leant back in a comfortable waiting room chair and fell asleep.

When he awoke, Soren was no longer in the hospital. He was lying on a hard surface in what appeared to be a grey tiled cell, with thick glass brick windows and a heavy door. His bed was a thin mattress, and he shivered under a rough blue blanket that had been placed over him. There was a smell of vomit in the room, and he had a faint memory of being sick into a metal toilet pan.

He sat up and rubbed his temples. This was going to hurt in the morning. If it wasn't already the morning. He swallowed. His throat felt and tasted like the bottom of a parrot's cage.

He stood and gently swayed until his balance had adjusted. He banged on the door. After a minute, he banged again.

When he began to hear the creak of the door, he returned to sit on the bed.

"The door is open, Mr Soren," said a uniformed police officer as she opened the door. "No need for aggression."

"Am I under arrest? What did I do?"

"No sir," said the officer. She was barely out of her teens, but obviously used to dealing with overnight drunks. "My Detective Inspector brought you here from St George's. Said you needed to sleep it off."

"When is it? What time?"

"It's just gone seven."

"When will Burman be back?"

"*Detective Inspector* Burman? I believe he's on shift at nine a.m. You're of course welcome to leave, but if you want to wait for him, I can get a breakfast brought in for you. It'll just be the same as the other overnights - eggs, bacon, beans, toast - from the cafe next door."

He swallowed hard at the chance of a fry up. "Hold the bacon. Will there be coffee?"

"Sir, I believe you are taking the piss," the officer said curtly. "But yes, since you are not under arrest, I shall bring you coffee too. It'll be instant, though. I'm not paying the price those fuckers charge next door." She smiled and almost curtseyed.

Soren grinned. "Thank you, and sorry. Just, hungover."

"I've seen it thousands of times. But the Boss said to treat you well. Otherwise I'd have zapped your ass by now," she indicated her taser with a grin.

Soren knew from short spells in jail during his dark five years that nothing happens quickly in custody. It would be an hour before breakfast came. By the time it did, Soren had attempted to clean himself up. He'd brushed his teeth with a tiny tube of paste, and a barely useable toothbrush which had broken into small pieces by the time he'd finished. They were designed to be weak, so inmates couldn't make a blade. The soap the custody sergeant provided had someone else's hair stuck to it.

Soren moved himself to the custody waiting room and swiped his feeds for any response to his story about the attack on Harrison. There wasn't much more than bits of sympathy from friends, wishing her a speedy recovery. He'd tried to swipe Harrison, but there was no reply. Chancing on the sympathy he'd received from Grey yesterday, he'd sent a message saying he'd be in late, and was going to visit Harrison on the way in.

Detective Inspector Miran Burman arrived early. He greeted Soren, and led him to an empty interview room.

"You weren't in any fit state to talk last night, so I brought you back here to sleep it off. Want to tell me what this is all about then? You said it was urgent."

"It is. I think we're in danger. Me, Mia Harrison and Amanda Ward."

"Amanda Ward, the national director at MinSoc? How do you know her? And what gives you the impression she's in danger?"

"We all are. Have you heard of something called Blue Team?"

"I don't think so."

"I think there's a threat from Blue Team against us three. Maybe anyone who works with Ward, or at MinSoc. Could be big, or could just be us?"

"Where are you getting this information, Mr Soren?" said Burman.

He hesitated. "I can't say."

"You can't say?"

"We just need protecting. Not me so much, but Amanda Ward. And Mia, she needs more. We've all been named."

"Back up, here," said Burman, with obvious impatience. "I asked you how you know Amanda Ward. How is she anything to do with you?"

"I can't answer that."

Burman pushed his seat away from the desk and stood.

"So, if I've got this right, you came into the hospital blind drunk last night, to tell me you were in danger. But you won't tell me why. And that some high profile figure you claim to know, but you can't tell me how, is also in danger, but you won't tell me why either? And you want me to act on this alone?

"Do you have any idea, Mr Soren, how busy the Metropolitan police is dealing with *actual* crime?"

"The attack on Harrison was a crime," bit back Soren.

"Yes, and I'd be over at St George's right now if I wasn't stuck here talking to you. So, you want to come clean and tell me what the hell is going on, or shall we say good day and you can pick *yourself* up off the floor next time?"

Soren considered his options.

Any use of the dark web was absolutely, categorically illegal. If he had viewed images, even accidentally, of child pornography, he had committed a crime. If he had read extremist literature, or instructions on how to carry out terrorist attacks, he had committed a crime. If he had read or seen information on how someone was planning to hurt or kill themselves, and not reported it, he had committed a crime.

He had created a login for himself on channels which would easily be regarded as the dark web. He had used it regularly, to try to understand what had happened to Grace, but also to actively track down the disappeared woman who killed his wife.

Although he was not under oath here, he knew that the officer now standing crossly in front of him would be obliged to take action if he knew. This situation could very quickly turn into an arrest, and that bed he'd slept on last night was just not comfortable enough for a repeat performance. He suspected a prison term would be less comfortable still.

"I am clearly wasting your time," Soren told him. "I wanted to tell you that Ward, and probably myself and Mia Harrison are under threat. I've done that. The rest is down to you. I can't speak any more without... what is it? Incriminating myself? So I'll leave it there.

He paused: "I'd like to leave now."

"You're sure, Mr Soren?"

The newsgatherer stood up. Burman sighed. They

walked in silence down the corridor, past the custody desk and to the door of the station. The pair shook hands. As he turned to leave, Detective Inspector Burman paused: "Blue Team?"

Their eyes met.

"Blue Team," said Soren.

21

———

Soren took a TriCab to SkyCloud, instead of visiting Harrison straight away. If Burman was on his way to the hospital, he didn't want another confrontation. When he arrived, he took a walk around the block to clear his head, then took a table at Carlos' to think through what he needed to tell Grey. And what he needed to keep to himself. He swiped Grey to tell him he was going to the hospital, to give him an excuse to be late.

He felt twitchy, unable to get Harrison's beating out of his mind, and the threats that had been made against him. Someone had their eye on him, and eventually they might strike. He couldn't help examining the faces of other customers, looking for someone watching him. He kept looking up through the window, to see if anyone was waiting. He'd have to keep himself in public, and only go out in daylight.

He'd become embroiled in the story he was supposed to be covering. Amanda Ward had said something about being in danger if he revealed the truth about her background. But he couldn't understand how the threats from Blue Team over the dark web could relate to that. And though she'd pleaded with him not to publish yet, she'd not threatened him with anything if he did. She was enjoying her place at the top of the halo charts just now, but that would pass. What goes up, always comes down. It wasn't worth spiking a good story for.

And yet.

She'd seemed desperate. She'd implied the whole of the Changemakers project might be at risk, and she was convinced the project was making the world a better place. Despite his concerns about the democratic implications of what the UN had asked the big tech companies to do, he couldn't help but admit that an era of peace, reasonableness and justice - in the UK at least - appeared to be coming over the horizon.

If that was because of Changemakers, then all power to them. A little nudge in the right direction. A butterfly's wings could cause a hurricane, and all that. But it could have been coming anyway. Things change. And all positive and progressive movements provoke a reactionary fightback.

Soren's slate buzzed, and he again broke his own rule of not using his screen when enjoying a solitary coffee at Carlos'. These were exceptional times.

It was a message from Grey: "Need you back in the office ASAP. Take a look at the feeds on your way from the hospital."

Ward swiped away the message and brought up the feeds.

"MinSoc reverses hate speech ban," ran a headline from InfoCom.

"Extremists back online after MinSoc climb down," ran another, from XLSMedia.

"National Director in the firing line after hate policy U-turn," another headline said.

He swiped away from the newsgatherers' feeds, and looked at the personal messages posted about MinSoc and Ward.

That Ward woman has let down all right minded people with her retreat.

MinSoc waste of space. Sack the Nat Dir. for giving in to social companies and extremists.

Flip Flop Ward should be out of a job.

Protest at MinSoc, calling for Amanda Ward to resign.

Soren swiped the personal feeds away, and brought up the groups' platforms. Already, some of the extremist groups that Amanda Ward had banned were back online. Their previous content was there, along with a flood of new comments about justice, freedom of speech and how MinSoc, enemy of the people, had been defeated.

Soren swiped a message to Amanda Ward: "You okay? What the hell is happening out there?"

He drained his coffee and left the cafe. After taking a moment to check his surroundings, he headed across the road to SkyCloud.

"What's going on?" Soren demanded the moment he reached his editor's office. He hadn't waited to knock or be invited in.

Grey was furious. "I should be asking you. It's been like this all morning. Since breakfast. Everyone got a release from MinSoc apart from us. Your friend Amanda Ward has pulled her ban on the extremist groups over the social. We've been played like idiots."

"The last I saw of her was when she dropped me at the hospital yesterday. I've messaged her just now," said Soren.

"We need to get on top of this, because right now we look like her biggest fans and she's totally turned us over. She's getting devil emojis, while we've still got her hovering under a halo. We are the last to the party, Soren. We should have published that fake history story, got ahead of her. What is she playing at?"

"Let me try to get hold of her again."

"We should publish the fake history, and expose that dogooder project she spoke about," said Grey, clenching his fists.

"What, and join her public battering? And put the Changemakers' project at risk, too. That was off the record."

"That's not our concern, it's now public interest. She's obviously failed the project herself. Any damage to her is no business of ours. Our job is to publish the truth."

"I think last time we had a conversation like this, Will, you said we needed to do journalism properly. We have to ask Amanda Ward for a personal response to the attacks against her."

"You're kidding me?" said Grey.

"And given what happened yesterday, I think I'm in a pretty good position to get the inside track."

There was a knock at the door. A twenty-something with headphones strung around her neck entered the room.

"This better be good," snapped Grey.

"It's the feeds," said the newsgatherer, who normally covered celebrity news. "Amanda Ward has been sacked."

Soren and Grey sat upright, and quickly leant into their slates. Soren was first to bring up the story, broken of course by InfoCom.

MinSoc National Director resigns over faked CV.

He spoke it out loud.

XLSMedia carried a similar newsline: *Shamed National Director faked her history to get top job at MinSoc.*

Ward sacked after admitting MinSoc policy against freedom of speech was wrong.

As they sat there, the feeds filled with further news of the resignation, all rehashes of the same basic information. Ward had either jumped or been pushed out of her job at MinSoc in the last hour. The line was that she had rushed in draconian rules to restrict freedom of speech, and had had no choice but to retreat on the policy because opposition to it had been so wide.

Resignation or sacking was inevitable.

The public feeds were making a meal of it. The resignation played right into the hands of those who Ward's policy had banned. The civil servant who would ban their freedom of speech or the 'news' as they saw it, was a liar. Untrustworthy. A manipulator of information herself.

She'd purposefully lied about her history. One rule for the powerful, another for everyone else. They speculated she'd gone against the government's will. That she was in league with special interest groups to get opposing voices banned; that she was being paid by this or that liberal group to blank out any criticism of them on the social.

But the charities and liberal pressure groups, the gay rights' groups, the womens' equality groups, the environmentalists were just as angry at Ward for her policy reversal. They too criticised her for lying about her past. Some more militant than others, but none were leaping to her defence.

There were lots of laughing emojis. A few devils and cackling witches. There were certainly no halos for the now former national director of the Ministry for Society and Communications.

Soren considered telling Grey about the Blue Team threat. But now it seemed everyone wanted a piece of the woman who had looked upon him with sympathy in the back of her Nissan yesterday, and gone out of her way to drop him at St George's.

"Mia!" Soren suddenly said aloud.

"What about her," replied Grey, looking up from his slate.

"I need to go to the hospital, discuss this with her. Perhaps she'll have a clue?" He was concerned about the threats he'd read last night.

"You just came from there."

"Like I said, *back* to the hospital. I'll try to get hold of Ward on the way, and Godspeed too. Maybe he's another way in."

"I'll get someone here to cover the bones of the story as it's emerging," said Grey. "But for now we'll keep what we know that's not yet in the public domain to ourselves. But you better produce Ward or Godspeed fast, otherwise I'll need you to go with the full Changemakers story by the end of the day. I'm taking a risk on this."

"I know you are, Will. If I can get hold of her, I think I can get Ward to speak."

When Soren reached the hospital, he noted the police BMW parked outside the main entrance. Burman was still here. Another facedown he'd have to endure. He looked again: neither of the two officers sat in the front of the car was the Detective Inspector he'd run up against that morning.

Another police officer was stationed outside Harrison's room. She stopped him, swiped his slate against hers for

ID, and then knocked to ask if Harrison wanted to see him.

Harrison was sitting upright. Her face was brighter, the bruises starting to fade. Some thick pillows propped up her left side. Awkwardly, she was swiping at her slate. She beckoned him to sit down without looking up.

"You got the news then?" he asked as he took up his place in the easy chair.

"Devil. Angry face. Bitch. Traitor. What has Ward done to herself?"

"I need to find that out," he said. "I've tried her a few times this morning, and Godspeed too. No response. The whole of MinSoc has gone to ground."

"People are really angry with her. Like, people who two days ago loved her. They're spitting."

"How can things flip so suddenly?"

"Because she let the haters back onto the internet?" suggested Harrison. "But it's got to be more than that."

Soren raised an eyebrow.

"I've been swiping these feeds all morning, ever since she pulled the social policy. The negative posts against her have just built and built. And with her sacking, they've gone wild. But have you noticed something?"

Soren looked at Harrison. She was super focused. He'd seen that look on her face before.

She continued swiping: "I've not seen one positive post about her. Not one sympathetic comment. Not one 'sad to see her go'. Not one 'she did her best'. Not one 'heart was in the right place'. It's all vitriol."

Harrison looked up for the first time, directly into Soren's eyes. "It's like the social is screening out anything positive about Amanda Ward. Her own rules are being used against her."

They said it together: "YoYo?"

Soren was first to speak, "This is why we need you back on your feet, Mia. Grey wants to join the piñata party, smashing what's left of Ward. We don't have long."

"I can't go anywhere," Harrison said, indicating her bandaged ribs and busted up face. "But if you can get me another slate, I might be able to work at twice the speed."

"Shouldn't you get some rest?"

"And miss our big story?"

"I'll get Grey to send over another slate," Soren replied. "And maybe another newsgatherer to help."

He stood, and made for the door. Before he opened it, he turned abruptly.

"Mia, there's another reason I came. I'm pretty certain the attack against you wasn't an accident. In fact, it was pre-planned."

"We thought as much," she looked scared, but not overly concerned. It couldn't get much worse I suppose. "How do you know?"

"I can't say - it's a lead I'm following up, but I need to be careful about what I tell the police. But you and Jessica, the girls, you need more protection. So does Amanda Ward I think."

"Should I really be worried?"

"Just look out for any reference on the feeds to SkyCloud, or you, me or Ward in particular. I think they're some maniac right wingers out there that are looking to vent at more than their slates. You're probably safer in hospital than anywhere else, right now."

"Okay, even more reason to stay put. Thanks, I'll let Jessica know. The kids are already placed out of reach."

Soren made for the door, but he turned back. He felt

himself somehow unable to leave her side. He stepped back into the room.

"Sorry, Mia. I forgot to ask. How are you getting on?"

"I'm grand. Jessica is looking after me."

"And about yesterday. I wanted to say thanks, you know..."

"Go away, Soren. We've a story to work on." But she smiled at him.

He left the hospital, noting the police officers still staking out the entrance from their BMW. He took a TriCab to his apartment. He couldn't work in the office, with Grey breathing down his neck. Besides, he wanted to contact Amanda Ward and the more direct channels weren't doing the job.

22

The TriCab dropped Soren a few blocks away from his apartment, so he could make it home without too much fanfare. If Blue Team had stalked him to his door previously, it was sensible to take precautions.

He tried to remember the play spy techniques he'd learned from the books he'd read when he was a kid. He stopped in front of large windows, trying to make out any reflection of someone following him while pretending to look at the goods inside. He stopped every now and again to tie his shoe laces and take a look around. But by the time he reached his building, he was confident that he could swipe through the front door unhindered.

Inside, he took a shower and put on some toast which he ate as he changed into clean clothes. He shoved the shirt and jeans he'd been wearing on top of his washing pile, built up to nearly a week now. Perhaps robots coming into the house to tidy up wouldn't be such a bad thing.

When Lucy was around, he seemed to produce less washing. He certainly smelled better. He looked around: his life had been tidier. He shook out his bed clothes, opened his living room blinds - when was the last time they'd let in sunlight? - and brushed up the broken bottle he'd thrown against the wall last night. The room smelled of whisky. He opened a window and sprayed some deodorant around the apartment. Lucy would have watched him, leaning against a door frame, arms crossed, shaking her head and smiling.

Grace had inherited her mother's tidy genes. She might have tried to be a goth, all dark makeup and ragged clothes, dull thumping music, but her bedroom was immaculate. Even her jet black bedsheets were pulled taught. That's the way they'd stayed until the police had turned up, looking for clues to her disappearance.

Soren stopped tidying and moved to his bedroom. He carefully swiped off his work slate, and pulled his legacy slate from the bottom drawer of his bedside table.

He swiped up the messaging app, and typed next to his fake name.

#ClariceKing: What's going on? I want to help, like you helped me.

He waited.

After a few minutes, he brought his legs up onto the bed and sat with the slate across his knees, leaning back into the pillows. He shuffled down and closed his eyes. He needed a few moments' concentration, to decide what his next steps should be. Was YoYo manipulating the social to damage Amanda Ward? And if so, how could he prove it?

He woke suddenly when the door system buzzed. It took him a moment to come round, and it was only on the second, longer buzz that he realised someone wanted him to answer his door. He stashed the slate in the bottom drawer. It was becoming dull outside; late afternoon, he estimated.

"Shit! Grey."

Another buzz.

"Fucking hell, I'm coming."

Soren went to his doorway and swiped open the CCTV that would show him who was at his apartment building door. But it wasn't Grey.

"Curtis, I need to come in. Can you let me in?" Amanda Ward was trying to speak formally, but he could tell by the heavy breathing it came with panic. She was looking around her as she spoke.

"Are you alone?" he said.

"Yes, I'm alone. Can you let me in?"

"Okay, close the door directly behind you. Second floor." He swiped open the building, and he listened through the entrance system as the door opened, then quickly slammed. The mechanism auto locked.

Shortly, he heard her knocking at his apartment, but waited until she buzzed his front door. He could then see a screen image of her waiting. She was alone, her hair soaked and messy, her face red.

He opened up and she rushed in, closing the door behind her. "Took your time," she said, taking off her heavy overcoat and shaking it vigorously. The rain fell over Soren's cheap carpeted floor.

"Do come in," he said, with only the slightest hint of sarcasm. "Where's Tom?"

"Can you not read, Curtis? I'm no longer national direc-tor. Tom's gone, it's all gone. Harry Godspeed has taken over." She pushed past him down the corridor, entering the living room. "What the hell have you done to me?"

He followed, admiring her brash manner.

"Nothing. I've not published a word. What are you talking about?"

"Then where has all this come from? The hate messages, the devil emojis. I didn't *do* anything. I trusted you to hold off. When we spoke it was off the record."

"I swear, I've not published. My colleague did a straightforward story, mirroring the other feeds, but we've put nothing else out. At least, not since I last looked. And anyway, you're the one who's reversed the policy. You've let hate speech back on the social, put those groups back into business. What were you thinking?"

"I didn't do it!" She was bellowing at him. "I didn't authorise any change. The withdrawal of the policy, the U-turn, it's nothing to do with me. MinSoc put that out, re-permitted those groups. Then put out the message I'd resigned. I've done no such thing. I had no idea Godspeed was going to be taking over. It's all happened without me."

"That's impossible," said Soren.

"Not in this social world, it isn't. First I heard was security guards coming to my office and asking me to leave the building. They gave me ten minutes, *ten minutes,* to leave. And they body searched me to ensure I wasn't taking any MinSoc property. I had to take a TriCab home. I've been trying to get hold of you."

"When we met last time, you talked about your safety," said Soren.

"Yes, you've read the feeds. They hate me from both sides, the extremists and the liberals. United against the devil Amanda Ward. And I haven't *done* anything."

There was panic in her voice, and she took some very deep breaths to calm herself.

"I took a cab home and talked to Roger and the boys. They've gone to our holiday home. I won't tell you where. They're safe, I think. I've tried Harry Godspeed, but he's not responding. Please, I need your help to call off the dogs."

"Like I said, we've not published anything. I had some-thing lined up, but it won't go out until six. What time is it?"

"Around four I think?"

"I need to swipe my editor and let him know. God, I hope he's kept his promise to hold the story. But I'm going to need you to back me up. And that means you need to show your face."

"I've no choice now, do I?"

"You make some coffee, I'll get in touch with him." He pointed to the kitchen, then went to find his slate. First, he swiped Harrison for backup and asked her to join in a group video conference with Grey. No time to explain.

He then prepared himself for a ball busting.

"Soren, where the hell have you been?" were Grey's first words. "The social is going mad over Ward, and I'm hanging by a thread about to publish our story. You promised me something for the six o'clocks. Neither of you have given me anything since this morning. Curtis, you've been switched off all afternoon. Mia, I guess you have a good excuse."

"Things are moving quickly," said Soren. Harrison nodded in agreement, though she knew nothing of what Soren was about to say. "There have been further develop-ments, and we're right on top of them. We can't publish yet. But it'll be worth it when we do."

"You keep telling me that," spat Grey. "All I see is a woman laid up in hospital and a man supposedly working from home, but looking like he's just woken up."

Ward returned from the kitchen, and placed a cup of black coffee on the table in front of Soren. "I couldn't find any milk," she said.

"Who was that?" said Harrison. Grey peered into his screen, trying to get a better view.

Soren budged along the sofa and Amanda Ward sat down beside him, crowding into the view of the slate's camera. She was drying her hair with a tea towel.

Grey and Harrison froze.

"My source," said Soren, simply.

"Oh, right," said Grey.

"Wait, are you two..?" said Harrison.

"No. Jesus, no," said Ward. She turned to Soren: "No offence." He grunted. "I'm working with Curtis here to, er, set the record straight."

"Why didn't you let me know, Curtis?" said Grey.

"Because this runs deep, and I'm trying to understand the whole story. I'm not sure Amanda understands what's going on either."

Everyone was quiet for a few beats. Grey was the first to speak.

"With respect, Mrs Ward, I'm not sure we have grounds to believe much of what you say, however friendly you've become with my colleague. You ban the extremists, then give them a free rein; you resign, then claim you got sacked; then you disappear and MinSoc goes to ground. Why should we trust you now?"

"I didn't reverse my policy. They did it over my head. MinSoc chucked me out, literally. Godspeed has become the new national director at MinSoc. Something has changed on the social, and I can't get any contact.

"Curtis and I go back," she looked across to him, "so I think we can work together to get to the bottom of this."

Grey looked across at Soren, and the two attempted to meet eye-to-eye through the video exchange. "Well?" asked the editor.

"I think she's right, Will. This is all developing as we

speak, and with Amanda here we're in the best position to find out what's going on."

Harrison added: "And you're sure you two aren't just, in cahoots, as it were?"

"My husband and children have moved to a safe house, Mrs Harrison. I believe yours have been moved too. This is bigger than a story. Our safety is at stake. You of all people know that. People really don't want the truth to get out. Mr Grey, it might be worth talking to your own security people."

"We don't have any," Grey said.

"Then get some. Or at least inform the security at your building to be extra vigilant." The tone was so strident Soren was surprised that Grey didn't salute, with a 'yes, Ma'am!'

After more discussion, Grey agreed that Harrison would work to try to break open MinSoc somehow, and to look again at YoYo and its possible role in the overnight change in Ward's status. Soren and Ward would do an on-the-record interview, using what she knew to get to the bottom of what might be happening to her.

"Mrs Ward, with all due respect, I'm giving you the benefit of the doubt this afternoon," Grey told her. "And that's because I trust Curtis and Mia, not because I trust you."

He swiped away before Ward had a chance to respond.

With the slate blank, the two no longer needed to sit so close. Ward retreated to an easy chair, leaving Soren on the sofa. They sipped their coffee in silence.

"So, where do we go from here?" she said.

"We should do our on-the-record interview," Soren said.

"Something Harrison and Grey can work with, while we look deeper into what's happening."

"I've nothing to lose now," said Ward. "We might as well."

Soren opened the voice recorder on his slate, and it began to transcribe into a document as Amanda Ward spoke.

He asked her about her real history, digging for detail. She told him again about being Junior Dean at Mansfield, then being stalked and recruited by what became known as the Changemakers programme. How the recruiters already knew everything about her worth knowing, and told her they believed she had the knowledge, attitude and charisma needed to bring about real change.

"They?" asked Soren.

"There were programme leaders, but it was made clear the whole initiative was run by big technology companies. The forerunners of the social. The ones that became Portico."

"They had the money and the information, the data, to understand some of the biggest challenges individual countries were facing, as well as global issues. Occasionally, big names would come to speak to some of the Changemakers as a group, but also one-to-one. Big names in the social world. I must have heard live inspirational talks by the leaders of all the major tech companies. Occasionally we'd get a politician too.

"The impression they gave, though it was never written down, was that they had been asked by UN leaders to find a new way through for politics, for the environment, for tackling poverty. The social companies had the democratic mandate to bring about the best social outcomes, even if they weren't overt about it. By commissioning what became Changemakers, they could bring it about at arm's length."

Soren supposed it was the same way as MI5, MI6 and the other security services worked. Governments commissioned their security services to protect the country and its citizens, but did not necessarily have day-to-day control of each programme, decision or tactics. They had to trust in the professionals to carry out their business, however murky. In the same way, the social - via Changemakers - had been given a free reign.

The mention of the social prompted Soren. How much control was exerted there by Ministries?

"You saw I was able to stop negative messages and posts, those coming from hate speech, those containing specific racist or homophobic words, right?"

Soren nodded.

"Anything is possible. The algorithms can be written any way that's required. Do you really think I got all of those positive halos by myself? The social was programmed to support the changes I made and the negative comments..."

"Criticism of your policies?"

"Yes, they were tempered. The algorithms allowed a minor amount, so things didn't look strange, but lots of the negativity about my policies was automatically removed."

"So, you not only banned hate speech, but also any criticism of your policy to ban hate speech."

"Not quite. The algorithm makes the decisions. It's programmed to judge the amount of control it should exert in order to bring about the best outcome. The algorithm didn't ban negative posts about the policies, it just restricted how far those messages could spread and to whom. To stop negativity getting *out of hand*. Of course, there's human intervention, but for the most part decisions are made by the social itself. It has the data in real time, it can monitor change far faster than any Ministry or even YoYo. It can model various futures, and advise us on measures to take."

Soren was astonished. "You mean it automatically bans and gives permission without human oversight?"

"Not as I understand it. Humans still set the parameters. I still sat in room after room with colleagues and advisors. Together we decided what level of harm we should be looking out for. What words should be banned. Which organisations were a threat.

"The algorithm just munches up what we feed it, and produces the best outcome. Including control of the negative attitudes towards the decisions it's trying to implement. To protect those decisions, I guess."

"And with Changemakers on the case, you're always bound to tell the algorithm to do the right thing, that's the idea?"

"That's where I get confused," said Amanda. "There was a time when I believed it was that way. We used the social and its data to get the information we needed to make good decisions about the future of our projects. But now, it's as if the social is in charge, and we're the ones reacting to it.

"It was supposed to be our greatest tool, gifted to the world by Portico. We learned to use the data and the computer modelling it allowed, to make good decisions. "

"But now it's turned against you?" said Soren.

"That's not possible. It may have turned against me, personally, because that's what the computer modelling for the future of the UK might have suggested. But it seems unlikely that it would propose one thing - the banning of the dark web, the cleaning up of the socials - then immediately overturn that decision, and propose the exact opposite. And hang me out to dry at the same time."

Soren added: "Plus, presumably people, human beings, don't *have* to do what the computer models tell it to do?"

"Of course not. Remember, once the initial Change-makers programme was over, we were sent back to our own countries to try to change things using the methods and models we'd developed, the use of social media and data analytics methods, to help us. Programmers had written basic analytic code that could be adapted to new situations as we found them. I think I trod the right line."

"Then, there's only one conclusion," said Soren. "Someone is out to get you. YoYo has turned against its own prodigy. I think this is the work of Lucas Simmons. He's a prime candidate for changing the way the wind blows, and God knows he had the resources."

"Lucas?" said Ward. "That's not possible. He was my personal mentor. My primary contact with Changemakers. I did a video call with him before launching the social changes. He's a straight guy. Genuine. He's been my biggest champion among the Portico leaders."

"If he's your friend and has the power you've just told me about, then he should be able to call off the dogs."

"We should go and see him. First thing, tomorrow morning," said Ward.

"Amanda, if Portico *is* out to get you, that's one thing. But you're incredibly unpopular on the social feeds now too, from the left and the right. We need to tread very carefully. And I need your absolute trust."

"You have it."

"I told you yesterday that my wife died in a car crash where we met, and that the social helped the woman who killed her to get away with it and disappear."

"I'm so sorry, Curtis."

"What I didn't tell you was that my teenage daughter, Grace... she died a few months later."

"Oh my God, that's awful. I'm so, so sorry. What... happened?"

"I've not been able to talk about it, until now. I've always been trying to work out why it happened. She was found, in a remote barn."

He still couldn't say the words.

"Oh no, oh Curtis." Ward moved across to Soren, and laid an arm across his shoulders. His whole trunk had sunk low as he spoke.

He took some breaths, and ran his palms down his face as if to wake himself up. He stood suddenly.

"I need to show you something." He left the living room, returning quickly with his legacy slate. He sat next to Ward and brought up his profile.

"Absolute discretion, right?"

Soren swiped through the dark web channels, and arrived at the self harm and suicide section.

"Ever since, I've been looking for a clue to why it happened. What would drive her to do what she did. How I failed."

"Curtis..." she began again, sympathy in her voice.

He ignored her. "These channels have given me an idea, but it's hard to see through the sorrow. And the goading. Shit heads come on here to try to *persuade* kids to hurt themselves. It's sick. The pictures, I can barely look at them. But I've kept coming back. Again and again. It's like an addiction, you understand?"

Ward nodded. She awkwardly placed her hand on his, half in sympathy and half so she could peer closer at the slate's flashing cursor. He brushed her away.

"Last week, I discovered this new channel." He typed in *TowardsDeath. "I thought it might be something useful."

He confirmed his choice, and a string of historical comments appeared.

Vitriol. Hatred. Numerous mentions of Blue Team. And threats. Threats against Amanda Ward and her family. And against Soren. Harrison and her family too.

Ward gasped as she read the comments, swiping at the slate to reveal more and more.

"What the hell is this?"

"To-Wards-Death - it's a channel on the dark web dedicated to," Soren paused for a moment, not quite able to say it, "dedicated to hatred of you and your policies."

"Oh God, this is awful," she said, frantically looking around, as if searching for Tom.

"Most of it is just sounding off, but some of it contains specifics. Your movements. Mine. Some of the posters on here knew about, maybe even planned, the attack on Mia."

"And you knew about it all the time? You could have prevented the attack."

"No, I couldn't. I only discovered it later that night. But I tried to tell the police afterwards. But couldn't reveal that I use *this*," he indicated his legacy slate. "You have some role to play in that, Amanda - zero tolerance, in any circumstances, ran your line. I've been monitoring it secretly, trying to keep on top of how real the threat is.

"And now the social is live again for the haters, they're venting online, and judging by the number of new posts on this TowardsDeath channel, they've been invigorated by their new found freedom."

The pair took a few minutes to browse the newest posts. Many of them, Soren told her, were reiterations of what he had seen before. But the change in MinSoc's social policy had clearly prompted a new attitude. Haters had been given freedom to hate again, and some had taken this as permission to take direct action against Ward.

Ward mumbled each one as she read them.

MinSoc bitch two faced, like we all knew she was

We win Ward, but she tried to wipe us out. Your turn now.

Where's her security guard now?

Ripe for the picking

Blue Team, assemble. Thoughts?

She turned to Soren. "Wow, people really hate me."

"No, it's not like that," said Soren. "Just a few angry freaks gathered in the one place. There's loads out there who love what you did, but they wouldn't chat about it here."

"And who is this Blue Team?" she asked.

"Crowd mentality, I'd guess. You should know all about that, from your PhD."

"Yes, I suppose so," she responded, after a moment. "Maybe some of the extremists on here have given themselves a name, a shared identity. Like a messed up version of Changemakers. But they don't have the capacity to question their own views, so congregate with others who won't challenge them. The classic echo chamber."

"They have theirs, we have ours. And no better place to echo than in the dark web," said Soren.

"Do you think they're a real threat?"

"I think they knew about Mia's attack, even if they didn't carry it out. It could be just three blokes in a pub, for all we know. Maybe they've never even met."

They continued to read, reaching the most recent posts.

Anyone know her current location?

Negative, but scouts are out and about.

"This is really scary, Curtis. We should call the police."

"What, and tell them we've spent the last half hour on the dark web? That'll go down lovely on the socials: the dark web you were in the process of eradicating. No one can know I have this access."

Ward stood and paced the room.

"I need to stay here. It's not safe out there. For either of us. It's dark. I'll take your bed. You can sleep on the sofa." She spoke quickly, jumbling her words together.

"Thanks very much," he shook his head at the gall of the woman.

"Jesus, I need a drink. What have you got?"

"I have McCrackens."

"Then I'll take a double." She waited, still pacing. Eventually Soren rose from the sofa and made for the kitchen, bringing back two glasses and a full bottle.

"I need to message Roger, let him know where I am. And Lucas Simmons, I'll arrange to see him tomorrow. Shit, how are we going to get there?"

Evidently, she expected the chief executive of YoYo to drop his work at her demand, despite her newfound social status as public enemy number one. Soren was impressed.

"Let's not get too panicked," he said, pouring the whisky. He handed her a glass. "If Blue Team wanted to harm you, they'd need to know where you are. And they're far less likely to attack in the day time. Simmons could just send a car. Let's try to get a bit of perspective."

They both sat and took a deep slug of the Scotch. "This'll help," she said.

Later, Ward took a shower. Soren gave her a pair of enormous jogging bottoms his wife had bought him but he'd never used and a decades old Radiohead t-shirt to wear in bed. While she was dressing, she'd video messaged with her husband and messaged Lucas Simmons. The YoYo chief executive hadn't yet replied.

She returned to the living room, and curled her legs under her on the sofa. Soren had made some more toast, the only food in the house, and the two drank and laughed a little about how earnest some of the pop bands had been back in the late 90's and early 2000's. The conversation came to a stop when it came full circle to Amy Winehouse in 2011, and the topic of how many musicians had died by their own hands. It was the year before Soren's daughter had been born.

"I really am sorry about your wife and daughter," Ward said, looking more comfortable with her hair now dry and loose, whisky in her belly. "When you're at my end - always looking at the good the social can do - you miss the damage we leave behind. I'm learning that the hard way now, aren't I?"

"It's not your fault, Amanda. The social and I, we just don't *fit*. I'll never be comfortable with it, because it robbed me of my family. It let the woman who killed Lucy off the hook. That I'll never forgive. But I'm living in a different age to what I knew. Just coping as best I can.

"There's just one thing I need to know," he added.

Ward waited.

"How do you delete yourself? The woman who killed Lucy. She disappeared. Her profile gone. Her messages disappeared. If we're all so embroiled in the social, how can she just have deleted herself?"

Ward stiffened a little.

"It would have been part of her relocation, her re-identity. The Ministry of Society and Communications has the power to instruct companies in the social to delete - or at least archive - certain accounts. For the sake of her safety, she would have needed pictures of her to be deleted, any implication of where her family lived."

"So you still have her original information? And where she was relocated to?" said Soren.

"I did have, before this morning. Now I'm locked out. But I wouldn't have given it to you in any circumstances. It would be highly illegal," Soren could tell she was treading carefully, "and unethical. She has a right to privacy. Remember, she was never convicted of anything..."

Soren interrupted. "She was guilty as hell, and got off exactly because of her status, the pressure of her followers."

"It's the way the justice system works, Curtis. There's nothing I can do about it. I'm so sorry, but I just couldn't."

She paused, before continuing: "I'm not sure I know anything anymore. There was a time when I thought I'd achieved national director by myself. Now, I'm not so sure whether I was just part of someone else's plan. From the moment I was recruited to Changemakers, maybe I gave up my freedom to think for myself."

"You're a very smart woman, Amanda. You were recruited for a reason."

"Recruited and used." She stared at the floor.

He held up the bottle, but she shook her head.

"No, you're right." He screwed the top onto the Scotch and took it to the kitchen. "Long day tomorrow."

There was a moment's uncomfortable silence between them.

"It's fine, Amanda, I've slept on this sofa more times than I've slept on that bed."

She stood and went into the bathroom, pulling the door closed behind her.

Soren considered his legacy slate. He could check out his usual haunts, once Amanda had gone to bed. But that would mean more whisky. More sadness. And the chance of being caught.

Amanda had brought a little warmth into his apartment. He realised she had been his first and only visitor. The first time he'd allowed someone even close to his personal space since Grace had gone. He felt guilt and sorrow, but also somehow a little lighter.

He closed the blinds, took a blanket from the cupboard, and lay down in an attempt to sleep.

23

Soren awoke to the sound of a knock at the window. Dragging himself from sleep, it took some time to realise how unlikely that was. A knock on a glass window, fifteen feet above ground.

The single knock came again, this time a little louder. He waited for his eyes to adjust to the dim light cast through the blind from the street. And for the grog from his sleep to ebb away. It was heading for midnight.

Knock.

There was no doubt about it. There was someone there, and they wanted in.

Stiff, he sat up on the sofa, then stood and made his way to the window and the blinds he'd pulled across. He bent open two slats to look between them, and gazed down to the street.

The large grey rock came whizzing towards him, bouncing off the double glazing, leaving the glass cracked. He stumbled back with the shock, tripped over and fell awkwardly against the coffee table with a huge bump as he hit the floor.

The next rock broke the window entirely, but the shatterproof glass left the shards intact and in place in the window pane. For now.

"Come out you fuckers," Soren heard from the street below him, as he lay on the floor below the window. He'd taken a blow to the temple from the corner of the coffee table. It hurt like hell.

Another solid object hit the window and the shattered glass began to fall out of the pane. Then Soren heard his door buzzer being pressed repeatedly, and heavy knocking on the front door of the building. Or was it someone's boot?

The buzzing continued. Again and again.

His bedroom door opened, and Amanda Ward stepped through.

"Curtis, what the hell...?" She turned on the living room light.

"Get down," he shouted.

She dropped to the floor, crying out a little. On her hands and knees, she moved the few metres over to Soren.

"You're bleeding," she said. "What's happening?"

He shushed her. "I don't know. But you've just let them know there's someone home."

Soren began to hear the entrance buzzers of other apartments going off. If someone let them through the front entrance, the next door they'd be kicking in would be his.

"Stay here," he said. He wasn't used to being an action hero. "Get under the table or something."

Instead, she followed him as he crawled towards his front door. He pushed across a security bolt at the bottom.

"The table?" It was Ward's suggestion, and a good one.

The buzzing continued, and so did the stones - sometimes very big stones - hitting the window. That meant there were at least two attackers.

Together, on their knees, they heaved the long, heavy coffee table towards the door, and propped it up on its side. It wasn't much, but it was something.

Soren leant against the wall, and pulled himself up by the door handle to steady himself. His mind whirled, and he slightly stumbled with dizziness from the head injury. He swiped the security screen, taking care to avoid opening the building entrance. He looked at the screen from the left, to ensure the camera couldn't see him.

A man with an iron rod, perhaps a crow bar, was intermittently bashing on the front door of the building, then pressing all the buzzers, saving an extra long one for his own apartment.

Suddenly, the man realised he was being watched and pressed his face up to the security camera. It came out as a wide, fishbowl image on Soren's screen. He was wearing a dark scarf around the bottom of his face, and a beanie hat on his head. And his eyes. They were narrowed in anger, and bloodshot with booze.

"Come out, you shit heads," he snarled. "I know you're in there and it's been a long time coming. Come out and get it, or we'll come in and give it to you. Either way, it's going down tonight."

Soren looked at Ward; she returned his glance. What now? Soren sure as hell wasn't going to buzz the guy in. Ward pulled herself up against the wall, pulled up her knees and buried her head between them.

The buzzing and the banging on the door below began again, and Soren swiped off.

"Aren't you trained for this kind of thing?" Soren asked Ward, as he slid down the wall next to her.

"What, hiding from nutcases determined to 'give it to

me'? No, we got basic self defence training at the Ministry, but I had security. I could swipe for backup…"

"Then swipe for it, for God's sake."

"But I'm no longer part of the Ministry, and don't come under their protection. They took my work slate away."

They'd been under attack for over five minutes and it wasn't getting any less intense.

"Then it's the police," said Soren. The glass took another blow, and shards fell into the room. The moment one of the neighbouring residents opened that front door, the stakes would rise considerably. A little more determined with that knowledge, Soren shuffled across to the sofa and picked up his work slate.

But it was too late. Soren heard the door downstairs bang open. It has either been opened by another resident, or a final whack with the crow bar had knocked the lock clean off. The rock throwing at the window stopped abruptly, only to be replaced by clumping footsteps up the stairs. At least two, probably three people. With one thing in mind.

Soren ran to the kitchen, and took a sharp steak knife from a draw. At the front door, he handed Ward a bread knife. He ran back to his slate, but his front door was already being pounded.

"Time to pay, bitch," a voice shouted from the other side, followed by a heavy swipe of the crowbar that made the door hinges rattle.

He ran over to where Ward was sitting, and pressed his back up against the table blocking the doorway. He opened his slate, and swiped for the emergency services. Before he could call, he heard the screech of tyres outside his building and car doors slamming.

Soren and Ward looked at each other in panic. *More of them.* They heard footsteps pounding up the stairs.

"STOP! Lay that bar down, so help me God I'll taze you." It was a woman's voice.

The banging abruptly stopped.

"Fuck you, copper."

"Both of you. Put your weapons down, and put your hands up." A male voice this time.

"Fucking black pig."

"Your choice." Then the sound of a man screeching in pain, as a heavy lump suddenly hit the floor.

"Hands up? That's good. Now, turn around and put your hands against the wall. Nice and slow. My colleague has her weapon aimed right at your balls."

They heard the jingle of metal, a thump against the wall, then a screech - the sound of a man whose arms were being twisted painfully behind his back. Then a reassuring ratchet sound that could only be handcuffs being pushed into place.

Silence.

Then a buzz at the door.

"Mr Soren, are you in there? Mrs Ward?"

He sat silently against the oak table.

"Mr Soren, this is PC Ryan Woodside from the Metropolitan Police. My colleague PC Toni Osei and I are going to take these scumbags downstairs and put them to bed. You should both wait here, with the door locked, until backup arrives."

Soren sat silently.

"Do you understand, Sir? Mrs Ward?"

He rose, and pressed the intercom. He swiped the screen. "Yes, thank you, we understand." The police officer peered closer to the screen.

"Are you hurt, sir?"

"I fell, that's all."

"Okay, stay put. We need to check the area, my colleagues will be arriving soon. I shall call an ambulance too, to check out that injury."

There was a great sound of shuffling, and some resistance from the attackers. Soren watched his screen as cuffs were put on the fallen man, who was beginning to recover from his tazeing but hadn't regained enough strength to fight. The officers pushed and dragged them down the stairs. The female officer gave one of them a minor punch in the guts.

In time, Soren heard his neighbours opening their doors, chatting about what had gone on. Someone knocked on his door, but he ignored them.

"I thought we'd be safe here," stuttered Ward, as she rose from her crouch beside the door. "Thank God you got through to the police."

Soren stumbled, and eventually sat on the sofa. "I didn't. They just turned up."

She went to the kitchen, ran a tea towel under the cold tap, and brought it to him. He folded it and pressed it against his forehead. Blood leaked across his eye and nose as he pressed.

He saw the look on her face, questioning.

"I didn't swipe the police. Someone else from the building must have."

"But they knew your name. The exact flat under attack. They knew I was here."

Soren sat staring at the floor, shaking his head. Blood dripped onto the carpet. The shock was starting to be replaced by searing pain across his left temple, and a pounding behind his eyes.

I need a drink.

In a short time, the pair heard more sirens in the distance, coming closer. New blue lights began to flash beneath the window, and Ward took a look out. The arresting officers were leaving, and an ambulance had arrived, along with two more officers - a man and a woman. No one seemed in much of a rush. On Ward's suggestion, Soren took the opportunity to place his legacy slate into his bedroom bottom drawer.

Eventually, his door buzzer sounded and he looked at the screen before allowing Detective Inspector Miran Burman and Sergeant Leanne Lee through the door.

While the paramedics patched up Soren's head, cleaning out the wound and attaching a few butterfly stitches, Burman helped himself to a straight backed chair and sat close to where Soren was being treated. Lee stood by the door, as if overseeing the whole scene.

"You want to tell me what happened?"

Soren braced himself against the pinching of skin, as the paramedic went about her work.

"We were attacked in my home. First, they were throwing great big stones through the window, then they tried to kick my door in."

"And Amanda Ward was staying here tonight?"

"For my safety," Ward said. "We'd identified there was a threat. I've been moved out of MinSoc, so lost my security."

"And your family?"

"Moved to a safe house," she said. "But the threat increased and I couldn't get out to them."

"I see." He didn't seem convinced.

"There was a credible threat against Amanda's life, perhaps mine too. I told you that, but you wouldn't listen," said Soren. "So I invited her to stay. I was trying to call you when we were attacked. But I get the feeling you were already on your way?"

"We may have had our eye on the property, on the threat," said Burman. He was choosing his words carefully. "But we had to be certain it was a real threat, so we take them down in the act."

"Take who down?" said Ward.

"Blue Team," said Burman simply.

"Blue Team?" said Ward.

"Now, we both know that's something you two don't want to talk about, don't we?" said Burman.

The paramedic kept her head down, securing a bandage around Soren's head with medical tape. Soren guessed lots of conversations between police and victims or perpetrators of crime went on over paramedics' heads.

Burman took more details of the attack, then stayed with Ward and Soren while Sergeant Lee took statements from others in the building. She returned to the apartment, and the officers compared notes.

"I think there's enough here to convict the thugs, certainly to keep them in custody. A forensic team will come to take pictures of your window and bashed in door."

"Do you think we need more protection?" asked Ward.

"Your family are secure, so is Mrs Harrison at St George's. This is a crime scene, and our intelligence suggests the perpetrators of the attack are in custody. All I can offer you is a cell at the station, if you want one."

"Not very intimate," Sergeant Lee added.

Burman gave her a reprimanding glance.

"You can give us a lift in your car," said Ward. "Head for the station, but I'll book us separate hotel rooms close by and you can drop us off."

As usual with Amanda Ward, it wasn't a question.

24

From the Bedford Hotel, close to Russell Square in central London, Soren and Ward took a TriCab out towards the east. They'd both slept late, then Soren had showered and changed his bandage to a spare one that the paramedic had left with him the night before.

They met at breakfast but were consumed in their slates. Soren was updating Harrison, sharing information about the attack and Blue Team, though he wouldn't tell her how he'd originally found out about them. She said she'd do some more research, and begin to work up a story. She'd also pass the information on to Grey, to see where he wanted to take it.

Harrison was still convinced YoYo was behind the massive drop in Amanda Ward's popularity, and they agreed the threat now meant pinning down Simmons was a priority.

Ward told Soren she'd been in touch with her husband and kids, and then with the diary secretary of Lucas Simmons. She had, she said, special status and could be very persuasive among his entourage. After all, she may have lost her job at MinSoc, but she was still a Change-maker. And Lucas Simmons' Changemaker at that.

"He's in London, and should be around the Village today," she told Soren over coffee and pastries. Soren took his usual, though hotel cinnamon loops were never as good or as fresh as Carlos'. "I've told his diary secretary I'm heading over, and he better make time for us."

"I suggest we keep the use of these to the minimum," said Soren, indicating his slate. "My guess is that YoYo is monitoring us both. How likely is it that someone with the right software could pinpoint our location right now?"

"One hundred percent," said Ward. "Geolocation has been possible without the consent of users for over a decade."

"What if we turn off our slates?"

"A little more difficult," she said. "It would leave a trace of our last movement, to this hotel. But it depends if anyone's looking for us: hackers, secret service, or one of the social companies, theoretically they could switch on our slates remotely and track us, if they got to them before we turned them off."

"So no point in just leaving them here then?"

"Not if we've already been hacked. And anyway, we pretty much need them to get anywhere and do anything." Ward shook her head. "We're slaves to them, and to the social…"

"Now you're seeing things from my perspective," said Soren. "Do you remember pounds and pence? Paying for things with the money in your pocket?" He indicated his slate. "Don't you wish we could just dump them? Go back a few decades and rethink?".

"In ten years' time, we'll be pining for *these* things," said Ward. She held up her own slate. "We'll be wishing the government couldn't read our minds, or that we'd not made the move to Mars because we thought the schools were better there."

Soren smiled, though his stomach twisted a little with the mention of schools. Family decisions. He took a big chunk of cinnamon loop, and spoke with his mouthful: "Let's hope some things never change." He held up the pastry, and crumbs dropped into his lap.

The TriCab pulled up to the entrance of the main YoYo building. The receptionist welcomed them by name, though Soren suspected he had pictures of them both on his screen and had been instructed to look out for them. He might even have been tracking their route towards the Village.

"Mr Simmons has made a space in his diary for you this morning, and has invited you to wait for him in our guest room."

Soren expected a small waiting room, but instead they were led directly to his office and the middle room where Soren and the chief executive had met before. Coffee had been provided.

They took their drinks to a large LCD screen, where today's news feeds were scrolling. Soren noticed headline news of his attack. Details were slim. The police had obviously not leaked, so Harrison's story was the only one getting traction: another of SkyCloud's most popular news-gatherers had been attacked by two thugs, but details of any motive were unknown. They were expected to be remanded in custody, while investigations continued.

Amanda Ward was not mentioned.

"Thanks for keeping my name out of it," Ward said as

they read the feed together. "I just want to disappear from the social for a while, let it all die down. Then I can bring my family home and we can decide what to do next with our lives."

"You're in the right place for that," said Soren. "Simmons can make you disappear completely."

She whispered: "There's no way he's done anything to harm my reputation."

"So, why are you whispering?" asked Soren, mocking her hushed tone.

"I'm not!" she said, overloud.

"Not what?"

The two turned from the screen to see Lucas Simmons. He was standing two metres behind them, pretending to read the feeds, but looking rather pleased with himself for surprising them.

Amanda Ward span round and Soren watched her almost leap towards Simmons and hug him. He held her tight, then at arm's length, a hand on each shoulder: a *haven't you grown* gesture of affection.

"Good to see you Amanda."

"It's been a couple of months," she said. "Nearly half a year, face-to-face."

"You've been doing very well at MinSoc."

"Until yesterday," she said. His face didn't flinch.

"And Mr Soren, very good to see you again."

Ward whipped round to look at Soren in the eye. "Again? You two know each other?"

"Only professionally," said Simmons. "Mr Soren came to interview me for a story. We left on good terms, didn't we

Curtis? Though, looks like you've had a recent disagreement with someone?"

Soren smiled, but said no more.

Simmons tried again: "What happened to you Amanda? Harry Godspeed has taken over?" He sounded genuinely concerned.

"That's what we're here to speak to you about," said Ward.

They took a seat.

Soren was first to speak: "Mr Simmons, last night Amanda and I were attacked. We think it was the result of her being suddenly made *persona non grata* on the social. The right wingers are free to attack her, and the lefties who admired her policies now hate her because they think she turned them over."

"We're not saying..." interjected Ward.

"We think the social is screening out anything positive about Amanda," said Soren. "As of this morning, Harry Godspeed is national director of MinSoc. All of a sudden it's halos for him all round. You have both told me it's possible to screen out comments, and we think YoYo - you, Mr Simmons - have something to do with this."

"I can assure you I don't," said Simmons, sitting up straight.

"Then someone else at YoYo?" attempted Ward.

"Not under my watch, Amanda. You know how committed I've been to you from the start. Any changes to the coding need to go directly through me, and our last move together was to ban those ten negative groups, and to set up the models to monitor and measure feedback."

"Well, someone in this Village has reversed that," said Soren. "The groups are back, and they're angry." He indicated his head. "My colleague was attacked too."

"I understand that, and you're right. I don't understand how the algorithms can have turned against you, without my intervention. But I too have seen a pronounced change this morning."

"So you've lost control of your own creation," said Soren.

"I've been in meetings all night and all this morning; we're trying to figure out how the social could have just created a U-turn as large as this with no human intervention."

"Explain that to us," said Ward.

"It's very complicated."

"We have all the time in the world."

Simmons sighed, and swiped his screen to cancel upcoming meetings. He asked the staff to bring more coffee, then to leave the room.

"I am presuming, at this point, Amanda, that you have told Mr Soren about our little project."

She nodded.

"Your anti democratic takeover of the world, yes she has," said Soren.

"That all depends on your perspective," said Simmons.

"Looks like it's working just fine, right now," said Soren, sitting back in his chair, crossing his legs and throwing his arms behind his head.

The three waited in silence. Ward offered Soren a look that he read as: *are you finished?*

Eventually Simmons continued: "The social was used strategically, but our main use of it wasn't to silence opposing voices. It was to bolster up the changes that we were proposing. And that always required human intervention. This isn't some scifi film. The robots are not in control."

Ward spoke up: "So if it's not the robots, it's a bad guy, right? Someone interfering with the social. Because I can't see why it could have turned against me so vociferously, nor so quickly."

"Rapidity, I can understand," said Simmons. "Things can move extremely fast on the social. It's thousands of chess boards running 24 hours a day, with millions of moves every second. Move your piece, and you've got checkmate before you've taken your hand away. But the change in the code, the turning against a particular individual, that would take someone to intervene."

"Someone in this Village, most likely," said Soren. "If not you. There's a lot at stake here, Mr Simmons, you've told me that yourself. You said you were worried about loss of control. Well, here it is, right in front of you."

Soren saw Ward's cross face, and observed her and Simmons exchange glances.

"I've told you, not in YoYo," said Simmons. "Change-makers was set up for the good. And Portico designed parts of the social to support it. I would never allow anything that would harm those aims."

Soren shook his head.

Simmons added: "Looks like I'm going to have to prove that to you."

He stood up and headed towards his private office space, beckoning them to follow. He swiped his slate against a sensor, and the door slid open. The glass wall opposite gave a view out over the branded fountain at the entrance to the whole YoYo complex.

Simmons took a picture frame from the wall and handed it to Soren.

"My name," he said, suddenly in a heavy eastern European accent, "is Lukas Simionis. This is my family. My grandfather here in the picture, Rokas Simionis, was one of the richest men in Lithuania. A giant in the fertiliser and pesticide industry. Simionis is a brand for farming goods in my home country."

Soren wasn't sure whether the YoYo boss was hamming up his accent, or merely relaxing his London tones.

"I came here in 2017, after the cauliflower revolution in my country," he continued.

Ward smiled, Soren laughed out loud then checked himself.

"*Kalafiorų revoliucija*. You may smile, but it was an important moment in my nation. A poor woman posted on Facebook about the outrageous price she had to pay for a single head of cauliflower. It marked the rapidly increasing price of simple goods in Lithuania, while salaries stayed the same.

"This in a country that was relatively rich among its neighbours. My grandfather and father were selling fertiliser all over Europe. The country was exporting produce at a high price, rather than feeding its own people. The post went viral. It started a revolution among the poor. A three day boycott of the biggest supermarkets. The government was spooked. They restructured the economy to make food affordable for the poorest.

"I was astounded by what the social had done in my country. It empowered people. Gave them a voice. I wanted to be part of this. So I came to the UK to get work in social media. Of course, with my father's money it wasn't difficult. But I worked hard. When I became more senior in YoYo, I found out about Changemakers and supported it. I became a mentor to Amanda. Eventually I became chief executive."

Simmons pulled another frame from the wall. He handed it to Amanda Ward.

It was a map of Lithuania. He leant over, and pointed to a small town in the southwest.

"Vilkaviškis," he said, sadly. "The home of the revolution. My home. And also the home of Rasalina Mazeika."

"The murdered girl?" said Soren. "You knew her?"

Ward took Simmons' arm in a comforting gesture.

"No, she was from the poorer district of Vilkaviškis, of course. And I, from the rich suburbs. But she *could* have been my sister. My wife. My own daughter. But for luck and money."

The three stared at the family picture. Soren imagined an extra woman in the image, the face featured in the over shared picture of Rasalina Mazeika in recent months. The talk of the social. Sensationalised. Dehumanised. Exploited.

Soren spoke: "And so this explains your about turn on social media. Why you finally agreed to implement Amanda's requests. To try to get rid of the dark web."

"Yes," Simmons said simply. "And why I wanted someone new to come in, to guide us. Someone who was not in love with the social as much as I thought I was."

A fully branded YoYo car took Simmons, Soren and Ward across the Village, and dropped them at the entrance to one of the large warehouses. Soren remembered this was where many of the coders were situated.

"You both, of course, know Adisa Zane," said Simmons as they disembarked. The driver of coding was waiting for them at the doors. He greeted them warmly, though Ward appeared surprised that Soren had already met the man personally.

Zane led them to a demonstration office. He docked his slate on the desk, and the display filled a large screen covering most of the far wall. Zane typed in three different passcodes, which all appeared as asterisks on the main screen.

"Amanda, can you recall when you first noticed the social appeared to have taken against you?" asked Simmons.

"As soon as I was ejected from the building at MinSoc. I was given ten minutes to leave the building, and I took a few minutes to look at the socials before packing up. Then they took my slate away."

"So, what time was that?" asked Zane.

"I don't know. Around half past ten?"

Zane looked at Simmons, who had turned to him.

Simmons said: "Can you be more specific, Amanda? Was it any earlier than ten thirty?"

"No, let's call it ten thirty a.m."

Zane swiped away at his slate, and various feeds began to scroll down the screen at breakneck speed.

"These are all the messages sent via our servers in the first minute from ten thirty yesterday," said Zane. "As you can see, there's many thousands of them. Now..." he worked away, swiping and mumbling to himself, "if we pin down any that mention you as a hashtag..." the messages slowed up to a trickle, "... we can see that - sorry - you're not very popular at that time yesterday."

Ward balked at the slurs.

#AmandaWard. Sack the Nat Director for u-turn

Which way is the wind blowing today #AmandaWard?

Bitch #AmandaWard backs down on Social

Simmons said, "I'm sorry you have to see this, Amanda."

"Can we go back in time?" asked Soren.

"Yes, it's a blunt instrument, but..." he swiped again. "Now the feeds are running from nine thirty. No particular negative emojis or words highlighted for hashtag Amanda Ward. Just neutral, or halos. Fast forward a little...."

The four watched the screen mesmerised, as hashtags about Amanda Ward scrolled up the screen at a rate slightly faster than they were able to read.

"There," Simmons called out.

Zane swiped his screen, and the feeds paused. Dotted around the comments were little red devil emojis and yellow angry faces.

"Now, back up," he said.

Zane swiped up the screen, and the messages travelled down. The first devil emoji appeared at two minutes past ten. Yesterday morning.

Why reverse a good thing, #AmandaWard. We hoped for better from you. 👿

Others had picked up the thread, sharing or adding their own negative opinions.

"That's the first reaction to the changes you announced. If we back up some more..." said Simmons.

Zane obliged, and the screen scrolled up again.

10.00 a.m.

MinSoc: Freedom of speech to be allowed on the socials. #AmandaWard says ban was mistake.

"I never did that!" Ward cried aloud. "I wasn't at my desk. I was..."

"Where?" said Simmons.

"I was with Curtis."

"I don't understand," Simmons responded.

Soren responded: "Amanda and I had a meeting, where I told her we were about to do a scoop about her past. That's when she told me about Changemakers, and a little of the truth about how you and MinSoc were manipulating the social."

"Only, we were by ourselves," said Ward. "I couldn't have

approved such a change. I was completely out of touch. Unless?"

"Tom?" said Soren.

"He was listening to every word." Ward said it with a resigned tone. "At the crossroads, and in the back of the car."

Simmons offered a questioning glance.

"He's my bodyguard."

"Was," added Soren.

"And he doesn't have any power over the social. He's just a decent guy whose job it was to look after me."

"Could he have been asked to spy on you?" asked Soren.

"Spy?" responded Ward incredulously. "This isn't the Ministry of Security. His job was to protect me, not to be involved in the work I do. He certainly wouldn't have been in touch with any hackers."

Simmons stopped the sniping: "We need to look deeper, then. Adisa, if you would?"

"Can we assume a devil emoji in the same post as #AmandaWard would have been screened out previously?" Soren asked.

He watched Simmons and Ward look at each other, hesitation in their glance.

"Yes, I think we can," said Simmons eventually.

"Jesus," said Soren.

"It's what we have to work with," said Simmons.

Zane split the screen into two. The feeds they were looking at on the left, and a complex series of letters, numbers and symbols on the right.

Zane scrolled up the computer coding, looking for time stamps. There weren't many, he said, because the main code was very rarely interfered with. Only to fix glitches and bugs, or to implement official policies. His and his colleagues' business wasn't to ask why, but to make the code changes that were required.

"Here," he said. "Compare the right and left hand of the screen."

The group stared at the right hand side of the screen, and then the left. Soren and Ward were unclear what they were looking at. About fifteen minutes before MinSoc had announced Ward's U-turn, there were a five or six paragraphs of numbers, symbols and words.

Zane approached the big screen and indicated a particular line buried in one of the paragraphs:

=("#AmandaWard" + ">:(" = permitted; ":innocent:" = notpermitted); ref: syntax 'permitted rules'

"This line," he said, "changes what's allowed to be said alongside the hashtag #AmandaWard. It reverses a previous ban on using a devil symbol, and stops the use of an angel emoji. The reference to permitted rules refers to another algorithm which prevents that post from appearing on our social platform."

Soren noticed Ward looked as confused as he was.

"This whole screen of text is altering how messages about you, Amanda, and your policies, are treated. This line is clearer, but most of the code is pulling phrases and rules from existing databases, and comparing them to make decisions about what should be stopped from publication."

"And it's that easy to interrupt someone's life," said Ward. "A few lines of code."

"You're not so keen now that you're on the receiving end," muttered Soren.

"It's not quite *easy*," said Simmons. "There are a very limited number of people who are able to make changes of this magnitude, and no coder can do it by themselves. They would have to be senior coders and have to be mirrored, like I explained to you, Curtis, last time you were here. They would be facing each other, checking each other's work. In this case, not just for mistake free coding, but that they were instructing the algorithm to do what they have been asked to do.

"And coding at this level would have to have someone of my own seniority in the room to sign off changes, using our own personal passwords," said Zane. "A rogue coder, working by themselves, just isn't possible at YoYo."

They all gazed at the code, as it sat there in white on black. It was somehow quite beautiful, like a leather encased book, thought Soren. Text running from line to line, leaving flowing wave like edges, broken up into separate groups.

'Words have more power than atom bombs.' Soren thought that might have been Einstein, but it could just as well be something he'd remembered from a film he watched as a kid. Either way, he'd posted it above his desk when he was an idealistic young journalist. Now he wondered whether lines of computer code had taken their place. If so, who had their finger on the button?

"So, someone here has made the changes, but you claim it wasn't under your watch," he said.

Simmons agreed. "A change like that would had to have come via me at least. Adisa, can you pull up access privileges?"

Zane returned to his seat, and swiped to open up a third column on the screen. Once again he scrolled to line up the timestamps of the changed code, and the MinSoc announcement.

"Much of this is everyday stuff coming from YoYo," he said, as he closed in on 9.15 a.m. "See the owner configuration codes 'T354-Reg' and 'T354-Mir'." Zane highlighted a few examples.

"That's a pair of coders in my office logging in to do some routine code cleaning." He continued scrolling up and down. "But this is strange."

He stopped, and highlighted a short line on the screen.

'09.30.32; E256-Sen'

"Isn't that a coding entry from Gum?" asked Simmons.

"I think so, but it doesn't have a mirror and it doesn't have a senior approval," said Zane. "And they logged out ten minutes later."

"Let me guess, the changes were made while they had access to the code." It was Ward who spoke.

Zane highlighted the MinSoc announcement, the change in code and the login and logout of 'E256-Sen'. They all lined up, with the MinSoc announcement happening just ten minutes after the coder had added the changes and logged out.

"Someone at Gum created the change," said Simmons. "But completely out of our usual security protocols."

"I don't understand," said Soren. "You said you had to approve high level changes to the social?"

"I do," said Simmons, "particularly when it pertains to events in sovereign issues. But it looks as if someone in Gum, in the United States, is interfering with our code."

"Shit, I have to warn Harry Godspeed," said Amanda suddenly. "He's taken over from me, so he's likely to get Tom as his bodyguard."

"Hold on," Soren turned to her. "If Harry Godspeed is within MinSoc, couldn't he be behind having you sacked? I imagine he knows the whole story."

"No," Ward snapped back. "Not Harry. It's the government that does the hiring and firing, he'd have no power to do that. Cover tracks, sure - we all do that, as you've seen. But only a Minister can hire and fire. Gum must be in league with a Minister somehow.

"And anyway, Harry would never - " she paused abruptly. She looked towards Simmons for assistance. Soren spotted it.

"Let me guess," Soren said. "Harry Godspeed is a Changemaker too."

25

Visiting time at St George's was nearly over when Soren arrived. Harrison was sitting up in an easy chair, wearing a sling over her right arm and with a plumped up cushion behind her back to prevent too much pressure on her fractured ribs.

"I'm just about ready to scream," she said, as he walked in. "These four walls are *making* me ill. I need to get back home and into the office. See something other than doctors and nurses, and hospital food."

"I brought you coffee," said Soren. He lay a cup on the side board and a paper bag containing shortbread from Carlos'.

"Any joy contacting Godspeed?" he asked.

"No, MinSoc is giving us the cold shoulder again. I've tried to dig more into his background, but his MinSoc biog is all surface. He's supposed to have spent time in Slovenia, but I couldn't find any evidence of him like I did with Amanda Ward. Can't prove he wasn't there, can't prove he was. No story, except that he must have stabbed Ward in the back pretty good to get to national director so quick."

"Ward claims not," said Soren. He closed the door. "Turns out he's a Changemaker too. They go back, she brought him into Changemakers when he joined the civil service. They're all in this secret club together, scratching each other's backs. With Ward thrown out of MinSoc, he's her natural heir. Changemakers stays in play."

"Lies within lies," said Harrison. "Makes for a better story."

"Only we can't publish it. We need to bring him on board. I suggest we use it, like I did with Ward, to get an admission. Ward's going to try to contact him."

"Sounds like you've been busy?"

"Do you have time to hear the whole story?"

She indicated her arm. "Where else am I going?"

Soren explained what had happened that morning, and how Gum was now the prime suspect in turning on Ward and changing the social's policy on hate speech.

One way or another, it had released the rage that had led to the attack on him and Ward in his apartment. It was likely the same group that had attacked Harrison before the change in policy, had now felt empowered to act more overtly. With positive news about Ward effectively banned on the social, and negative messages practically encouraged, the danger to Ward, and towards Soren and Harrison, was increased.

At least the police were now aware of the threat. Ward was about to be shipped out to be with her husband at a safe house, with some police protection in tow. From there, she would keep in touch.

She'd also promised to contact as many other Change-makers as she could. They'd be interested in what was happening to the great project, she had said, and many would be keen to help. Some might even go on the record, now everything was in flux.

"The next step was to pin down exactly who is in control of the social," Soren said. "YoYo thought it was, but they've discovered the code is being manipulated by others too. The whole Changemakers project, if not Portico itself, seems to be falling apart."

"Which is no bad thing for democracy," said Harrison.

"We've all been lied to for so long," said Soren. "Our own governments lied to us years ago and let the social companies take over. We need to expose that. I saw it today - they have unbelievable power. And our leaders gave it to them."

"This is starting to sound like the scoop of the century," said Harrison.

"If we can find out who's manipulating the code from the United States, and who's feeding Gum our information, it really is. Spies. Interference in the UK's sovereignty. Even our democracy at stake. It's a major scandal," said Soren.

"I want at it," said Harrison. "Instead, I'm stuck in here until this evening. They're going to release me, they say."

"You can still be pretty useful. I'll keep feeding you updates in real time, you write and tweak, keep Will happy. And when it's time, I promise, you get to push 'go'."

"I'll settle for that."

"In the meantime, I wanted to run something by you. And I know you're genius enough to help me find a way to make it happen."

Lucas Simmons pulled the blinds on his inner office, and locked the door with his slate. Outside his three compartment suite, a screen would have lit up warning that the chief executive of YoYo was not to be disturbed in any circumstances. He'd dismissed his personal secretary early, once she'd been instructed to make the connections he needed.

Simmons sat at his desk beneath the family photo and the map of his home country. He took a deep toke on a cigar flavoured vape, and waited for his slate to light up. Once it did, he wafted away the steam, and swiped open the conversation.

"Julian, very good to see you," he said. The name Julian Renfrew, CEO Talk, ran across the bottom of his video cast.

"Lucas, you too. It has been a while. But not too long that I can say I'm delighted to be meeting before I'm even in work. Could this not have waited until our next monthly conference call?"

"I don't think so. I'll explain in a moment."

Another face appeared on screen. Louise Burgher, CEO, Wonderfish.

"Louise, thanks for taking the call," said Simmons.

"Julian. Good to see you Lucas, though a little more notice would have been appreciated. No sign of..."

Another face appeared, with a ding on Simmons' slate. Bradley Leyton, CEO, Gum Corporation.

"Bradley, thanks for joining us."

"What the hell is this about, Simmons?"

"Thanks all of you for joining me. I do know it's an inconvenient time for you guys on the West Coast. It's the end of the day here for me. I appreciate your time and that this isn't part of our normal meeting schedule."

"Let's make it quick then, Lucas," said Renfrew.

"You'll all be aware of how turbulent politics has become suddenly over here in the UK," he said. "Our social has been flip flopping all over the place."

His compadres were quiet.

"I had my coders investigate some of the interventions in

social posting, and we've detected some illegal interference. Someone has been manipulating our codes, to support or turn against civil servants who work for our government."

"Illegal?" said Bradley Leyton.

"Well, not what we would all hope for," Simmons corrected himself. "Are we all on secure lines?"

The other three nodded.

"I think someone is attempting to influence the people of the UK, outside of the Changemakers programme. You know outside intervention is strictly banned, we agreed that from the start. Our agents can make minor changes, to promote certain policies, but wholesale change from outside compromises a country's sovereignty."

"You're saying someone has hacked the system," said Burgher. "I seriously doubt that. Our code security is the strongest in the world. We advise the US military on coding, for God's sake. Every penny people spend through the Wonderfish network is triple protected."

"I'm aware of that, but the fact is that our code here has been compromised. And we've been able to pin down the details."

Leyton quickly asked: "What kind of details?"

Simmons took a breath. "That at least once, probably a number of times, someone from Gum - your organisation, Bradley - has interfered with our codes. That is interference from a foreign company, and we agreed that would not be allowed. It goes against the whole spirit of what Change-makers and Portico was set up to do."

"You're accusing my company of espionage!" said Leyton. "I will not have this. Julian, Louise, what do you say?"

"Not you, Bradley," said Simmons. "But I have the logins that indicate it came from your organisation."

Louise Burgher spoke up: "Lucas, we set up that programme together, we've spent billions on it, and we were asked to set our own rules. The governments trusted us, and I think we've done well doing the work they wanted to keep at arm's length. Why would anyone at Gum want to put that in jeopardy?"

Renfrew added: "We've influenced our own government's affairs to the maximum degree, without needing to interfere in yours."

"I am about to be hung out to dry here," said Simmons, pleading. "Journalists here know about Changemakers. They know about our power to manipulate the social. They've examples, *exact examples*, of algorithms and codes being changed, and the outcomes we've created. It's enough to bring down the whole project."

The four leaders of the world's biggest companies on the web sat in silence for a moment.

"Then maybe it's time to let it go," said Leyton eventually. "Let them write their stories. For too long we've put social good above our own company's interest. My shareholders are breathing down my neck every day. I'm sure it's the same for you all. They want to know why we continue to put so much money under 'philanthropic projects' on our accounts."

"You've lost the point, Bradley," said Burgher. "Changemakers has allowed us to prosper. None of us can say we've not taken advantage of putting the right people into the right places. It's great for our bottom lines."

"It's gone too far," he responded. "We've worked together for a long time, but how long do you expect it to go on for? Governments gave us a mandate, but it wasn't forever. Time to hand back the power, and start doing what we really want."

"So you're going off programme?" said Simmons.

"Programme? What programme?" snapped Leyton. "The measures Amanda Ward brought in could do serious damage to my company in the UK. It could affect confidence in searching or buying from our advertisers. Do you know how big a chunk of money pornography and gambling advertising makes for my company? Ward's policies were moving in the direction of banning those freedoms."

"I never mentioned Amanda Ward," said Simmons.

"Leyton?" said Burgher, CEO of Wonderfish.

"Sure," the CEO of Gum's tone became belligerent. "We might have been taking a close look at what she's doing over there. Amanda Ward got lots of good traction for banning people with strong opinions from the social. People over here in the US are starting to demand the same. Many of our customers, going about their legal business, would be banned if we gave in. There's no democracy in that, and no profit either."

"So, you changed the code, got her fired, and began a hate campaign against her?" said Simmons. "People here are getting hurt."

"People always get hurt," he replied, his voice raised. "Do you think our predecessors were able to install a new government in East Burundi without sidelining some folk who believed the land was theirs?"

"I think we need to take stock," said Renfrew. "If this gets out, the social will explode. Our governments will come down on us with legislation so strong we won't be able to breathe. It'll be the end of Portico, perhaps the end of our companies."

"Bradley, you've fucked everything up," said Burgher.

"We've always taken decisions unanimously," said Simmons. "That's what Portico has always been about."

"We can put it right," said Renfrew, CEO of Talk. "But we all need to be on board. Lucas, how close are these journalists to publishing?"

"Very close," the chief executive of YoYo responded. "But I think I can hold them back. I can tell them we'll give a full account, if they agree to sit on the story until we at Portico have met face-to-face."

Burgher responded: "Then we need to work out a united response. A good spin on a controversial story. A dedication to openness, and some way of making it clear that the sharing of data, and the implementation of Changemakers, was for the greater good."

"I don't know," said Leyton. "I still think we need to change the way we're going about things here. Enough of the bowing down. Governments use us to their own ends, we should be fighting back. They've taken enough from us already."

"And they have the power to take it *all* from us," said Lucas Simmons. "We have to work in partnership with them. At the end of the day, the administrations in the US or the UK could pull the plug. And that'll be the lights going off for us all."

"I don't agree. We need to meet up. In the next few days," said Leyton. "We should all clear our diaries. Understood?"

"Agreed," said Renfrew. "We need to discuss what next for Portico. But no going rogue. Wherever we're going, it's a join decision."

Louise Burgher nodded: "Until then, we stay united. If you can persuade the journalists not to publish, or to tell the story our way, we might even come out with a halo."

The other three agreed.

Simmons concluded by making eye contact with the Gum boss: "Bradley, I need to trust you on this. Keep your fingers out of my code. Keep your nose out of the UK's sovereign business. It's our democracy. You deal with your own. God knows, you need to."

Leyton harrumphed, but eventually said: "At least until our face-to-face, I agree."

The four swiped off, with halfhearted salutations.

Simmons placed his head in his hands for a long time, the dull light from his slate reflecting off his fingers. Eventually, he lifted his head and placed his slate aside.

"Enough for you?" he said.

Soren and Harrison nodded.

Soren swiped his slate to stop the recording.

"Do you think Bradley Leyton will keep his word," he said.

"I seriously doubt it," said Simmons.

Grey was impatient, but there was excitement in his voice too. Soren and Harrison, with her arm still in a sling, sat opposite him in his office. Apart from an overnight advertising editor, the rest of the SkyCloud staff had gone home.

"Tell me everything that you have."

Soren took first turn: "We have a huge, multi layered story about how big tech companies have been able to influence, even control, government policies for at least a decade.

"The former national director of MinSoc has gone on the record, saying she was part of Changemakers. And admitting with the connivance of the Ministry and YoYo at least, that she has published false information about her history. The current national director of MinSoc, Harry Godspeed, was also a Changemaker and faked his history too. He's being protected by his Ministry, but I've had a message from Amanda Ward saying she's going to have a private meeting with him. Hopefully we'll get a response.

"We have the chief executive of YoYo offering an official response - not apologising, but arguing he and the other chief executives that make up Portico were asked to take these actions by the UN - arguing they've done a pretty damn good job. That's all the first angle."

"Second," said Harrison, "we have the fact that social media has been manipulated to allow and disallow specific criticism of MinSoc, and we can presume other Ministries, to manipulate public opinion and actions, to further the aims of the social companies and to support the secretive Changemakers project.

"This is beyond what Ward had pledged to do; which was to begin to rid the social of negative and bullying behaviour, and to ban certain groups. She and others took measures to ensure her policies weren't criticised or questioned on the social. It's likely this caused a virtuous circle in praise of her policies, which later exploded when those policies were reversed, under the influence of Gum."

"Which brings us to the third part of the story," said Soren. "The banning of certain interest groups from the social, Ward's initiative, and the reversing of that, apparently by MinSoc. The CEO of Gum, Bradley Leyton, has directly allowed interference with the social, screening out any positive messaging about Amanda Ward, and actively promoting hate messages about her. That opened up a real threat to Ward and her family, as well as those around her. Including me and this organisation. Probably the attack on Harrison too. It also interfered with national sovereignty, the right for the UK to govern itself and establish its own rules."

Grey sat back in his chair, impressed.

"Lots of information, a bit of conjecture. But who's the

real bad guy? Why should our audience care? Most of them know the price they pay for the convenience of the social."

"I think that's the sovereignty issue," said Harrison. "We may live in a global society, but we're still a small set of islands and a relatively tight community. We like our little place, and we don't like others interfering in our affairs without our permission."

"Kind of a flip side to British imperialism since the dawn of time," grumbled Soren.

Harrison continued: "Whether with US government approval or not, we've been able to prove a major US company, Gum, has taken direct action to interfere in our sovereign democracy. Not just to influence it - the US has always been working at that - but to actually subvert it, and steer it on a particular course in their favour. There's your bad guy. And Lucas Simmons at YoYo is severely pissed off about it. He's on the record as saying so. "

Soren added: "Yep, it's Simmons' job to interfere in our democracy, not the US'."

Grey rolled his eyes. "How long will it take you to get it all together?"

"Mia's already done a lot of the writing work from hospital. I think we need to work overnight, and publish in the morning."

"Overnight?"

"Remember, we're on California time now. It's mid morning there. By the time we publish, it'll be their night time - perfect for us. We also have to act quickly in case Gum puts out its own version of events. They have a lot more traction than we do, and we've seen how they can manipulate code in their favour. Simmons may have persuaded Bradley Leyton to hold back, but we can't trust him. He's pissing blood."

"Are you up for this, Mia?" Grey asked.

"I wouldn't miss a moment," she said.

"Then we're all on duty. I can check things as you go along. I'm also going to have to make a call to our lawyers - to see what we can and can't say. How far that secret recording you made is in the public interest. If it's a no go, we'll have to go with 'anonymous sources' which will weaken the story.

"If there's any sniff of Gum trying to get the spring on us, then we'll publish what the lawyer has been able to clear, then add to it as it's written and checked."

The three sat there grinning. Reviewing fashion accessories, this was not.

26

Grey had called in an overnight newsgatherer to work with Harrison and Soren throughout the night, proofreading, checking facts and names. Grey also asked her to keep an eye on the feeds for emerging trends that SkyCloud would normally be covering.

Grey also asked her to keep an eye out for any mention of MinSoc, Amanda Ward, Gum or anything else connected to the story.

Grey himself kept in touch with the company's lawyer - the first time the legal firm had ever been asked for an opinion from SkyCloud, despite the heavy yearly retainer. By asking the lawyer to work overnight too, Grey was determined to get his money's worth.

Apart from collecting coffee and buns from Carlos' when it opened at 7 a.m., the overnighter would not be allowed to leave the office until the story was published. Any staff arriving before publication would also be subject to the lock in.

Soren wrote some sample copy, and wrote up some official questions to be put to the newly instated director at

MinSoc, Harry Godspeed. Ward had agreed to pass this onto him. Soren didn't expect an official response, but Godspeed might be persuaded to break ranks like Ward had.

Throughout the night, Soren had noticed his editor becoming more tetchy. He and Harrison had been too busy to worry much about whether Portico would leak a spoiler before they'd had a chance to publish, but it appeared to be all Grey could think about. A public statement from any of the Portico big four would eat up headlines from any smaller newsgathering organisation like SkyCloud. Their story would then be seen as irrelevant.

He kept coming over to where Soren was working to express these worries. It gave the newsgatherer a chance to exercise his mind at first, instead of staring at his screen. Finally, though, he had to ask Grey to step back.

"If we're going to get in before they do, then we have to publish by nine," he told Grey. "I think that's not going to happen if Harrison and I don't really concentrate."

"Why don't you take a doze?" suggested Harrison. "If we pull this off, it's going to be a big day tomorrow."

Grey returned to his office. It was 4 a.m., but Soren was wired. He and Harrison kept flipping looks to each other, ones of satisfaction, though his companion was clearly in pain from her ribs and arm.

The two had agreed on a structure, along the lines they'd presented to Grey the night before. Soren decided to take on the story of Amanda Ward's background, her position and the loss of it at MinSoc, as well as the attack at his home. He'd write from a personal perspective, adding some drama to an otherwise quite technical piece.

Harrison would take on the social: how MinSoc and YoYo had worked together to go further than Ward had announced, and how criticism of her policies would be screened out. She'd also write about Changemakers, and its foundation by the pre-Portico companies. That Ward and Godspeed were members. There was still hope Godspeed would provide an admission or quote.

Finally, they would both write about Gum's interference which led to Ward's sacking, and squarely lay the blame for that on Gum's chief executive, Bradley Leyton.

Grey said the lawyer had advised them not to include parts of the sound file in the story. They'd argued and debated it, but knew the power of Gum and its legal department would blow them out of the water. With more time, they might be able to find a legal way through, so they decided to hold the voice recording as a backup story to give the it more legs later in the week. For now, they'd go with 'unnamed trusted sources', which the lawyer had agreed to.

When they'd finished first drafts, they swapped to check each other's work, tighten it up, and add anything that had been missed. Just like the coders, Soren thought.

By just after 7 a.m., when the overnight staffer had brought coffee and buns, Soren and Harrison joined Grey in his office.

The editor hadn't taken her advice to sleep. It showed on his face and in the slump of his shoulders. He'd been stuck to the screen, he told them, unable to take his gaze off the feeds.

"I don't understand why they're being so quiet if they know we're about to launch such a huge story about them," he said.

"Maybe they don't quite know what we've got?" suggested Harrison.

Grey rubbed his temple, and then drew his eyes together with his thumb and forefinger. "The biggest tech companies in the world, with a GPS chip in every device, don't know we're about to launch a big story about them? When we've as good as told them we are?"

"Or Simmons told Leyton that he's successfully persuaded us to hold the story," Soren added.

"Maybe they're waiting for us to publish, and they're ready with a rapid rebuttal for every point?" said Harrison.

"I think we need to up the stakes somehow," said Soren.

Grey looked puzzled.

Soren continued: "We need to make a call for change. Direct this to the government. So not just criticism of Portico, but something bigger. Go beyond setting out facts that they can deny, excuse or just plain ignore."

"This is where you come in, Will," said Harrison.

"Me?"

"You need to write an editorial piece," Soren said. "Like the newspapers used to have. A short, demanding statement, on behalf of independent journalism. Our democracy has been harmed. Our ability to tell the truth hampered."

"We will be silenced no more," added Harrison.

"Time to return to total freedom of the press, and a legally binding end to manipulating the social in favour of government policies," said Grey.

"We tried to do the good thing, and work alongside government and the social companies, but the victim has been the truth. We kept our side of the bargain; they've lied and cheated and failed to keep theirs," said Harrison.

"Powerful stuff," said Grey. "Can you write down what we just came up with?"

"If you'll sign it off," she said.

Soren knew this was difficult for his editor. It could mean the end of SkyCloud. In a way, the editorial was going against what most people really wanted: an easy, non controversial life, where decisions were made without them having to get all cross about politics. They wanted fashion, and movies, and cooking, and sports chat. And to be offered amazing products they didn't know they wanted, at prices they couldn't believe. Advertisers would give SkyCloud the widest berth if it started publishing political manifestos, trying to say what was important rather than what people wanted.

"I'll do it," said Grey. "We've come this far, I don't think we have a choice. SkyCloud has a decent reach and influence. It's brought in lots of readers, and kept us all in work. It's time to use the power *we* have."

He looked at his slate.

"We have fifteen minutes. I'll give a final check over of your articles, if you write my editorial for me. Make it as forceful as you like. We only have one shot at this so might as well go all in."

"This is the right thing to do," said Soren. "I'm proud of you..."

"Why are you both still here?" Grey responded, checking the feeds again.

At 8.50 a.m., Grey's office was packed. The staffers at SkyCloud had been briefed that something big was about to happen, but few really understood what their colleagues had been working on for the last few days. Nor, thought Soren, did they know the possible implications for their jobs.

Gossip newsgatherers, advertising copywriters and even salespeople gathered outside Grey's office. They stood whispering, while Grey - with Soren and Harrison gazing over his shoulder - mumbled over his slate, making minor changes here and there, to their resistance or approval. The lawyer had sent a few 'must do' changes.

There were five articles in total, each with photographs of key players, or illustrations about how the social worked. Three on each of the core scandals, a summary introduction to the whole series, and Grey's editorial. Despite his protestations, Soren had insisted it should feature a photo of him to add weight to his words.

For the last fifteen minutes, they'd pinned down the headlines for the series.

Portico Scandal: How the US meddled in our democracy #PorticoScandal

Then,

#PorticoScandal: Ten years of secret 'Changemakers' project

#PorticoScandal: US tampering with social leads to violent backlash

#PorticoScandal: The personal stories behind the scandal

#PorticoScandal: Editor demands return of free journalism

"Not a bad night's work," said Soren. Within the melee of excitement, he began to feel a deep sorrow. He remembered the confrontation with Amanda Ward at the crossroads, the first emotional pull he'd felt for five years when they were both attacked at his apartment.

This story, the relationship he'd built with Harrison and Ward, had given him a reason to go on. An outlet for his grief for Lucy and Grace. Seeing Harrison laid up in hospital had offered him a view of what he had missed when his family had been torn away from him - the opportunity to support, to care, to worry, to fight. With seconds counting down to publication, he felt *alive*. Behind Grey's chair, and out of view of the rest of the office, he took Harrison's hand and squeezed it tightly. She returned the gesture.

Grey planned to swipe the stories out, one by one, sixty

seconds apart from 9 a.m. The digital clock in the right hand corner of his slate slipped past 8.59 a.m.

He cued up the summary story, ready to swipe it across. Around 9 a.m. was the time when most viewers checked their slates, just before they started work. It was peak time to launch.

"Suppose we better do this," said Grey.

"If you don't, I'll do it for you," said Soren, half leaning over towards his slate.

"It's done," he said. He swiped the story across to the SkyCloud feed, and waited for it to register - a matter of milliseconds.

It failed to appear on the feed.

He swiped again. Maybe he'd missed the window, Soren thought.

Nothing.

"Bastards," said Soren.

"Hold on," said Grey. He swiped across the second story.

It didn't appear on the feed either. He swiped across the third and fourth, together.

Neither of them ran on the SkyCloud feed.

"They've manipulated the codes to screen out the story," said Soren.

The rest of the SkyCloud staff looked at each other puzzled.

"Everyone, back to your desks," shouted Grey. He could barely hold back his anger. They filed out, back to their stations, gossiping and raising their eyebrows.

"Will, can you type this?" asked Harrison.

"#HarryGodspeed cocaine." He looked puzzled, but nodded.

He swiped it across. Nothing.

Grey looked up at Soren and Harrison.

"So what do we do now?"

They took a break. Harrison checked in with her wife, while Soren put in a call to Amanda Ward. Grey just stared at the wall, apart from occasionally checking the feeds to see if their massive scoop had somehow made it through.

They met again in Grey's office.

"Well, at least we know one thing," said Soren.

Harrison finished his statement: "Godspeed is the leak."

Soren explained: "I talked to Ward. She briefed Godspeed last night face to face, as Harrison had suggested. They're both Changemakers and were colleagues at MinSoc, so it was natural he'd listen to her. She told me she gave him the full story we were going to tell, in as much detail as she could. And she gave him a first draft of the actual copy I'd already written about him and his involvement in the Changemakers project. Only the copy I gave her contained a deliberate mistake. I wrote that he had been a habitual user of cocaine at the time he joined the programme. Certainly not what the national director of MinSoc would want in his biog."

Grey appeared puzzled. "Do we have proof of that? I don't remember sending that to the lawyer."

"No idea. We were never going to publish it. We just sent the accusation to Godspeed." said Soren. "But it proved to us that he had that accusation in his hands."

"And when he passed it to Gum, it screened out of the slightest sniff of him and cocaine on the socials," Harrison said.

"You suspected him all along," said Grey.

"What can I say?" said Soren. "And now we have an extra angle to our story: the current national director of MinSoc is actively censoring us to protect his own professional reputation, as well as the whole Changemakers story."

"That's all great," said Harrison. "But how the hell are we going to get the story out?"

"You worry about pinning down Godspeed further, and if you can do it, add him to our story in big bold type as in league with Gum," said Grey. "I'm supposed to be the publisher around here. I'll worry about getting the story out."

27

"You know this is highly illegal," said Adisa Zane.

Lucas Simmons and Curtis Soren stood behind him as he sat again at his coding slate, projecting onto the big screen on the wall.

"I take full responsibility," said Simmons. "I think I'm in sufficient trouble when all this goes down."

Zane nodded.

"So, Amanda Ward said she spoke face to face with Godspeed at around nine last night. So, we need to see what Godspeed was up to not long after that," said Soren.

"Can you bring up any movements on the YoYo network by Godspeed?" asked Simmons.

Zane swiped at his slate, quicker than Soren could follow. He explained: "Because we host MinSoc's slate accounts, we can track his location."

A map appeared. It pinpointed Godspeed's slate in a pub close to Highbury Park in north London at 9 p.m.

"He switched it off, at nine fifteen. No geolocation."

"Okay, so let's assume he met Ward in the pub, they turned off their slates, then chatted in the pub or went for a walk around the park. Somewhere perfect to share secrets," said Soren.

"Forty five minutes later, Godspeed's slate is back on. He's travelling in his MinSoc car, from Highbury back towards the Ministry. From what I can see, his bodyguard is with him."

"Tom, we can presume?" said Soren. "Can we pick up any communications from Godspeed's slate?"

"You sure?" asked Zane, looking up at his boss.

"Like I said, my responsibility."

Zane brought up another window, and typed in some codes that were impossible for Soren to understand.

"During the journey, there's a video call put through to a London IP address - perhaps his home. Maybe his partner saying he'll be late home?" said Zane. "Then there's a very short one..."

They waited as Zane double checked: "To Los Angeles."

"Gum HQ," said Simmons.

"If we then go back to his slate location," said Zane, indicating the other half of the big screen, "it goes out of contact again at eleven pm, outside the Marriot Hotel at St. Pancras station. He switches it off."

"The Marriot? There, every room has its own private slate," said Soren.

"It's a business hotel. There must be hundreds of slates online there at any one time, communicating all over the world, each with extra security built in for business negotiations," said Zane.

"Perfectly invisible, in a crowd of people wanting to keep their conversations secret," said Simmons.

The chief executive of YoYo released a deep sigh, and stared out of the window. Soren and Zane waited patiently for Simmons to gather his thoughts.

He shook his head. "I've known Harry for five years. I never took him for a fake. He and Amanda were both my charges, if you like. We all worked well together. Chemistry. I'm sure he believed in Changemakers as much as we do."

"Maybe he just liked the idea of national director more?" offered Soren.

"No, that's not how he was. Harry was recruited because we believed he was a man with ambition, but one we could trust. And all the work we did together, every moment, was about building relationships."

Soren spoke again: "Amanda said some Changemakers didn't make the grade? Maybe he just took longer to show?"

Simmons spoke slowly. "No. I failed to keep him on side. That was my primary job. To nurture, to help him believe in the best we could do."

"People go rogue."

"Changemakers don't go rogue, Curtis."

"It's not your fault."

"Maybe, maybe not," said Simmons. "But what has happened has put Amanda and others in physical danger. I bear responsibility for that. And Rasalina Mazeika. And I have to put it right."

Simmons stood suddenly, and approached Zane's desk. He turned to Soren.

"Do you have enough to publish?"

"If Godspeed hadn't slipped up and put in that first call to the US, it might be pure conjecture," said Soren. "But that first call is pretty good grounds to indicate his next move was to make a second secure call from the Marriot to the US."

Simmons turned to his chief coder, determined now rather than emotional.

"Can you confirm that short call to Los Angeles was to somewhere within Gum?"

He placed his hand on Zane's shoulder. A kind, fatherly gesture.

"And check whether any code changes were made after that call, to prevent posts containing keywords from Mr Soren's story appearing on our platform," he added.

Zane cracked his knuckles, and began swiping.

Soren and Simmons took coffee in the chief executive's private office. The line of enquiry had run just as they had expected: Godspeed's short call had been to someone in the Gum complex and not long after, Zane had discovered, the code had been changed in the main social algorithm.

But the Gum coder had been extra careful this time, Zane had explained. Instead of putting the terms they wanted screening out into the code itself, the algorithm was to refer to an external table of specific terms as part of its process.

The table, he supposed, would be hosted on a private server at Gum. It could only be changed on site, and that meant it could be kept entirely locked from others. It could also be changed in real time by a human coder. The 'mother' code didn't have to be changed at all.

Zane had told Simmons he thought the coder who had created the table hosted at Gum was mocking them, in a coder type gag. They had called the protocol table Icarus, the name of the boy in the Greek myth who flew too close to the sun with wax coated wings. The wax melted and he fell to his death.

Unless Zane could break the military grade protection that had been built into this referral to Icarus, there was nothing they could do to stop the screening process, preventing any posts containing phrases or ideas contained within the table. Zane had helped design the security system himself; the chances of breaking it, he'd told them, were zero.

Simmons topped up Soren's coffee.

"Why has Bradley Leyton gone rogue on the Change-makers' project, and started interfering with the social to disrupt it?" Soren asked.

"You were in the room. You heard him. I guess programme wasn't running the way he had envisaged. I guess he has just run out of patience, or lost belief that we were really making a difference or making enough money."

"What about the other companies in Portico?"

"They didn't seem too distressed by it, did they. But then it's not their country being tampered with. Call it sparring, if you like. We used to do it by briefing against each other. Or planting spies in each other's companies. It kept us all on our toes. But Gum has gone too far. They're reaping the benefits of bending UK government's policies to their own ends."

"Do you think the other pillars of Portico would support you, if you called for Gum to be somehow reprimanded, or drawn back? Threatened with sanctions, or something?"

"Unlikely," said Simmons. "What kind of sanctions could we impose? We stand as a four, but Gum has always been the most powerful. Bradley Leyton is a hard ass. He has the most users, the biggest population and the most money. He's not afraid to throw his weight around. And the US government stands by him, of course, because all the parties rely on Gum's functionality."

Soren stared out of the window. He didn't know whether

to gamble. Had Simmons come far enough along to take the extra step?

"He demanded a face-to-face?" Soren ventured.

"Yes, he wants us all to meet. That's not happened for two years. I think he's going to suggest the formal wrapping up of Portico, probably Changemakers too. Actually, suggest is probably not strong enough. I'm certain he will. If he pulls out, some of our biggest joint projects will fall by the wayside, or be put back a decade."

"Where's the meeting?"

"It hasn't been arranged, but I know he'll be pushing for it. The man likes to vent as you saw."

Soren hesitated. "Could you bring them all here?"

"That would certainly make sense," said Simmons. "We're the ones under fire, I'd get the opportunity to show the damage that's been done. Plus I'd be on home turf."

"How long would it take to organise?"

"Why do I feel like you're twisting my arm here?" replied Simmons.

"Because, I am. I saw you in that meeting. You're proud of what Changemakers has achieved. And you don't like being double crossed. You were commissioned by the UN to bring about a better future, and that's now been betrayed. After all your hard work..."

"Okay, I get it," said Simmons.

Soren picked up his coffee and leant back in his easy chair. "How long would a private jet take to fly from Los Angeles to London?"

"These days, nine hours, maybe eight."

"And presumably, the tech is developed enough for contact from that jet with the ground throughout the flight?"

"Yes, by KA band satellite, which Leyton's Dreamliner is

bound to have," said Simmons. "But I know he sleeps on the overnight flights, because he suffers incredible jet lag. He likes to stay on California time wherever he is."

Soren finished his thought: "So, theoretically, Leyton could be out of contact with his company for, say, five hours during night time in California, if he was to fly over here to meet you?"

"Yeah, he can't get much done while Silicon Valley is asleep," said Simmons.

They sat in silence. Soren wanted to make the man sweat a little, before he spoke again.

"Mr Simmons, our story does not put you or your company in a good light. The way our readers will see it, you've been at the heart of a secretive anti democratic plot to control their decision making, and their lives, over a number of years."

"I can see how they would see it that way," said Simmons.

"But you've spoken to us on the record, and said that you now want to make things right. You'll be more transparent, you will better balance freedom of speech with the need to monitor and ban those who would seek to exploit your tools for violent and extremist purposes, post vile content and bully and coerce others. You're re-committing to the Changemakers programme - but this time with the public's support, if and when it's offered."

"That's about the size of it, I suppose," Simmons didn't look hopeful.

"I think your connection to Rasalina Mazeika, and your about turn after her killing, could show you as a sympathetic figure." Soren gestured dramatically above his head. "I can see the halos now, if we're able to tell *that* story."

"It's not about halos for me anymore, Curtis, it's

about doing the right thing. I have all the money I need, I've done my share. Not everything went perfectly, but I do believe we were only doing what we were asked to do."

"So you have nothing to lose, and if you gain, well, that's a bonus," concluded Soren.

"I'll be satisfied not to be hanged and flogged," he smiled.

Soren made the man wait for a minute longer. He took an exaggerated last deep drag on his coffee.

"What is it you want me to do?" Simmons finally said.

"Talk to Portico," Soren said. "Bring Leyton over here to kiss and make up. Plan for the future of Portico, like you agreed in the meeting."

"And that's all?"

"Far from it. Let me talk to Adisa Zane again. My editor is working on an idea to get the story out, but it's probably going to take some coding muscle and some real time action."

"I'll get my diary secretary onto it now," said Simmons. Soren stood to leave.

"I like the way you operate, Curtis. When all this is over, if I'm not in a prison cell, will you reconsider?"

"Reconsider?"

"Coming to work for me?"

Soren let out a full belly laugh. It felt good to release some tension.

"Not a chance, Lucas. Not a chance."

"Do you remember print publishing, Mia?" Grey was asking Harrison a question he thought she might not even understand.

"I'm not sure," she said. "I think I may have read about it once, in a magazine. Is that the right word? 'Mag-a-zine'?"

Soren laughed. Grey was not impressed.

"Ten years ago, Soren and I started working on the *London Herald*. It had started off as a serious printed newspaper, but ended up as distributed for free across the capital. It was full of adverts by the time it collapsed. The actual news inside took about three minutes to read in the end, just about as long as the journey from one tube stop to another."

"I remember the papers piled up at the stations as a teenager," said Harrison. "And chucked in gutters."

"Probably where they belonged by then," said Soren.

"There was something pure about print though, wasn't there Curtis?" said Grey. "The smell of it."

Soren watched Harrison roll her eyes.

"The weight of it. It exuded authority. No matter how many were put in the rubbish or recycled. Someone, somewhere, would have a copy, the real physical object."

"Okay, old men, where are we going with this?" interrupted Harrison.

"I think we should create a printed edition of our story," said Grey. "Call it a 'SkyCloud Special Edition', if you like. Something to surprise people, something people can smell, and feel, and will actually read. And then talk about in real life. Not just over the social."

"Something that can't be erased at the swipe of a slate," added Soren, getting the gist.

"But how?" asked Harrison. "The bulk newsprint works have all closed down, the tech has moved on. We don't even have a printer in this office, everything is done on slate. Last time I saw a photocopier was at school."

"I'm not suggesting we do a print run from this office," said Grey. "We've got really strong stories. And we still need to add in Godspeed too, which gives it all a far sharper edge. Bulk print does still exist, but it's all used for packaging these days. If we can use one of our own designers to create it, then use our advertisers' print capability, we could create something to be given out on street corners."

"Like an old pamphlet, by Samuel Pepys," said Soren.

"Who?" said Grey. He didn't wait for an answer.

"But who would fund that?" said Soren. "I suspect you don't have the money. Publishing online is cheap. On paper, I think not. And we'd have to pay people to distribute it.

"Advertisers would run a mile from stumping up cash to run an advert in such a subversive medium as print, let alone surrounded by the copy we're planning to put out."

Silence.

"Unless we went for the ultimate contradiction," said Harrison brightly.

The other two looked in her direction.

"We get YoYo to sponsor our special edition. The ulti-mate online platform goes offline for a day."

"Impossible," said Grey, sharply. "The story features Simmons, Ward and Godspeed, all interfering with the social, all connected to Portico and YoYo. Any sniff of YoYo or MinSoc would reek of more corruption, and compromise the story. Readers wouldn't know who to believe. It would give Gum the easiest hit to discredit us."

"You sound very different from a few weeks ago. I think I like it," said Soren. "And you're right. It's enough that we're working with YoYo at all, without having to take hard currency from them to publish."

"Fine," said Harrison, obviously offended. She turned away from her colleagues, and looked out of the glass panel which overlooked the rest of the open plan SkyCloud office.

The two men exchanged glances, half embarrassed, half

entertained. At least she'd had an idea, thought Soren. He couldn't even pay his rent.

He was about to apologise, when he saw in the reflection a small smile grow from the scowl and then spread across her face into a grin. She turned back to them.

"You say you've got the best advertising sellers in the business right here, Will?"

"Best on what I can afford to pay them," he said.

"They know our audience inside out, top to bottom?"

"That's their job."

"Then I think I have the answer." She had their full attention. "And you, Soren, are going to absolutely love it."

"Go on," said Soren.

"Crowd funding."

"Who's going to pay to read a story before they know what it is?" asked Soren.

This time it was Harrison's turn to dramatically roll her eyes.

"The sniff of print? The weight of paper? I thought you knew all about this business," she said.

Half an hour later, Harrison was standing before SkyCloud's handful of online sales staff, and their advertising coding and design colleagues.

Soren watched from the side. He was sitting against a table, his arms crossed, nodding gently as she spoke.

She had wit and confidence, but the subtle tones to make the people she was speaking to feel good about themselves. He'd felt that charm lately, and envied Jessica for the comfort Harrison must bring to their family.

"You may not really know me, I'm kind of new here," she told the small crowd. Most wore the office uniform of jeans, incredible hair and rings through their noses. Harrison dressed smarter. She looked good centre stage, despite her arm still sitting in a sling.

"As you can see, I kind of got beat up the other day. I won't go into the detail, but it was because I work *here*. And I try to tell the truth," she said.

Grey shuffled uncomfortably from his position next to Soren.

"There's not an awful lot of truth around these days, and I'm sure you're all as bored as I am with our jobs." Grey shuffled again.

"We write drivel about fashion, celebrities, perfume, gadgets, and then you lucky people get to contact advertisers and ask them to run ads or sponsor features about them."

The staff looked at each other, and Soren detected they either weren't bothered by what they'd been told, or just accepted it as an accurate description of their job. He detected a hesitation in Harrison's voice, and gave her a subtle nod of encouragement.

"You'll know we have a policy here, that we don't deal in fake products. And I think that's a good thing, and I praise our editor Will Grey for that policy." She turned to him. "We don't write about, or take adverts about, nor share, nor publish, the usual crap about miracle cures, UFO sightings, conspiracy theories, healing crystals, quasi-religious prophecies. Fodder for the gullible."

Grey nodded at this. He'd never explicitly stated the policy, but it was implied by the stories he chose to run and the products he allowed on site.

"It's fair to say, our competitors make big money out of that stuff. It's one of the biggest industries on the social, but we've always put principle before profit."

The group nodded along, and all looked at Grey, who tried to look directly at Harrison to prevent any reaction. Soren nudged him in the side, and Grey finally acknowledged his colleagues with embarrassed gratitude.

Harrison continued: "Well, now we do have a conspiracy theory. Only the unique thing about *our* conspiracy theory is that it is true. And like the classic conspiracy theory that the social loves so much, our conspiracy theory really is being hushed up by those in power."

The small group laughed. They'd seen the three try to launch the story the day before, when Grey had swiped it into the feeds. They'd seen it disappear as quick as he could swipe. They'd then been dismissed, without understanding why. Soren saw a few faces paying more attention, as the staff began to understand what Harrison was implying.

"What we want you to do, is what you do best," she said. "We would like you to create an advertising campaign. But this time promising to reveal the biggest of conspiracies. The secrets your own government doesn't want people to know. Secrets that will shock, and anger and alarm. And confirm to our readers that they've been cheated and lied to all along."

She was gesturing expansively, emphasising the horror of the tale they would be telling.

"All the great conspiracy stuff that our readers will love, but we've never given them before," said Grey, adding weight to what Harrison was saying.

"But we won't give any detail," her voice dropped to a whisper. "Just advertising. Landing pages. Sign up boxes. We'll build the mystery. Stoke the conspiracy. And here's the key. We'll promise them we will reveal all, every single fact, in a special exclusive report for their eyes only."

The group shuffled, clearly excited by the prospect.

"And all it will cost them," she said. "Is just five slate coin, paid in advance. You know how to sell that. It's less than a cup of coffee. Half the cost of a bus trip."

"We need thousands of sign ups," said Grey, more firmly. "Coders, you can use your skills to make sure anyone who shows an interest follows through into a sale. Make it one-swipe payment, easy as possible. We have some great design capability for online, so work together please."

He continued: "We may face some opposition from other interested parties, so you'll need to dress up the offer in a variety of ways. All promising to reveal the truth, for next to nothing. Be as creative as you can. And if you find your adverts suddenly disappear, create new ones, use a different design, a different idea. Once we have the swipes, we will have the contacts we need to send out the secret report in one massive mailing."

"And place the adverts where they'll get seen," said Harrison. "Not just our feeds, but as many of the others as we can. The boss has allocated some budget, and you know how to get the discounts."

Grey stared at her. Soren knew he had not promised any funding to advertise externally. He was amused as he watched his editor try to hold his smile.

"Any questions?" asked Harrison, with a firm tone that assumed there would not be. The group shuffled in their usual meek way. But faces showed they were excited by the prospect of the next few hours.

She turned towards Grey in an exaggerated way, bowed a little to him, then turned back to the group.

"Why are you all still here?"

28

The scene, thought Soren, was something akin to what he'd seen when he was a kid. When NASA was launching a space rocket and everyone was glued to the TV. Busy rows of people behind screens, with a large master screen at the front.

There was only one way to do this: a full on assault on the social. Adisa Zane had figured out how it would work, and Simmons had directed his best technical staff to set up the operations room overnight.

Zane's eyes shone as he showed them around.

"These guys are my best coders," he said, introducing a row of three trendy looking kids, with flyaway hair and loud attire, but the social awkwardness of shy teenagers. They nodded, embarrassed.

"I've set you up on this desk, Mrs Harrison. You can slot in your own slate. And you, Mr Soren, next to her. Mr Grey, I've given you a desk and a slate mount."

Soren looked in awe at what had been created.

"If you don't mind, myself and Mr Simmons will be at

the back, but my screen will be reflected on the big screen in front."

They all took their seats.

"This is all pretty straightforward stuff, in terms of tracking traction," he told the group. They looked up at the big screen. "I've created an example. If I search for the keyword 'Weather UK', you'll see every appearance of that query, and any relating to it, across the main social platforms, in real time."

Soren watched as a swarm of tiny red dots appeared against a map of the UK, they swooped and circled like a crowd of starlings over a bridge. They spent moments concentrated in particular areas, then moved across the map. A cluster of lights would appear up above a city, then a minute later gradually begin to fade.

"That fading," he said, "reflects a rush of queries on that topic, or perhaps a temporary trend that slowly ebbs away as fewer people are interested. I suspect one of the main feeds put out a warm weather warning in a few cities, and users checked it on their commute to work."

It was fascinating. And easy for Soren to see the power of information and how it spreads. With models like this, advertisers could preen and target their advertising, and test it in real time, probing for traction, sharing, measuring success and reporting back to their bosses within an hour or two.

MinSoc had obviously used the modelling to track its announcements on the social, and to see what comments and keywords made the most progress, then learned from that.

"I suppose the algorithm learns from what we're seeing, then pushes the information in the correct direction," said Harrison.

"Exactly so," said Zane. "That's how trends are built. Say a reader finds a beach is particularly quiet or beautiful today. Maybe posts a picture and a boast. It's a good day for a day by the sea today, right? We've just seen how interested people are in the weather."

He zoomed in on the coast of Essex, and in turn the seaside towns of Clacton, Frinton, Brightlingsea and Southend. "Here's where they're posting about the beaches right now."

A few red pixels appeared in each seaside town, a smattering along the coast where beaches existed.

"Well, an advertiser might have pre-written marketing that targets that particular area when those keywords come up. The algorithm then runs their adverts, attempting to persuade a punter to buy from their particular shop: say ice cream, or sunscreen, or to eat at their restaurant for lunch."

Zane continued: "And this model can be built to screen in and out particular demographics - gender, sexuality, ethnicity, location, relationship status, pretty much anything you'd care to mention."

"Anything that users have shared with the platforms, willingly or without knowing it," said Soren.

"A mix of all the above," said Zane.

He cleared the screen, and the group looked up again at a blank map of the UK, with only the biggest cities marked.

"I'm now going to use the keyword #*PorticoScandal*, which was in the titles of your articles," said Zane. He swiped above his screen.

One tiny red pixel momentarily lit, in east London, then disappeared.

"See, it tracked the input of my term, but the post was immediately erased. That's the code which has been tampered with, automatically erasing the mention. It didn't exist long enough for it to appear on anyone's slate. It entered the servers - that's why it lit up - but was immediately taken down."

Soren marvelled at the tech, while Harrison let out an audible 'wow'.

It was Simmons' turn to speak.

"What we have before us is the assumption that Gum has interrogated every aspect of our story as delivered to them by Godspeed. For all we know, if Gum has been able to access our own servers, they had pretty much every word you wrote."

"And since we published an hour ago, they definitely have every word," said Harrison.

"Correct again. They may now have created code that screens out any mention of keywords in the articles, or keywords derived by artificial intelligence from those articles."

"You mean it's not just a list of keywords that the algorithm is looking for?" asked Soren.

"No, it'll be looking at the words and perhaps using other words that say or imply the same thing," said Simmons.

"How the hell will we get the story out then?"

"We can't delete the terms themselves, because they will have been hard coded in the Icarus table, on site at Gum," said Zane. "The mother code asks Icarus whether to publish a particular post, and we can't do anything about it. My team can try to put some glitches in the mother code, or try to circumvent the instruction to refer to Icarus. But we can't rely on code alone. We need to be cleverer than that."

Simmons completed the thought: "Computers are great at processing quickly, and AI can also be pretty effective. But code will only take us so far. That's why you wordsmiths are here. We need new ideas, new words, turns of phrase, clever ways of getting the story read that can cheat the code."

"Look for their slip ups. Exploit holes in their armour," said Zane. "We need to get social users to open a download of your story on their slate. Not a web hosted version. The report that you guys have produced. Once that's open, the code can't prevent them from reading it. It might stop them from sounding off online about the contents afterwards, but if it's open, it exists."

"And the best bit of all of this," said Harrison, "is that if readers don't get the Special Report we've promised them, we've pre-warned them there is a conspiracy that is trying to prevent the truth coming out. And then they try to comment on that, their own words will be banned too. All strength to our story."

"Genius," said Simmons.

Soren spoke up: "We also now have a hard copy of the Special Report. It's been printed, funded by more than 2,000 people who can't wait for the amazing revelations we're about to deliver into their inbox. The printed report is waiting for pick up from printers in seven major UK cities. There are dozens of pizza delivery staff, their jobs squeezed by TriCabs, more than keen to distribute it on street corners. Thanks to the gig economy, we recruited them all in about ten minutes."

"Amanda Ward has been in touch with a number of Changemakers, and many have agreed to support our efforts here," Simmons added. "She's waiting to receive your report, so she can swipe it out to each of them. They all have heavy followings and influence in the UK and worldwide, so should gain some rapid traction on our behalf. Words are our weapon here. Our job here is to get the story out, and hope it gains traction online or offline, preferably both.

Once it starts, it will grow. And we'll see all that up there. On the screen."

The room buzzed a little as members of the crew shuffled around in their seats, compared notes, or asked for clarifications. Eventually the room came to a hush.

"So, when do we get started?" Soren said.

Zane swiped at his screen, and a swarm of coloured dots moving in different directions appeared against the distinctive east coast profile of the United States. In a search box, Zane typed a code, and the lights disappeared except for a single flashing green one, slowly edging towards the eastern edge of Quebec, Canada.

"Leyton's plane," Zane said simply. "Another ten minutes and he'll be off the coast, and hopefully he'll take the opportunity to sleep. That's our best time to launch."

"I think we can allow the hard copies to be released from the printers, but it's your call Will," Simmons said.

"What, do you want me to drop a red flag or something?" said Harrison. "Just get on with it."

"Okay, let's swipe the printers then," said Grey. They all tensed. He began swiping at his screen.

The room was silent as Zane pulled up the UK map again. It was blank. Thirty seconds later, a few pixels of red blinked on - then quickly back off again.

"Manchester, Birmingham and London," said Zane. "But screened out, as soon as they posted."

"Hold on, who posted? The couriers can't have started delivering yet?" said Soren.

"The couriers themselves," said Grey. "Or the printing staff - they were on strict instructions not to communicate about the material until officially released."

"So, our early adopters have already been screened out?" said Soren.

"It's too early to say," said Zane. "Let's see how this first step develops. We're still waiting for Leyton to clear the coast."

The group watched as more tiny red flashes appeared in the cities where the printers were located, no more than twenty. They disappeared as quickly as they came, and certainly weren't multiplying or swirling around like the weather warning tag.

Simmons said: "Don't worry, this is what we expected. A few lone posters using the basic keywords in your report are likely to be screened out by the Icarus table. The couriers haven't even started to distribute the pamphlets yet."

For five more minutes, the group watched in silence at a blank screen. Soren was itching to begin publishing to the subscribers who'd paid a fiver for their Special Report.

A red pin prick appeared in the centre of London, then a few others swirled around it.

"There," said Zane. "There's a bit of traction. The first courier must have started giving them out."

He zoomed in on London

The red dots grew by about two at a time, four, six, eight, right in central London - and then flashes of red further across the city, presumably in response to those initial posts.

Zane flipped to a CCTV camera he'd accessed at Oxford Circus, the tourist centre of London. Two couriers, in high visability jackets, were pressing booklets into the hands of puzzled tourists and commuters. A few were reading them as they tried to walk through the crowds, then stopping to swipe their slates.

He flipped back to the map, then zoomed out to encompass the major cities where the pamphlet was being given out. Tiny smatterings of red dots appeared as they had in London, but none were sticking, nor multiplying on a mass scale. The odd one appeared, here or there, outside of the main cities, but the countryside quickly went back into darkness.

"It's going to take time for the printed pamphlets to find their legs," said the SkyCloud editor, in a tone which Soren detected as hopeful. "And the pamphlets are only part of our strategy, remember? We're informing people with a hundred thousand copies, that's a hundred thousand people out there over the next few hours, most of whom will be on our side. We already suspected any online communication about it would be closed down."

"If anything," said Simmons, "it proves our strategy. We need to be creative about the techniques we use, and the words and phrases we use to circumvent the screening code."

"Then there's no reason we can't mail our 2,000 funders with their eagerly awaited Special Report?" said Soren.

"Given Bradley Leyton is heading over the Atlantic now, I'd say this was the ideal time," said Zane.

Soren swiped a message back to the coders at SkyCloud, who were poised to push the email out to subscribers. The sales staff had come up with the idea of a 'secure wrapper' to emphasise how secret and valuable the report really was to potential buyers. Each subscriber would need their own specific passcode, sent in advance, to open their individual copy of the report. It was easy to code, and proved an absolute hit with the conspiracy theorist audience they'd targeted. And it would take some time for Gum to clock on to what they'd done.

They watched the screen impatiently. The tiny number of pamphlet flashes continued to wink, but any traction was short lived.

Then suddenly, the whole dark room suddenly lit up

red. Tiny dots appeared across the UK, creating a flickering that was almost uncomfortable to watch. Soren estimated around three or four hundred reports had been opened, and maybe half of these had immediately messaged, posted about it or passed it on.

He watched with a smile, as those lights flickered off again just as quickly. Having your own post 'disappeared' from the social would be perfect proof to the suspicious subscribers that what they were reading was spot on truth.

"It's working," said Soren. "They're opening the special report, reading and sharing their opinion about its contents."

There was an excited atmosphere in the room, as the flickering continued. Soren knew a single pixel of light that then went out was a message or a post screened out on the social, but it gave him hope that so many subscribers were actually reading and trying to comment on the report they'd sent. They'd be getting traction offline, even though their online distribution was being deleted as quickly as it could spread.

He only wished he could see which pin pricks had been created by the subscribers and which by the hard copy distribution. He suddenly felt he could get into all of this tracking and analytics for his stories. He looked up to see Harrison, who was offering him a smile.

"You get it now, old man?" she said.

"Okay, now is prime time for us to go all in," said Zane. "Nothing is sticking just yet, but we may be able to find some keywords that get some serious traction. Meantime, we'll try to circumvent the screening code."

The driver of coding's colleagues took this as their marker, and started prodding and swiping away at their screens.

"We have their blocking code isolated," said one of the coders. Over their shoulders, Soren could see a mix of white text on black backgrounds, open on various windows. He tried to remember what Zane had said about their role. It would be like a plumber, diverting water around a blockage in a pipe. That blockage was Icarus. He stood mesmerised by the code for minutes.

"Okay, and now we've opened up the channel beneath it," the coder said.

On the big screen, the red pixels stayed lit for five or ten seconds longer than they had before, enough to show some traction. The posters comments were staying online for longer than they had been, before somehow they were being taken down again. More time online meant more viewers, and potentially more re-posts or more people adding their own opinions. Snowballing their story.

Zane turned to Soren and Harrison: "Okay, you folk need to be writing posts and messages. Get as many of those pixels lit as possible, for as long as possible, in case Gum tries to interfere with the code again."

Soren spoke up: "And I'll ask Amanda Ward to release the Changemakers. Let's see if their reputation for influence is as good as it's supposed to be." It was a single swipe.

Then the two SkyCloud newsgatherers started writing the most sensational headlines they could, attaching the PDF document, and releasing it into the social.

Government scandal hits social.

Your voice, banned by MinSoc, screened out by Gum.

Street protests threat over scandal on social.

YoYo treachery: the real truth revealed.

Five part guide to the biggest internet scam in history.

... and so they continued.

Soren watched as pixels began to light as each of the

stories went out into the social. He could see some areas really sticking, before disappearing.

"We've opened up our sluice," said Zane. "Everything you write is going through. By the looks of the code, they're trying to edit theirs as fast as we can put stuff out. But we've managed to get round Icarus and out into the world.

Excited, Soren and Harrison kept on writing.

Social chiefs admit cheating the public, top brass may resign.

"Hey," said the chief executive of YoYo, "I've promised no such thing."

"Anything to get through," said Soren, enjoying himself.

MinSoc in disarray, as truth about social companies revealed. Dirty tricks on the social.

Soren looked up at the big screen. He was beginning to see a slight swirling of the red pixels as they came on, stayed around for longer, then eventually went off. It was happening over their target cities, but also in places across the UK they hadn't specifically targeted.

"Wait," said Zane. "Let's see what it does for a moment. We need to see if it's become infectious."

They watched the screen for thirty seconds. The swirls slowly reduced, then like water down a plug hole, disappeared into nothing. Quickly they were looking again at a near black screen, with just occasional pin pricks of red.

Zane spoke up, while still swiping and typing at his slate: "They've placed Icarus elsewhere in the main social code. Above our blockage. And the same Icarus syntax is being placed elsewhere too. But really quickly."

"What are you talking about?" said Soren.

"The worst news," said Zane. "I think they've placed a virus into the code, to reproduce the call on the Icarus table. It's now multiplying randomly across the mother code."

"Meaning we can't just circumvent it?" asked Soren, more desperately.

"The faster we code, the faster their virus will spread," said Zane. "They've only a few lines of code, and all traffic is running through that. Only now they've got that same bit of code repeating itself, all over the social."

"They saw us coming," said Grey.

"They were holding back, rather than launching a pre-emptive strike," said Simmons. "Not a strategy I'd expect from Bradley Leyton."

"But maybe one we might expect from Godspeed?" said Soren. "Our only hope then is to bring down Icarus."

"Impossible," said Zane, shaking his head. "Like I said, the table is protected by military grade security. Stronger even. We can't delete or edit it, and besides, you can bet the code would switch to another security protected table in milliseconds. An exact copy of Icarus. We need to outwit the table itself. Think about ideas and words you haven't used in any stories, or in posts so far. Ones that the table hasn't been pre-geared to screen out."

The whole group looked up at the next-to-blank screen. It had gone back to showing maybe five or six red pixels at a time. All the online traction they'd had was now being screened out.

Soren considered their position. Whoever put together Icarus must have really forensically analysed their story, from the moment it was first swiped into the social. Not only using their report's keywords, but ones like them or meaning the same thing. Even the same ideas. Gum had been at least two steps ahead of them before they'd even sat down. They'd been modelling this battle for at least the last 24 hours, with the most sophisticated AI and some of the sharpest brains on the planet.

No wonder Leyton was confident enough to sleep for six hours.

Harrison started typing and swiping at her slate. He watched her for a moment.

Showdown for the social.

Join the social revolution.

Something suspicious in your feeds?

She wrote: *Nigerian general in need of funds to expose real story.*

He laughed out loud at that one. Then he had an idea of his own, and it was her turn to look over at his screen.

Soshial report: downlode now

Scandle in Goverment

"You're spelling that wrong," she said.

"Yup."

"Clever bugger."

She tried a few.

MinnsSock in disaray

Screned by Minstry

The dark screen began to light up again. Everyone likes a dumb spelling mistake on the social, and anyone even slightly amused or offended by a sloppy posting like that would share for the hell of it. Some wouldn't even notice the difference.

They weren't swirls of pixels, but there was definitely some traction there. Icarus hadn't accounted for spelling mistakes.

"And what about short text," said Harrison. She spoke aloud, but now she was concentrated on her screen.

She tried a few:

Soc wnts 2 surrndr

LOL at Minnsoc disses

More red lights emerged in major cities, then swirled a little before disappearing.

"Posts with emojis?" asked Soren.

"Might as well," said Harrison.

They both tried a few, and watched as corresponding red pixels appeared and spread slightly on the map, before disappearing.

Soren tried a few more misspellings, while Harrison swiped across some more short texts. But the posts had begun to get far less traction. They flashed on and off, as quickly as they had before.

"Wait, I want to try something," said Zane.

They watched on the big screen as the chief coder opened a window that showed the posts they'd been swiping into the social. He scrolled back, mumbling to himself, then typed:

Scandle in Goverment

"We've done that one," said Soren, watching the screen.

It registered one single red light in east London, then disappeared.

"Shit" said Zane and Simmons together.

Soren then understood what was going on.

"It's learning from us," he said.

"I think so," said Zane. "Icarus must be an algorithm, not just a table. That's just too sneaky. It's not just a static list of words and phrases to screen out. There's a process going on, and it's hard coded behind a security fence."

"What the hell?" said Harrison.

"If only I'd have thought of it," said Zane. "We send out a post containing seemingly random words, or misspelled words - ones that don't appear in the Icarus table - but when that post is opened, it reveals that it is carrying terms referring to our story. Then those random words are added to Icarus, preventing them from being shared again."

Soren thought for a moment: "In other words, we're giving more power to Icarus by trying to outsmart it. We're handing our strategy to them - on a slate." No one laughed.

"That is *some* code," said Zane, shaking his head again.

Soren thought it was the first time the driver of coding had shown concern about what was taking place in that dark room.

Harrison spoke up: "I've had a swipe from Ward. She says her contacts' posts are being screened out too. Some didn't get the report through at all."

Everyone stared at the big screen and watched it gradually go dark again. It occurred to Soren that trying to circulate the scandal so heavy handedly was exactly what Gum had been expecting. It had worked perfectly against them.

Not only had every smart idea they'd come up with in the dark room got itself screened out, but the public - the ones out there trying to share their shock at the story - they'd done Bradley Leyton's work for him.

Every word of outrage they'd shared when passing on the story would have run through the Icarus algorithm, silencing itself.

Absolute genius.

Soren's eyes hurt. They had become glazed over from staring through the dark for red pin pricks. They'd gone back to five or six appearing at any one time. No one was speaking, all lost in their own worlds.

"Do we know how many posts we actually got," said Soren. He knew it was a useless question. Zane had imagined a screen lit up with constant red lights. At best they'd seen a few swirls, quickly narrowing into nothing.

Zane checked: "Over 4,500 individual posts or shares,

not including repeats or multiswipes." He didn't need to mention that the spread of posts on the weather had registered at nearly a third of a million at any one time, and stuck there in swirls bright enough to bathe the whole room in a red glow.

Nowhere near enough. There had been no traction. It wasn't even a trend. Even with their biggest hit in the last hour, it wouldn't even have registered on most of the social users' top ten stories.

If it wasn't online, it didn't exist. The pamphlets were being circulated, but their numbers were comparatively minuscule. And insignificant next to the awesome power of Icarus to prevent discussion of its contents. Tomorrow's fish and chip wrapping.

Tonight's more like.

The last red pixel went out, above the city of Manchester. Their story was dead. It would have rattled some cages, but without a means to communicate their anger, it would wash away as people got on with their lives.

"Well, so much for that," said Soren. He slammed his fists on the table, then stood up and picked up his coat and slate.

"I'm sorry," said Simmons. "We'll find another way through. We are doing our best."

"Your best is not good enough, is it? It never was. I always thought you'd created a monster. But this is worse. Now you can't even control your own beast."

Harrison stood. "Soren, that's not fair. Where are you going?"

"Away," he said, swinging round as if he was about to launch a punch at someone. "Back to where I was. Before this."

He spat out the words, and gestured helplessly at the naive little control room they'd set up.

"There must be another way," said Grey.

"Not for me. I'm out. I was always out, I don't know why I ever thought I could be part of this."

He slammed the door behind him, hard enough for the large black screen to shudder.

29

The McCracken tasted scorching and strong. Soren looked across the bar to the mirror behind. He was tired, worn down. Perhaps Ned had taken his drink from one of the illegal stashes Soren knew he saved for customers like him on especially miserable occasions. Back to the strength of the old days, before government started to interfere. Before near-to-teenage health obsessives started lecturing everyone about how to go about their private lives. Repeating those health messages that seemed to be so popular on the social. Suspiciously popular, Soren now wondered. With the Ministries so close to the social companies, nothing could be trusted online.

He looked around the dim bar with comfort. Ned sat on his stool in the corner, ready to pour. It was otherwise empty. The last time Soren had been here, he'd been joined by Amanda Ward.

If she'd not joined him that night, would the outcome have been the same? And the rest of the world tick-ticking along like it always did. The last few weeks of work a whisper that no one would hear? The public. The Great

British People. Oblivious. Or more likely indifferent to what was happening under their noses.

After Lucy had died, and his daughter had killed herself, Soren had gone away. The hum of Thailand, Vietnam, Cambodia. He was looking for escape from high technology. Desperate for colour, vibrancy, change, difference. Warmth to numb the pain.

There, those who were poor became poorer still. Beggars at every corner. People queued outside high tech factories, hoping they had arrived early enough to get work that day. And taking home just enough change to spend on a jug of jasmine rice or lentils to feed their families.

Those who had money spent it. On slates, music players, motorbikes. One humid and close evening in Koh Rong, close to a busy market square, a kid revving a petrol powered scooter had brushed past him, causing Soren to tumble into the gutter. The kid had been swiping at his screen at twenty miles per hour. The collision caused the boy to swerve, and the scooter wheels slipped beneath him in the dust.

The machine span to a stop, but the boy was barely grazed. His bare head had not hit the ground. He lay there laughing out loud. Then he sat up, slate still in hand and took pictures. First of his battered ride, then of his own knees, his jeans ripped from them, his skin dotted with a little grit. He swiped the pictures from his screen, then picked up his scooter, tested the ignition, and was gone.

No one offered to help Soren. No one had rushed to the boy's assistance. They were too busy reaching for their slates to record the scene, or were too enraptured by their screens to register anything had happened at all.

Soren had stumbled to a bar for a seat to steady his nerves. The waiter brought him some sour Cambodian rice whisky that tasted like piss. And charged him twice the normal price for the pleasure.

You can go wherever you like, but you can never escape yourself. Perhaps that's how Grace felt. What future without her mother? After the death of Lucy, nothing could ever be the same again.

He'd come back from Asia because he'd run out of energy. He couldn't run away from himself. Grace had been braver. At least she could be bothered to do something.

He admired her. It disgusted him.

He tapped his glass on the bar. Ned held up the bottle. He'd take a double. If it was the special stuff, it would cost a lot. And he'd know about it in the morning.

An hour later, the newsgatherer stumbled out of a TriCab and up his apartment steps. Before entering the building, he looked around him. Ward had been here. His home had been attacked with bricks. The police had come. He'd scrambled around on the floor. Shoved a table against the door. Cowered as the police had arrived.

What a fucking hero.

He spat, then giggled to himself as he swiped his way through the front of the building. He took the steps to the second floor slowly, clinging to the bannister. Craters had been left in his front door by the thugs who'd tried to take it down. He pressed his forehead against the door and traced the indents with the tips of his fingers. He could stay there all night. Resting, tracing. If the Met hadn't shown up, these ridges would have been in his head. And Ward's.

He pulled himself up on the doorknob, and swiped at the sensor. His front door opened and he fell inside. The table was still pushed to the side, leaning up on its edge. The broken window had been boarded up by a cheap handyman the police had called. It shook noisily, even though the breeze outside was mild.

He trod around the upturned table and went to the bathroom to pee. The glare of the bathroom light made him dizzy and he dropped to his knees.

The vomit was not a surprise. The filthy mix of smoky McCrackens, his cinnamon vape... and could he detect that sour Cambodian whisky?

No solids. He couldn't remember the last time he'd eaten. The thought of doing so made him retch again, but what was to come had already been purged from his body. The muscles of his stomach heaved painfully.

Soren stood, moved to the kitchen, ran the tap into a glass, rinsed his mouth and spat out the remains of bile. He filled the kettle and looked for coffee.

As he waited for the boil, he went to his own bedroom and threw his vomit stained jacket onto the bed.

He couldn't help but swipe his slate to see if anything had changed at YoYo since he'd left. No message from Harrison, Simmons, Ward or Zane.

He swiped up the feeds, then retched. Fiercely vomited the glass of water he'd just drunk.

The real secret: Newsgatherer's wife died at the wheel while texting

"NO! NO!" he shouted at the screen.

There was more.

Dead mother was online moments before fatal crash

Mother's careless driving causes crash, truth finally told

Soren screamed. It was a howl of helplessness, mixed with anger. A brutal screech.

Tragic tale of suicide daughter, rejected by father after mother's death

School girl hangs herself after mum's texting death

There were pictures of both women. Beautiful pictures. One from Lucy's former work profile. Another from Grace's secondary school year book.

Soren's heart thumped, his eyes began to water, his face ran hot and red. "You fuckers. Oh, you fuckers," he screamed. Only MinSoc had the trial information, which had been deleted along with the profile of the woman who had killed his wife. Godspeed and Gum had put the information out to discredit him. Or was it to punish?

He rocked forwards and backwards on the edge of the bed. He stood and flung his slate as hard as he could against the wall. The screen cracked as it hit concrete and plaster, then dropped to the floor. Soren leaned back onto his bed, curled into a ball, and shook with pain. Wailing. Suffering, rocking himself in unbearable agony.

He lay there for ten minutes, maybe more. Then he sat up, swung his legs over the side of the bed and leaned over to reach for his legacy slate from the bottom drawer. He swiped open the screen, entering the correct password after a couple of tries through blurred salty eyes.

He scrolled through using the arrow key on his slate: *AskingForIt. *Choke. He brought up the channels he'd used before: *CuttingRemarks. *SpectatorsOf.

He read to suffer. He read to understand. He read to punish himself.

He hurt. In his burned throat and throbbing head. In his battered feet and tired legs. In his heart, in his core. In his eyes, burned from tears and alcohol and memories of Cambodian whisky.

He pressed the reverse key, and browsed some more. *OKComputer *AnimalNitrate.

He typed: *OKComputer.

He read.

Computer hacking. Secret codes. Military plans. Terrorist plots. Post after post by loners, sitting in their pants in darkened rooms, trying to break open the US government, or a bank, or a corporation. Just for the hell of it. Just because they can. Just because, with their digits and symbols and letters and dots and dashes, they believe they somehow have power.

And here, in this dark channel, they don't have to justify it to anyone. It's fun. A challenge. A freaky hobby, with little personal goal apart from the achievement of breaking someone else right open.

These hackers could be anyone in the street. The boy who runs the cleaning machine for TriCabs as a night job. The girl who presses the buttons on the machine which churns out 'home made' pizzas ready for delivery, Soren thought. No one knows them. They don't know each other. But they're there. Working alone. Celebrating together. Here on the dark web, where nobody knows their name.

Soren held his breath for moment. He opened his SkyCloud account on the illegal slate. Irresponsible. Careless. Only he didn't care. And he didn't feel responsible. Someone else can care. Someone else can be responsible.

NEWPOST, he typed.

He copied and pasted a text from his SkyCloud account and moved it across the secret *OKComputer channel. He returned to his SkyCloud window and picked up the Special Report. He dropped it into the *OKComputer channel too. Without hesitation, he swiped the words and the report into the dark web. The screen renewed, and there it was. His story, exposing the Gum conspiracy, every detail promised in the attachment.

He didn't wait for the post to be erased. He retreated, then navigated to other channels. Soren spent ten minutes swiping and posting the same news and report into random dark places, first fuelled by adrenaline, picking very specific channels, then later posting wherever he saw a flashing cursor.

Sex, animals, pornography, drugs, trafficking, self harm. He would be lambasted for posting off topic. The sickos who ran the channels could go fuck themselves. He'd already lost. Words were not weapons, they were a waste. Might as well spread a bit more shit about.

Disgusted, he pressed the button at the top of his legacy slate to turn it off, then picked up his other slate from the floor. He carried both to the kitchen. He looked around, opening drawers at random, eventually finding what he was looking for. The heavy wooden rolling pin these crappy made-to-bore apartments came with as part of their starter packs. He'd never used it.

He placed the legacy slate in the sink, lifted the thick rolling pin high and brought it smashing down onto the screen. It shattered on the first blow. He brought the rolling pin back and hammered again. Then again. Glass flew from the slate around the sink, tiny pieces flew out and hit Soren in the neck, the hands, the face. They felt like mosquito bites.

Pleasurable tiny cuts.

He hammered again and again, until the slate started to crack across the middle. The broken screen revealed a thin green circuit board beneath. Tiny components like little beetles crawled across its surface. Minute worms of wire fell out and he chased them blow after blow.

The slate broke into two pieces, connected only by two thin pieces of silver cord. He flung the wrecked machine towards the waste bin, where it bounced against the wall and cast more tiny shards across the kitchen floor. Then he set about his other slate with the same blunt wooden tool.

Later he ran the tap, washing glass, and plastic, and wire and circuit board down the plug hole, using the rolling pin to break up larger pieces. The rest he gathered up and dumped into the bin.

He walked out of the kitchen, feeling the crunch of tiny broken parts beneath his shoes. He spotted a larger component that had escaped the violence and kicked it across the living room. It came to a halt only when it hit the boarded up window and dropped to the floor.

Sweat ran down his forehead, which he wiped away with the same tea towel Ward had used to dry her hair. He returned to his bedroom, kicked off his shoes and lay down.

Minutes later, breathing heavily, he was asleep.

30

Soren dreamed his door was being kicked in. There was a frantic buzzing on his intercom system, and he and Ward were crouched behind the table, leaning up against it trying to prevent the thugs from breaking into the flat. He dreamed of the rolling pin, and the heaving hammering sound it made as he'd smashed his slates to pieces. He dreamed of vomit rising in his stomach, and blood flowing from the cut above his eye, as the buzzing continued.

Again and again and again.

Soren was panicking. He was gulping for air. He couldn't breathe.

He woke with a desperate gasp for oxygen. The nightmare had cut off his air supply, terrified him into rigidity, stopped his lungs from pulling. At least it felt that way.

"Oh God!" He pulled his hand to his forehead, and wiped away the sweat. He breathed heavily, filling his lungs again, then settled for a moment half awake.

The buzzing began again and then a hammering on his door. His eyes sprang open and he checked himself. He was no longer asleep.

His stomach lurched as he pulled himself up from the bed. He pushed back the covers that he'd pulled onto himself during the night. He stumbled out of his room, still fully clothed and gazed around. Broken glass. A coffee table on its side. The stench of vomit, sweat and whisky.

The door buzzed again, then the hammering.

For a moment he thought of the rolling pin, then remembered he and Ward had had knives when they were attacked before. Or was that in the dream? He approached the door and swiped open the security screen.

"Curtis, what the hell?"

It was Harrison. He swiped the screen, unlatching his front door, but didn't bother to wait. He was heading for the sofa by the time she pushed the door herself and entered his living room. He slumped down, and closed his eyes.

"Nice place you got here," she said. "Kept lovely and clean. Apart from the broken glass and stink of vomit. Jesus, Soren."

He growled, leant back and rested his stiff neck on the sofa. He groaned with the ache. Running his fingers through his hair, the strands stuck together with sweat and grease. Maybe something more gross.

"Coffee this way, I presume," she said, moving towards the kitchen. He heard her muttering as her shoes crunched over tiny shards of glass, and she switched on the kettle. A cupboard door opened and closed, and he heard the sound of a cup being moved around on the counter.

"Looks like you've had quite a party," she called from the kitchen. "Been baking?"

The kettle boiled, and he heard the fridge door open then slam shut. "Animal," he heard her mutter.

She brought in black coffees, struggling with her one arm still in a sling. She sat next to him and gave him his drink. Dry coffee granules from the night before's abandoned brew floated at the top. He stared at them, then took a sip, chewing the grains and swallowing.

"Where the hell have you been, Soren?" she asked. "What happened in the kitchen?"

"I had a disagreement with an old slate of mine," he said, staring at the ceiling. His forehead pulsated. "And some whisky."

"I've been trying to contact you most of the night, but you've been off grid." She reached over, and picked up the remaining component of his slate that had hit the window board last night, a small shard of motherboard with two tiny red beetles surviving on its edge. She looked impressed. "Guess we have the rolling pin to thank for this?"

She pulled her own slate from her bag.

Soren stood, and turned away from her heading for the bathroom.

"I've told you, Mia, I'm finished. I'm sure you've read all about Lucy and Grace on the social. And no, I don't want to talk about it. I just want to drink. So if you don't mind, there's the door."

"Go wash your face, change your shirt," she said, "and come back with a smile on your face."

He turned.

Harrison turned her screen round to him. It showed an outline of the UK, with tiny red dots flashing all over it, swarming and circling and repeating.

He approached.

"Oh, no you don't," she said, turning the slate back towards herself. Her face glowed red from its reflection. "Bathroom first. And for God's sake, brush your teeth."

By the time he had returned ten minutes later, in a new

shirt hastily refreshed with deodorant, Harrison had brought up a number of feeds on her slate.

"Our story is trending," she said. "We're top of every feed. People are outraged. You can practically feel the social shaking with rage."

He didn't want to look. But couldn't help himself. "What happened?" said Soren.

"We're still trying to work that out. After you left, we spent more time chucking everything at the socials, trying to make something stick. Then suddenly, out of nowhere, the map started showing some traction."

Soren stared at her slate.

"It was minuscule at first, and kept disappearing like before. We thought it was another false dawn. But then it started to build, and suddenly...." She swiped at her screen, and the map glowed red again. "It's been like this since about three this morning. You missed the action during your late night... baking. Zane has his coders looking into it, trying to figure out what landed."

"How's it panning out on the ground," said Soren.

Harrison swiped back to the feeds. "In real life? Protests outside MinSoc, for a start. Calls on Godspeed to resign and for Ward to be investigated. Godspeed has gone to ground, no response from the Ministry at all. An official statement from the Prime Minister is due at midday. Calls for a complete boycott of the social - obviously for only half a day - but still. There isn't an adult in the UK who hasn't seen our little pamphlet online or in their hands, and half of them are commenting on it."

"Freely?" asked Soren.

"Every comment seems to be getting through. It's open season on MinSoc, Gum, Bradley Leyton, Portico, the whole lot. And you, Mr Soren, are getting halos. As am I. *Blush*."

She made the hashtag sign with two fingers of each hand, and fluttered her eyelids, an immature but endearing gesture.

"Well done, Mia." He said it without celebration. "You did it. I got fucked."

"*You* did it," said Harrison. "You just missed the fun part. Though looks like you had your own party. And those nasty headlines about Lucy and Grace? They're gone. Disappeared.

"Don't ask me how. Once we'd started to get some traction, Adisa Zane said he was going off for a break. The man doesn't stop, so make of that what you will." She smiled.

Soren stared at Harrison, mouth open.

"Time to get ship shape as we need to check in with the boss to decide what our next move will be. The other news-gatherers are already asking *us* for interviews."

"I need a shower." he said, his eyes staring and worn out. "Do you mind?"

"On the contrary," she said. "I insist. Meanwhile, I'll get any updates and swipe for a TriCab."

The pair took the car to YoYo, where Grey was waiting for them in the control room. He'd stayed on site, he told them, in accommodation that was better than his own home. Simmons and Zane were waiting for them too. Freshly made coffee and cinnamon loops had been prepared for Soren's arrival.

There was an air of celebration about the room, and Grey shook Soren's hand when he entered. Zane took his place, and they all gazed up at the screen. It was bathed in red lights. To the side, social feeds ran with tags including #MinSocScandal, #SkyCloudExpose and the ironic #BoycottTheSocial.

"It looks as if Gum just turned around and retreated

during the night," said Zane. "One minute we were banned, then suddenly everything was getting through."

"Something really strange happened," said Grey. "You couldn't visit a website, or post on the social, without our report - our Special Report - appearing on your screen. It was like a virus."

Soren didn't understand. "Posters were eventually able to share the report?"

"More than that - they got it even if they didn't want it. Watch this." Zane began swiping at his screen, mirrored again in mega size before them all. He opened a search page and typed in *"Weather UK"*.

The Weather Channel's web page emerged, but then immediately a pop-up box hovered before it. *The Social Scandal of the Decade,* ran the text. There was a digital clock below it, running with just over eight hours left. Then a moment later, a PDF document appeared on the screen. Their report.

"It doesn't matter whether you're searching for cupcakes, car batteries or ordering a TriCab, you get the same response," said Zane.

"How is that happening?" asked Soren.

"The coders discovered it early this morning. Someone, maybe a hacking group, has got into our code."

"This operation, the pop-up, has been hardwired into the social. It's not an addition, it's like it's concreted in. You can't go round it like we tried to do with Icarus," said Simmons.

"That takes some serious code, like nothing I've ever seen," said Zane. ""It has all the hallmarks of classic hacking," said Zane. "Not just taking things down, but overemphasising the hacker's powers - like the ticking clock. After that appeared, Gum started pulling its code. Every reference to Icarus disappeared. It wiped itself out. Covering its tracks, if you like. If you look at the code now, Icarus doesn't exist. It never did."

"And the timer?" said Soren.

"My guess is whatever the hackers planted will self destruct and disappear when the clock runs down. Then the social will be able to run as it did," replied Simmons. He held a tone of authority, thought Soren.

"The hackers have given us enough breathing room to get our house in order. Now it's my responsibility to take it forward in the best way we can. Transparently, and with consent. I need to get the other pillars of Portico on board. Or at least two of them. I hope it won't be so difficult this time around."

Soren left with Harrison, but not before shaking the hand of Lucas Simmons. The head of YoYo raised his eyebrows as they did, but Soren shook his head. "It's still a no," he said, and they both laughed.

He turned to Adisa Zane, held the man's hand and slowly bowed his head in respect. He mouthed the words *thank you* and squeezed his fingers gently.

Soren and Harrison decided to leave the Village on foot. Soren never wanted to see the YoYo logo again, let alone travel in one of its cars. For a moment they sat on the steps of the entrance to the building in silence. He pulled out his vape.

They watched the fountain as water from the Lee tumbled over the glowing sculpture. Soren blew out, creating a cloud in front of his face. When it cleared, he watched a slow moving BMW approaching the roundabout.

"You need to leave, Harrison," he said, calmly. "Please, let me deal with this."

"I don't understand. We haven't committed any crime."

"You haven't," he said. He pulled out a picture of his wife and teenage daughter, the last he'd taken of them. The last physical memory of them he owned, before everything went digital. He showed it to her. "Go be with your family. I need to be with mine."

"Okay, but we'll catch up later. Download?"

"I'll need a new slate for that," Soren said.

"A clean one?" she said.

He smiled. She turned and walked away towards the lake.

The BMW circled the fountain, then came to stop where he sat.

Detective Inspector Miran Burman and Sergeant Leanne Lee stepped out.

"Mr Curtis Soren?" asked Burman.

Soren put his vape into his pocket, along with the photograph. He held his hands and wrists out in front of him, nodding in assent. "You know I am."

"I'm arresting you on suspicion of accessing illegal parts of the internet, the so called 'dark web'. You have the right to remain silent, but anything you do say may be recorded and used against you in a court of law," he said.

"Would you care to step into the vehicle, Mr Soren?" asked Sergeant Lee.

He dropped his hands, embarrassed, and nodded again. Burman opened the passenger door for him, before taking the driver's side. Lee sat in the back.

"Mr Soren, I need to remind you that under the Crime Prevention Rapidity Act of 2023, I have the right to convert this car into a custody suite. Now you are under arrest, I am implementing that right. You are under caution. Everything we discuss will be recorded, and you will be sent a transcript as per your rights."

"I understand," said Soren. "I think we've done this before."

"I then have the power to decide whether to press charges directly, or to pass your case, after further investigations, to the prosecution office to consider."

"Again, I understand," said Soren.

"For the record, Mr Curtis Soren has consented to be interviewed under the Act of 2023 in this vehicle, time coded and stamped as per this recording. He is being interviewed by myself, Detective Inspector Miran Burman, and my colleague, Sergeant Leanne Lee."

"Confirmed," said Lee.

Silence for a beat.

"Mr Soren, we have reason to believe you have, in the last six months, accessed the so called dark web. And that you have used fake personas to communicate over social media? Can you please confirm that this is the case?"

He stared out of the window, watching the cascading water and Mia heading off towards the lake behind it. "Yes, I can confirm that," he said.

"And can you confirm," said Burman, "that your actions took place with the understanding that you were breaking the law."

"Yes," said Soren. He closed his eyes and held the picture of Lucy and Grace in his mind.

"And can you please confirm that when doing so, your intention was to act only as a newsgatherer doing their job, a mitigating circumstance for accessing the dark web?"

Soren opened his eyes. Burman smiled and nodded to him as if to say: *go with this.*

Soren paused a moment.

"Sir?" asked Sergeant Lee, from the rear of the vehicle.

Soren said: "I can confirm that my actions were conscious, but judged only to bring about a public good. To back up evidence I already had for highlighting a greater crime."

"And that there was no other way to successfully collaborate the information that was necessary to bring about that outcome?" said Burman.

Soren suddenly understood: "Yes, what you said. I am not a newsgatherer. I am a *journalist*. And in my professional journalistic opinion, there was no other way to confirm the story I was investigating."

Burman paused.

"I see. In that case, Mr Soren, I see no reason why this interview should continue, nor that any prosecution could proceed with a reasonable possibility of success. This interview is therefore concluded at the time and location identified on this recording. I have made the relevant notes, and with my Sergeant's consent, conclude this should be the end of the matter."

"I agree, DI Burman," said Lee from the back.

Burman swiped his screen.

Sergeant Lee stepped out of the car. She walked around the vehicle, and opened Soren's door.

"Sir?"

Soren and Burman shook hands. "Thank you."

He stepped out, and Lee sat where he had. She looked up, and for the first time smiled warmly at him. Soren stood in silence as she closed the door, and watched as the electric BMW slowly drove away.

· · ·

The private jet arrived at London Heathrow. An irate Bradley Leyton stepped out of his Dreamliner and onto the tarmac. He'd woken a hour ago and had been on the feeds and communicating with his office since. All kinds of shit had hit the fan while he had been airborne.

As he walked towards the terminal building, he barked orders at his staff.

"Get Simmons on the slate now! I want Godspeed waiting for me at the Marriot when I get there. Get me some proper breakfast. And a breakdown of the feeds, every one of them. What are they saying about us? How much shit has Simmons got us into?"

They chased him along the tarmac, responding with 'Yes sirs' in turn. His private bodyguard walked two paces behind.

Airport staff met Leyton at the terminal door, and invited him into a plush waiting room. On a wide screen, feeds revealing aspects of the story ran wild. He turned away from them, and stared out of the window towards planes landing and taking off.

His personal assistant brought him coffee and took his breakfast order. Below, he watched baggage being unloaded from the Dreamliner.

The door of the private arrival suite opened, and a stout, bearded man in a smart border security uniform entered.

"Can I see your passports please?"

Leyton waved him away, towards his assistant. She swiped up Leyton's passport on her slate, as well as her own and the two other staff travelling with the Gum party. The border officer swiped his own slate against each passport, thanked the room and welcomed them to the UK.

"When you are ready, please leave by this door," he said, before exiting himself.

Leyton sank the rest of his coffee, and told his assistant he'd take breakfast on the way to London in a private car. They gathered, before leaving the room the way the border control officer had.

In an anteroom, two smartly dressed police officers were waiting. Behind them were two airport police officers, each conspicuously armed.

A police officer stepped towards Leyton.

His bodyguard took a step forward too, attempting to block his way. The officer with the rifle spoke loudly and directly.

"Please step aside, sir." He walked forward, clasped his rifle and gestured to the bodyguard, who rapidly took a step back.

"Mr Bradley Leyton, welcome to the UK," said the officer. "You have just crossed the border of Great Britain, and into the jurisdiction of the London Metropolitan Police. I'm *delighted* to inform you that you are hereby under arrest for direct interference with UK democracy; interference with sovereign UK affairs; and for illegally manipulating communications pertaining to UK citizens and the UK Ministry of Society and Communications."

"What the fuck is this?" said Leyton. The armed officer stepped a little closer.

"You have the right to remain silent," he said.

Less than 150 metres away, through stud walls and the busy aisles of perfume and high end luggage and clothing shops, Harry Godspeed hurried towards Gate 34, to catch Delta Airlines DAL3416 to Los Angeles International.

He'd rushed through security, which was not difficult for first class passengers. He'd booked his flight in the early hours of that morning, then left home without packing more than a few basic clothes, his biometric passport and a toothbrush.

His slate, with the secret login for ClariceKing, he'd left in a litter bin at Paddington station before boarding a fast train to Heathrow. His partner would follow on.

When he reached LA, he would take an electric cab to Silicon Valley. There, a new job, a new apartment, and new life were supposed to be waiting.

31

Soren hired a long distance car, and picked it up on the outskirts of south west London, near Richmond Park. He had asked Harrison along for the company, and if he was honest with himself, moral support. It would be a long trip to where he was heading. They took a TriCab out to the park, where Soren picked up the car and slotted in his new slate. A top-of-the-range one, with a brighter screen and more applications. It fitted smoothly into the TriCab mount.

These types of cars, the ones using the roads that were still shared by the fewer and fewer fossil fuelled vehicles, still required a driver. The slate would do most of the work, but the driver still needed to be aware of poor roads and non guided vehicles. Soren had to keep his hands on his slate, in case he had to override the self drive and take over.

He kept his eyes on the road, and it took him twenty minutes to settle into the responsibility of driving again, albeit passively. It had been a decade since he'd got behind the wheel and self consciously *driven* a car.

Destination West Lulworth.

Soren had looked up the location. It appeared to be as

beautiful and peaceful as he'd feared. A famous cove, with its own windless beach. Not too many years ago it was an almost completely enclosed bay. There had been a single opening to the Atlantic, which had created a perfectly calm inland lake where wildlife had thrived. A mini ecosystem of its own, warmer than the open sea.

Some of the beach had been lost as sea levels had risen over the last ten years, but it was still rated as one of the most beautiful areas of coast in that part of the country. A 'real gem' said one of the review sites. According to the social, it was a haven for retirees, dog walkers, gentle sailing and peaceful beachside strolls.

The sea had not risen enough to fill a close by arch in ancient rocks, through which swimmers would still paddle daily, hoping - as the legend had it - to extend their lifespan. The idea that the woman who had killed his wife, and for whom he blamed the death of his daughter, should have been placed close to there under a different name, to escape justice, saddened him. He no longer had the strength to be angered by it.

After the Portico scandal, it was the only thing he had asked of Ward. He told the now reinstated national director of MinSoc he had nothing to exchange, no promise to make. Only that he wanted, he needed, to know where this woman had been placed. Where she was living out the rest of her life in peace, while his own wife and daughter remained ashes he had never collected from the crematorium.

For a short time, Ward had resisted. She didn't have that data. She wouldn't be able to find it. Soren had thought that unlikely and said so. Ward had then taken a different attitude. Sharing those details would be illegal. Ethically questionable? Soren offered her no more than a mutter and a raised eyebrow.

Bradley Leyton had been released almost immediately, and was back in the United States lambasting the Met police and Ministry of Security for false imprisonment. It hadn't been in Ward's power to keep him in custody. The 'special relationship' between the UK and the US had just been too strong and the Prime Minister had ordered his release as soon as he'd heard about it.

Leyton had been back on his own private jet before any prosecutor had had even a sniff of the case against him. But for a moment, thought Soren, he had been exposed.

Ridiculed.

WonderFish, YoYo and Talk had all made public statements about Changemakers, and that everything would be entirely transparent from now on. They had condemned Gum in the strongest terms, and named Bradley Leyton specifically. He and Godspeed were the villains of the piece, as far as the social was concerned.

The real dark side of the social had been revealed, ran the line. The control, the biggest cheat we'd all allowed. Anyone who cared to look now knew the social did not exist to look after their interests.

Soren hoped the mistake would not be repeated.

He suspected it would.

Past Southampton, the motorway petered out and he and Harrison continued their journey on the A31. The fast moving electric and legacy traffic was replaced with tractors, including some electric models, and heavily loaded lorries heading for the ports of the south west. The pair decided to pull off the main road, and to head into the New Forest for lunch.

Close to Lyndhurst they spotted the first herd of wild ponies. By the time they'd reached a recommended pub in Brockenhurst, the grey, brown and dirty black ponies at the side of country roads, even in the road, had become a common sight.

Their electric car didn't quite know how to react when the horses were so close to the road, so Soren took control to gently steer around them while Harrison pressed her nose against the window. As close to a horse as she'd ever been.

The intention had been to visit Lulworth Cove just to see the ancient arch, but the deviation through the New Forest had set Soren back an hour at least. If they were to return to London afterwards, they would have to press on.

The name and address of the woman had been delivered to Soren's apartment, in the middle of the night, while he was asleep. For the third night running, he'd slept well. Without the fug of alcohol. The note had been handwritten, on a plain piece of paper. No stamp. No logo.

After lunch, they rejoined the main road through the national park, and pressed on past Bournemouth, Wareham and Wool, places which sounded like they came from adventure stories, where kids embarked on wild adventures to find pirate treasure.

By 3 p.m., they had arrived at Burngate, a small village from which Soren could see the sea in one direction and the tall tower of Lulworth Castle in the other. It was the kind of place where you could become anonymous. This was an area replete with second homes, bed and breakfasts, small country hotels. A place to be invisible.

Burngate did not turn out to be the ancient, quaint village its name suggested. Mostly it was factory buildings, industrial estates and a sewerage works. What was once an army barracks had been transformed into rows of nearly new, neat but unremarkable semi detached houses, the roads named after regiments who had served in and around the area.

Soren pulled up outside 21 Bermuda Road, a small house that was the mirror image of the one attached to it at 23. It had a slim drive, upon which was parked a runaround electric car. There was a small alcove window, next to a fading blue door, over which hung a small porch. The tiny lawn next to the drive was unkempt, but not messy.

"Are you sure you want to do this?" asked Harrison.

He wasn't, but he'd made the commitment. It might be his only chance to meet the woman. It had been a long journey, and despite the beauty and calm, he craved the city. Was being stranded out here an escape for the woman? Or was it really her punishment?

"I think I need to," Soren replied. "You okay to wait here?"

"Take it easy, Curtis. Ten minutes, and I'm coming in after you." She was joking, but the tone implied a serious threat if he lingered too long.

The walk across the pavement, then up the drive to the front door was a long one. He was in no rush, and still undecided whether he should be there at all. He stared at his shoes as he walked.

What would he say to her? Did he just want to know why? Did he want an admission of guilt? An apology? Or maybe just to see her face. And if she was smiling, to wipe it away by forcing her to realise the damage she had done.

Was still doing.

By the time he reached the door, it had begun to open slowly. He looked up to see it open wider, and an older man looked towards him in silence. He wore jeans two sizes too big for him, a baggy jumper torn at the sleeve. His hair was grey, and thinning in patches. His breathing was heavy and the doorway smelled of tobacco.

They stood in silence. When the man spoke, it was in a

373

voice grazed with years of smoking, heavy with a West Country accent.

"We don't get many visitors, but we got a message. I thought you would turn up soon."

"Mr Wallace?"

"Mr Soren. You're here, hoping to meet my wife?"

"Felicity, is it?" Soren said, his throat felt dry.

"She's not well." He sighed it, rather than spoke.

Soren considered. "I've come a long way."

He opened the door wider, and Soren stepped into the house. It was dusty and smoky. The stained wallpaper looked far older than the house had looked from the outside. The carpet crunched underfoot. It felt close and dark. Claustrophobic.

The man led Soren through the house, along a dark corridor which opened up on a tiny, greasy kitchen. Then through the kitchen, to a plastic lean-to full of barely looked after plants, garden tools, broken rusty bike parts and old pots.

"She likes to sit here, watching the birds," he said.

Soren looked out at a rotting bird table, sitting in the centre of a blank rectangle of overgrown, moss filled grass. There were no birds.

Mr Wallace coughed. Soren wasn't sure whether it was his smoking, or a signal. He turned towards the man, who indicated his wife. The thin, transparent skinned woman sat deep in a wicker chair, with a blanket over her knees. She wore a thick knitted cardigan, loose threads hanging from the sleeves. Her dull grey hair was lank and long, her face almost as grey. She stared out at the bird table.

"Felicity," he said. His tone was that of an adult addressing a young child. He coughed again. "A kind man has come to see you. A visitor from London."

Her head turned slightly at the sound of his voice, but then back to the bird table. The movement was barely noticeable.

"Lon-don," he repeated a little louder, but she did not move.

He turned to Soren, gesturing towards her. "I never get any sense out of her these days." He tapped his head at the temple. "Early onset, doctor says. She was halfway there when we met. I'm not long behind."

He coughed dramatically, uncontrollably, pulled some deep breaths, then reached for a packet of cigarettes from his pocket. The woman did not move. He lit a cigarette and poked the packet in Soren's direction.

"No, I quit. A long time ago," he said. Soren paused. "And, well, sorry."

The man coughed again. "Me too," he said.

Soren stayed for a minute longer. The three staring into the garden in silence, waiting for a bird to land and take some seed. It never did.

Soren thanked the man again, then left the house. The man waited in the doorway and Soren felt the weight of his gaze as he left.

He walked down the drive, opened the door of the hire and sat next to Harrison. They sat quietly, staring at the house he'd just stepped out of. Its owner had closed the door.

"Maybe we should visit that cove after all," said Soren. "Take a walk on the beach before the sea totally destroys it?"

"Maybe we should," said Harrison.

Soren swiped his new slate to start the vehicle. They pulled away.

* * *

Thank you for reading Portico.

I hope you have been entertained, perhaps challenged and that you would like to read more of my writing.

You can get a free book by signing up to my website, below.

It would make a real difference to me if you were able to please leave a review of Portico on your social media, share your recommendation of it with your friends, and please write an honest review on Amazon, Goodreads or any other review platform you use.

Thank you for reading!
Gideon Burrows

www.gideon-burrows.com

ALSO BY GIDEON BURROWS

A man on the edge.

A young woman in mortal danger.

Matt Carron is a man losing control. Overwhelmed by change, unable to cope with fatherhood, desperate not to lose his wife.

A mysterious doctor puts everything Matt has at risk, forcing him to make the most terrifying choices of his life.

What would you decide?

Safecry is a thrilling tale about coercive control, resilience and the deepest challenges we face.

Coming Spring 2021

ALSO BY GIDEON BURROWS

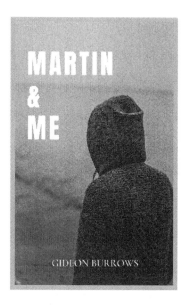

In 1998, Gideon Burrows became involved in the campaign against British arms sales to some of the world's dodgiest regimes.

It was a journey that took him onto the streets all around Europe, into arms fairs, into police cells, outside arms company dinners, getting thrown out of shareholder meetings and up in court facing two years for stopping a train full of arms dealers.

As he became more and more involved in the protest movement, Gideon struck relationships with fellow campaigners that were to last a life-time.

Martin & Me is the difficult tale of one of those relationships. It was one that didn't last. But it did end up being life-changing.

Get Martin & Me www.gideon-burrows.com

ACKNOWLEDGMENTS

Thanks to all those who have supported this project, particularly my wife Sarah Mole who put up with every twist and turn. Thanks to my wonderful editor Barney Jeffries who challenged me to create a believable near future.

Thanks to my fantastic B-Team who stopped me going getting ahead of myself. Thanks to my well deserved 'unaware mentor' Joanna Penn at The Creative Penn.

Printed in Poland
by Amazon Fulfillment
Poland Sp. z o.o., Wrocław